A Thread Between Lives

R Leonowicz

COPYRIGHT © 2025

All rights are reserved. No part of this book may be reproduced, distributed, or transmitted in any form or by any means, including photocopying, recording, or other electronic or mechanical methods, without the prior written permission of the author, except in the case of brief quotations embodied in critical reviews and certain other noncommercial uses permitted by copyright law. For permission requests, write to the author at the address provided in the acknowledgments section of this book.

Printed in the United States of America

First Printing Edition, 2025

I S B N: 9798268749892

Dedication

For my parents;

John & Alma Rita Majcherek

With love always.

Author's Note

A Thread Between Lives was my first romance novel, and it's also my favorite piece. I've incorporated a little bit of myself into each character, so my close friends may catch subtle glimpses of me or a trait from my own life—a life that is constantly changing with the people I meet and the journey my path presents.

I hope I captured the authentic compassion and devilish humor—and, of course, the not-so-pretty times when life wielded jealousy and anger for all the wrong reasons. My greatest hope is that you, the reader, will connect with these characters and be open to the boundless possibilities that true love can offer.

Sincerely,

Rita

Table of Contents

Part I 1
Jake and Claire 1
Detroit Modern Day 1
Chapter One 2
Chapter Two 8
Chapter Three 18
Chapter Four 27
Chapter Five 32
Chapter Six 40
Chapter Seven 49
Chapter Eight 63
Chapter Nine 72
Chapter Ten 82
Chapter Eleven 88
Part II 92
Stephen and Elly 92
New Orleans 1800's 92
Chapter Twelve 93
Chapter Thirteen 98
Chapter Fourteen 104
Chapter Fifteen 112
Chapter Sixteen 116
Chapter Seventeen 124
Chapter Eighteen 137
Chapter Nineteen 147
Chapter Twenty 162
Chapter Twenty One 168
Chapter Twenty Two 179

Chapter Twenty Three 191
Chapter Twenty Four 200
Chapter Twenty Five 207
Chapter Twenty Six 216
Chapter Twenty Seven 223
Chapter Twenty Eight 228
Chapter Twenty Nine 251
Part III 259
Jake, Claire, Stephen and Elly 259
Past and Present day 259
Chapter Thirty 260
Chapter Thirty-one 270
Chapter Thirty-Two 276
Chapter Thirty-Three 283
Chapter Thirty-Four 297
Chapter Thirty-Five 303
Chapter Thirty-Six 316
Chapter Thirty-Seven 336

Part I
Jake and Claire
Detroit Modern Day

CHAPTER ONE

The moonlight casts a silvery glow over the cold cobblestone streets, illuminating the French-trimmed buildings of the town Jake Miller calls home. Birmingham is a quiet enclave of upper-class residents, a world apart from Detroit's restless energy. Close enough for an hour's commute into the city's pulse, yet distant enough to forget its creeping poverty and crime, it offers an illusion of serenity—one Jake barely notices.

Lying still in his bed, his arms crossed over his forehead as though shielding himself from unseen demons, Jake stares at the ceiling. Sleep evades him, replaced by nameless faces and distant places that flood his mind. Shadows of thoughts that don't feel like his own stir within him, unsettling and relentless.

Frustrated, he rolls over, punches the pillow, and presses his head into its familiar indentation, bracing himself for the exhaustion morning will bring.

At last, sleep takes him. His mind drifts to places he knows only in dreams, where a soft melody plays, guiding him deeper into the unknown.

The sky churns with tormented shades of black and gray, thick clouds drifting past the luminous full moon. Rain pounds relentlessly, splashing into puddles that have pooled on the sodden grass.

A young man, drenched to the bone, kneels in the downpour, cradling a woman's lifeless body in his trembling arms. Her breath has faded, her stillness absolute. Desperation contorts his face as he tilts his head back, rain streaming down his cheeks, and cries out a single name—"Elly!" His voice is swallowed by the storm, lost to the heavens.

He buries his face into the woman's cold neck, his body rocking back and forth in anguish. Shadows gather around him—silent figures standing just beyond reach, their faces blurred, their presence neither threatening nor comforting. They watch, unmoving, as grief consumes him.

Then, from the void, a voice speaks.

Stephen."

Jake jolts awake, his chest heaving, eyes wide with shock. His body is slick with sweat, his pillow damp beneath him. His hands tremble as he struggles to grasp the fragments of his dream—hazy yet haunting, a sorrow that lingers in his chest like a weight he cannot shake.

An ache settles deep within him, hollow and unrelenting. He closes his eyes, willing himself back into the comfort of sleep, hoping a few more stolen moments of rest will be enough to face the day ahead.

After a brief hesitation, Jake throws off the covers and heads to the bathroom. As he leans over the sink, he pauses, catching his reflection in the mirror. He studies himself—a face he knows well, yet somehow feels detached from.

Dark brown hair, hazel eyes, and dimples that soften the sharp angles of his jaw. He's always been modest, never considering himself particularly remarkable, though others have insisted otherwise. His naturally athletic build—a firm chest, well-defined arms—is more a stroke of luck than discipline; he rarely works out.

Pushing aside his thoughts, he steps into the shower, letting the hot water wash away the remnants of his restless night. Minutes later, he emerges, throwing on his ceil blue hospital scrubs and a pair of Reebok tennis shoes.

In the kitchen, he pours himself a cup of coffee, the rich aroma filling the quiet space. Before heading out, he sprinkles fish food into his small aquarium, watching Oscar and Lillian—his two goldfish —dart eagerly toward the floating flakes. Morning, guys," he murmurs. Their small, simple existence is oddly comforting.

With plenty of time to spare, Jake steps outside, locking the door behind him. He s never late. Ever. The thought of being stuck in traffic or catching the eye of a lurking patrol officer in the school zone fuels his habit of always leaving early.

As he settles into his car and pulls onto the road, his thoughts drift back to his dreams. They feel so vivid—more like memories than figments of his imagination. Flashes of unfamiliar faces, overwhelming emotions—fear, anger, despair—flood over him, though he can t quite place why.

Driving down Main Street, Jake notices an old man panhandling on the street corner. Their eyes meet, and something shifts. A strange pull.

The old man doesn t look away. He just watches.

Even after Jake passes him, the unease lingers. He glances in the rearview mirror. The old man is still staring, as if waiting—expecting—something from him.

A chill crawls up Jake s spine.

Had he seen this man before?

Had he dreamed of him?

A sharp honk from the car behind jolts Jake from his thoughts. He shakes his head, forcing a breath. It s just a synapse, he tells himself. The brain misfiring, trying to reconcile delayed signals—déjà vu, nothing more.

Still, as he continues down the road, he can t shake the feeling that something... isn t right.

Jake's black Lincoln Navigator eases into the "Doctors Only" parking area of Mercy General Hospital, a 450-bed facility with a bustling emergency department—especially on chaotic Friday and Saturday nights.

It's eight o'clock sharp. Morning rounds begin in thirty minutes, just enough time for Jake to check his mailbox, grab a much-needed cup of coffee, and meet with the three residents assigned to the emergency medicine department.

Inside, the hospital hums with early morning activity. Nurses move briskly through the corridors, patients' voices murmur behind half-drawn curtains, and the overhead paging system crackles to life. Behind the nurse's station on the first floor, Jake reaches for his white lab coat, the embroidered letters reading Jake Miller, M.D. The pockets, as always, are stuffed—gum wrappers, a dog-eared emergency medicine guide, and his much-worn stethoscope.

Maggie, the charge nurse, smirks as she pats him on the back.

"When are you finally going to wash that jacket?"

Jake grins. "Tonight. I promise."

Maggie rolls her eyes. "Yeah, yeah. Heard that one before. Have a good day, Dr. Miller." She waves as she walks off, already busy with her morning tasks.

Jake chuckles before heading to the call room for morning report. The week has been long, and his desk—buried beneath stacks of patient charts—is proof of that. Lately, he's found himself spending more time drowning in paperwork while his residents handle the hands-on patient care. He doesn't mind teaching, but he misses the personal connection—the assessments, the conversations, the moments of humanity between the chaos.

Because if there's one thing Jake Miller is never short on, it's compassion.

For the past two years, Dr. Jake Miller has served as Medical Director of the Emergency Room at Mercy General Hospital. At just 32 years old, he is one of the youngest members of the Medical Board of Directors, actively participating in teaching, mentoring, and giving lectures.

Jake's schedule is grueling—three full 24-hour shifts in the ER each week, plus two eight-hour administrative shifts—but he thrives in the fast-paced environment. Unlike some of his colleagues, who bask in the prestige of their titles, Jake remains approachable and down-to-earth. He's confident in his skills, secure in his competency, and uninterested in playing the role of an "elite" physician.

His reputation extends beyond his medical expertise. Among the hospital's staff, he's known as a "hot catch"—an attractive, successful bachelor who, despite the many nurses who have tried to lure him in, remains decidedly single.

At 8:30 sharp, two of the three residents arrive for morning report. The third, Julie Jacobson, will predictably be exactly ten minutes late—as always. Soon, she'll come rushing through the door, out of breath, her long black hair pulled back in a Nike sweatband, clad in a skin-tight running suit and sneakers. Without fail, she'll boast about shaving two minutes off her five-mile jog to work.

Julie is a fourth-year resident from a long lineage of doctors. After this final year, she plans to join her father's family practice in Bloomsdale, an affluent suburb on the wealthier side of town.

Mike Wilson, tall and athletic with blond hair and a build more suited for basketball than medicine, is another resident. His bedside manner is blunt and unpolished, his personality better suited for the cutthroat world of surgery, which he plans to pursue next year.

Then there's Marcia Fuller—sharp brown eyes, deep auburn hair, and an intensity that makes you feel like she can see right through your soul. Unlike her peers, Marcia fought her way through medical school, working as a student teacher and picking up odd jobs just to pay the bills.

Jake has taken special notice of her career. He believes she has the potential to surpass all of her peers—maybe even him. And if she weren't under his supervision, he's certain he'd pursue something more than friendship.

For now, though, their relationship remains strictly professional—except for their weekly lunch at Hogan's Café every Friday afternoon, where conversation shifts from medical cases to easy companionship.

For Jake, it's the one hour of the week that feels less like work and more like something else entirely.

CHAPTER TWO

Claire... Claire Strauss?"

The voice calls from behind a half-open, tinted window—gray, impersonal, revealing nothing of the speaker inside. From their vantage point, they can see into the waiting area, but no one on the outside can see in.

Yes, right here," a soft, hesitant voice responds.

Claire stands and walks toward the window, where a receptionist hands her a clipboard filled with forms for her appointment with Dr. Royce Webster. With a polite nod, she turns away and sinks back into her seat, setting the clipboard on her lap.

Reaching into her black backpack-style purse, she rummages through a clutter of crumpled notes and paper scraps in search of her wallet. A few scribbled reminders spill onto the floor—tiny, fleeting remnants of her sometimes chaotic life. Claire s world is a paradox: elegant yet unorganized, refined yet cluttered.

By trade, Claire is a violin instructor, running a family-owned music shop alongside her brother. The store has been in their family for generations, its legacy traced back to a long line of gifted musicians. Their family tree, meticulously researched, revealed a direct connection to the 18th century, with whispers of a distant ancestor who was once a cousin of Mozart himself.

For Claire, music is more than a career—it s a sanctuary. Each note that flows from her violin is an extension of her soul, a melody woven with longing, passion, and comfort.

With a steadying breath, she completes the insurance forms and hands them back to the receptionist. Minutes pass. Then, with a soft creak, the exam room door opens.

Claire, follow me, please... right this way."

A nurse leads her down a quiet hallway and into a brightly lit office. The room is pristine—its walls stark white, adorned with an intricate Gothic-style border that adds a touch of sophistication.

On the far wall, a series of oak-framed credentials hang neatly, each bearing the same name:

Dr. Royce Webster, Doctor of Psychology.

The matching oak desk reinforces the room s sense of prestige, a silent testament to Dr. Webster s success and meticulous nature. Claire s stomach tightens. Suddenly, she isn t sure she s made the right decision in coming here today.

Before she can talk herself out of it, the door swings open again.

Dr. Webster steps inside. His presence is composed yet inviting, his handshake firm but warm.

As their hands briefly clasp, Claire exhales—a deep, unsteady breath she hadn t realized she was holding.

Dr. Webster settled into his chair, pulling a pair of eyeglasses from his shirt pocket. As he unfolded them and placed them on the bridge of his nose, he opened the folder in front of him, his gaze shifting between its contents and Claire.

He cleared his throat, then began in a measured tone, summarizing what he had reviewed in her chart.

Let s see... You re thirty years old. A music teacher—violin, very nice." His voice held an air of polite interest before he continued. You ve been struggling with sleep, experiencing repeated dreams—some of them recurring since childhood. Lately, they've been getting worse, keeping you up at night."

Dr. Webster paused, his sharp eyes lingering on Claire as if he were trying to see beyond her words, past the surface, into something deeper.

She shifted slightly in her chair, rubbing her hands together. "Yes... They feel so real, but I don't recognize anyone in them. Except—" She hesitated. "There is one man. His face is always unclear, but... every time I dream of him, more of his features come into focus. It's like a puzzle, and I'm slowly putting the pieces together."

Dr. Webster made a small note in her file, then leaned forward, shifting the direction of the conversation.

He began asking about her childhood—simple questions at first. Was she a happy child? How many siblings did she have?

Then, unexpectedly, he threw in unrelated questions—about politics, religion, and personal beliefs. Claire wasn't sure if he was trying to be conversational or if this was part of some deeper psychological evaluation. Either way, the tactic was effective. By the time their hour-long session was nearing its end, Claire felt mentally drained.

Dr. Webster closed the folder with a quiet snap and folded his hands together.

"Claire, I'd like to place you in a dream study program."

She blinked. "A dream study?"

"Yes." His expression remained neutral, clinical. "You would stay overnight in a designated room where we could monitor your sleep patterns and conduct some tests."

Her body tensed. "What kind of tests?"

A flicker of apprehension crept into her voice.

Dr. Webster folded his hands on the desk and spoke in a calm, reassuring tone.

"First, I'd like to run some blood tests—just to make sure everything is balanced and rule out any underlying medical causes for your sleep disturbances. Then, while you're here, we'll attach small electrodes to your forehead to monitor your brain waves as you sleep. I assure you, it's completely harmless."

Claire exhaled slowly, considering the proposal. "I'm not accomplishing much sleeping in my own bed anyway, so... I suppose it couldn't hurt. How long would I need to stay?"

"Typically about two weeks." Dr. Webster nodded. "I'll meet with you regularly to review the data and discuss any progress in understanding your dreams."

She bit her lip, weighing her options. "Thank you. I really need to put an end to this and move on with my life. It's frustrating—not knowing why these dreams keep coming back."

"That's exactly what we're here to help with." Dr. Webster stood, extending his hand. "Stop by the nurse's station on your way out—she'll draw your blood and help you get set up for the study. In the meantime, try to relax and trust the process."

Claire shook his hand, appreciating his firm but warm grip, and left the office feeling cautiously hopeful.

On her way home, Claire stopped by a small, family-owned grocery store tucked beneath the old high-rise buildings downtown. The scent of freshly baked bread and ripe produce greeted her as she stepped inside.

From across the store, she spotted a man standing on a ladder, replacing a light bulb.

"Hello, Tim," she called out.

Tim looked down from the ladder, his face breaking into a broad, familiar grin. "Well, if it isn't Claire Strauss!"

She watched as he carefully steadied himself before climbing down. At nearly 290 pounds, with a mop of naturally curly, dishwater-blonde hair and striking blue eyes, Tim was hard to miss. Deep creases feathered from the corners of his eyes—evidence of years of smiling too much, if that was even possible.

As he stepped onto solid ground, Claire's memory flickered—an old snapshot from childhood. She could suddenly see the young, curly-haired boy she and her brother Bobby used to run through the neighborhood with, laughing, playing, dreaming.

A wave of nostalgia swept over her.

"How's Bobby and the family?" Tim asked, his voice warm with familiarity.

Claire smiled, shifting the basket on her arm. "Bobby's doing alright. He doesn't seem to have much free time these days—he's coaching little league this season."

Tim chuckled, shaking his head. "Still finding ways to stay busy, huh? Tell him to give me a call when he has a chance. A few of the guys and I are going camping next weekend—I'd love for him to join."

Claire nodded. "I'll let him know."

Bobby was her only sibling, and Tim had been one of his closest friends since childhood. While many kids from their neighborhood had left for college and never returned, Bobby and Tim had inherited their families' businesses, carrying on the legacy expected of them.

Claire sometimes felt a twinge of unease around Tim—not because he wasn't a good man, but because of the unspoken history between them. He had asked her out when they were younger, and she had always gently declined. She'd always seen him more as a protective older brother than a romantic interest. Still, she sometimes wondered if he had never married because a small part of him had held on to the hope that one day she would change her mind.

But Tim never let those old feelings get in the way of their friendship. He remained kind, steady, and loyal—to Bobby, to Claire, and to the community.

After a few more minutes of small talk, Claire wandered through the aisles, picking up what she needed. She never made grocery lists. Instead, she simply strolled the familiar shelves, grabbing whatever caught her eye. Since she lived only a short walk away, forgetting something was never a big deal.

Before heading to the register, she tossed a few cans of cat food into her basket for her little companion, Lucy.

"That should do it," she said, placing her items on the counter.

Tim rang her up, and after exchanging goodbyes, Claire stepped back onto the bustling city street.

Just a few doors down from the grocery store sat a charming little florist shop, its display bursting with fresh bouquets. The scent of roses and lilies drifted into the sidewalk, blending with the aroma of baked bread from the nearby café.

As Claire passed, a familiar voice called out.

"How are you today, dear?"

She turned to see Mrs. Sellars, the elderly florist, smiling at her from behind the counter. Her silver hair was pinned in its usual neat bun, and her bright green apron was dusted with pollen.

"I'm doing fine, Mrs. Sellars. And you?"

"Oh, excellent! I have a beautiful bundle of fresh flowers for you. They just arrived from the gardens this morning."

Claire grinned, reaching into her bag. "Perfect. I'll take them."

She handed the old woman two crisp dollar bills and accepted the bouquet, inhaling the delicate fragrance. Flowers had always brightened up her apartment—and her mood.

As she continued her walk home, the city hummed around her. The weight of her dreams, her past, and her uncertainties still lingered, but for a moment, the simple pleasures of fresh flowers and familiar faces made life feel just a little lighter.

Mrs. Sellars never changed her price when selling flowers to Claire, no matter what she charged her other customers. Claire was a loyal patron, and the elderly florist had long since taken a liking to her.

Claire cherished the presence of fresh flowers in her home. Their delicate fragrance filled the air, weaving through her daily life like a gentle reminder of beauty and tranquility. Each time she brought home a bouquet, she carefully divided it between two vases—one for the kitchen, where the morning light made the petals glow, and the other for her bedroom, where their soft presence greeted her upon waking.

It was a small ritual, but one that gave her a sense of peace.

"Thank you, dear. Goodbye," Mrs. Sellars said warmly, her hands dusted with pollen.

Claire smiled, adjusting the flowers in her arms. "Thank you, Mrs. Sellars. I'll stop by again soon."

She waved as she walked away, her footsteps light against the pavement.

A little further down the street, the familiar sight of the "Strauss Music Shop" came into view. The sign hanging above the sidewalk was a relic of the past—its gold-carved lettering gleamed softly, and beneath it, the words *Established 1849* stood as a quiet testament to the family's long musical lineage.

The sight always gave Claire a warm, safe feeling. No matter where life took her, this place was home.

Between the music shop and the bakery next door, a narrow entryway led to her apartment. She stepped into the alcove, shielding herself from the afternoon bustle, and pressed a familiar sequence of numbers into the keypad. A soft beep, and then the door clicked open.

Inside, the small corridor was quiet, lit by a single overhead bulb. Two mailboxes were fixed to the wall, one for her and one for Bobby, though he rarely checked his. The wooden staircase ahead stretched three flights up, its edges worn from years of footsteps. Claire's flat was on the second level, directly above the music shop.

The metal door, secured with three deadbolts—a common feature in the old apartments above the shops.

Claire's apartment was small but inviting—a space perfectly suited for one person and a feline companion. Though modest in size, it held a quiet charm, a fusion of old-world elegance and modern comfort.

Years ago, while Claire was finishing music school up north in Lansing, she had rented out the apartment to a young architect. She had granted him the freedom to make improvements, and he had done so with great care. His touch had transformed the space, breathing new life into its walls.

The sterile overhead lighting was replaced with a warm, soft system that cast a gentle glow across the rooms. But during the day, natural light poured in from the expansive wall windows, filling the space with golden warmth. One wall had been stripped bare, revealing a stunning backdrop of original brick, giving the apartment an industrial yet intimate feel. The floors—once covered in worn carpeting—were restored to their original hardwood, polished to a rich sheen that reflected the light beautifully.

In the kitchen and bathroom, the architect had installed custom maple cabinets, their natural wood grain lending a touch of rustic elegance. The bathroom itself was a masterpiece, featuring an antique European-style bathtub with gleaming brass fixtures—a relic from another era, adding a sense of timelessness to the space.

Claire often marveled at the transformation, grateful for the care he had put into what he called *his playground, his learning experience*. Before he moved out, he had shown her the before-and-after photos, capturing the apartment s evolution as a piece of his portfolio.

She had since filled the space with her own touch, a curated collection of antiques from her travels across Europe. Each piece had a story, a memory attached, yet somehow, despite their mismatched origins, they blended together harmoniously.

But the heart of the apartment—the place where Claire felt most at peace—was by the large window overlooking Main Street and the entrance to the music shop below. There, in the corner, stood a sturdy wooden music stand, draped with an assortment of sheet music. Resting beside it was her violin, cradled on a handcrafted stand that her grandfather had given her one Christmas.

On restless nights, when sleep evaded her and the echoes of her dreams lingered too vividly in her mind, she would rise, take her violin in hand, and let her fingers dance along the strings. She played the melodies that whispered to her in her sleep—haunting, beautiful tunes that she could never quite remember in the morning.

After putting away her groceries, Claire filled a kettle with water and set it to boil on the stove. The thought of a steaming cup of apple spice tea and a long, hot bath felt like a small slice of heaven after the day she had.

The warm water enveloped her as she sank into the antique tub, the scent of lavender and chamomile rising with the steam. The tension in her muscles eased as she let her mind drift, trying not to think about the appointment, the questions, or the dreams that awaited her that night.

Freshly bathed and wrapped in a thick robe, Claire settled onto her leather couch, pulling a soft, knitted blanket over her lap. She cupped her tea in both hands, savoring the rich blend of cinnamon and apple as its warmth spread through her chest.

Lucy, the cat who seemed to believe she was anything but feline, gracefully leaped onto the couch and curled up beside her, purring softly. Claire smiled, stroking Lucy s fur absentmindedly as she reached for her mystery novel. For the first time that day, she took a deep, steadying breath, letting the calm wash over her.

But she knew it wouldn t last.

The night was coming.

And with it, the dreams would return.

CHAPTER THREE

After finishing his morning rounds and exchanging pleasantries with a few fellow physicians, Jake made his way to his office. A small but comfortable space, it held only the essentials—a sturdy desk piled with patient charts and a soft leather couch perfect for quick naps.

The window behind his desk overlooked the hospital's garden courtyard, where bright bursts of flowers added a touch of warmth to the otherwise sterile environment. On the walls hung his diplomas, medical certifications, and a painting he had picked up at an art auction hosted by the Cancer Association. The artwork—a pirate ship braving a stormy sea—had captivated him with its bold strokes of blue and green. Something about the scene soothed him, reminding him that even in chaos, there was beauty.

A soft knock at the door broke his focus. Marcia peered inside, a playful smile on her face.

"Hey, what about some dinner?"

Jake shook his head. "Sorry, I'm on call tonight. ER duty in half an hour. I'll have to grab a cold sandwich from the cafeteria later."

Marcia rolled her eyes, tilting her head. "Okay, but you don't know what you're missing. I was going to buy."

Jake hesitated, then grinned. "Wait—how about a quick cup of coffee? That is... if you're still buying?"

She laughed. "Sure, let's go."

The hospital rooftop was one of the few places where staff could steal a moment of peace. Vending machines lined the wall, and a handful of plastic chairs offered a modest seating area beneath the open sky.

As they sipped their coffee, Jake found himself contemplating whether he should confide in Marcia about the strange dreams that had been haunting him lately. He valued their professional friendship—would opening up about something so personal be crossing a line?

He exhaled, shaking off the thought. Not now. Not here.

Instead, he steered the conversation toward work, burying the unease beneath layers of routine.

At 5:30 pm, Jake stepped into the emergency room, scanning the board behind the nurse's station to see which resident would be working alongside him tonight. Julie Jacobson. He nodded to himself, then grabbed a stack of clipboards and approached the charge nurse.

Carla Briggs, a stern but dependable retired military nurse, greeted him with a small smile.

"Good evening, Dr. Miller. So far, it's been a quiet night. Dr. Jacobson is finishing up with the last patient now. I'll call you if things pick up, but for now, this should keep you busy."

She handed him a few charts of recently discharged patients for review.

"Thanks, Carla. I'll be in the sleep room," Jake said, waving as he turned away.

Just outside the emergency room doors, tucked around the corner, was the doctors' sleep room—a small, functional space with a bed, nightstand, and a television. A second door led to a modest bathroom with a shower. Fresh linens and towels were replenished daily, but nothing could quite mask the room's persistent musty scent, reminiscent of old sneakers.

Jake chose to ignore the thought of how many exhausted doctors had cycled through before him. Instead, he settled at the tiny desk, flicked on the reading light, and opened the first of several patient charts.

Early Morning Hours

Sometime in the night, exhaustion had won. Jake's head rested on the desk, cheek pressed against an open chart, a thin trail of drool escaping the corner of his mouth. Beneath his closed eyelids, his eyes darted back and forth in restless REM sleep.

Then—the phone rang.

The sharp, jarring sound jolted him upright. His heart pounded as he looked around in confusion before grabbing the receiver.

"Dr. Miller," he mumbled, voice thick with sleep.

"We have a Code Three arriving in less than five minutes. We need you in the ER."

Jake rubbed his eyes, his mind scrambling to shake off the fog of sleep.

"Yes, thank you. I'll be right there," Jake said, hanging up the phone.

For a moment, he sat still, trying to grasp the remnants of his dream. A soft melody lingered in his mind—a tune both haunting and beautiful. He concentrated, hoping to hold onto the fleeting images.

An open balcony. Thick red velvet curtains billowing in the wind, the kind found in grand colonial mansions. Outside, a woman stood, her silhouette barely visible through the darkness. The curtains flared wildly as a sweet voice—unfamiliar, yet strangely intimate—whispered a name.

"Jonathan."

Jake frowned. He didn t know a Jonathan. And he certainly didn t recognize the woman s voice.

Before he could dwell on it, the phone rang again. This time, he didn t answer. Duty called.

Emergency Response

Jake strode into the trauma room, grabbing a pair of gloves and a yellow protective gown to shield his scrubs. Near the pharmacy cart, a nurse quickly briefed him on the incoming case.

"We have an 84-year-old female, coming in from home. Past medical history of pneumonia—she s in severe respiratory distress, possibly congestive heart failure. Heart rate s in the 130s, respirations 45, BP is 70 over 50. Coarse breath sounds, oxygen saturation at 83% even on 100% oxygen. She s awake but not coherent. Her private nurse is with her in the ambulance. We re trying to reach her daughter to confirm a DNR order. Her son, Congressman Rohn, is vacationing in the Caymans, and we re attempting to notify him as well."

Jake nodded, processing the information just as the stretcher burst through the doors.

The elderly woman before him was frail and ghostly pale, deep wrinkles carving through her sagging skin. Her lips were tinged blue. Despite her condition, someone had taken care to brush her bleach-blonde hair, streaked with gray, neatly back. She wore an elegant French silk nightgown, trimmed with delicate lace along the collar—an odd contrast to the sterile surroundings.

An oxygen mask covered her mouth, and cardiac leads peeked out from beneath her gown.

Dr. Miller," Mark Frost, the paramedic, began, patient is an 84-year-old female, severe respiratory distress, probable CHF…"

He repeated the report almost verbatim.

"Her name is Margaret Williams-Rohn, widow of the late Judge Rohn," Mark said, meeting Jake s eyes.

Jake gave a curt nod. "Do we have confirmation on the DNR?"

"Not yet, Dr. Miller. We re still checking," Carla replied.

The team swiftly transferred Margaret from the ambulance stretcher to the hospital gurney, moving with practiced precision. Each person knew their role, and Jake, as the lead, wasted no time. He maneuvered to the head of the bed and began his assessment.

Carla stepped out to verify the DNR and speak with Margaret s private nurse about her medications. Meanwhile, Jake leaned in slightly, offering a reassuring smile.

"Margaret, I m Dr. Miller. We re taking care of you."

Margaret s breathing was labored, her frail body restless from the lack of oxygen. Her lips moved, forming incoherent whispers, before she turned her face away.

Jake continued his examination, speaking aloud so the nurse could transcribe his findings.

"Breath sounds equal, coarse rhonchi present. Heart sounds muffled and distant. I need a chest X-ray, stat. Order a CBC, Chem 7, Glucose, and ABG. Call respiratory for a ventilator. Have an intubation tray ready—size six endotracheal tube."

Just as he finished, Carla returned.

"DNR confirmed. Her daughter is en route. She asked that we keep her mother comfortable but take no heroic measures."

Jake nodded solemnly. "Start an IV and administer two milligrams of morphine."

"Right away, Dr. Miller."

He turned back to Margaret, his voice softer now. "Your daughter is on her way, Margaret. She'll be here soon. We're giving you something for the pain—it'll help you rest."

As he spoke, he felt a gentle pressure—Margaret's frail fingers tightening around his hand. Then, a soft sound drifted from her lips.

A melody.

Jake froze.

The tune was eerily familiar.

His pulse quickened as he recognized it—the same haunting melody from his dreams.

Without thinking, he carefully lowered Margaret's oxygen mask to hear her more clearly. The humming grew steadier, filling the sterile air of the trauma room. Then, Margaret's eyelids fluttered open.

For the first time, she spoke clearly.

Margaret's lips moved one final time, her voice barely a whisper.

"I can see you, Stephen... you're almost there. Keep searching for me."

A faint smile touched her face, as if she saw something—or someone—beyond the room. Then, her eyes drifted shut.

The cardiac monitor emitted a long, piercing tone.

Jake didn't move. His fingers remained wrapped around Margaret's frail hand as the life faded from her body. The final breath escaped her lips, and a stillness settled over the room.

The alarms blared.

Margaret's daughter rushed in, her eyes instantly locking onto her mother's lifeless form.

Jake turned to the nurse. "Turn off the monitors, please."

The shrill sound cut out, leaving only the quiet hum of the fluorescent lights. He turned toward Margaret's daughter, his voice gentle yet firm.

"I'm very sorry for your loss. I'll leave you with your mother to say your goodbyes."

The young woman stepped forward, her movements slow, almost hesitant. Then, as if something broke inside her, she collapsed onto the gurney, gathering her mother's frail body into her arms. Soft, choked sobs filled the space where Margaret's voice had been just moments ago.

Jake inhaled sharply, a familiar lump tightening in his throat. No matter how many times he had stood in this exact moment, it never got easier. It was never just another case.

He peeled off his gloves and tossed them into the open trash can, the snap of latex barely audible over the quiet crying. He turned toward the doorway, hesitated.

A glance back.

The daughter held Margaret as though she could somehow bring her warmth back. The sight made Jake's chest tighten.

With slow steps, he made his way to the counter, sinking into the chair at the dictation desk. He braced his elbow on the hard surface, fingers threading through his hair, gripping the back of his neck. His head felt heavy, weighted by something more than exhaustion.

A deep sigh escaped him.

His eyes locked on a distant point, unseeing. His mind was already drifting, retracing his steps, replaying the moment he had walked into the trauma room after that phone call.

It was a habit—one he could never shake. A loop in his head, checking, rechecking. Did he miss anything? Was there something more he could have done?

But tonight, his thoughts weren t just on medicine.

They were on Margaret.

And the words she had spoken with her last breath.

As Jake reached the end of his mental replay, just before Margaret had drawn her final breath, two things stood out—the melody she had been humming and her last words.

She had gripped his hand with unexpected strength, her gaze locking onto his with an intensity that made him pause. It was as if, in that moment, she recognized someone. Not just a doctor standing at her bedside, but someone she had known before.

Jake had seen countless patients in various states of delirium. At 84 years old, Margaret s mind had likely blurred the past with the present. Her failing lungs had deprived her brain of oxygen, distorting reality.

Jake was a doctor. He knew how to rationalize things.

The humming. The cryptic words. The way she had looked at him.

There was an explanation. There was always a logical explanation.

He forced himself to push the thought aside.

With a steadying breath, he finished his notes and informed the nurse to call the morgue. Margaret's daughter had already gone home. The emergency room had fallen silent again, the chaos of life and death momentarily stilled.

Jake walked past the curtained-off section where her body lay. He hesitated.

Something made him stop.

Slowly, he reached for the curtain and pulled it back.

There she was. Still. Pale. Gone.

His eyes lingered on her face. He studied her delicate features, trying to recall if he had ever seen her before. Was there any connection?

He tried to imagine her alive, vibrant, full of laughter. He searched for something—a flicker of recognition.

Nothing.

With a quiet sigh, he let the curtain fall back into place.

Jake walked back to the sleep room, kicked off his shoes, and crawled into bed, still dressed in his scrubs. The moment his head hit the pillow, his eyelids grew heavy. The last thing he remembered before drifting into sleep was the lingering echo of Margaret's melody.

CHAPTER FOUR

The orchestra swells with the delicate strains of Mozart, each note weaving through the air like a whispered secret. The conductor, dressed in a black tail tuxedo, moves with effortless grace, his baton carving strokes of elegance through the symphony.

Above the polished black-and-white marble floor, dozens of crystal chandeliers glisten, their candlelit glow casting a golden shimmer across the vast ballroom. The walls are adorned with masterpieces, each encased in exquisitely carved frames, silent witnesses to the evening's enchantment.

Men, impeccably groomed in crisp white shirts and black tuxedos, glide with effortless charm, twirling their partners across the floor. The women's gowns shimmer in an array of styles—some draped off their shoulders, others adorned with delicate silk shawls. A few hold fine linen fans, hiding soft laughter behind them as they steal glances across the room.

Laughter ripples like champagne bubbles, and for a moment, Claire feels weightless—as if she is floating above them, unseen.

Her eyelids flutter in REM as she dreams of the scent of fresh-cut flowers and fine champagne lingering in the air. A soft breeze brushes her face as she glides through the space, untethered.

Then, across the ballroom, she sees him.

A man stands alone, his tall figure turned away, gazing at a portrait on the wall. The painting is breathtaking—a beautiful young woman in a deep red gown, a single flower resting in her hands.

Claire's heart quickens. Who is he?

Slowly, he begins to turn.

But as his face starts to emerge from the shadows, a dense mist swirls between them, obscuring him. Claire strains, desperately trying to push through the haze, to see him, to reach him—

But the harder she tries, the farther away he feels.

Bang!

A sharp noise jolts Claire awake. Blinking against the dim glow of the room, she scans her surroundings, searching for the culprit.

Her eyes land on Lucy.

The mischievous gray tabby perches near the edge of the table, her tail flicking with feigned innocence. A teacup lies on its side, the soft rattle of porcelain still lingering in the air.

"Come here, you naughty girl," Claire murmurs, scooping Lucy into her arms. The kitten purrs in protest, rubbing her cheek against Claire's chin before melting into affection.

Lucy has always been a climber—restless, curious. Claire found her as a tiny stray while walking through the Michigan State University campus during her college years. Pets weren't allowed in the dorms, but she couldn't leave Lucy to fend for herself. With a little persuasion, she convinced her roommate that sneaking in a kitten was far better than letting her roam the streets alone.

Now, years later, Lucy is still causing mischief.

Claire glances at the clock—12:30 am. She must have dozed off on the couch. Stretching her toned arms above her head, she yawns, pushing back her long blonde hair with both hands. Her body feels limber, a result of the daily aerobics routine she never misses.

She leans forward, resting her elbows on her knees, her chin nestled in one hand. This is her deep-thinking mode.

The dream lingers in her mind like a half-remembered melody. She can still hear the strains of Mozart, see the swirl of gowns, the gleam of chandeliers. And the portrait—the man.

Who was he?

She picks up a pen and a scrap of paper, scribbling down fragmented notes:

Music. Mozart. Ballroom. Dancing. Portrait. Man.

But no matter how hard she tries, his face remains just out of reach, a silhouette behind a veil. Each time she feels on the verge of clarity, the image slips away.

She exhales sharply, frustrated.

These cryptic details will later be transcribed into her notebook, the one where she collects pieces of dreams.

Claire rises from the couch, her mind still adrift in the lingering notes of her dream. A pull—an unshakable longing—guides her to the far corner of the room, where her instruments and books reside.

Her fingers trace the polished wood of her violin, its presence as familiar to her as breathing. With practiced ease, she lifts the instrument to her shoulder, nestling her chin into place. The bow feels natural in her grip, an extension of herself.

She begins to tune.

A slow, deliberate stroke across E, then A, D, and finally G. Small adjustments follow—precise, instinctive—until the notes ring true. Only when she is satisfied does she allow herself to begin.

The melody from her dream spills into reality.

Claire has always had a gift—an ear finely attuned to music. If she hears a tune, she can replicate it effortlessly, coaxing it into existence with delicate precision.

But this piece is different.

The notes feel familiar yet elusive, like something forgotten but never truly lost. Her eyes drift shut as she plays, letting the music envelop her. The melancholy melody tugs at something deep inside—a yearning, an ache, as if reaching for something just beyond her grasp.

Who was the man in her dream?

The question lingers as her fingers dance across the strings. The hauntingly beautiful tune fills the room, yet remains unheard by the world beyond. Claire had the foresight to attach a silencer to her violin, ensuring that these late-night performances wouldn t disturb her neighbors.

She plays for a while longer, repeating the same passage, hoping for a revelation—a moment of clarity that never comes. Fatigue settles in.

With a sigh, she draws the bow to a stop. She takes a soft cloth, gently wiping away the fine dust of resin before returning her violin to its wooden stand.

Claire crosses the room, picking up the empty teacup from the table. She shuts off the table lamp, plunging the space into quiet dimness.

A stop by the kitchen—the clink of porcelain as she sets the cup in the sink. Then, barefoot steps shuffle toward the bedroom.

She pauses by the couch. Lucy stirs, her tail curling lazily.

Goodnight, Lucy," Claire whispers.

CHAPTER FIVE

The rest of the night in the emergency room was uneventful—just a couple of patients with minor injuries. Dr. Julie Jacobson, the attending resident, handled any new arrivals, giving the attending physician a chance to get some rest.

Jake appreciated working with the residents. He remembered all too well those grueling, sleepless nights, doing what they called "scut" work—the endless tasks that came with the job.

By 7:30 am, he was up again, showered, and making his way to the second-floor doctors' lounge.

Inside, the familiar hum of morning conversations blended with the scent of fresh coffee and warm bagels. Jake headed toward the snack line, a section set aside exclusively for doctors and residents.

As he reached for a bagel with cream cheese, followed by two bananas and a large glass of orange juice, his gaze landed on Marcia and Mike Wilson, sitting in the back of the lounge.

Marcia waved him over.

Jake gave a quick nod, acknowledging her, before heading in their direction. As soon as he set his tray down, Mike reached out his hand for a handshake.

"Hey, Dr. Miller," Mike said with a grin. "Heard you had a nice, quiet night?"

Julie had just left, having filled Marcia and Mike in on everything that had happened in the ER overnight, including Margaret's case.

Jake took a bite of his bagel and nodded absentmindedly.

Before he could even swallow and respond, Mike had already shifted the conversation—naturally steering it toward himself.

Jake listened, smiling slightly as he chewed. His eyes flicked up to Marcia, and as their gazes met, he raised his eyebrows—their silent way of teasing each other about Mike's habit of making every discussion revolve around him.

After a short while, they all got up and dispersed, leaving their empty trays and coffee cups behind.

A Long Day, A Soothing Drive

Jake spent the next few hours clearing out paperwork, reducing the ever-growing stack of patient charts on his desk.

Later, he attended a lecture on Emergency Fluid Therapy and Electrolytes, given by one of the second-year residents, before wrapping up the day with a quick meeting with the hospital administrator.

By the time he finally stepped out of the hospital and into the parking lot, it was 3:30 pm.

The air smelled faintly of rain, and puddles reflected the muted light of the overcast sky. Though the sun tried to break through, thick clouds clung stubbornly above.

Yawning, Jake slid into his Lincoln Navigator, relishing the feeling of finally being off duty. He tapped the controls on his steering column, switching to the CD player.

The opening notes of *Phantom of the Opera* poured from his custom Bose speakers, filling the cabin with sweeping orchestral sound.

This was his escape—his hour-long drive home to Birmingham, where he could unwind with his symphony collection.

As the music swelled, his hands instinctively lifted, mirroring the sweeping motions of an orchestra conductor.

It was a habit that had never left him.

As a child, he had dreamed of conducting. He'd pull a cape over his shoulders, fasten it at the neck, and place his grandfather's old black top hat on his head.

Then, he'd carefully arrange his stuffed animals and toys in neat rows on his bed, standing before them as if they were an audience in a grand concert hall.

With a pencil in one hand, he would wave his arms theatrically, leading an imaginary orchestra in a breathtaking performance.

At the end, he would remove his hat, take a deep bow, and bask in the silent applause of his plush companions.

As Jake continued his drive home, his thoughts drifted back to Margaret—the elderly woman who had died on his watch last night.

"Stephen."

The name she had whispered lingered in his mind.

He pictured her daughter, cradling her mother's lifeless body, her sobs shaking through the sterile hospital air.

Jake swallowed hard as the memory pulled him further—past Margaret, past last night, past the hospital walls—back to his own mother.

Her fading breath.

The hospital machines.

The words he never had the chance to say.

His chest tightened, and he clenched the steering wheel.

The music, once soothing, now stirred emotions he wished would stay buried.

Jake pulled into his driveway, exhaling as he shut off the engine.

Grabbing his lab coat and briefcase from the back seat, he stepped out just as the front door swung open.

Maria Hernandez, a small, sturdy Hispanic woman with streaks of gray in her thick black hair, stood in the doorway, smiling warmly.

"*Como está, Doctor Jake?*" she greeted him, her voice rich with familiarity.

Jake smiled despite himself and leaned down to place a small kiss on her cheek.

"*Gracias, Maria. You're the best. Be careful going home.*"

Maria waved him off with a knowing look.

"*Sí, sí, you rest now. I see you tomorrow.*"

She wobbled slightly as she made her way down the sidewalk, her gait unsteady but determined.

As Jake stepped into his house, the crisp scent of lemon Lysol greeted him, mingling with the faint aroma of freshly cut daisies.

The plush gray carpet bore neat vacuum lines, each path a silent reminder of Maria's care.

She had done most of the decorating—Jake would buy things, and Maria would move them around until they "felt right."

A crystal vase sat centered on the kitchen table, holding a bouquet of daisies. Simple, yet bright.

His eyes landed on a familiar note stuck to the fridge:

"Pot roast and potatoes on a plate for you in the icebox."

Maria's careful handwriting.

Jake opened the fridge, retrieved the plate, and grabbed a cold beer before making his way to the living room.

Collapsing onto the couch, he flipped on the television, just in time for the evening news.

His gaze drifted to the answering machine beside him—no blinking green light. No messages.

Good.

He ate absentmindedly, his thoughts lingering on the events of the day.

Margaret.

Her daughter.

"Stephen."

The names and faces blurred together in his mind.

The empty plate rested on his lap, but he made no move to take it to the kitchen. He was too accustomed to someone cleaning up after him.

After a long, scalding shower, Jake pulled on a pair of boxers and slid into bed.

The clock read 6:00 pm—early, but he didn't care.

The weight of the day pressed against his chest, and as his head hit the pillow, sleep pulled him under almost instantly.

The night was dark, the moon casting long shadows over the cobblestone path. The towering colonial mansion stood like a silent sentinel, its white walls stark against the night.

From a second-floor balcony, a faint flicker of light danced, escaping from behind heavy red velvet drapes.

Inside, the glow of the fireplace cast shifting shadows along the walls.

A man stood before the fire, his hands gripping the mantel, his back to the balcony.

He did not move.

The flames reflected in his dark eyes, creating a wild, almost untamed expression.

Somewhere in the house, faint music echoed through the halls—soft yet eerily familiar.

From the balcony, a woman's voice cut through the stillness.

"Jonathan?"

No response.

The man continued to stare into the flames, motionless.

The woman stepped into the room. The light from the fire illuminated her figure, but her face remained a haze—unrecognizable.

She brought a trembling hand to her lips and whispered, Stephen."

A flicker of fear crossed her expression as she turned away, as if regretting speaking at all.

The woman s cascading black curls were pulled back with delicate ribbons, framing her smooth skin.

Her red satin gown clung to her waist, its low-cut neckline revealing the curve of her collarbone. A golden heart pendant dangled between the pearls wrapped around her throat.

She turned to leave—

But before she could take a step, his hands were on her. Large, strong fingers encircled her arms, his knuckles white with tension.

She gasped, struggling, but his grip only tightened.

He shook her, like a predator testing its prey.

Tears welled in her eyes.

"Please," she pleaded.

Her fear only seemed to fuel his anger.

Jake lay still, trapped in the dream s grip.

His heart pounded. His breaths came in deep, ragged gasps.

Anger burned within him, overwhelming, suffocating.

He clenched the bedsheets—fingers tightening as if grasping something unseen.

Then—he let go.

The woman collapsed to the ground, weeping.

Jake s eyes snapped open.

His chest rose and fell rapidly as if he had just sprinted up flights of stairs.

The room was dark.

A dull hum filled the silence—the ceiling fan spinning above him, round and round.

Jake turned his head—1:00 am.

He lay still, staring into nothingness, his pulse gradually slowing.

Beneath him, his pillow was damp with sweat.

He exhaled, shutting his eyes, willing sleep to take him once more.

CHAPTER SIX

The custom vertical blinds were pulled open, letting golden sunlight spill into the room. The sky was a crisp, cloudless blue, and the hum of the city slowly stirred awake—the occasional revving engine, distant honks, and a loud radio blasting from a passing car.

Claire had cracked open two of the four large windows, welcoming the crisp morning air before the city heat took over. This was her favorite time of day—the brief, peaceful hours before the sun reached its peak, before the air became thick and heavy. Soon enough, she'd shut the windows and rely on the air conditioner to keep the flat comfortable.

She stood in front of the television, mid-aerobics routine, moving with precision. Her hair was pulled back into a high ponytail, strands clinging to her damp forehead. Black spandex shorts hugged her toned frame, and a white Nike sports bra soaked up the sweat from her intense workout.

Her breaths were steady, focused. Her muscles burned, but she welcomed the sensation. She had climbed from beginner to intermediate, and now the advanced steps barely fazed her. Her movements were sharp, practiced—second nature.

She was deep into her cooldown when the sharp chime of the doorbell broke her rhythm.

Without stopping, she trotted to the intercom near the door, still keeping time with the cooldown steps.

"Hello?" she said, pressing the button.

A slight crackle, then a familiar voice responded.

"Open up, Sis. It's me."

Claire exhaled, pressing the button to unlock the downstairs entrance. She turned the deadbolt on the front door, then walked over to switch off the television.

Grabbing a clean towel, she draped it around her neck, wiping away the sweat as she waited.

Just as Claire wiped the last of the sweat from her forehead, the front door swung open.

Bobby walked in with easy familiarity, stepping over to give Claire a quick peck on the cheek before heading straight for the kitchen. Without a word, he opened a cabinet, grabbed a cup, and poured himself some coffee from the still-steaming pot.

Claire smirked. "You could at least pretend you came to see me and not just for free coffee."

Bobby chuckled, settling into a chair at the small kitchen table. "Why mess with tradition?"

Claire grabbed her own cup and joined him. Her muscles were still warm from her workout, and the rich aroma of coffee was a welcome comfort.

Bobby, with his blonde hair, blue eyes, and lanky six-foot frame, had often been mistaken for Claire's twin when they were kids. She had always been grateful for the way he looked out for her, especially during those long, restless nights. Whenever she woke up from her nightmares, Bobby was always there—reading to her, talking to her, doing whatever it took to help her forget.

"What's on your schedule today?" Bobby asked, his gaze drifting toward the large windows.

Claire exhaled. "I have a session with Kristen—Rosemary's niece—at noon. Then I'm meeting the girls to play at the coffee shop. And tonight, I start my dream study at the clinic."

She lifted her arms, resting her hands on the back of her head as she tried to shake off the unease creeping in. "The more I think about it, Bobby, the less sure I am about doing this study."

Bobby looked at her, his expression knowing. "Claire, you've been having these dreams since we were kids. You should have outgrown them by now." His voice softened. "You need to do this. It might help you find some answers."

Claire traced the rim of her coffee cup with her thumb. "That's what scares me. What if I don't find the answers? Or worse—what if I find the wrong ones?"

Bobby gave her a reassuring smile. "Give it a chance. You owe it to yourself."

A pause settled between them before he added, "Want me to check on Lucy while you're gone?"

Claire shook her head. "She'll be fine. I don't have to be at the clinic until nine tonight, but thanks."

Draining the last of her coffee, she stood and walked to the sink, rinsing out her cup. She stared at the water swirling down the drain, forcing herself to push away the lingering doubt.

Alright," she declared, shaking off the weight of her thoughts. Enough is enough. I need to shower, and you need to open the store."

Bobby chuckled, standing as well. Fair enough. But don t back out, Claire. Not this time."

Claire forced a small smile as she watched him go, her stomach twisting.

Bobby poured himself another cup of coffee for the road. Alright, I can take a hint. See you downstairs."

Claire smirked as he walked out, the door clicking shut behind him. She turned the locks, then sighed, rolling her shoulders.

As she made her way toward the bathroom, she peeled off her sweat-dampened clothes, dropping them carelessly along the way. A hot shower would be the perfect reset before the day ahead.

The small bells jingled as Claire stepped into Strauss Music, the familiar chime greeting her like an old friend.

Morning sunlight poured through the shop s floor-to-ceiling windows, casting long beams across the original hardwood floors—worn smooth from decades of musicians and dreamers passing through.

Gold lettering spelling out "Strauss Music" gleamed on the glass, framing the elegant display inside: a black grand piano sat center stage, its polished surface reflecting the light. A guitar rested on a stand beside it, and nearby, a drum set and other instruments added to the shop s charm.

Behind the main counter, a cash register and computer sat waiting, while a door in the back led to extra inventory. To the side, a small soundproof glass room served as a dedicated space for music lessons.

Claire made her way to the cork bulletin board, her fingers trailing down the list of appointments. Kristin Hall—12:00 pm.

Just as she turned around, the front door swung open. Rosemary and Kristin walked in, the little bells jingling again.

Claire, you look fabulous! I just love your hair," Rosemary gushed, embracing her warmly.

Claire smiled. You always say that."

Well, it s always true." Rosemary turned to her niece, handing over a small violin case. You ready for your lesson, sweetheart?"

Kristin nodded shyly.

Claire crouched slightly, offering a reassuring smile. We re gonna have fun today, I promise."

How long do I have with her?" Claire asked, straightening up.

Oh, about an hour," Rosemary replied, adjusting the strap of her purse. I have a few errands to run, then I ll be back."

Claire waved as Rosemary walked out, then turned to Kristin with an encouraging grin.

Alright, let s get started."

So, Kristin, ready to get started?" Claire said with a warm smile.

Kristin nodded, gripping her violin case a little tighter as Claire led her into the small soundproof glass room.

For the next hour, Claire worked with gentle patience, adjusting Kristin s posture and hand position as she held the violin. Relax your wrist a little," she said, demonstrating. It ll help your bowing feel smoother."

Kristin followed her lead, her small fingers adjusting accordingly.

They played together—D, E, F, and G—long full strokes, then switching to half strokes. The room filled with the soft, measured notes of the violin, occasionally interrupted by Claire's encouraging corrections.

By the end of the session, Claire handed Kristin a study booklet. "Practice these exercises this week," she said. "I know they're tricky, but I promise, they'll help you improve."

Kristin tucked the booklet into her violin case just as Rosemary arrived.

"How'd she do?" Rosemary asked as she stepped inside.

"She's got a great ear," Claire said, smiling at Kristin. "If she keeps practicing, she'll be playing full songs in no time."

Rosemary beamed. "That's wonderful. We'll see you next week, same time?"

"Sounds great." Claire walked them to the door, waving as they disappeared into the bustle of Main Street.

Claire turned back into the shop, finding Bobby hunched over the finance books at the counter. She walked up behind him and patted his back.

"So," she teased, "are we broke yet?"

Bobby smirked, rubbing his temple. "Not yet, thanks to that baby grand piano you sold the other day. Now, just sell five more and we can retire."

Claire rolled her eyes. "Yeah, yeah. Do I have any messages?"

Bobby glanced at the desk. "Not that I know of."

"Alright then, I'm off to meet the girls at the coffee shop." Claire grabbed her violin case, slinging the strap over her shoulder as she stepped outside.

The city buzzed with energy—pedestrians weaving through sidewalks, cars honking at intersections, and the scent of fresh bread wafting from the bakery down the street.

She raised a hand to flag down a cab, and within seconds, one pulled up.

Sliding into the back seat, she said, Mission s Coffee Shop, Riverside Drive."

The driver nodded, and the cab pulled away from the curb.

Claire stepped into Mission s Coffee Shop, the rich aroma of freshly brewed espresso mingling with the faint scent of aged books and cinnamon pastries. The place had its own kind of charm—old, mismatched couches, colorful thrift-store pillows, and walls adorned with local artwork, each piece tagged with a price in the corner. The chalkboard menu above the circular bar listed homemade soups, fresh-baked bread, and an array of teas, coffees, and cocktails.

She spotted Katherine and Renee already set up in their usual corner. Katherine s silver flute rested on her lap, and Renee was tuning her mandolin, fingers deftly adjusting the strings.

The trio had met at Michigan State University, their shared love for music forging a bond that lasted beyond college. They had made a pact—every other week, no matter how busy life got, they would meet here to play, unwind, and catch up.

Katherine s sister owned the coffee shop, which meant they always got their prime pick of time slots.

Claire waved to them, but before heading over, she stopped at the bar.

One espresso, please," she said, tapping the counter lightly.

The barista, a tall guy with a scruffy beard and a coffee-stained apron, nodded and started preparing her drink.

A moment later, Claire picked up her cup and walked toward the corner.

Sorry I m late, traffic was horrible today." She set her violin case down and took a quick sip of espresso, letting the warmth chase away the lingering chill from outside.

As Claire set her violin case down, Katherine walked over and wrapped her in a warm hug.

Not a problem, I just got here myself," she said, stepping back with a smile.

From her seat, Renee grinned. Hey girl, I m glad you made it. I actually have a new piece I want us to try tonight—if you re up for it?"

Claire s eyebrows lifted with curiosity. Ooh, did you write it yourself?"

Renee nodded and handed a copy of the sheet music to both Claire and Katherine. Yeah, I ve been working on it for a while, but I need your thoughts."

The three of them studied the arrangement, their fingers tracing the notes as they murmured about the flow of the piece. Claire admired Renee s composition style, always rich with emotion yet technically refined.

After a moment, Claire set the music down and stretched her arms. Alright, let s give it a shot—but can we also play Greensleeves ? I ve been itching to perform that one again."

Katherine s face lit up with excitement. Yes! You know I love Ralph Vaughan Williams. That s a perfect choice."

Renee tapped her mandolin. Agreed. But let s try my piece first while it s fresh. Then we can close with Greensleeves.'"

With that, they settled onto their wooden stools, adjusting their instruments and positioning their music stands. Claire tucked her violin under her chin, her bow hovering just above the strings.

Katherine inhaled deeply, lifting her flute. Alright, girls—let s make some magic."

And with the first soft, deliberate notes, the coffee shop transformed into a symphony of warmth and harmony.

CHAPTER SEVEN

Jake slept in until 8:30 am, the weight of exhaustion still pressing against his body as he finally rolled out of bed. With slow, heavy steps, he shuffled into the kitchen, rubbing the sleep from his eyes. The rich aroma of brewing coffee filled the air, a small but welcome comfort.

Yawning, he stepped onto the front porch, still clad in his denim blue boxers and a white T-shirt. The cool morning breeze brushed against his skin as he bent down to grab the morning newspaper. Without a second glance at the quiet street, he retreated back inside, where he poured himself a steaming cup of coffee and unfolded the paper across the kitchen table.

The back door creaked open.

Maria stepped inside, her gaze immediately landing on him. His messy, tousled hair, the shadow of stubble lining his jaw, his bare feet on the tiled floor—he looked rugged, unpolished in a way that made him seem more human than the composed doctor she usually saw.

"Good morning, Dr. Jake," She smiled, setting her things down. "How did you sleep last night?"

Jake returned the smile, though there was something guarded in his expression.

"Like a baby," he lied. "I was really tired."

The words came easily, but the truth sat heavy in his chest.

The dreams had come again.

He never spoke about them. Not to Maria. Not to anyone.

His father—a disciplined man with a military background—had ingrained in him from an early age:

"Be strong, son. Don't let people see your weakness."

Weakness. That's what his dreams felt like—something out of his control, something that made him vulnerable. And vulnerability had never been an option.

As a child, Jake had tried once. He had gathered the courage to tell his parents about the dreams. But they had been too busy to listen. Or maybe they had heard him and dismissed it, believing it wasn't worth their concern.

Either way, the message was clear.

He had learned, just as with so many other things that troubled him, to keep it to himself.

Maria wiped her hands on a kitchen towel and glanced at Jake.

"Dr. Jake, can I make you some eggs and bacon?"

Jake looked up from his coffee, nodding.

"That would be nice. Thank you, Maria."

She smiled and got to work, moving seamlessly around the kitchen—cracking eggs, sizzling bacon, cleaning as she cooked, just as she always did. The rhythmic clatter of utensils and the rich aroma of breakfast filled the air, but Jake was only half-aware.

He sat at the table, the newspaper spread before him, idly turning the pages. Headlines and articles blurred together until—

A name stopped him.

Margaret William-Rohn.

Jake's breath hitched.

He sat staring at the obituary section, his fingers tightening slightly around the edges of the page. The black-and-white print swam before his eyes as memories pushed their way to the surface—

A young woman, tears streaming down her face, arms wrapped tightly around her mother. The raw, unfiltered pain in her sobs. The weight of grief so heavy, it seemed to pull the air from the room.

Jake exhaled slowly, his stomach knotting. He didn't need to read the obituary to know what it would say.

But he did.

His eyes dropped to the text beneath her name.

William-Rohn

Margaret Elizabeth William-Rohn, born December 3rd, 1912, in Birmingham Heights, Michigan, entered into rest on Thursday, September 7th. Mrs. William-Rohn was a lifelong member of the Birmingham Chapel of Christ and a member of the Knights of Columbus. A beloved mother and grandmother, she will be missed by her family. She was preceded in death by her husband, Judge Carlton Rohn. She is survived by her son, Congressman Robert Rohn, and wife, Diane, with children Becky and David. Her daughter, Elizabeth William-Rohn, and other loving relatives and friends. The family will receive friends on Thursday from 8 am to 4 pm at The Silverspruce Estates. Services will be held at

Birmingham Chapel of Christ on Friday morning at 11 am. Those desiring to make a memorial contribution may do so to the Arthritis Foundation or any of the many Foundations that Mrs. William-Rohn supported. Please contact Executive Estate 5677 E. Ave Birmingham, Michigan 48955.

Maria wiped the counter and glanced at Jake, noticing his distant stare.

Are you alright, Dr. Jake?"

Jake blinked, snapping back from his thoughts.

Yeah," he replied, voice quieter than usual. This woman—Margaret William-Rohn—she came into the ER the other night while I was on shift." He tapped the obituary.

Maria sighed. Oh, what a shame. I don t know how you do it, Dr. Jake—working around all that sickness and death. I d be depressed all the time." She shook her head as she continued cleaning. You have a warm heart, though. It takes a special kind of person to do healing."

Jake gave a small nod, but something about Margaret s death unsettled him.

Doctors learned early on that death was part of the job. You did what you could; you had compassion, but you didn t let it consume you. You moved on.

And yet—this time felt different.

His eyes drifted back to the obituary. The funeral was scheduled for today. Without fully understanding why, he decided he had to go.

As he finished breakfast, his mind flashed back to Margaret in the ER. Her final words echoed in his thoughts.

Then—the dream.

That same voice, over and over. Calling a name.

"Stephen."

Jake inhaled sharply and shook his head, as if physically trying to dislodge the thought.

Maria cleared the last of the dishes. " I ll see you later, Dr. Jake."

He barely heard her.

After showering, Jake dressed in a crisp, short-sleeved white shirt and khaki pants. He had a few errands to run before lunch with Marcia, but his mind remained fixated on Margaret's funeral.

By the time he arrived at the cemetery, the service was nearly over. He stood at the back, silent.

Rows of mourners lined the gravesite. Many influential faces were present—lawyers, judges, and city officials. Off to the side, a television news crew filmed a segment, likely for the evening news.

Jake s eyes landed on Judge Walker, standing with his wife. He had taken office after Judge Rohn s passing.

Then, near the casket, he saw her.

The young woman from the ER.

Margaret s daughter.

She sat in a chair at the front, dressed in a sleek black dress, a matching hat with a delicate veil covering her face.

After the service ended, Jake hesitated before stepping forward. The young woman stood near the casket, shaking hands with mourners offering their condolences.

Taking a breath, he approached her.

Miss Rohn," he said gently.

She turned to him, her eyes still hidden behind the delicate black veil.

Jake extended his hands, taking hers between his. Her fingers were cold.

I just wanted to say again how very sorry I am for your loss. My deepest condolences to you and your family."

For a moment, she studied him in silence. Then, just as he started to turn away, she spoke.

Wait... I m sorry. I didn t recognize you at first. Are you the doctor who cared for my mother that night?"

Jake stopped and turned back to her.

Yes," he said. I was the attending physician."

A flicker of something—gratitude, sorrow, exhaustion—passed across her face.

Thank you for taking care of her."

Jake nodded solemnly. I wish I could have done more."

Miss Rohn gave a faint, sad smile. She was very ill. You did what you could."

Jake hesitated, debating whether or not to say what was on his mind. Finally, he asked:

Miss Rohn... did your mother know a man named Stephen?"

Her expression shifted. Confusion.

Stephen?" she repeated.

Yes. She mentioned the name shortly before she passed away."

Miss Rohn frowned, her brows drawing together beneath the veil. "I don't believe she ever mentioned anyone by that name to me."

Jake studied her face, searching for any trace of recognition. Nothing.

"I could be mistaken," he admitted. "I just thought I'd ask. I hope I didn't disturb you."

She exhaled softly, the weight of grief visible in her posture. "No, you're fine. Thank you for coming, Dr. Miller."

With that, she turned away, accepting an embrace from another family friend.

Jake watched her for a moment longer before finally heading toward his vehicle.

As he walked across the cemetery lawn, a voice called out behind him.

"Jake? Jake Miller?"

Jake turned, his eyes narrowing at the approaching figure.

It took him a second to recognize him.

Royce Webster.

A grin spread across Royce's face. "Hey! It is you. Man, I haven't seen you in ages."

Jake shook his hand firmly. "Royce. Wow. It's been a long time."

Royce chuckled. "Too long."

Jake and Royce had been close in medical school, but after graduation, life had pulled them in separate directions.

It's great to see you, Jake." Royce clapped him on the shoulder. Still working the ER at Mercy?"

Jake nodded. Yeah, got a board position last year. Things are looking good."

Royce raised an impressed eyebrow. That's great. Glad to hear it."

Jake smirked. What about you? Private practice?"

Yeah," Royce said. I'm running a sleep and dream study. We get some state funding, but most of the costs come from private pay or insurance."

Sounds like things are going well for you."

Royce glanced around at the departing mourners, taking in their designer suits and dark sunglasses. So, what brings you here today? Didn't know you kept up with this crowd."

Jake exhaled. I was on duty the night Margaret came into the ER."

Royce gave him a sideways look. Wow, must be nice to attend the funerals of every patient who dies on your shift." His tone was lighthearted, but Jake caught the teasing edge beneath it.

Jake shook his head. No, this was different. I don't know why, but I felt like I needed to be here." He hesitated. Lately... I've been having these strange dreams."

Royce's expression shifted. Interest. Curiosity. Something else.

How do you mean—'strange?'" he asked, suddenly serious.

Jake rubbed the back of his neck. I don't know. Just the same ones, over and over."

Before Royce could respond, a buzzing sound came from his pocket. He pulled out his phone, glanced at the screen, and sighed.

Damn. I hate to do this, but I ve gotta run." He reached into his jacket and handed Jake a business card. Come see me sometime. We can catch up—and maybe talk more about those dreams."

Jake took the card but forced a grin. I ll give you a call to catch up, but I m not sure about analyzing my subconscious. It s not that bad."

Royce smirked. You might be surprised."

As Jake turned to leave, a thought struck him.

Hey, by the way, what are you doing here?"

Royce gave a half-smile. I m dating Elizabeth Rohn."

Jake s eyebrows lifted.

I ll catch you up on it later." Royce waved, heading toward a sleek black limousine.

Jake stood there for a moment, watching his old friend walk away.

What the hell made him bring up the dreams? He hadn t told anyone. Not Maria. Not even himself, really.

But now, saying it out loud made them feel more... real.

He exhaled, slipped Royce s card into his front pocket, and headed toward his SUV.

Before pulling out of the cemetery, Jake picked up his phone and dialed the emergency room at Mercy General.

Emergency department, may I help you?" A voice crackled through the speaker.

This is Dr. Miller. Can I speak with Dr. Fuller?"

One moment, Dr. Miller." A small click, then hold music.

Seconds later, Marcia's familiar voice came on the line. "This is Dr. Fuller."

Jake sighed dramatically. "Doctor, I have a horrible, unbearable pain."

Marcia chuckled. "Oh? Where exactly?"

"It's everywhere," Jake groaned. "Every time I touch here—ouch! And here—ouch!"

Marcia played along. "Well, sir, my expert medical opinion? Stop touching those places."

Jake grinned. "I think the pain might go away if we have lunch. Can you escape?"

"I think I can manage. Hogan's in thirty minutes?"

"Perfect. See you soon."

Change of Plans

Jake arrived at Hogan's Café first, only to find the door locked. A handwritten note hung in the window:

"Closed due to a broken water pipe."

Great.

A few minutes later, Marcia pulled up, rolling down her window. "You're kidding, right?"

Jake gestured at the sign. "Nope. Looks like we're out of luck."

Marcia groaned. "And I was craving their sandwiches."

Jake glanced around. "Want to try somewhere else?"

"What about that coffee shop on Riverside? Mission's Coffee?"

"Never been, but I'm game."

She hopped out of her car, and Jake slid his arm around her back, gently guiding her down the sidewalk. Let s go."

It was a short five-minute walk before they stood in front of a sign reading:

"Mission s Coffee Shop."

Jake pulled open the door, grinning. Ladies first."

Jake held the door open with a teasing grin. Why thank you, are you sure your weak, achy body can handle that door?" Marcia quipped, stepping inside.

He chuckled. Barely, but I m pushing through."

They followed the sign pointing to the "Order Here" counter, where a young man with a pierced nose ring greeted them.

Marcia ordered a ham and cheese sandwich on wheat, with pickles and a raspberry iced tea.

Jake went for a club sandwich and a soft drink. After paying, they grabbed a numbered table flag and scanned the café for a seat.

Let s sit by the window," Marcia suggested.

Alright. Hey, what do you think—should I get one of those nose rings?" Jake smirked.

Marcia gave him a playful look. You re in a funny mood. Holding out any secrets?"

Jake shook his head. No secrets. Just exhausted—haven t been sleeping well lately."

They settled into their seats, the café s cozy atmosphere wrapping around them. Soft couches and pillows gave the space a warm, inviting feel. Across the room, a small trio of women played violin, flute, and mandolin.

A familiar melody floated through the air—"Greensleeves."

Marcia sighed. I love this song."

Jake took that as a cue to fall silent, letting the music settle between them. His gaze drifted to the violinist. Something about her presence felt familiar.

As if sensing his eyes, Claire looked up.

For a fleeting second, their eyes met.

A strange pull tightened in Jake s chest.

Flustered, he broke eye contact, suddenly very interested in the whereabouts of their food. But Claire kept watching him, her bow gliding effortlessly across the strings.

She didn t know why she was so drawn to him.

His smile. His eyes. There was something there. A whisper of recognition.

Or maybe it was just the music, stirring feelings she couldn t quite explain.

Jake had always been a little shy when it came to women. He d dated a few over the years, but since his career took off, romance had taken a backseat. Long hours at the hospital didn t leave much room for dating—not that he actively tried.

Marcia, ever perceptive, noticed the lingering eye contact between Jake and the violinist. But she didn t comment. Instead, she let the moment pass, allowing the soft music to fill the space between them.

Their food arrived, and they ate in comfortable silence, the melodies of the café trio providing a soothing backdrop.

Jake deliberately avoided looking at Claire again. It wouldn't feel right to steal glances at another woman while sitting across from Marcia. But that didn't stop the thought from creeping in—Claire was breathtakingly beautiful.

He shook the feeling off and focused on lunch.

"Great meal. I'm absolutely stuffed," Marcia sighed, leaning back in her chair. "This place is good. Now that I've got a full belly, I sure could go for a nap."

"Too bad someone has to go back to work," Jake teased.

Marcia smirked. "I can hear the sympathy in your voice, you monster." She crumpled her napkin and playfully tossed it at him.

They both stood, ready to leave. Jake hesitated for a moment, letting Marcia walk ahead. Just before stepping out, he stole one last glance at Claire.

She was already looking at him.

For a brief second, their eyes met again. Jake offered her a quick smile—nothing more, nothing less. Then he stepped out the door, feeling something stir inside him.

It had been a while since he felt the thrill of spontaneous attraction.

He walked Marcia back to the emergency room entrance.

"Thanks for lunch. Same time next week? Hopefully, Hogan's won't be closed," she said as they reached the automatic doors.

"Sounds good. Try not to work too hard—I'll call you."

She gave him a casual wave before disappearing inside.

Jake turned toward the doctors' parking garage, pulling Royce's business card from his pocket as he walked. Seeing Royce again had brought back memories—the endless hours they spent quizzing each other on bones, arteries, and veins. Medical school had been brutal, but they'd leaned on each other to get through it.

Sliding into the driver's seat, Jake tucked Royce's card under the strap of his sun visor.

As he pulled out of the garage, he turned on his instrumental CD. His thoughts drifted back to the coffee shop. To Claire.

For a split second, he considered turning around. Going back.

But he didn't.

Instead, he slowly eased onto the highway, leaving the city behind as he made his way home to the quiet suburbs of Birmingham.

CHAPTER EIGHT

Carrying a small overnight bag and a pillow, Claire stepped through the door marked *Sleep Study Clinic*, followed by the name *Dr. Royce Webster*. A faint scent of antiseptic lingered in the air, mingling with the softer, warmer notes of fresh linens.

An older woman in a crisp white nursing uniform greeted her with a gentle smile. Hello, can I get your name, please?"

Claire Strauss. I have an appointment for the dream study tonight." Claire shifted the pillow in her arms, her voice tinged with unease. I feel a little lost not having my cat with me while I sleep."

The nurse chuckled softly. No problem, dear. We ll take good care of you tonight. I m glad you brought your own pillow—it might help you settle in. Just so you know, the first night can be tricky. Most people don t sleep as deeply as they normally would."

Claire offered a small smile. I don t know, I m pretty tired. I usually fall asleep easily."

That s good to hear. Come this way, and I ll show you to your room."

The nurse led her down a quiet hallway lined with several doors, their numbers discreetly labeled. The soft hum of machines drifted from behind one of them. At the end of the hall, the nurse opened a door to Claire's room.

The space was surprisingly cozy, decorated in soothing earth tones. A double bed sat in the center, dressed in crisp white sheets, two plush pillows, and a goose-down comforter. To one side stood a small wooden nightstand with a reading lamp, and across from the bed, a dresser with a large mirror. On top of the dresser sat a glass pitcher filled with ice water, a matching glass turned neatly upside down beside it.

"Another door led to a private bathroom. You'll find fresh towels in there," the nurse explained. "And just so you know, while there are small video cameras in the corners of your room, there are none in the bathroom. The technician won't start recording until you're in bed and ready to sleep."

Claire nodded, absorbing the details. The presence of the cameras made her stomach tighten, but she reminded herself that it was all part of the study.

"Take your time settling in," the nurse added. "If you need anything, just press the call button by the bed."

With that, she left the room, closing the door softly behind her.

Claire let out a slow breath and glanced around. A phone sat on the nightstand next to the television. The sign next to it read: *Outgoing calls only. Incoming emergency calls permitted after evening hours.*

After a long day, Claire stepped into the bathroom, letting the hot shower soothe her nerves. Steam curled around her, enveloping her in warmth. She had made a special trip to the store earlier that day, purchasing a new pair of pajamas just for this experience—soft, lightweight, and a shade of blue that reminded her of a calm sky.

Once dried off and dressed, she nestled herself into bed, sinking into the plush comforter. The unfamiliar setting still felt strange, but the warmth of the blankets made it easier to relax.

A sudden knock at the door startled her.

Yes?" Claire called, not bothering to get up.

The door creaked open, and the nurse reentered, carrying a squeeze bottle and a bundle of thin wires in her hands. I just need to attach some leads to monitor your sleep patterns," she said with a reassuring smile.

Claire shifted slightly against the pillows. Alright. Do I need to sit up?"

No, you re fine just as you are. This will only take a second."

The nurse stepped closer. Can you hold your hair back from your face?"

Claire tucked her hair behind her ears as the nurse dabbed a cool solution onto her temples and forehead. A slight tingling sensation followed as tiny wires were gently pressed into place, the liquid acting as an adhesive.

Don t worry, dear, this will wash off easily," the nurse assured her.

With practiced efficiency, she connected the other ends of the wires to a small monitoring box attached to the headboard.

Alright, all set. Sleep tight, dear," the nurse said as she made her way to the door.

Thank you. Good night," Claire replied, watching as the door clicked shut behind her.

She sighed and reached for the reading light, flicking it on. The warm glow softened the dim room as she opened her book, but the absence of Lucy—her cat—left a hollow space beside her. A cup of tea would have been comforting, but she knew she should try to sleep soon.

Time slipped by, the words on the page blurring as her eyelids grew heavier. She yawned, stretching her arms before deciding to call it a night.

Before turning off the light, Claire glanced at the cameras and gave a small wave, imagining the technician on the other end catching the moment. The thought made her smile.

She settled into the pillows, her breathing slowing.

Good night, Lucy," she murmured softly, the familiar words a final tether to home.

With that, she closed her eyes, letting sleep take her.

The orchestra plays a waltz, its lilting melody weaving through the grand ballroom. The room is alive with laughter and movement, gowns swirling in time with the music. Chandeliers cast a golden glow over the elegantly decorated space, illuminating the faces of guests who dance and chatter with effortless grace.

Claire finds herself in the midst of it all—no longer floating above the crowd as in past dreams, but fully present within it. Yet something is different. She doesn t feel her feet moving, but she glides effortlessly through the people, as if carried by an unseen force.

Voices surround her, snippets of conversation flitting past like wisps of silk. Lovely ball, my dear." "Smashing, darling." "Delightful ball, Elly."

Elly?

The name echoes in her mind. No one calls her Claire. It is as if she is seeing through another woman s eyes, inhabiting a body that is not her own. A sense of familiarity lingers, yet she is calm, poised—almost as if she belongs here.

The men in the room turn to gaze at her with admiration; the women whisper behind gloved hands. She moves with quiet purpose, her steps unhurried as she scans the room. She is searching for someone.

And then she sees him.

Across the polished floor, a tall man stands with his back to her, dark hair neatly styled, posture straight. He is studying a portrait—a striking woman in a crimson gown, dark hair cascading over her shoulders, a single white flower resting in her hand.

Something stirs within Claire. A deep, inexplicable pull.

The man turns.

Their eyes meet.

A sharp breath catches in her throat. Her pulse quickens. A warmth spreads through her, tingling through every fiber of her being. She has never seen his face clearly before—not in any of the dreams. His features were always blurred, indistinct. But now, in this moment, they come into focus.

And Claire feels her heart begin to sink.

This dream was different. It was clearer, sharper—so vivid that Claire felt as if she were truly there. But more than that, this time, the people in her dream saw *her*, acknowledged her presence as if she had always belonged.

She saw *him*.

The young man stood tall, his brown hair neatly combed, his hazel eyes warm and filled with something she couldn't quite name. He smiled—a gentle yet captivating expression that deepened the dimples on each side of his mouth. He was dashing, dressed in a crisp white tuxedo shirt, a black cummerbund, and a long-tailed tuxedo that accentuated his regal presence.

And he was walking toward her.

Claire felt herself moving too, drawn to him, unable to look away. Their eyes locked, never wavering, never daring to break the connection. The sounds of the grand ballroom faded away, swallowed by the relentless pounding of her heart. It was the only thing she could hear now—its rhythm quickening, echoing inside her chest as they neared each other.

Almost close enough to touch.

Then—*a jolt*.

A sudden, firm grip on her arm. The pressure was so real, so strong, that it startled her.

A voice.

A name.

"Elly."

Claire's eyes flew open.

The room was dark, save for the dim glow of the bedside lamp. Her breathing was uneven, her pulse still racing. But the pressure on her arm—it remained.

"Claire, Claire, dear. Can you hear me?" a voice called softly.

She turned her head. The nurse stood beside her, gently shaking her arm—the very place she had felt the grip in her dream.

"Yes, yes. I'm awake," Claire mumbled, her voice tinged with irritation and lingering confusion. "What's wrong?"

"I'm sorry to wake you, but we need to talk for a minute," the nurse said, her tone urgent but calm. "What do you remember? Speak quickly—I'm recording this."

Claire blinked, trying to gather her thoughts. I remember the name... *Elly*," she said slowly. I think... people were calling me that." A flicker of the dream returned, sharp and undeniable. I saw him this time. I *really* saw him. He was tall, very handsome, brown hair, hazel eyes... dimples on both sides of his mouth. He was looking at a portrait." She paused, then added, The woman in the portrait—she was wearing a red dress and holding a flower."

The nurse leaned in slightly. Was she wearing anything else? A ribbon? Jewelry?"

Claire shut her eyes, searching the fragments of her memory. Then—*there it was.*

Yes," she whispered. She had a necklace. White pearls... and a gold heart hanging within the pearls."

The nurse made a small sound of acknowledgment, scribbling something down.

It felt like I was inside this woman," Claire continued. Like I *was* Elly. Everyone knew her. She was looking for the man—*him*—the one admiring the picture. Their eyes met, and then... I woke up."

The nurse nodded. Alright, dear, you did well. I won t wake you again tonight." She hesitated. Would you like some water?"

Claire exhaled deeply, the weight of the dream still pressing against her. No," she murmured, lying back down. I think I ll just go back to sleep."

The nurse quietly exited the room, shutting the door behind her. Claire lay motionless in the darkness, her mind racing. *His face.* She had never been able to see it before tonight. But now, the image was clear—his hazel eyes, his warm smile, the dimples on either side of his mouth.

She squeezed her eyes shut, hoping to drift back into the dream, to return to that ballroom, to him.

But the rest of the night was nothing more than frustrating replays—each time, the same moment over and over. She and the man walking toward each other, their eyes locked, an invisible force drawing them closer. And then—nothing. She could never reach him.

When Claire finally woke, the clock read 8:00 am. She groaned, rubbing the sleep from her eyes, a sense of unfinished business weighing heavily on her. It felt as if she had been pulled away just when she was on the verge of something *important*.

As she gathered herself to leave, Dr. Webster intercepted her in the hallway.

Claire," he greeted, offering a reassuring smile. I heard you made some progress in your dreams last night?"

She sighed, adjusting the strap of her bag. I guess so. But I can t help feeling frustrated. I keep getting stuck in the same place. No matter how hard I try, I can t seem to move past it."

Dr. Webster nodded thoughtfully. That s completely normal. Dreams are complex, especially when the subconscious is trying to process something significant. Don t push yourself too hard. From my experience, these things tend to unfold naturally. I think you ll find the answers you re looking for soon enough."

Alright, thank you, Dr. Webster. I ll be back tonight." Claire gave a small wave before turning away.

The clinic had allowed her to leave her suitcase in the room she d slept in, reassuring her that she would stay in the same space for the duration of the study. Somehow, that small comfort helped ground her.

Stepping outside, she paused on the sidewalk, tilting her face toward the sky. The warm sunlight kissed her skin, a stark contrast to the lingering unease twisting inside her. It was a beautiful day, yet something felt *off*. Out of sync.

Her routine was already disrupted—no morning aerobics, no familiar rhythm to start her day. The next two weeks would be a departure from everything normal. But it wasn't just the shift in routine that unsettled her.

It was *him*.

The man from her dream.

His face was so vivid, so real—more than just a figment of her imagination. He looked *familiar*, yet she couldn't place him. Had she seen him before? Or was her mind playing tricks on her?

Then there was the way she had *felt*. The intense pull, the rapid heartbeat, the fluttering sensation that still lingered deep in her chest. No dream had ever left her feeling this way. It was overwhelming, almost *exasperating*.

She exhaled sharply, trying to shake the thoughts from her mind. But even as she raised a hand to hail a cab, she knew the feeling wouldn't fade so easily.

Because when she closed her eyes, she could still see his.

CHAPTER NINE

The night was weary. A full, luminous moon cast shifting shadows as tree branches swayed across the cobblestone paths outside the great white mansion. Thick clouds rolled overhead, concealing the stars, while distant thunder rumbled, and jagged streaks of lightning momentarily illuminated the tormented sky.

Music drifted through the heavy night air, its melody soft yet sorrowful, seeping from behind the towering walls of the grand estate. On the balcony, a young woman stood, her elegant white evening gown billowing slightly in the wind. Her delicate hands clutched a lace handkerchief to her lips, her shoulders trembling as silent tears traced glistening trails down her cheeks. She leaned against the balcony's ornate railing, staring out into the darkness as though searching for something—or someone—that was just out of reach.

A sudden movement behind her.

The tall French doors leading to the dimly lit room swung open, and the red velvet curtains thrashed against the walls as the storm's breath swept through. A man stepped onto the balcony, his presence both commanding and intimate. Firelight flickered behind him, casting long, restless shadows that danced upon the stone floor.

A THREAD BETWEEN LIVES

He approached her soundlessly, placing his hands gently on her arms, his touch warm despite the night's chill. The woman did not turn, did not flinch—only stood frozen in place, still lost in the darkness beyond the garden. Slowly, his fingers traced down her arms and back up again in a slow, deliberate motion. His lips hovered close to the back of her head, her dark tresses brushing against his mouth with each breath he took.

Then, in a voice as soft as the night wind, he whispered, "I am very sorry, my dear Elly. I love you with all my heart."

Elly inhaled sharply, closing her eyes as though the words themselves were painful. She bit her lip, forcing back the sob that threatened to escape. The lace handkerchief trembled in her grasp.

The man leaned in closer, his breath warm against her ear. "Jonathan cannot touch what we have. You are mine, Elly. I can give you everything."

His voice, once a gentle caress, grew steadier—more insistent. "You do love me, Elly?"

A beat of silence.

"Don't you?"

Elly trembled, her breath catching in her throat as she gave a slow, reluctant nod. She could not find the words, but she did not have to. Stephen's arms encircled her, his embrace firm, possessive. He pressed against her, his warmth contrasting with the cold night air.

"I know you do," he murmured, his lips close to her ear. "Now, shall we join the guests in the ballroom? Remember, this gala is for you, my dear."

Elly turned from the balcony, slipping away from him like a ghost. Her gown whispered against the floor as she stepped into the dimly lit room.

Stephen, go ahead and join the guests. I need to freshen up."

Stephen hesitated for only a second before offering a polite smile. Yes, of course. But don t be long, my dear."

Elly nodded again instead of replying, her fingers tightening around the lace handkerchief in her hand.

Stephen studied her for a moment, then turned on his heel and exited the room. His polished shoes echoed against the wooden floor as he strode down the long corridor, heading toward the grand double staircase that overlooked the ballroom.

At the top of the stairs, Stephen stopped, his hands gripping the polished railing. Below, the ballroom glittered in opulence. Crystal chandeliers cast a golden glow over the black and white marble floors, their light reflecting in the delicate clink of champagne glasses and the swirl of silk gowns. The air buzzed with soft laughter and elegant conversation, punctuated by the gentle notes of a waltz played by a grand orchestra.

Stephen s gaze traveled over the crowd, scanning faces—dancers twirling in perfect rhythm, dignitaries locked in polite discussion, women laughing behind lace fans. Then, his eyes landed on the figure he was searching for.

A young man stood alone, gazing at a portrait hanging on the far wall.

The painting was of Elly.

Rendered in exquisite detail, the artist had captured the delicate curve of her jaw, the warmth in her deep-set eyes, the whisper of sadness that seemed to cling to her expression. She looked almost alive, her painted gaze heavy with unspoken words.

Stephen descended the staircase, his stride purposeful, weaving through the elegant throng.

When he reached the young man, he stopped beside him, standing shoulder to shoulder, mirroring his posture. Crossing his arms behind his back, Stephen gazed up at the portrait, his tone smooth yet edged with something darker.

A lovely portrait of my wife, would you not say? Beautiful, is she not?"

The young man did not turn his head, his gaze remaining fixed on the painting. His voice was calm, measured.

Yes, it is a fine piece of work, sir. I am sure you are delighted to own her."

Stephen's lips curled into a slow smile, though there was no amusement in his expression.

Finally, he turned his head, fixing the man beside him with a piercing stare.

Hear this, Jonathan," he said in a low, steady voice. I love my wife, and she returns my affection. Leave her alone, or trouble will follow." Stephen glared at Jonathan and promptly returned to the crowd.

Elly followed the same path down the long hallway that Stephen had taken just minutes earlier. Reaching the railing, she peered down into the bustling crowd, scanning for someone. As she swept her gaze across the room, an older woman waved up at her.

"Elly, dear! Come down and join us," the woman called, her voice carrying above the noise.

Elly hesitated before offering a small wave in return, acknowledging the invitation but not committing.

Meanwhile, Stephen, standing about ten feet from the woman, heard her call Elly's name. His eyes instinctively searched the balcony until he spotted her. He watched as she descended the staircase, moving with a quiet urgency. A friend from his fox hunting circle approached, engaging him in conversation, but Stephen's attention remained divided. He continued to glance back, keeping a watchful eye on Elly.

Elly reached the ground floor, slipping past the older woman with a fleeting smile and a raised hand, gesturing for patience. She moved gracefully through the crowd, nodding at acquaintances who spoke to her in passing, though her focus never wavered. She was searching—searching for one man.

And then, she found him.

Jonathan stood before her portrait, the one Stephen had commissioned from a renowned artist. He studied it intently, unaware that she was now watching him just as closely.

Elly's breath hitched. Jonathan turned, scanning the room until his gaze locked onto hers. The air between them tightened. The music played on, couples danced, conversation buzzed around them—but for Elly and Jonathan, none of it existed. Only their eyes held each other.

Slowly, they began to move, stepping toward one another, the crowd parting as if by some unseen force. Neither broke the connection, each step drawing them closer.

Stephen, still in conversation, caught sight of Elly changing direction. A familiar unease gripped him. He followed her gaze—and then, he saw Jonathan. His pulse quickened, a hot wave of anger crashing over him. Without a word, he abandoned his hunting companion and strode forward, his pace quickening.

Elly and Jonathan were only feet apart now. Neither noticed Stephen's approach.

She was just within arm's reach when—

Stephen's hand clamped around Elly's arm. With controlled ease, he turned her to face him, his grip firm yet practiced. His voice was warm, but his flushed face betrayed him.

"My dear, I've been looking for you," he said, a smile curving his lips. "May I have this dance with my lovely wife?"

"Of course," Elly says as Stephen escorts her toward the dance floor. But as she follows, she turns her head, her gaze lingering on Jonathan. He remains where he stands—alone—returning her stare.

Beep. Beep. Beep.

The sharp noise blares from the tiny alarm clock on the table beside Jake's bed. With a groggy stretch, he swings an arm over and shuts it off without opening his eyes. A deep yawn escapes him as he slowly blinks awake, his vision adjusting to the dim morning light.

Instinctively, he glances at the clock—9:00 a.m. Just as he had set it.

Jake doesn't have to work today, but he has a racquetball match scheduled for 10:00 a.m. with Mike Wilson, one of the residents in his building. Every now and then, the two would meet for some friendly competition.

Lying there, Jake's mind drifts back to his dream. This one felt different—more vivid than the others. The faces, usually blurred and distant, were clear this time. He had names to go with them. He could see them. And with that clarity came emotion—anger, jealousy—so intense that he woke up feeling drained.

With a heavy sigh, Jake rubs a hand down his face, from forehead to chin, as if trying to wipe away the remnants of the dream. He swings his legs over the side of the bed, stretches, and forces himself up.

A quick shower shakes off the last traces of sleep. He throws on a pair of sweatpants and a T-shirt before grabbing his backpack, stuffing it with his racquet, a few balls, and a towel.

In the kitchen, the scent of fresh coffee lingers. Maria has already been by, leaving a bagel for him on a plate. Balancing a steaming cup of coffee in one hand, he clamps the bagel between his teeth and grabs his keys with the other.

Jake slings his backpack over his shoulder as he steps outside. Tossing it into the backseat, he slides into the driver's seat and heads toward the gym—a solid thirty-minute drive.

Mike lives in the city, so they always choose a spot halfway between them. It's routine.

Mike was already at the gym when Jake arrived. After flashing his membership card to the woman at the front desk, Jake scanned the weight room.

It didn't take long to spot Mike—a tall man in his late twenties with blonde hair. His height made him stand out in any crowd.

Jake smirked as he approached. "Hey."

Mike turned, grinning. "Hey, Dr. Miller. Ready to lose ten bucks today?"

Jake sighed. "You know I hate it when you call me that. Just call me Jake."

"I know. That's why I do it," Mike said with a laugh.

Jake shook his head, playing along. "As for that ten bucks... I think you'll be the one walking out of here a little lighter today." He gestured toward the court.

For the next hour, they battled it out, both playing well. By the time a knock on the door signaled the end of their session, Jake had won two games over Mike.

Jake extended his hand. "Good game."

"Yeah, yeah. I think you were cheating—messing up the score," Mike teased as he shook Jake's hand.

Jake grinned. "Pay up. I've got lunch plans." He held out his hand expectantly.

Mike sighed, pulling out his wallet. "Fair's fair. But I'm calling for a rematch. Gotta restore my dignity."

They headed toward the locker room, but before they could part ways, Mike's tone shifted.

"Hey, Dr. Miller, I've got a question for you. If you don't mind."

Jake stopped walking, sensing the change in Mike's demeanor. "Sure. What's on your mind?"

Mike hesitated. "Nothing's bothering me. I was just wondering... You and Marcia seem pretty close, right?"

Jake raised an eyebrow. "We have a good working relationship."

Mike nodded but pressed on. "You're friends outside of work too, though. Right?"

Jake crossed his arms. "Mike, just ask your question." His tone was firm now. He wasn't sure where this was going, but he had a feeling he wasn't going to like it.

"I was wondering... do you know if she's seeing anyone?" Mike asked, his tone casual but laced with curiosity. "I'm thinking about asking her out, but I wasn't sure if she's already dating someone. Since you two are close, I figured you might know."

Jake hesitated for a moment. "Honestly, Mike, I'm not sure. We grab lunch sometimes, and we've been to a few art exhibits together, but we don't really talk about personal stuff."

Mike nodded. "Got it. Do you think you could feel it out? You know, just casually check if she'd be interested?"

Jake let out a small sigh. "I don't know... I don't really want to intrude on her personal life. But I can drop your name in conversation, see how she reacts. No promises, though."

Mike grinned. "That works for me. Let me know if you hear anything." He clapped Jake on the back as he walked off. "See you later, Dr. Miller."

Jake stayed at the gym for another hour, walking on the treadmill. He wasn't much of a workout enthusiast, but since he was already there and had no other plans, he figured he'd make use of the time.

On his way home, he pulled into a Dairy Queen drive-thru and ordered a country basket, a large shake, and a banana split for dessert. He planned to take it home and catch the end of the baseball game playing that night. Jake was an avid fan, with the Detroit Tigers and Texas Rangers being his favorite teams.

Pulling into his driveway, he grabbed his food and headed inside. He set his meal on the table, switched on the TV, and flipped to the game. It was the fourth inning—Detroit was up by six. Jake dug into his banana split first, since it had already started melting, and he didn't want to put it in the freezer. Once he finished his meal, he settled in to watch the rest of the game. Detroit won.

Afterward, he moved to the second bedroom, which he had converted into an office. He powered on his laptop and opened a Word document, scrolling through his files until he found "Resident Evaluations." With some evaluations due next week, he decided to spend

80

the afternoon catching up on paperwork—something he often did in his downtime.

For the next five hours, Jake worked steadily, only pausing to stretch and grab a drink. By the time he shut down his computer, the sun had set.

Stepping onto his front porch, he took in the stillness of the night. The sidewalks were empty, and the rhythmic hum of crickets filled the air. Jake inhaled deeply, savoring the cool breeze against his skin. He loved this time of day—the quiet, the peace. No frantic calls from the ER. No sick children needing his help. No late-night drunks needing stitches. Just stillness.

And for now, that was enough.

CHAPTER TEN

The yellow cab pulled up in front of the music shop. Claire handed the driver some cash, waving off the change before stepping onto the sidewalk.

She owned a Honda Accord—kept in pristine condition, mostly because it spent most of its time in storage. She only took it out for long trips or weekend getaways. For daily travel, she preferred cabs and public transit. Even back in East Lansing during college, she had relied on buses and her bicycle to get around campus.

For as long as she could remember, Claire had dreamed of settling in Europe. Paris and Rome had always been her favorite destinations. If she had to choose, though, Paris would win. The grandeur of its museums, the breathtaking art, and the elegance of the Opera House had captivated her. She loved the charm of the city s countless cafés lining the boulevards, the thought of sitting in a park near the Eiffel Tower—watching people pass by, or losing herself in a good book. These simple pleasures soothed her soul. To Claire, Paris had to be the most beautiful city in the world.

Snapping back to the present, she stepped inside the music shop, the familiar chime of the bell overhead greeting her.

Hello, Bobby," Claire said as she walked toward the counter.

"Why, hello back at you, sis," Bobby replied, setting aside his calculator. He tilted his head. "Well? How was your night away from home?"

Claire exhaled and leaned against the counter. "It was... alright. Except for being woken up in the middle of the night. They were monitoring my brain waves, and whenever I reached deep dream sleep, they woke me up." She shook her head. "It was strange, though—I remembered more than I usually do. I could actually *see* the people in my dream. Their faces weren't blurry this time. And I could hear names—people were calling me *Elly*."

Bobby frowned slightly. "Elly?"

Claire nodded. "Yeah. It felt like I was someone else entirely, living through her eyes. Feeling emotions I've never felt before." She paused, rubbing her arms as if shaking off a chill. "I don't know, Bobby. These dreams... they're getting stranger."

"Sounds like this is working out," Bobby said.

"Maybe... I just don't know. I wish I had never started having these weird dreams. Sometimes, they're really scary." Claire exhaled, rubbing her arms. Then, shaking off the thought, she said, "Hey, I'm going to run up and see Lucy. Then I'll come back down and relieve you for the day. I don't have any students, and you need a break, big brother!"

"I'm not going to argue with that—especially if you bring me a cup of coffee when you return," Bobby said with a grin.

"Sure thing." Claire smiled before heading out of the music shop.

In the corridor, she stopped to check her mail. She sifted through a handful of junk mail before her fingers landed on a letter addressed to her—from Pierre Cambier, postmarked from France. Her heart gave a small leap.

83

She opened the door to her flat and called out, "Lucy?" as she set the mail down on the table, keeping only Pierre's letter in her hand.

"Here, Lucy girl!" A tiny furball darted toward her, rubbing against her leg. Claire bent down, scooping up her cat. "There you are, sweetheart. Did you miss your mommy?" She stroked Lucy's soft fur and kissed the top of her head. "I missed you too. Let's get you some food."

She set Lucy down and opened a small can of cat food, scooping it into a bowl before placing it on the floor. Lucy wasted no time devouring it.

Claire put on a pot of coffee, then sat at the kitchen table, unfolding the letter from Pierre.

Dear Claire,

We have missed you so much! When do you think you can spare some time to come work with us? Donnell and I are opening a new shop featuring pieces from local artists—it's going to be marvelous.

Trish is coming from New York next month. She'll be staying with us for two weeks, helping us get everything started. It's going to be a lot of work, and we could really use your talent. Besides, we miss you.

I know you love it here, so give it some thought and see what you think. I can guarantee you superb tickets to the Opera—I have an inside connection at the ticket office.

Paris is beautiful this time of year, as I hope you'll remember.

Call me.

Regards,

Pierre

Claire smiled as she read the letter. She had met Pierre about six years ago while backpacking across Europe. Pierre was born in France but had spent much of his life wandering the world, living on a generous trust fund he had inherited from his grandmother. He had been traveling across Europe when he met Claire and her friend at a brewery in Munich. After that, he followed their route through the Swiss Alps and across Italy.

Pierre spoke English fluently, having lived in New York for two years while attending school—though he had eventually dropped out. Claire had always thought of Pierre as an eccentric artist. He was incredibly talented and had a flair for dramatizing everything. His travels had made him worldly and cultured, something Claire admired.

Over the years, she had kept in touch with Pierre and usually stayed with him when she visited Europe. He had even visited her once in Detroit. They had crossed the bridge into Windsor, Canada, and taken a train up to Toronto. While Pierre had enjoyed Canada, he hadn't been a big fan of Detroit.

Claire gave the idea a quick thought, wishing she could find the time to go. But with the sleep study and her responsibilities at the music shop, she didn't see how she could fit it in. With a sigh, she folded the letter and placed it on the table with the rest of her mail.

Lucy had finished her meal and was now purring as she followed Claire into the kitchen.

"Lucy, I'm sorry, but I have to leave again," Claire said, giving the cat a quick scratch behind the ears. She poured two cups of coffee and headed back out the front door to return to the music shop.

"Here you go," Claire said, handing a cup to Bobby.

"What a lifesaver. I should just break down and buy a coffeepot, huh?" Bobby said with a grin.

"What? That would be too easy, Mr. Complicated." Claire smirked. "Hey, I got a letter from Pierre today."

"The guy from Paris?" Bobby asked.

"Yeah. He wants me to help him open an art shop."

"Sounds like fun. What do you think?" Bobby said, closing the receipt book he had been working on.

"I d love to go, but I just don t have the time. Maybe next year," Claire said with a hint of regret.

Bobby opened a desk drawer, pulled out his keys, and grabbed his coffee. As he walked toward the door, he said, "I m out of here. See you tomorrow. Sweet dreams—again—at the clinic."

"Bye," Claire called, waving as he left.

Claire walked around the music shop, checking out the displays. About once a month, she would clean the pianos and instruments on display, ensuring they remained in pristine condition. She never had trouble finding things to do around the shop. Between managing inventory and handling daily maintenance—such as cleaning the bathrooms and mopping the floors—both she and Bobby stayed busy.

The shop had been slow that day. Only a few customers had come in to browse, and aside from selling a clarinet earlier in the afternoon, business had been quiet. By six o clock, Claire decided to close up for the evening.

She headed upstairs to her flat to spend some time with Lucy. After greeting her cat, she popped a frozen dinner into the microwave. As she waited, a sense of hesitation crept in. The thought of going back to the clinic that night unsettled her—sleeping in a strange bed while being observed made her uneasy. A fleeting idea crossed her mind about skipping the session altogether, but after a quick mental debate, she couldn t find a justifiable reason to back out.

Sighing, Claire finished her dinner, cleaned up the kitchen, and prepared to leave. Then, with some reluctance, she started her journey back to the clinic.

CHAPTER ELEVEN

Claire returned to her assigned room at the clinic, exhaustion settling into her bones. She took a long, hot shower, letting the steam soothe her tense muscles. When she emerged, the nurse on duty was waiting, carefully placing the tiny wires on her forehead—just as she had done the night before—to monitor her sleep patterns.

After the nurse left, Claire curled up in bed with her book, hoping to read until sleep overtook her. But as she turned off the light and lay in the quiet darkness, her mind wandered. She thought about the researchers sitting behind the monitors, watching her sleep, analyzing her every movement. Then, her thoughts shifted to the man from her dreams—the one with the striking features and a familiar yet elusive presence. Who was he? Why did he feel so real? The questions lingered as her eyelids grew heavy, and she slowly drifted into unconsciousness.

The soft hum of an orchestra fills the air, playing a graceful waltz. Laughter and conversation ripple through the grand ballroom, where elegantly dressed guests move in rhythmic harmony. The men are clad in crisp tuxedos, the women in flowing ballroom gowns adorned with intricate embroidery. The decor, the candlelit chandeliers, the grand paintings adorning the walls—it all suggests the late 18th century.

Claire finds herself back in this world, a place she has dreamt of before. She moves through the room, drawn toward a man standing before a portrait of a woman—Elly. Their eyes meet, and a surge of recognition floods through her. Her heart pounds and her stomach tightens with nervous anticipation. They step closer, inches from touching, when suddenly, a firm hand grasps Elly's arm, yanking her away.

"Elly, my dear, I've been looking for you." Stephen's voice is warm but tinged with something unspoken. His face is flushed as he reaches for her hand. "May I have this dance with my lovely wife?"

Elly hesitates for only a moment before offering a polite smile. "Of course."

Stephen leads her onto the dance floor, gently but purposefully steering her away from the man she was just about to meet. As they begin to waltz, she glances back over her shoulder. The stranger still stands where she left him, watching.

"You look lovely tonight, Elly," Stephen says, his voice softer now.

"Thank you," she replies, keeping her words brief.

"These people are here for you, my darling. They are our friends, our guests. They adore you, as do I." His expression shifts—his eyes darken, yet a deep sincerity lingers in his gaze.

"I know, Stephen," Elly murmurs, turning her face away. "You are a wonderful man, and you do too much for me—things I do not deserve."

Stephen tightens his hold on her waist. "My darling, you deserve more."

She stops moving. "I'm tired," she says softly. "May I retire for the evening? I'd like to go to my chambers and rest." A slight tremor laces her voice as she adds, "Please send Dora to prepare my bath."

Stephen studies her for a moment, his fingers still intertwined with hers. Slowly, he releases her.

Claire." A voice cuts through the dream. A hand shakes her shoulder gently.

Claire gasps awake, disoriented. The room is dim, and the nurse stands over her, holding a tape recorder. Wake up, dear," the nurse says. Tell me what you were dreaming about."

Claire blinks rapidly, realizing her pillow is damp with tears. She lifts a trembling hand to her cheek—she s still crying, though she doesn t understand why.

It s so hard," she whispers, her voice thick with emotion. I love Jonathan. I long for his touch, his kisses. But I m devastating Stephen. He s so hurt... so angry." A fresh wave of fear grips her. I m terrified of his jealousy. I m frightened for Jonathan. For myself."

She swallows hard, struggling to control her tears. I don t want to hurt Stephen. I do love him... but my desires for Jonathan—I can t deny them."

The nurse s voice remains steady. You re doing good. Keep going. What else do you remember?"

I m married to Stephen, but he knows how I feel about Jonathan. He s so angry, so hurt. He would never let me leave him." Claire s voice trembles. Elly... she s beautiful. I saw her reflection in a mirror. But the strangest part was—it wasn t my reflection. It was hers. It was like looking at myself, yet not myself. How is that possible?"

She presses her fingers against her temple, frustration building. Why am I dreaming this? Are these people real? Did this really happen? Why does it feel so intense, so... familiar? I wake up crying, feeling everything as if I lived it." She exhales sharply, her chest tight with emotion. I just need to understand."

The nurse, calm and steady, places a reassuring hand on Claire s shoulder. I don t have all the answers, Claire. But Dr. Webster will review the tapes. He'll research the people in your dreams and help you make sense of them. He's a good doctor. Be patient, my dear—you're doing wonderfully. And remember, this is only your second night."

Claire lets out a weary sigh. "You're right. I just... I either need to understand why I'm having these dreams, or they need to stop. Either way, I just want some peace." She sinks back into the pillows, pulling the comforter over her.

The nurse offers a gentle smile. "Get some rest. We'll see what Dr. Webster thinks in the morning." She stands, tucking the tape recorder away, and heads for the door.

"Good night," Claire murmurs, her voice barely above a whisper.

The door clicks shut, and Claire stares at the ceiling, her mind still racing. Sleep doesn't come as easily as she wishes.

Part II
Stephen and Elly
New Orleans 1800's

CHAPTER TWELVE

The year was 1830. New Orleans was booming—ranked as the fourth-largest city in the United States. Ships docked daily at its busy ports, bringing settlers from Europe in search of freedom and fortune in the new world. August was the hottest time of year. The relentless sun-baked trash and waste piled high on the streets, while the heavy scent of rot and fish drifted from the murky waters of the Mississippi. The city was expanding rapidly, and the steamboat traffic churning up and down the river only added to the congestion. Newcomers poured in, their hearts filled with hopes and dreams.

Among the city's elite stood Samuel Bentley. In his late fifties, Samuel was a portly man with thick gray hair, a full beard, and a drooping mustache. Wire-rimmed glasses perched precariously on his nose as he spoke, often while holding a lit cigar. The ever-present scent of whiskey clung to him like a second skin. Samuel was one of the wealthiest men in New Orleans, a status earned not just by his own endeavors, but through generations of family foresight. His great-grandparents had acquired large tracts of rural land when it was still cheap and undeveloped. That land now formed the foundation of Samuel's immense wealth.

Samuel resided with his wife, Carolyn, and their three sons—Stephen, Grant, and Chestin—on the northern edge of town near the shores of Lake Pontchartrain. His sprawling estate encompassed over three hundred acres, where he cultivated tobacco and cotton. Though he also bred thoroughbreds, that was more of a passion project than a business. Much of his land was either rented out or sold to the highest bidder. Between tenant income and his booming agricultural operations, Samuel's fortune continued to grow year after year.

Samuel purchased slaves from traders who arrived by boat, bringing Africans forced into bondage. Alongside these transactions, he also acquired white laborers known as indentured servants—individuals from Europe who, facing dire conditions at home, had agreed to work for a period of three to seven years in exchange for passage to the Americas. This system, while different in structure and outcome, still placed people under grueling and often exploitative conditions.

On his estate, Samuel employed both enslaved Africans and indentured servants in a variety of roles—cooks, household servants, stable hands, and, most extensively, field workers who planted, harvested, and processed his tobacco and cotton crops. The system provided him with a steady source of low-cost labor, fueling the continued growth of his wealth.

Though a shrewd and successful businessman, Samuel distinguished himself from many of his contemporaries in how he treated those in his service. He avoided the cruelty that was rampant during that era, choosing instead to provide his enslaved workers with adequate food, reasonable living quarters, and, when possible, efforts to keep families intact. Once, he even paid triple the usual price to ensure a married African couple would not be separated—an act seen as rare, if not radical, in his time. Samuel believed that contentment led to productivity and loyalty. In his eyes, a strong, healthy, and emotionally stable worker—enslaved or not—was a sound investment.

Occasionally, when a white indentured servant completed their contract, Samuel would help them purchase land—sometimes offering a parcel from his own holdings. With wealth, land, and influence at his disposal, there was little Samuel Bentley could not do.

Samuel s home was a grand plantation-style mansion perched atop a gentle hill, shaded by a canopy of towering oak trees. These mighty oaks also lined the cobblestone path that stretched from the wrought iron front gates to the stately front porch. Behind the house lay a manicured garden filled with trimmed hedges, vibrant flowers, and a graceful fountain at its center. Winding cobblestone paths circled the fountain, inviting quiet strolls through the lush greenery.

The front façade of the mansion boasted two grand wooden doors that opened into a wide entryway. Four massive white pillars rose from the porch floor to the high ceiling, giving the estate an air of regality. The porch itself wrapped fully around the home, allowing guests and family alike to walk in a complete circle without ever stepping onto the grass. It was, without question, the largest and most lavish estate in all of New Orleans.

Samuel's father had once commissioned a renowned architect from England to design the mansion. Construction took seven years, followed by an additional two to complete the elaborate gardens and sprawling stables. Samuel, an avid lover of horses, took great pride in his stables. He owned over a hundred thoroughbreds, and often spent hours observing the trainer's work, quietly admiring the animals' strength and grace.

Stephen, the eldest of Samuel's three sons, was a fine young man—tall and slender, with hazel eyes and brown hair that curled slightly at the ends. At twenty-two, he had completed his higher education and returned home to assist in managing the plantation. Stephen was devoted to his family and, following in his father's footsteps, knew that one day the full weight of the estate would rest on his shoulders. His two younger brothers were expected to follow a similar path: education abroad, then a potential return to the family estate, where each would inherit a portion of the vast holdings. Yet, Stephen would be the primary heir, destined to carry on the Bentley legacy.

Carolyn, their mother, was a woman of refined grace and elegance. Her pampered life was evident in her smooth, unweathered skin, her manicured nails, and the careful attention she gave to her appearance. She adored the arts, literature, and music, and took charge of all social gatherings held at the estate. Carolyn concerned herself little with the business or operations beyond the mansion walls. Her domain was the household itself, overseeing the servants, cooks, and attendants. Though she remained distant from the broader workings of the plantation, her management of the domestic sphere was a full-time role in its own right.

Carolyn was putting the final touches on preparations for the evening s grand gala, which would take place in the mansion s opulent ballroom. The event promised to be the highlight of the season, with seventy-five distinguished guests expected—prominent lawyers, politicians, and influential families among them.

One family, in particular, stood out on the guest list: Antonio Cortez, his wife Theresa, and their daughter Elena. Antonio was a man of considerable influence who had arrived from Spain just three years prior and had quickly made a name for himself in New Orleans. A wealthy merchant, he imported silver and gold from Spain and traded in other precious metals throughout the Americas.

Though the Cortez home was smaller than the Bentley estate, it was still the second-largest residence in New Orleans—a testament to Antonio s financial stature. Unlike many others who leased their land, Antonio negotiated a fair deal with Samuel and purchased his property outright, paying in cash. Samuel respected his shrewd yet honorable business sense. Over the past three years, Antonio had strategically opened shops across the city, offering fine imported goods, and had multiplied his wealth tenfold. Samuel saw great potential in aligning the two families and was eager to deepen their business ties.

Antonio had only one child—a daughter named Elena, though she preferred to be called Elly. She was strikingly beautiful, with a soft, sun-kissed complexion and long, flowing black hair that curled naturally at the ends. Her dark brown eyes held a quiet allure, and her presence exuded both elegance and mystery. Well-educated and cultured, Elly had been raised with grace and refinement.

Samuel's intent for the evening extended beyond business. He planned to approach Antonio about a potential marriage agreement between Stephen and Elly. The match, he believed, would benefit both families greatly—uniting two fortunes and securing influence across both domestic and foreign ventures.

Stephen had seen Elly before at various social functions—brief encounters, always surrounded by chaperones or mingling guests. Her beauty had left a lasting impression on him, but they had never shared a private moment. Stephen's days had been filled with studies and responsibilities on the plantation, leaving little time for courtship or romance. The idea that his father was planning his future stirred a mix of emotions—nervousness, uncertainty, but also a spark of curiosity and desire.

The servants worked tirelessly in the days leading up to the gala. Every hand on the estate—cooks, maids, stable boys, and gardeners—pulled together to create an atmosphere of elegance and abundance. The aroma of fresh pastries and roasted meats filled the air, mingling with the scent of cut flowers brought in from the garden. Silver was polished until it gleamed, crystal glasses lined up in perfect rows, and the ballroom floors shone like glass under the soft golden candlelight.

The Bentley family held a significant social role in the rapidly growing city of New Orleans. Owning the majority of the land in the surrounding area, they were considered a pillar of prosperity and influence. At this moment in time, life on the plantation felt harmonious—secure, predictable, and graced by privilege.

CHAPTER THIRTEEN

Dozens of beeswax candles glowed brightly from the chandeliers above, casting a warm light over the polished marble floors of the elegant ballroom. Well-dressed men and women arrived by horse-drawn carriages at the Bentley mansion, their presence adding to the evening s grandeur. On one side of the room, a long table displayed an array of freshly baked pastries and hors d'oeuvres. Servants dressed in crisp white coats and black trousers moved gracefully through the crowd, offering glasses of champagne and finely crafted cocktails.

As the guests arrived, Samuel and Carolyn stood at the entrance to greet them. To be invited to a Bentley gala was a mark of high esteem. These gatherings were not just social events—they were prestigious occasions where the influential and the beautiful mingled. Carolyn would often extend invitations to the talented actors from the town playhouse or renowned musicians performing at the Opera House in New Orleans. Captains of docked ships were also welcomed, often bringing with them news from Europe or names of distinguished travelers soon to arrive from abroad.

Not long after the orchestra began to play, Antonio Cortez arrived with his beautiful wife and daughter. They stepped into the grand entryway where Samuel and Carolyn stood to receive them. Samuel extended his hand warmly.

My good friend—and his lovely family. How are you?" Samuel greeted.

We are very well, thank you. This is a grand gala," Antonio replied.

Carolyn kissed Theresa and Elly on the cheek in turn.

We're so pleased to see you tonight," Carolyn said, then turned to Elly with a smile. You look radiant this evening, my dear."

Thank you, Mrs. Bentley. That is very kind of you," Elly replied shyly.

Come, enjoy yourselves. The evening is still young," Samuel said as he led them toward a table near the edge of the dance floor. Antonio, Theresa, and Elly followed, taking in the sights and sounds of the vibrant celebration.

Instead of returning to greet the rest of the guests, Samuel and Carolyn stepped onto the dance floor. Samuel waved up to the orchestra, signaling them to begin a waltz. In a playful gesture, he swept Carolyn into a dance. The crowd applauded, and many couples soon joined them, filling the floor with elegant movement and laughter.

Stephen did not care much for large crowds. The noise, the constant chatter, the press of people—it always made him uneasy. So he waited, lingering upstairs until the ballroom had already filled and the festivities were well underway. When he finally descended, he moved quietly to a far corner of the room, seeking solitude among the splendor. From there, he watched the swirl of elegant gowns and tailored suits, the blur of spinning dancers and laughter that echoed through the grand hall.

He was just about to turn and disappear once more into the quiet shadows when his gaze landed on a sight that rooted him in place.

There, seated alone with graceful poise, was Elly Cortez.

She was watching the dance floor, her expression calm and thoughtful as she waited patiently for her parents, now spinning together among the other couples. There was something in the stillness of her—serene yet magnetic—that stirred something deep in Stephen. His heart fluttered unexpectedly as if her presence had awakened something dormant within him.

He had always known of the unspoken plans—those whispered agreements between his father and Elly s. But Elly, as far as he knew, was unaware of such discussions. She was untouched by those expectations, and to Stephen, that made her all the more genuine.

Summoning a rare burst of courage, he stepped away from the wall and walked toward her. Each step made his heart beat faster, his thoughts clashing with anticipation and fear of saying the wrong thing.

When he finally stood before her, she looked up. Her eyes met his with a soft, curious gaze.

Hello, Miss Cortez. I m Stephen Bentley," he said, his voice steady though his heart raced.

Yes, I know," she replied with a gentle smile. You may call me Elly."

He smiled back, caught off guard by the ease of her warmth. Are you doing alright? May I get you something?"

No, I m fine. Thank you for asking," she said kindly.

Stephen lingered beside her table, unsure of whether to sit or say something more. He glanced around the ballroom, searching for words that didn t feel forced. But in her presence, everything seemed to vanish—the music, the crowd, even the sense of time. All he could focus on was her. Her beauty held him captive, especially her lips, which curved softly when she smiled. His thoughts ran wild—he imagined what it would be like to kiss her and quickly tried to banish the idea before it showed in his expression.

Just as he turned to speak again, Elly opened her mouth at the same time.

They both paused.

"I'm sorry—" they said in unison.

Stephen chuckled lightly. "You first," he offered, his smile widening as he looked into her eyes.

"I was going to ask about your gardens. I heard you have an array of plants and flowers—some that your mother imported from the islands," Elly said.

"Yes," Stephen chuckled softly. "She does have a love for large things—the gardens, the house... and these grand festivities."

"Would you like to see the gardens?" he asked, half-nervous, half-hopeful.

"That would be lovely. If it's not a bother."

"Not at all. Allow me."

He reached for her hand, gently escorting her toward the glass doors that led outside. The touch of her soft skin sent a shiver through him, a quiet tremble that sparked something alive within him—something he hadn't felt for anyone before. As they stepped through the doors, the warm light from the ballroom faded behind them, replaced by the soft flicker of candlelight glowing along the cobblestone path. Overhead, the moon cast a pale silver light, illuminating the garden in a dreamlike hue.

"What a lovely place," Elly said, pausing to breathe in deeply. "I love the smell of flowers."

She closed her eyes for a moment and smiled, letting the fragrant air wash over her. Stephen had wandered these gardens hundreds of times, but tonight they looked different. They shimmered with a kind of magic he had never noticed—because Elly was there. He watched her move gently among the flowers, touching their petals, lifting them toward her face, breathing in their fragrance with a sense of wonder.

And in that moment, he knew. His father's plans for marriage between him and Elly no longer felt like duty or arrangement—they felt right. Nothing, no one, had ever stirred such feeling in him before.

He walked toward her quietly and reached for her hand.

The suddenness startled her, but she did not pull away. Instead, she became still—more attentive to the young man standing alone with her beneath the stars.

"Elly," Stephen said, his tone shifting to something more serious. "I need to ask you something."

"Yes? What is it, Stephen?"

"Will you marry me?" he said, his voice soft, almost a whisper.

Elly's breath caught. She pulled her hand away and turned, her brows rising in disbelief. Then, almost involuntarily, she let out a small laugh, uncertain whether he could be serious.

"What do you mean, 'Will I marry you'? How can you ask something like that of a perfect stranger?" she asked. "I must say... I feel offended by your jest. I thought you to be more of a gentleman, Mr. Bentley."

Stephen looked stricken. "I'm not joking. I've never been more serious in my life," he said. "Elly, I adore you. I want you to become my wife. Our fathers are to speak of it tonight. They... they hope for our union."

I can't believe this," she said, her voice a mix of hurt and disbelief. You know nothing about me, nor I of you. My father would never allow such an arrangement without my consent. Please... take me back to the ballroom."

Without waiting for a reply, she turned and walked several steps ahead of him.

I m sorry if I ve upset you," Stephen called softly behind her.

But Elly didn t answer. She walked back through the doors and into the warmth of the party. At her family s table, Theresa sat alone, eyes scanning the room. She looked up and smiled faintly as Elly returned and sat beside her. Elly leaned in, shaking her head gently as she spoke to her mother.

Stephen stood just outside the open doorway, watching from the shadows.

Across the room, his father Samuel, stood beside Antonio Cortez. They were deep in conversation. Samuel held a glass of whiskey in one hand and a half-burned cigar in the other. As Antonio glanced toward his daughter, Stephen saw him nod and gesture in agreement.

Stephen s heart sank.

He had the sudden urge to rush in—to stop his father before the question was even asked. But Elly s reaction echoed in his mind, and something inside him held him back. She wasn t ready. Perhaps she never would be.

Instead, Stephen turned and stepped quietly into the night, away from the music and the lights. He walked back into the garden, the moon still shining above him, and sat alone in the cool silence.

CHAPTER FOURTEEN

The marriage between Stephen and Elly was inevitable. An agreement arranged by their fathers had settled the matter: the wedding would take place in the fall. The ceremony would be held at Saint Louis Cathedral, followed by a grand gathering in the gardens of the Bentley estate. Afterward, the couple would live together at the Bentley mansion.

Elly, however, strongly objected. Her father, Antonio, refused to change his mind. He believed he knew what was best for her future—better than she did. But Elly had dreams of her own. She longed to attend school and travel to Spain. Marriage, especially one that would tether her to plantation life, was the last thing she wanted. She loved the theater, and the idea of becoming an actress had even crossed her mind. Anything, she thought, would be better than a life dictated by obligation.

At eighteen, she felt her future slipping away before it had even begun. She barely knew Stephen and couldn t imagine building a life with someone she hadn t chosen herself. Elly wanted to fall in love—to feel the rush of it, the joy, the freedom. She didn t want love assigned to her like a chore.

After countless hours pleading with her father, her resistance wore thin. Defeated and exhausted, Elly gave in. Her body went numb at the thought of marriage, yet this was what her family wanted. And so, she must obey—even if it came at the cost of her own happiness.

Elly reluctantly agreed to marry Stephen.

Throughout the rest of the summer, Theresa and Carolyn met constantly to plan the wedding. It would be far from simple—it was to be the most glorious event of the year, the grandest celebration anyone in the region had seen. Guests from all over were expected, and no detail would be left untouched.

Stephen had called upon Elly many times during the summer, but she always found ways to avoid him. She hoped that if she kept her distance, he might grow frustrated and call off the engagement. But he didn't. Instead, he remained patient.

Day after day, he tried to reach her heart in quiet ways. He would send flowers, cut fresh from the gardens by the estate's gardener—roses, lilies, even wildflowers, whatever he thought might please her. Sometimes he didn't even attempt to see her. He would simply leave the bouquet on her window ledge, perfectly arranged, where she couldn't help but see them.

Stephen's intentions were clear. He wanted her to know he was devoted, that he would be gentle, steady, and true. It was as if Elly occupied every corner of his thoughts. And the more she kept him at a distance, the more determined he became to win her heart—not just her hand.

Summer faded, and with it came the changing of the leaves and the tightening of time. It was now just two weeks until the wedding.

Elly had gone out riding early that morning—an attempt to feel free, if only for a little while. The mare she rode was her wedding gift from the Bentley estate, a chestnut horse with a smooth gait and calm temperament. She rode along the riverside beside the pasture, where the wind played through the tall grass and the sun danced on the water. After some time, she slowed her horse to a stop and let it lower its head to drink from the river.

The peaceful silence was suddenly broken by the sound of galloping hooves behind her. She straightened and turned in the saddle, her breath catching slightly.

Stephen.

He approached on his black stallion, the horse powerful and majestic as it moved toward her. With a gentle tug on the reins, Stephen brought the horse to a halt beside her and leaned forward slightly, trying to catch her eyes.

Elly," he said softly, catching his breath. I hoped I d find you here."

Steady, boy," Stephen murmured, leaning forward to pat his stallion s neck. The horse snorted softly and settled beneath him.

Good day, Elly," he said, his voice warm but cautious.

Good day, Stephen." Elly turned slightly in the saddle. You startled me—I didn t think anyone else would be out this far."

I apologize," he said sincerely. I didn t mean to frighten you. I often ride here when I want quiet—when I need space away from the plantation." He paused, studying her face. Are you alright?"

Yes, I m fine," Elly replied, her gaze drifting back to the river. The current moved lazily along the rocks, reflecting the golden hues of early evening.

Stephen hesitated for a moment, then cleared his throat.

Elly, may I ask you something?"

His voice was different this time—gentler, and more deliberate. The question made her turn toward him, surprised by the gravity in his tone.

Yes, what is it, Stephen?"

He looked at her with quiet intensity. "Do you think... you could ever love me?" He paused, his brow furrowed, his voice vulnerable. "I know this isn't the marriage you wanted. I know you didn't choose me. But do you think, in time, you might grow to love me?"

Elly stared at him. There was a raw honesty in his face—something tender and unsure. He didn't look like the man she imagined marrying. He looked like someone trying to build something fragile and real out of nothing.

She didn't know what to say.

He looked so sincere. The way he sat tall on his black stallion, eyes full of hope and uncertainty, it made her chest ache. Maybe it was pity. Or maybe... maybe it was something else. A seed, not yet sprouted.

"I don't despise you," she said softly. "I'm just... not in love with you. Not yet. But I think—maybe in time—I could be."

Stephen nodded slowly, a glimmer of relief flashing across his face.

"You are a good man, Stephen. But can you really live with me, knowing I'm not in love with you? Promise me to keep in mind that you may not find happiness with me. I don't want to hurt you, however your dream of happiness doesn't always come or can found be in others. "

He smiled, small and honest. "I can. I promise to give you everything you need—everything you want. I'll be honest with you. I'll be faithful. And in time, I believe your heart will change. That... I can live with."

They sat in silence for a moment, the river murmuring nearby, horses shifting beneath them.

"It's getting late," he said, glancing at the sky. "Shall I ride back with you?"

Yes," Elly said with a small nod, gathering her reins. That would be nice."

She gave her horse a gentle nudge, and Stephen followed, his stallion moving in step beside her. They rode back toward the estate in quiet companionship, two silhouettes against the setting sun—bound by fate, and now perhaps by something more.

The days passed swiftly, and though Elly had still not fully embraced the life that awaited her, she began to accept it. The decision her father had made was no longer met with the same resistance in her heart. She started to feel a quiet resignation, an acceptance that perhaps this life, though not of her choosing, could still offer something of value. She even found herself participating in the final preparations for the wedding with Carolyn. The buzz of excitement, the chatter of the guests, and the constant stream of visitors eager to admire the bride-to-be began to lift her spirits, despite the lingering uncertainty.

Elly s wedding gown, a delicate lace and satin creation, had been passed down through generations—worn first by her grandmother, then her mother, and now it was hers. The gown was beautiful, with intricate lacework that danced in the light, and satin that shimmered with every step. It was an heirloom of love and sacrifice, but to Elly, it felt like a reminder of the life she hadn t chosen, a life she was still learning to accept.

Though the wedding approached with its bright promises and sparkling expectations, Elly's thoughts often returned to the image of Stephen on his black stallion—the way his pleading eyes had looked into hers, filled with hope and longing. She tried to hold onto that image, hoping that perhaps the more she thought of him, the more she might begin to feel something more than the quiet affection that had started to grow in the space between them.

On the wedding day, Elly complied with her father s wishes, standing before the grand altar at the Bentley mansion in front of a sea of guests, family, and friends. The ceremony was nothing short of magnificent—the grandest event the estate had ever seen. Stephen stood beside her, the look in his eyes one of pure adoration. And though Elly gave him her vows, there was an emptiness in her heart that she couldn t quite fill.

That night, as husband and wife, they shared their first night together. Elly gave him her body, but her heart—still a fragile, closed thing—remained untouched. Stephen adored her with all his being. He whispered his promises of love and protection into the quiet of the night, his voice firm, yet tender. To him, she was everything—his heart, his soul, his very reason for living. There could be no other woman who would ever hold the place in his life that Elly did.

He knew, deep down, that winning her love would take time. But he was patient. He had always been patient. Stephen lavished her with gifts—beautiful dresses from the finest European designers, jewelry that glittered like stars, and flowers, always flowers. Each morning, when Elly awoke, fresh blooms would greet her, carefully arranged in vases beside her bed. Stephen hoped that through these little acts, he could touch her heart, show her the depth of his devotion.

But beneath the surface of all the grand gestures, Stephen worked tirelessly. With Samuel ill and unable to oversee the plantation, Stephen had to take on more responsibility. He worked from dawn to dusk, ensuring that the estate ran smoothly, even as his thoughts often strayed to Elly. He believed with all his heart that, given time, she would come to love him as he loved her.

With Chestin s return from school, Stephen found himself less tethered to the plantation, his responsibilities growing more each day. The plantation was flourishing under Stephen s guidance, and with the arrival of Chestin, Stephen was confident the business would continue to expand. Together, they began to handle the intricate balance of managing crops and dealing with the legalities that came with the land, while also assisting their father in business matters in New Orleans.

Stephen's frequent trips to the city became more regular, leaving Elly behind in the quiet solitude of the Bentley mansion. He had become deeply involved in Antonio's family business, and with the absence of other heirs, Antonio had made it clear that Stephen would play a key role in his future plans. It was an opportunity Stephen could not refuse, and though he had agreed to take on the mantle, it took him away from Elly more than ever.

Elly didn't mind his absence. In fact, it brought her a strange sense of relief. She had never wanted this life—had never wanted to be bound by the duties of a plantation wife. With Stephen gone, she could find her own peace, her own distractions. Her days were filled with projects, most of which involved organizing grand events with Carolyn, who had become a close companion. They spent hours planning the upcoming balls, and Carolyn, ever the gracious hostess, shared the secrets of creating the perfect celebration—how to ensure the guests were entertained and what the latest trends were in the world of society and etiquette.

Every week, Theresa would visit from town, joining the two women in the garden for tea, gossip, and discussion of the latest news. Though Elly's heart felt disconnected from her new life, the daily routines of her mother and Carolyn helped fill the silence. Theresa's tales from the shops, her accounts of the whispers in town, painted a vivid picture of a city divided. The talk of Voodoo and black magic that permeated the air intrigued Elly, though it also unsettled her. Rumors swirled about rituals and dark practices from Africa—stories passed down through the slaves that had been brought to New Orleans—and it seemed that every corner of the city had its own secret.

New Orleans itself was a city at war within. Creoles, blacks, and immigrants clashed, their political and religious views a constant source of tension. The plantation, with its quiet, ordered existence, felt like an isolated world in the middle of this growing chaos. While the city grappled with its identity, Elly felt increasingly removed, as though the outside world was moving on without her. The gossip that traveled through the city—whispers of upheaval, of change, of cultural battles—was both a mystery and a warning. And though Elly did not know it, she was on the precipice of a much larger world than the one she had ever imagined.

Stephen s absence seemed to open a door within her heart, one that was not only filled with the fear of what she had lost but also the curiosity of what might be found beyond the gates of the plantation. The days spent on the estate with Carolyn and her mother were filled with calm, but Elly could feel a growing sense of unrest deep within her, a restlessness that would not be so easily silenced.

CHAPTER FIFTEEN

Several years had quietly passed at the Bentley mansion. Samuel was gone now—lost to respiratory complications after a battle with pneumonia. He'd refused to give up his cigars, stubborn to the end. In fact, he died exactly the way he wanted: a lit cigar in one hand, a glass of whiskey in the other.

Stephen hadn't left his father's side during the two weeks Samuel lingered between life and death. When the end came, all three sons—Stephen, Chestin, and Grant—were there. Grant had returned home from school and decided to stay on, helping his brothers with the plantation. It was the first time in years the three had lived under the same roof again.

Samuel's final words were soft, barely audible murmurs. But they were words of peace. He died a happy man, proud of his sons and the legacy he'd helped build. He'd created a fortune and a name to pass down, and he knew it.

Life at the plantation continued, albeit with a quieter rhythm.

Carolyn took over the household, managing the servants with practiced grace. Elly assisted when she could, though she preferred solitude. More often than not, she could be found tucked away with a book or venturing into town for the occasional play, opera, or cultural event. Stephen accompanied her when his schedule allowed, though those moments became increasingly rare.

Burdened by mounting responsibilities, Stephen handed off much of the day-to-day plantation management to Chestin. The change allowed him to spend more time working closely with Antonio, whose demands had grown more intense with each passing week.

Chestin had met a lovely young woman named Veronica while away at school. They married soon after and welcomed a child not long thereafter. Wanting some independence, Chestin had a modest country home built on five acres of the plantation—close enough to remain connected, yet far enough to start a household of his own.

As the middle son, Chestin was two years younger than Stephen. He lacked the striking features of his brothers—shorter in stature and carrying a bit of extra weight—but what he lacked in appearance, he made up for in integrity. He was solid, dependable, and honest, the kind of man whose strength lay in quiet consistency. Stephen trusted him deeply and relied heavily on his help in managing the plantation's daily operations.

There had never been any tension among the brothers over land or money. They were raised to work hard and to share—united by the same goals their father had instilled in them. They would not allow power or greed to divide them.

Though Samuel's will named Stephen the sole beneficiary, he didn't hesitate to divide the property into three equal shares after their father's death. The brothers agreed to continue working together in partnership.

Stephen and his family remained in the main house, along with Carolyn, who oversaw the home as she always had. It was her wish to be buried beside Samuel in the family cemetery when the time came. Grant, the youngest, had the option to either stay at the mansion or build a house of his own. For now, he chose the comfort and convenience of the mansion.

Grant was strikingly handsome, favoring his mother's features—wavy blonde hair, hazel eyes, and a chiseled jawline. His body was lean and strong, shaped by years of riding horses and boxing. There was a rugged charm about him, a "bad boy" quality that made him both captivating and unpredictable.

At nineteen, Grant led a carefree life. He worked hard on the plantation by day, but by night, he'd ride into town to gamble at the local saloons. He smoked cigars, drank whiskey like his father, and often returned home at dawn—sometimes with a black eye from a brawl. He rarely came out the worse for wear; he could more than hold his own in a fight.

The local sheriff knew him by name. On occasion, Grant would be locked up for the night just to sober up. Stephen kept a close watch over his younger brother, feeling a deep responsibility for him—perhaps more than was necessary. Grant was, after all, legally an adult. But Carolyn had long since lost any influence over her youngest son, and Stephen had taken on the role of protector by default.

Whenever Carolyn tried to scold Grant for his reckless behavior, Samuel would quickly cut her off with a casual, "Let the boy be." It frustrated her. Deep down, she believed Samuel's indulgence only encouraged Grant to live life on the wild side—and while she loved her youngest son dearly, his choices often filled her with dread.

Grant was well-known among the young women who worked and socialized in the saloons each night. Handsome, charming, and wealthy, he was considered one of the most eligible bachelors in the region. With his easy smile and magnetic personality, he seduced more than a few into his bed. But he had no interest in settling down. The thought of committing to one woman felt like a cage. Grant was young, unburdened, and eager to taste all the pleasures life had to offer—especially the ones that came wrapped in mystery or mischief.

From time to time, Grant took Stephen's place and escorted Elly to the playhouse. New Orleans could be dangerous for a woman alone, and he never minded stepping in—at least not outwardly. He would smile politely, even while tugging uncomfortably at his collar and stiff bow tie. Elly appreciated his company, and though he rarely understood the performances, he never let on.

Occasionally, after a show, Elly would agree to join him for a drink at one of the more reputable saloons. She noticed the shift in him the moment they stepped inside. His eyes lit up with boyish excitement, as if the room itself welcomed him home. Grant belonged to the night. The flicker of gas lamps, the clink of whiskey glasses, the hum of laughter and music—this was his playground.

CHAPTER SIXTEEN

Stephen and Elly had been married for eight years now. Despite their deep bond, they had been unable to conceive a child and had long since abandoned hope. The silence of their home, while peaceful, sometimes echoed with the absence of what might have been.

Chestin, on the other hand, enjoyed a thriving, fertile marriage. He and Veronica had just welcomed their fifth child—a son named Samuel Edgar Bentley. After four daughters, the arrival of a boy brought immense joy to the family. Carolyn, especially, was thrilled by the news. The baby's name, a tribute to her late husband, made her heart swell with pride and sorrow.

Carolyn had been in declining health for the past year. She was no longer able to move around the estate as freely as she once had, but she remained mentally sharp and emotionally anchored. Almost daily, she would have a carriage bring her to the family cemetery. There, in the quiet afternoon light, she'd sit in a chair placed beside Samuel's grave. A teacup in hand, she spoke aloud to the cold stone engraved with his name, as if he were seated beside her, listening.

The Bentley plantation held the distinction of being the only property in New Orleans legally permitted to conduct underground burials. Situated inland on the north side of town, it was immune to the swampy water tables that plagued the rest of the region. Within the city limits, above-ground crypts and vaults were the norm—but the Bentleys were buried in the earth, among cotton fields and long southern winds.

The view from Samuel s gravesite was a remarkable one. Cotton fields stretched out like a pale green sea, and in the far distance, the silhouette of the mansion could be seen standing like a quiet sentinel. When the wind picked up, it would pass through Carolyn s thick gray hair, tied neatly into a ponytail, and she d close her eyes and smile. This was where she would rest, and this, she knew, was the view she wanted to carry with her on her final day.

Meanwhile, Stephen s responsibilities had grown nearly unmanageable. Since taking over Antonio s shops in town, he had been working long hours, balancing the needs of the plantation with his growing business ventures. The daily ride across the city was punishing—hot, jarring, and time-consuming-so—so Stephen eventually purchased a small one-bedroom flat in town to ease the strain.

Grant often stayed there as well, usually when he had been out drinking too late and needed a place to crash. Sometimes he helped Stephen with shop management and errands, but his unpredictable lifestyle made it difficult for Stephen to rely on him fully. While Grant wasn t lazy—he worked hard when asked—his priorities remained far different from those of his older brothers. He lacked the seriousness and focus that defined both Stephen and Chestin.

Still, Stephen tried to include him when he could. He couldn t help but feel a lingering sense of responsibility for Grant, especially with their mother s health declining and so much of the family legacy at stake.

Stephen carried a quiet sorrow in his heart. He wasn t spending as much time with Elly as he wanted, and the distance between them seemed to widen with each passing year. They still shared dinners when she was in town—after a play or an afternoon of shopping—but rather than growing closer, Stephen often felt like they were drifting apart. He adored her—her beauty, her flair, her spirit—but the absence of a child between them left a silent ache in him. It was a space he couldn't fill, no matter how much he loved her.

One particular morning, Stephen awoke alone in his flat in town. The memory of Elly lingered in his thoughts—her voice, her smile, the scent of her perfume—and he found himself aching to be near her. The storm that had raged through the night had finally passed, and puddles glistened along the streets. The sun had just begun to peek over the hills, casting a pale light through the windowpanes.

He made a decision: the town could wait. Today, he would go home.

Slipping on his coat, Stephen tucked a brown-wrapped parcel beneath it, shielding it from the damp morning air. Inside was a gift for Elly—a stunning red satin dress he had purchased from a French dressmaker who had recently opened a boutique in the Quarter. Lavishing Elly with gifts was something Stephen had never ceased to do, no matter how busy his life became. Every morning, he still had the gardener place fresh flowers in her room, a silent gesture of devotion.

As he rode through the front gates of the Bentley estate, the morning light broke fully over the land. Dew and rain still clung to the grass and trees, catching the sunlight and scattering it in golden shards across the fields. Stephen's heart stirred at the beauty of the scene, at the peace of being home.

He dismounted in front of the house, handing the reins of his stallion to a waiting servant.

"Good mornin', Sir," said Jacob, the older Black man who had served the family for decades.

Good morning, Jacob," Stephen replied, brushing the wet from his coat. Please see to my horse. Is Mrs. Bentley still in her quarters?"

Yes, sir. The house is quiet," Jacob said with a nod as he took the reins.

Stephen offered a small smile and pulled the package from beneath his coat. He stepped inside, boots echoing softly on the polished floor as he made his way up the long grand staircase. At the end of the hall, he paused in front of Elly s door. Gently, he knocked.

When he pushed the door open, he saw her already awake. The curtains had been drawn back, letting golden morning light spill into the room. Elly sat up in bed, the covers drawn to her waist, her hair softly tousled. She turned her head as he entered.

Stephen stepped forward, the package still in his hands, a quiet eagerness in his expression.

Stephen, what a surprise. I thought you had work in town?" Elly said, eyebrows raised as he stepped inside.

I do," he replied softly, but I wanted to see you." He held out the neatly wrapped brown package. I thought you might like this."

Elly took it, her expression curious as she began to untie the string. Stephen watched her with quiet anticipation, then glanced around the room. His eyes landed on the small vase by the window—empty.

He blinked, frowning.

No flowers this morning?" he asked, his voice low, but already tinged with sharpness.

Elly looked over, seemingly unbothered. Hmm. You re right. That s odd," she said, her tone light, distracted by the gift in her hands.

Stephen's tired body pulsed with sudden heat. He had made the long, muddy ride just to be with her, driven by love, guilt, and longing. That single detail—the missing flowers—felt like a betrayal of everything he tried to hold together.

His hands clenched.

He turned on his heel and stormed out, the package still unopened in Elly's lap.

"Jacob! Where are the servants?" Stephen's voice boomed through the hallway. His boots struck the floor like gunfire as he charged down the staircase. Startled murmurs rose from the corners of the house. Doors creaked open. Faces appeared, uncertain and afraid.

One young maid, no more than fifteen, dropped to her knees and began to cry, overwhelmed by the sound and fury. She had never heard Stephen raise his voice—until now.

He burst through the back doors into the garden, his eyes wild. The storm had left the grounds soaked. A man stood at the bench washing down gardening tools, whistling softly to himself.

Stephen marched toward him, livid.

"What is the meaning of this?" he shouted. "I have one request—one—and you can't fulfill your duty?"

The gardener looked up, startled, water dripping from the trowel in his hands. Stephen was already grabbing the rose shears from the bench, pacing in a tight circle around him, pointing with the sharp tool like a weapon.

"My wife wakes up, and there are no flowers in her room. That's all I ask. Every single morning! How hard is that?"

The gardener swallowed hard and removed his worn hat, clutching it in both hands. His head bowed.

Master Bentley... I m sorry, sir. The rain last night—it soaked the beds. I was fixin to get to them first thing. I didn t mean no disrespect."

Stephen stood over him, breathing heavily, chest rising and falling as the weight of his anger caught up with him. The shears trembled in his hand.

There was a long, terrible pause. Then Stephen dropped the shears back on the bench with a loud clatter and walked away, silent now, shame rising in the place of rage.

Stephen stormed into the garden, fury still burning through him. He marched to the rose bushes and began cutting stems with unsteady hands, unaware of the sharp thorns slicing into his skin. Blood welled up from his palms and fingers, but he paid it no mind. He moved with single-minded focus, yanking a dozen blooms from the bush, red petals clinging to his damp coat.

Clutching the bundle of roses, his hands raw and bleeding, Stephen strode back into the house. Servants watched in silence from shadowed corners, their eyes wide, whispering nervously among themselves. No one dared approach him.

He climbed the grand staircase two steps at a time and pushed open Elly s door.

She sat upright in bed, startled. Stephen?"

Without a word, he crossed the room and placed the roses into the empty vase. Crimson droplets fell onto the table, blooming on the polished wood like tiny blossoms of their own.

Elly s eyes widened as she saw the blood running down his hands.

Oh my Goodness—Stephen!"

She leapt from the bed and rushed to him. Grabbing a towel from the vanity, she gently wrapped it around his torn hands, pressing them to her chest to stop the bleeding. Her voice was low and steady, though her eyes shone with alarm.

"What are you doing?" she whispered. "Are you alright?"

Stephen stood still, head bowed, rain-soaked clothes clinging to him. The fury had drained from him, replaced by something heavier, fragile and exposed.

His voice cracked. "I don't know."

He still wouldn't meet her eyes. His shoulders slumped, and he looked down, the towel now spotted with red. "I try so hard, Elly. I love you so much. But I don't think you'll ever love me the way I love you."

Tears welled in his eyes, and one finally rolled down his cheek, disappearing into the collar of his coat.

"I need you. I'm afraid of losing you," he whispered. "But I don't know what else to do. I don't know how to make you love me."

At last, he looked up. His face was flushed, his expression raw.

Elly's heart ached at the sight of him—wounded, not just in his hands but in his soul. Her own tears spilled freely now. She reached for him, pressing her forehead to his, still holding his hands close to her chest.

"Stephen," she said softly, "I do love you. I have for a very long time."

She brushed her cheek against his, her voice trembling.

"You don't have to try so hard. You've given me everything a woman could dream of. I don't want riches—I want you. Just you."

Stephen let out a shaky breath and rested his head on her shoulder. Her arms wrapped around him, anchoring him, forgiving him. His chest rose and fell with quiet sobs, the kind that had been waiting far too long to escape.

I m so sorry for my actions," he whispered.

Elly just held him tighter, not needing anything else.

Don t worry, my darling. Everything will be alright," Elly whispered as she guided Stephen to the bed.

He was weary—his shoulders heavy with more than just the weight of a long ride or his wounded hands. Elly removed his boots and called softly for a servant to bring bandages and antiseptic. When the supplies arrived, she accepted them quietly and closed the door behind her, leaving the world beyond them to fade.

She undressed Stephen gently, lifting the damp fabric from his skin as if it were fragile. The silence between them wasn t cold—it was full of unspoken words, years of distant affection now drawing closer.

Elly wrapped his injured hands with slow care, holding them within her delicate fingers. When she finished, she stood back, letting the sunlight wash over her as it poured through the window. The light seemed to gather around her as if drawn to her stillness.

Her eyes met Stephen s. There was no fear in them now, only quiet resolve. She reached up and untied her silk nightgown, letting it fall. For the first time, she stood before him with nothing held back.

Stephen s breath caught. He had always seen her as beautiful, but never like this—unshielded, vulnerable, present. It wasn t just her body that was revealed, but her trust.

Elly stepped forward and climbed gently onto the bed, curling against his side, resting her head on his chest. He wrapped his arms around her, cradling her close. They didn t speak. They didn t need to.

Their closeness grew slowly, naturally, like a fire stirred back to life from embers long thought to be fading. Each movement, each breath, each touch was deliberate, tender, and filled with meaning.

What passed between them that morning was not only passion, but the beginning of something deeper, healing, a rediscovery.

Hours later, Elly slept beside him, her features soft and peaceful. Stephen watched her with a heart so full it ached. Her lips, parted in sleep, were tinted with a natural rose, and her cheeks glowed with a warmth he had never seen before.

In that moment, Stephen knew she loved him—not because of gifts or gestures, but because she had let him in. At last, he had found the connection he had longed for.

Not in the grandness of romance, but in the quiet truth of their closeness.

CHAPTER SEVENTEEN

The following year, Carolyn passed away. A servant found her in bed on a cold November morning—breathless and still. Her face bore a peaceful expression, and Stephen took comfort in believing she had gone to a place where she felt welcomed and at peace. Death was never something Carolyn had feared. She had lived a long, fulfilling life.

In the wake of her passing, Elly became the sole manager of the household and its staff.

Winter arrived quickly and harshly. It was a bitter season, both in weather and in spirit. Carolyn's absence weighed heavily on the family during the holidays. Christmas, once filled with warmth and laughter, was quiet and subdued. Many of the servants had fallen into a deep sadness. Carolyn had treated them with dignity and affection; to them, she was not just an employer, but a friend. Her absence left a hollow space in the halls of the mansion—and in their hearts.

But spring eventually returned, as it always did, bringing with it softer breezes and renewed energy. The hard winter had passed, and with it, the sharpest edge of grief began to dull. Life on the plantation gradually resumed its rhythm. The family, though changed, began to move forward.

Over the years, Carolyn had carefully trained Elly in the art of household management and the importance of maintaining a presence in the public eye. Hosting galas was not just about celebration—it was a symbol of status, a way to remain connected with prominent neighbors and business partners. Elly had watched and learned diligently, and now, she felt ready to carry that legacy forward.

It had been several years since the Bentley mansion hosted a grand event. With new purpose, Elly decided to plan her first gala.

She retrieved the old invitation rosters from Carolyn's desk and began assembling a guest list. She contacted the orchestra from the Opera House and set a date—April, when the flowers would be in bloom and the evenings mild.

The event would be a masquerade ball. Elly gave precise instructions to the cooks and servants for the elaborate preparations. The household bustled with activity once again. She had the staff gather feathers and craft elegant masks for the guests—vibrant and whimsical for the women, each attached to a delicate handle, and simpler, ribbon-tied masks for the men.

Wanting to share the joy of the project, Elly invited Veronica to help. Over the years, the two women had grown close. Though Veronica's hands were full with the children, she appreciated being included. It was exciting to be part of something creative and festive.

Carolyn had loved Veronica like a daughter, but it had always been Elly who held a special place in her heart—something unspoken, but understood.

Elly had entrusted Grant with several invitations to extend to his circle of acquaintances, though she had been clear: this would be a reputable affair, and he was to keep that in mind when selecting guests. Grant, however, had a history of mingling with questionable characters in saloons and had already been led astray in a few dubious business dealings. Both Stephen and Elly worried about the company he kept—but Grant remained unapologetically drawn to a life of easy pleasures and unpredictable adventures.

The evening of the gala arrived in a swirl of anticipation. Everything was set perfectly.

The musicians arrived early, tuning their instruments as the sun dipped below the horizon. Inside the mansion, a grand spread awaited the guests—delicate pastries, fresh fruits, and aged cheeses arranged with exquisite care upon gleaming silver platters. Champagne chilled in crystal buckets, and the finest wines from town lined the bar alongside bottles of aged whisky, brandy, and scotch.

The Bentley mansion radiated elegance. Every room was open and glowing with soft, golden light. Crystal chandeliers sparkled above the black-and-white marble floors, each tile waxed and polished to a mirror-like shine. Small tables encircled the dance floor, each one draped with handmade lace tablecloths imported from Italy.

Elly had worried that Stephen might not return from town in time—his day had been full of business meetings. It mattered to her deeply that he stand beside her when the guests arrived. Fortunately, he made it back just in time to change into his formal attire. For the evening, he selected a sleek black mask adorned with three white feathers on one side, subtle yet striking.

Elly wore the red satin dress Stephen had brought her from France. The neckline dipped low in the front, revealing a graceful curve of cleavage. Her mask, custom-made to match, featured soft red feathers that fanned elegantly above her brow.

Just before the first guests arrived, Stephen found Elly in the center of the ballroom. The warm candlelight shimmered off her dress as she stood beneath the chandelier, a vision of poise and anticipation. He approached her, silent for a moment, simply taking her in.

I have something for you, my dear," Stephen said, his voice warm and deliberate as he handed Elly a small velvet box tied with a silk bow.

Stephen, you spoil me," Elly said with a smile, undoing the ribbon. Inside, nestled in satin, lay a string of luminous pearls crowned with a delicate gold heart pendant.

It s beautiful," she whispered, touched by the gesture.

Not as beautiful as the lady who wears it," he replied, his eyes fixed on her. Allow me?"

She handed the necklace back to him and turned, sweeping her hair aside. He fastened the clasp gently behind her neck, then she turned to face him.

What do you think?" she asked, tilting her chin slightly.

Absolutely captivating," he said, his gaze lingering on her eyes longer than propriety might allow at a public gathering.

You do too much for me," she murmured, glancing away toward the flurry of activity in the ballroom where servants were making final adjustments to the tables.

It appears the first of our guests have arrived," Stephen said, nodding toward a couple entering the ballroom s grand archway.

Together, they moved to greet them.

Marcus and Vivian, lovely to see you both," Stephen said, extending a hand to Marcus and bowing to kiss Vivian s hand with polished grace.

Bravo! This is fabulous! A masquerade—who would have thought?" Marcus exclaimed, eyes dancing beneath his half-mask.

Splendid idea, darling," Vivian chimed in, directing her compliment to Elly. Her own mask glittered with tiny emeralds, a perfect match to her gown.

As the minutes passed, the mansion buzzed with voices and laughter. Guests filled the rooms, swirling into conversation and drink, the air humming with excitement and mystery. When all had arrived, Elly gently instructed everyone to don their masks, veiling identities and adding a playful, provocative air to the festivities.

Later in the evening, Grant made his entrance with two unfamiliar men. Stephen caught sight of them as they crossed the marble threshold—

Grant's companions were well-dressed but carried themselves with a casual defiance that made Stephen wary.

"Stephen, I'd like you to meet Jonathan Tate and Clyde Parker," Grant said. "They're opening a new playhouse in the French Quarter. Jonathan's a director—just arrived from England last month."

Stephen extended his hand with a cordial nod. "Nice to meet you both. Sounds like... stimulating work."

His tone was flat, courteous but cool. He barely glanced at the men before his eyes drifted toward the crowd, already distracted. To Stephen, theater and its artistic pursuits belonged in a world far removed from labor and legacy. With a tight smile, he excused himself and walked off, leaving the trio standing near the entry.

Grant chuckled softly, turning to his companions. "Apologies, my brother doesn't spend much time in theaters. Or anywhere he can't make a deal."

"No offense taken," Jonathan said with a laugh. "Not everyone appreciates the stage."

"Well then," Clyde grinned, "show us to the whiskey and the women you so generously promised."

With a knowing smirk, Grant led them toward the bar, the three men disappearing into the clamor of masks, crystal glasses, and candlelight.

Elly returned from the kitchen, where she had ensured the cooks stayed on schedule with the fresh pastries and that no last-minute disasters loomed. Carolyn had once handled these matters with grace and poise, and Elly now felt the weight of that legacy on her shoulders.

As she stepped back into the ballroom, she paused. The scene before her was breathtaking—guests swirling across the marble floor in elegant attire, their faces hidden behind colorful masks, the soft glow of chandeliers reflecting in crystal goblets. The music swelled, and laughter chimed like bells in the air.

Her eyes scanned the room—until they caught on a man watching her.

He stood near the bar, medium height, with thick dark hair and a confident posture. His black feathered mask was striking, but what stood out more was the single white rose pinned to his lapel. When he realized she'd seen him staring, he didn't look away. Instead, he raised his glass in a silent toast and smiled, nodding in her direction.

Elly, unsure who he was beneath the mask, returned a polite nod before disappearing into the crowd.

Across the ballroom, Grant had seen the interaction. He walked up to the man—Jonathan—and slung a friendly arm around his shoulder.

"Beautiful," Grant said, grinning. "But taken."

"Oh, but they're never truly taken," Jonathan quipped, his voice playful.

"That one is," Grant replied with a chuckle.

"And the taken beauty's name?"

"Elly. Elly Bentley. She's Stephen's wife."

Jonathan let out a low whistle. "Ah... I see. My mistake. Still—you can't blame a man for noticing."

"Come on then," Grant said, steering him away. "Let me show you who's not off-limits."

As they moved across the floor, Jonathan cast one last glance over his shoulder at Elly. She hadn't noticed.

Elly continued weaving through the crowd until she found Stephen in conversation with a young man.

"Elly, my dear," Stephen said, waving her over, "I want you to meet Pedro Santiago. He's an artist from Spain—I'm hoping to commission a portrait of you."

Elly smiled graciously and extended her hand. "Pleasure to meet you, Mr. Santiago."

"Ah, the pleasure is mine," Pedro replied, taking her hand lightly. He looked her over thoughtfully, not with rudeness but with the calculating eye of a painter studying his subject. "Exquisite. Your eyes, your hair—it would be an honor to capture such beauty on canvas."

"Good," Stephen said, clapping Pedro on the shoulder. "Let's meet in town this week to finalize the details."

Turning to Elly, he added, "I'd love for you to wear this very dress for the portrait. You look absolutely stunning tonight, my dear."

"Of course, I will," Elly said softly as she reached for Stephen's hands.

"Come with me." She led him toward the dance floor.

There was no music playing yet. The crowd parted for them, stepping aside as Elly guided Stephen by the hand to the center of the room. Once they reached their mark, Elly turned to the conductor. With a graceful lift of her arm, she signaled him to begin.

Mozart's *Violin Concerto No. 3* filled the hall—the delicate notes echoing with elegance. It was Stephen's favorite.

"Shall we dance?" Elly asked, smiling up at him.

Applause rippled through the crowd as the music swelled. The couple began to move, twirling with effortless grace. Stephen held Elly close, his hand firm yet gentle on her waist. They seemed to float, completely attuned to each other.

At the bar, Jonathan watched with a whiskey in hand. His gaze was fixed on Elly, mesmerized by the way she moved—elegant, seductive, radiant under the golden lights. Her dark brown eyes kept lifting to Stephen, filled with warmth and affection.

Jonathan's chest tightened. He envied Stephen deeply—the man who held her heart, her attention, her touch. Elly's graceful poise stirred something within him, something aching and unresolved. A vision flickered through his mind: her lips on his. The more he drank, the more vivid and insistent these fantasies became.

Overwhelmed, Jonathan stepped out into the night, seeking relief in the garden. He found a secluded spot beneath a tree, away from the footpath, and sank to the ground. With the whiskey still in hand, he stared up at the full moon, his thoughts consumed by the woman he could not have.

Back inside, the dance ended. Stephen excused himself to speak with a business partner, leaving Elly to mingle among the guests. But the crowded room felt stifling, and she needed a breath of air. Slipping out quietly, she made her way to the gardens.

She stopped by the fountain, gazing down at the lily pads drifting across the water's surface. The moonlight bathed her in silver, casting soft shadows across her shoulders. She folded her arms against the evening chill.

From his spot beneath the tree, Jonathan saw her—just a silhouette at first, framed in moonlight. But he knew immediately. It was Elly.

The same woman who had haunted his thoughts.

Still wearing his mask, Jonathan rose unsteadily and approached. His footsteps were nearly silent in the grass, and when he spoke, Elly startled, spinning to face the masked figure emerging from the darkness.

Excuse me—I didn't mean to startle you," Jonathan said gently.

You didn't frighten me," Elly replied, though her voice betrayed the slight tremble of surprise. What are you doing out here?"

I needed some fresh air," he said, glancing up at the night sky. I love this time of year—when the air is crisp and cool. Your gardens are splendid."

Thank you." Elly studied him in the moonlight. His dark brown eyes held a quiet intensity, and his jet-black hair framed a face both handsome and enigmatic. The mask added to his mystique, giving him the air of a gentleman from another time.

Do I know you?" she asked, her curiosity piqued.

I'm afraid not. We haven't been properly introduced." He extended a hand politely. Jonathan Tate. Grant invited me to join him this evening."

Ah, Grant," Elly said with a smile, recognizing the name.

Jonathan laughed softly, glancing away before returning his gaze to hers. From your tone, I gather you're not entirely fond of Grant's choice in company?"

No, it's not that," she said quickly. It's just... Grant lives a rather wild life. It's exhausting trying to keep up with him. But he's a wonderful brother-in-law—I love him dearly."

He is a good man," Jonathan agreed.

Are you enjoying yourself tonight?" Elly asked, smoothing a hand down her dress.

Very much so. You've thrown quite the extravagant masked ball."

Thank you." Elly looked away, slightly flustered. A strange feeling stirred inside her—a nervous flutter she couldn't quite place. She wasn't used to feeling off-balance in conversations, especially not with men.

I should get back," she said after a pause. "There are still guests I need to attend to. It was very nice to meet you, Jonathan."

The pleasure is mine, I assure you." Jonathan took her hand and bowed slightly, brushing his lips across her knuckles.

The warmth of his kiss lingered. It was a simple gesture, one she'd experienced many times, yet something about this moment unsettled her—softly, inexplicably.

She gently withdrew her hand and offered a polite wave as she turned and walked back toward the house. Her thoughts raced.

Why did that feel... different? she wondered. Why him?

Back inside, the party had begun to wind down. Some guests were gathering their coats, saying goodbyes as the midnight hour crept closer.

After the last guest had gone and the grand ballroom fell into silence, Elly remained seated alone amid the stillness. The servants had long since retired, knowing they would rise early to erase the traces of the night's celebration. By morning, the floors would gleam, the glasses would vanish, and not a single rose petal would betray the memory of the masquerade.

It had been a beautiful evening. Elegant, timeless, and filled with laughter. Yet now, in the hush that followed, the room felt like a memory slipping quietly into the past.

Elly's gaze wandered through the shadows, her thoughts drifting to Samuel and Carolyn. She could almost see them—greeting guests with warmth, dancing arm in arm beneath the chandeliers. A soft ache bloomed in her chest. They had been so good to her. She hoped they would be proud that she had carried on the tradition they so loved.

A THREAD BETWEEN LIVES

Her thoughts turned to her own parents—Antonio and Theresa. They were still alive, but time had bent their backs and slowed their steps. They hadn't come tonight. Antonio was too weak to travel, and Theresa refused to leave his side. Elly missed them dearly and resolved to visit them tomorrow.

As her eyes swept across the ballroom, they paused at the bar—the very spot where Jonathan had stood. She remembered the moment he lifted his glass in her direction, the boldness in his eyes, the way he had nodded after catching her watching him. There had been something unspoken in that exchange—something curious, almost magnetic.

Elly smiled faintly, then shook her head, rising from her chair. The echo of her footsteps followed her as she left the ballroom and climbed the stairs to her room.

She and Stephen did not share a bedroom. There were two master suites in the mansion now. After Samuel's death, Elly had redecorated his suite and made it her own. Stephen, however, had chosen not to move into Carolyn's. He'd cleaned it out—removed her clothes—but left everything else intact, preserving it like a shrine to the past. Instead, he remained in the bedroom he had occupied since childhood, a space that now offered a clear view of the stables.

Stephen loved to sit by the window and watch the stable hands train the new horses, a habit left over from boyhood. Over time, he and Elly had settled into their arrangement. Late in the evenings, Stephen would come to her room. Sometimes just to talk. Other times, to be more intimate. Their connection was comfortable, dependable. They understood one another. They knew what to expect.

And yet, Elly had never felt that burning passion for him.

She had married a man she wasn't in love with. Over the years, she had come to love him deeply—genuinely—but not in the way she had once dreamed of. She often wondered what might have been, had she been given a choice.

Would she have loved Stephen differently if they had met under other circumstances? If he had courted her properly, wooed her like the suitors in fairy tales?

Stephen was everything a woman should want—handsome, kind, generous. Her mind knew this. But her heart... her heart remained uncertain.

These thoughts haunted her, especially on quiet nights like this. And the burden of unanswered questions weighed heavier with each passing year.

CHAPTER EIGHTEEN

New Orleans transformed into a bustling city after sunset. Bourbon Street came alive, becoming the city's main attraction. Narrow streets were lined on both sides with saloons and guesthouses. The air reeked of stale liquor and bodily waste. People huddled together in the dim alleyways branching off from the main road. It was not a safe place to be after dark.

A night patrol officer strolled the street, dressed in blue and carrying a wooden nightstick, hoping his presence alone would deter troublemakers. Women in tight dresses with feather boas draped around their necks worked the streets, offering their bodies in exchange for money and fleeting pleasure. Jazz music floated through the steamy night air, while horse-drawn carriages clattered along the cobblestone streets, ferrying people to and from the city s vibrant core.

Elly maintained a permanent box seat at the town playhouse. Located on the second level to the right of the stage, the box was arranged to seat her and three guests. In earlier days, her mother and Carolyn often joined her, with Grant occasionally serving as their chaperone. Stephen, on the other hand, never particularly enjoyed the theater. He would attend if Elly insisted, but otherwise, he preferred to occupy himself elsewhere.

Tonight, Grant was her escort to the evening s performance. They arrived by carriage and were greeted at the entrance by a man distributing playbills. They entered just a few minutes before the show began—Elly disliked arriving too early. Disorderly men in the cheaper seats below would sometimes shout up toward the balcony patrons, and the heavy cigar smoke rising from the lower level often gave her headaches. The old building s ventilation system left much to be desired.

They were then escorted up a grand staircase. The wooden floors were covered with plush red carpeting. The playhouse carried a musty scent, a mixture of age and history. Large velvet drapes lined the walls, adding to the heavy, theatrical atmosphere. On the second level was the balcony, overlooking the stage below. The wooden railing of the balcony was hand-carved and painted a deep gold. Masterful paintings from the Renaissance era adorned the walls, each one a testament to elegance and taste.

Elly and Grant entered their private box. The two extra seats, unused that evening, were promptly removed to give them more room to relax and enjoy the performance. Below the stage sat a recessed area, lower than the main floor seating—this was where the orchestra performed. The pit remained dimly lit, revealing only the silhouettes of musicians as they played.

The play unfolded in four acts, with a short intermission following the second. When the final curtain fell, all the actors assembled on stage to bow and offer their thanks. The director joined them for the final bow and the ceremonial closing of the curtain.

Good evening Mrs. Bentley" Jonathan kissed her hand as he bowed to her.

Grant" he reaches for Grants hand to shake.

Great work Jonathan, it was a wonderful play" Grant says.

Very nice work. I did not know you were a director" Elly says looking at Jonathan. Yes, one of my many secrets that I keep" Jonathan teases. Elly looked at him in a puzzled manner. She was not sure what to think about the comment he just made.

I didn't know you two had met before?" Grant questioned speaking to Elly and Jonathan.

Yes, we met at the masquerade" Elly replies.

A lovely masquerade at that" Jonathan says as he looks at Elly.

Grant continued a conversation with Jonathan for a few minutes as they were talking Elly looked around acting as if she was not quite interested in what they were saying. She could feel Jonathan's eyes upon her, as he would listen to Grant then reply to what he had said. Jonathan had dark brown eyes; they were so dark they almost looked black. He had a flirtatious smile and manner about him when he talked. The way he looked deep into her eyes caused a flutter that tickled her stomach. She felt nervous in his presence. What are your plans for the evening? Would you like to go have a drink?" Jonathan said as he looked at both of them.

Elly was about to shake her head no, when Grant eagerly asks.

That sounds great, would you mind Elly?"

I really should not." Elly resists.

Just one drink. Come on you deserve to relax. I will take you home right after" Grant pleads.

Alright, just one drink" Elly says.

Jonathan holds his arm out to escort Elly as they leave.

Jonathan followed their horse drawn carriage to a small pub at the end of Basin Street about one block north of the French Quarter. This was a more quiet low key area a lot of the local Jazz artists would play at these back street brothels some even found fame here. The particular place where Jonathan had led them was to a narrow alley then down a small flight of stairs. A man was standing in the entryway leaning against the door smoking a cigar his hat pulled down low on his forehead almost to the point were you could not see his eyes. Jonathan walked by him first and the man nodded at him allowing us to enter. Grant had never taken Elly to this place before, it was a little bit outside of the area were Elly had felt comfortable. Tales of black magic, witches, and voodoo were poplar during this time. The only comforting thought was that, two men who knew this sort of lifestyle; escorted her.

As they stepped into the smoke-filled room, a few customers at the bar turned their heads to glance at the newcomers. The trio was slightly overdressed, having come straight from the theater. After a moment s curiosity, the patrons returned to their drinks and conversations.

The room was packed, with every table occupied. Jonathan surveyed the room until his eyes settled on a table where two men were seated. He walked over and casually tossed a silver coin onto the table. One of the men picked it up, inspected it, then exchanged a look with his companion. They stood, taking their drinks with them, and left without a word.

Jonathan carried himself with calm confidence—fearless and sure. He pulled out a chair for Elly, who sat down gracefully. Grant fetched two more chairs and placed them around the table, taking a seat beside Elly. Jonathan remained standing for a moment longer.

Elly, what is your pleasure?" he asked with a smile.

Elly blinked, caught off guard. She looked at him with confusion.

What would you like to drink?" Jonathan clarified.

Oh! Just a glass of tea… or water, please," she replied quickly.

Grant?" Jonathan turned to him.

Double scotch," Grant said. Make sure it s the good stuff."

"I'll return shortly," Jonathan said, offering a charming smile as he locked eyes with Elly for a beat before heading to the bar.

Elly leaned slightly toward Grant. "Your friend is quite the character," she said softly.

Grant nodded. "Yes, but he's a good man. He works hard and truly loves what he does. He used to act back in England, you know."

At the bar, Jonathan leaned casually against the counter and relayed their order to the bartender. While he waited, a young woman approached him. She wore a short red dancing dress with a matching boa draped around her neck. Without hesitation, she wrapped her arms around his neck and whispered something into his ear.

Jonathan responded with a grin, murmuring something back. She gave him a playful pout before dropping her arms. As she turned to walk away, she glanced toward the table where Elly and Grant sat.

Elly had seen the interaction but quickly turned her gaze, pretending not to notice what had just transpired between them.

"Jonathan is a lady's man, isn't he?" Elly asked Grant, leaning in slightly. "He has that certain look about him."

Grant chuckled. "He's harmless. A little flirtatious, but harmless. But you're right—the women do like him."

Just then, Jonathan returned, setting their drinks down on the table.

"Thank you," Elly said politely.

"So, Mrs. Bentley, did you enjoy the play?" Jonathan asked as he took his seat.

"Please, call me Elly. And yes, it was delightful. I especially loved Act Two."

"Ah, yes—when the brave warrior finds his way back to his love. That's a favorite among the ladies," Jonathan replied with a knowing smile. He studied her face for a moment. "You know, you have beautiful features—a lovely smile. Have you ever thought about acting?"

Elly laughed softly, shaking her head. "No, I don't have that kind of talent. I'd much rather watch. But thank you for saying that."

"Well, keep it in mind. I could always use a fresh face—and a beautiful woman," Jonathan said with a playful grin.

"Oh, I bet you can," Elly replied teasingly.

"Yes," Grant chimed in, smiling. "Jonathan doesn't get enough fresh young women falling all over his stage. That's all he gets. He never leaves any for me when I'm out with him."

Jonathan laughed. "Grant is teasing, of course. But really—think about it. I wouldn't start you with anything too difficult. Just a few lines, to see how you do."

Elly hesitated, then nodded. "Alright. I'll give it some thought."

Once again, the conversation shifted back to Jonathan and Grant. Elly sipped her tea and listened patiently. But she could feel Jonathan's dark eyes lingering on her. That same flutter returned in her chest—an odd weakness she didn't like, and one she couldn't explain.

The feeling unsettled her.

"Excuse me, please—where is the powder room?" Elly asked, interrupting their exchange.

Both men stood as she rose.

"Right behind that door," Grant said, pointing toward a door near the side of the bar.

"Would you like me to walk you over?" he offered.

No, I'll be fine. Thank you," Elly replied with a small smile, then walked off toward the restroom.

After entering through the first door, Elly found herself in a narrow hallway leading to another door. Just as she reached it, the woman who had been speaking privately with Jonathan at the bar emerged. Their eyes met. The woman glared at her with a smirk, still chewing gum.

As they passed, nearly shoulder to shoulder, the woman leaned slightly toward Elly and muttered, "Good catch, sweetie. Now see if you can keep him."

Her voice dripped with sarcasm. Elly stood still, stunned, and watched as the woman continued down the hall and out into the bar area without another glance.

She remained frozen for a moment, processing the comment. *What did she mean by that?* Elly wondered. *Who was a good catch? Grant—her brother-in-law? Or Jonathan—a man she barely knew?*

She shook her head, brushing off the comment. *The woman must've mistaken me for someone else,* she reasoned, and continued on to the powder room.

After freshening up, Elly returned to the table. Both men stood again as she approached and took her seat.

"It's getting late," Elly said, adjusting her gloves. "I really must be going now."

"Is everything alright?" Jonathan asked, watching her closely.

"Oh, yes," she replied with a polite smile. "I had a lovely evening. I just need to get back—it's a long ride home."

"You and Grant are more than welcome to stay at my château," Jonathan offered, his tone smooth and generous.

No, that s not necessary," she said, shaking her head. "Thank you, though. The play was wonderful. I hope to see more of your work now that the playhouse has a new director."

"I ll do my best to deliver," he said. "I have another production scheduled in a few months. I ll send you notice once it s ready."

Grant stood and extended his hand to help Elly from her seat.

"Let me go call for the carriage," he said. "Jonathan, would you mind walking Elly to the door? I ll just be a minute."

"Of course," Jonathan replied.

He offered his arm, and Elly hesitated just briefly before accepting it. Together, they walked slowly toward the door.

"I truly hope you ll consider my offer," Jonathan said in a low, deliberate voice. His head tilted slightly down, but his eyes looked up at her through thick lashes. There was something undeniably seductive in his gaze—controlled, practiced. Elly had no doubt this charm had worked on other women before.

She told herself she wouldn t fall under his spell. And yet, her knees felt unsteady, and a slight tremble betrayed her hand as he took it in his own.

"I really am too busy," she replied, trying to keep her voice firm. "But I do appreciate your kind words. Good night, Jonathan."

They had just stepped outside, and the sound of a horse-drawn carriage approaching signaled their ride. She turned to walk away, but Jonathan still held her hand. He didn t let go. When she looked back at him, he bowed slightly and brought her hand to his lips. The kiss was slow, deliberate. His warm breath and the wet press of his lips against her skin sent a shiver down her spine. His eyes remained fixed on hers as he lifted his eyebrows, a subtle gesture of mischief or intent—Elly couldn't quite tell.

She quickly pulled her hand away and stepped up into the carriage. "Good night," she said again, more briskly.

Grant was already inside and reached to steady her by the arm as she climbed in. As the carriage started to roll forward, he leaned his head out the window.

"Jonathan, I'll call on you tomorrow night, alright?" Grant called.

"Yes, my friend. All right," Jonathan answered, waving. He remained standing in the street, watching the carriage disappear into the night.

A few moments later, Elly glanced over her shoulder. She could still see the silhouette of a man watching them—watching her. She turned back around to find Grant's eyes on her. Not wanting him to read anything in her expression, she quickly broke the silence.

"Jonathan is a different sort of man," she said.

"Did you like him?" Grant asked, his voice casual but curious.

Elly hesitated. Was his question as innocent as it sounded?

"Did you think Jonathan was all right?" he clarified. "He's a lot of fun. He's saved me more than once after a few too many drinks. Looks out for me."

Elly nodded, realizing Grant had no idea about the confusing, magnetic feelings she'd experienced around Jonathan.

"Yes," she said. "He's... all right. He directed a good performance."

The rest of the ride passed in relative silence, broken only by the sound of wheels hitting uneven stones, jolting them side to side. Elly sat quietly, letting her mind wander—back to the moment Jonathan kissed her hand. She could still feel it: the warmth, the stir deep within her.

Excitement, and guilt.

She had always been faithful to Stephen—devoted, even. And yet, Stephen had never ignited this strange, burning sensation inside her.

Elly shut her eyes, forcing herself to think of other *things. No, she* told herself. Jonathan cannot stay in my mind. I won t allow it.

CHAPTER NINETEEN

A few days had passed since the play Elly and Grant had attended. Elly kept herself distracted, determined not to revisit the strange feelings that had overwhelmed her that night. She refused to dwell on them. Instead, she buried herself in her many tasks, and during her spare moments, she rode her horse along the pastures near the lake, letting the steady rhythm of hooves on earth quiet her mind.

Today, Stephen had arranged a meeting for her with Pedro Santiago, the painter he had commissioned for her portrait. Pedro arrived at the Bentley mansion shortly after noon, his two young apprentices in tow, carrying canvases, brushes, and boxes of oils and pastels.

Pedro wasted no time. With his easel being set up and his paints prepared by the apprentices, he had Elly stand before him. He circled her slowly, inspecting her posture, tilting his head thoughtfully as he evaluated her from every angle. From time to time, he paused, looked at the windows, then muttered to himself about the lighting.

Unsatisfied with the natural light, he directed his apprentices to arrange candles to correct the shadows. Then, he asked Elly to change into the red dress she would wear in the painting. Once she returned, he positioned a wooden stool near the window, guiding her to sit. Elly shifted her body slightly to the side, keeping her head turned forward, just as he directed.

Pedro continued circling her, moving her long hair over her shoulders, then back again, testing different visual balances. Around her neck, Elly wore the necklace Stephen had given her the night of the masquerade ball. The jewels caught the sunlight and glimmered where the beams hit just right.

Pedro was known for his meticulous process. He murmured repeatedly, No, no, it s not right," prompting his apprentices to adjust the background—fabrics, drapes, even the tilt of a chair in the corner. Still unsatisfied, he stood in thought, rubbing his chin.

Then, one of the apprentices noticed a bouquet of twelve white roses on the table beside the sofa. He plucked a single rose from the vase, gently shook off the water droplets, and handed it to Elly. She held it lightly in front of her, the crisp white petals standing out against the deep red of her dress.

Pedro s eyes widened. He clapped his hands together and laughed with delight.

Yes, yes! That is it. Wonderful!" he exclaimed. Now—let us begin."

The preparations had taken well over an hour, and Elly was already growing tired from sitting so still on the stool. Pedro made a few final adjustments to the paints his apprentice had mixed, carefully inspecting each color before finally beginning his masterpiece.

They worked for another two hours, allowing Elly only short breaks to stand and stretch. Pedro was deeply serious about his work, consumed with an artist s pride and precision. He could paint for hours without stopping—his endurance far surpassing that of most of his subjects. It was always the sitter who needed rest before he did.

When he finally called it a day, Pedro left his paints and canvas at the mansion, issuing strict instructions to the household staff. No one was to touch his materials, and under no circumstance was the sheet covering the portrait to be lifted. Do not disturb anything," he warned. Not until I return."

He informed Elly that he would be back early the next morning, prepared to work several more uninterrupted hours. She agreed only to appease Stephen—truthfully, she had little interest in having a portrait of herself at all.

After Pedro had gone, Elly decided to go for a ride. The long morning indoors had left her restless, and she needed fresh air and motion to shake off the stiffness. She made her way to her room and quickly changed into her riding attire. She slipped on her dark brown leather boots, which reached just below her knees—part of a wardrobe she had imported from England. In fact, most of Elly s belongings were imported, carefully selected from across Europe, with no expense spared. Though the local tailors were competent enough, Elly still preferred her trusted suppliers abroad.

She had already asked the stable hand to have her horse saddled and ready by the front steps.

When Elly finished dressing, she stepped outside to find Jacob waiting with her horse. The gray dappled stallion stood tall and alert, his coat gleaming in the sunlight as Jacob gave him a final brush-down.

Thank you, Jacob. I ll return in about an hour," Elly said, taking the reins from the black servant s hands.

Yes em, you be careful now, ma am. She s feelin frisky today," Jacob replied, holding the horse steady as Elly mounted with practiced grace.

I will," she assured him, settling herself sidesaddle and taking up the reins. With a gentle nudge of her heel, the stallion moved forward, and Elly rode off.

She preferred the elegance of English riding—something she d trained in as a young girl under the guidance of a professional champion rider. That instructor had long since returned to England, and no one else had quite measured up to his skill.

The afternoon was cool, though the sun offered a touch of warmth. Still, Elly found herself wishing she had worn a jacket. The pasture stretched out before her, empty and quiet. The grass, touched by the recent cold, had turned a golden hay color. Trees dotted the land, some beginning to show the pale green of new growth while others remained bare, skeletal against the sky.

She guided her horse toward one of her favorite places by Lake Pontchartrain—a secluded spot she often visited when she needed peace. It was quiet, just as she liked it. But as she sat still upon her mount, she caught the sound of laughter and splashing drifting from beyond the trees.

Curious, she gave a light tug on the reins and nudged her horse forward, walking slowly around the bend. The voices grew clearer, and one of them she instantly recognized—Grant s.

As she rounded the trees, she saw him and Jonathan standing at the water s edge, fishing poles in hand. Jonathan was holding up his line with a twelve-inch catfish dangling from the hook, its tail flapping wildly. Grant, drenched from the waist down, laughed as he wiped the water from his arms—evidence that he d helped wrestle the slippery fish from the shallows.

The men stopped laughing abruptly when they saw Elly perched on her horse, looking down at them with an unreadable expression.

Jonathan was the first to speak. Hello."

What in the world are you two up to?" Elly asked, a light smile playing on her lips as she watched their antics.

"Hello, Elly," Grant greeted her with a grin, brushing some of the water off his clothes.

"Don't tell me that little fish got the best of you two strong men," she teased, her voice lilting with amusement.

"Yes, well, I'm sure he'll be thinking that—when I'm eating him for dinner tonight," Jonathan quipped.

"I think you'll need to catch quite a few more of his brothers and sisters if you're planning to serve catfish for dinner," she replied with a soft laugh.

Grant gave her a mock-serious look. "Why don't you come show us poor souls how a professional catches fish?" He knew that Elly had gone fishing with Stephen on occasion and had even caught a few herself.

"Oh, I'd hate to interrupt your obvious expertise," Elly said, still smiling. "You seem to have things well under control—or should I say, the fish has you under control."

The two men exchanged a look and broke into laughter. Grant splashed a bit of water in her direction, but it fell short of reaching her.

"What brings you out this way?" Jonathan asked, shading his eyes from the sun with one hand as he looked up at her.

Elly glanced down at him, taking in the way the light caught his features. He wasn't dressed formally, but in rugged outdoor attire—thick wool trousers held up by suspenders, black leather boots just below the knee, and a faded blue denim shirt with the sleeves rolled halfway up his arms. His dark, tousled hair lifted slightly in the breeze. There was a rugged charm about him that made her chest tighten, though she pushed the feeling down.

"I needed some fresh air," she said evenly. "I enjoy riding out here by the lake."

"Hey Elly, could you let the cook know Jonathan and I will be staying for dinner?" Grant called out, casually.

"Elly hesitated. Oh... of course." She hesitated again, just for a second too long.

The thought of Jonathan—this man who stirred emotions in her she tried hard to suppress—sitting across from her at the dinner table unsettled her more than she cared to admit. But she was determined not to let anything show. She quickly added with a lighter tone, "Although I don't think we'll be having catfish."

"All right, that's enough. Or I'll have to come up there, drag you off that horse, and use you as bait," Grant called up to her with a laugh.

"Good day, boys," Elly replied playfully. She turned her horse and gave it a light kick, riding off and leaving them behind with a faint smile on her lips.

Elly decided to return home. She wanted to freshen up before dinner.

Jacob was waiting out front, just as she had expected. It had been about an hour since she left. Elly dismounted gracefully, handing him the reins with a pat and a soft kiss on the horse's snout.

"Be good to her," she said as she walked toward the front entrance.

"I will, ma'am," Jacob replied, leading the horse away.

Elly stopped by the kitchen to inform the staff that Grant and his companion would be staying for dinner. Then she made her way upstairs to her room. She asked her attendant to run a hot bath while she selected a wardrobe for the evening.

The warm water was a welcome comfort as Elly leaned back into the tub, soaking her smooth skin. She closed her eyes, letting herself relax completely, the heat easing the tension from her muscles.

But even in this moment of peace, her mind betrayed her.

She found herself recalling the scene by the lake—Grant and Jonathan fishing, laughing like carefree boys. She could clearly picture Jonathan's face, the way his smile curled slightly on one side, and the depth in his dark brown eyes as he looked up at her. The memory stirred something inside her.

No," she whispered to herself, splashing water onto her face. She would not let herself think of him anymore. She would not.

After dressing, there was a knock at the door.

Yes?" Elly responded.

Mrs. Bentley, dinner will be ready to serve in half an hour. Will that be satisfactory?" came a voice from outside.

Elly crossed the room and opened the door. Dora, her attendant, stood there politely waiting.

That will be fine, Dora. Thank you," Elly said with a nod. Dora gave a small curtsy and disappeared down the hall.

Have Grant and his guest arrived yet?" Elly asked.

Yes, madam. They're freshening up as we speak," Dora replied politely.

Half an hour will be fine. Thank you," Elly said, closing the door gently.

After finishing her evening attire, Elly descended the grand staircase. In the library, she found Grant, Jonathan, and Stephen seated with drinks in hand, engaged in light conversation. As she entered the room, all three men rose to their feet.

Elly wore a stunning emerald green satin dress, the lace trimming the neckline and sleeves with delicate detail. Her hair was neatly pulled back and tied with a matching green ribbon.

Stephen approached and kissed her gently on the cheek. Elly, my dear, have you met Jonathan Tate?" he asked.

Yes," Elly replied with a gracious nod. He directed the marvelous play that Grant and I attended last week."

A pleasure to see you again, Mrs. Bentley," Jonathan said, his gaze meeting hers.

Elly s eyes lingered on his for a moment before quickly turning away. Please, call me Elly."

Of course—my apologies," Jonathan said softly.

What s for dinner—catfish?" Grant teased with a grin.

Oh, let s not start that again," Elly said with a light laugh, which was echoed by both Grant and Jonathan.

Stephen smiled faintly, unsure of the joke that had brought them such amusement.

I believe dinner is ready. Shall we?" Stephen offered, extending his arm and leading the way toward the dining room.

They followed him into the elegantly prepared space. Fine china gleamed under the soft light of the chandelier, and crystal glasses sparkled at each place setting. Silverware was arranged with precision, and a grand floral arrangement served as the centerpiece, bursting with color and fragrance.

The table, large enough to seat twelve, had been set only for four. Stephen took his seat at one end, Elly at the other. Grant and Jonathan sat along the side, across from one another in the middle, allowing for easy conversation among them all.

During dinner, the three men dominated the conversation. Elly sat quietly, eating her meal and glancing between them as they spoke. She made a conscious effort not to look at Jonathan, though on several occasions she could feel his gaze lingering on her. Stephen noticed it too. Each time he caught Jonathan looking toward Elly, he would steer the discussion—often bringing up Jonathan's work or politics—to redirect his attention.

To Stephen, Elly seemed oblivious to the glances. She remained composed and disinterested, giving no sign that Jonathan's presence affected her in the slightest. Her posture was poised, her demeanor cool and indifferent, as though Jonathan Tate were just another guest at the table.

When dinner concluded, they returned to the library. The men lit cigars and poured glasses of whiskey. Elly, sensing she had played her part, quietly excused herself and retired to her chambers.

Hours passed, along with several glasses of whiskey. Eventually, Stephen excused himself as well, needing rest before his early trip into town. The hour had grown late, and Grant, concerned for Jonathan's journey back, offered him a guestroom for the night. Jonathan accepted the offer graciously.

Grant led him upstairs to one of the guest suites on the second level of the mansion. He informed the servants to see to Jonathan's needs and ensure his comfort. After a brief goodnight, the two men parted ways.

Jonathan entered the candlelit room. The warm glow flickered across the ornate walls and polished wood furniture. A basin of fresh water and a towel awaited him on the nightstand, along with a small cube of lye soap. He removed his shirt, splashing water on his face and shoulders, wiping under his arms. The cool water revived him slightly as the lingering aroma of cigars and whiskey clung faintly to the air.

Alone now, and with the house quiet, Jonathan moved slowly, his mind still replaying glimpses of the evening—Elly's eyes, her reserved smile, and the unspoken tension that lingered like a hidden current beneath the surface of dinner.

After a brief wash, Jonathan dried off with the towel, savoring the coolness of the air against his bare skin. The house was slightly chilled—a welcome contrast that he knew would help him sleep. Leaving his shirt off, he wandered to the window, where he gazed down into the gardens. The moonlight spilled silver across the hedges and over the marble fountain, turning the scene into a painting of shadows and light. A restless wind blew through the trees, stirring the leaves and sending flowers swaying in a dance. The soft whistle of the breeze played against the windowpane like a lullaby.

Jonathan removed his boots and reclined across the bed, still in his trousers. The candlelight flickered on the ceiling, but it was the image of Elly that lit his thoughts—her laughter, her poise, the subtle way she avoided his gaze at dinner. He closed his eyes, but desire had made a bed in his mind, and sleep was slow to follow.

Across the house, Elly stirred in her bed. She had not known Jonathan would be staying the night. Her sleep had been shallow and uneasy, broken by a dream she couldn't recall but that had jolted her awake. Her skin burned lightly, a sheen of sweat gathered at her collarbone and neck. She lay still in the dark, eyes open, but rest would not return.

Pushing back the sheets, she rose and padded barefoot to the window. The glass was cool beneath her hand—a soothing contrast to her heated skin. Below, the garden glowed beneath the full moon, and the wind tossed the blooms like dancers in a waltz. Drawn to the air and quiet, she decided to step outside.

Wearing only her thin white nightgown, she walked softly through the corridor, her long hair unbound. The house was hushed. All the servants had retired, and Stephen's room was dark; the door closed, the man undoubtedly asleep. Elly assumed that Grant and Jonathan had returned to town, perhaps for cards or the company of women. She felt secure in the stillness.

She stepped through the doors leading to the garden and crossed the lawn to the fountain. The night air pressed against her body, rushing beneath her gown in gentle waves. It was exhilarating, almost daring—standing there, barefoot and nearly translucent in the moonlight.

She leaned over the edge of the fountain, tilting her face up to the stars. Then, slowly, she dipped her hand into the water and lifted a palmful to her neck. The coolness ran down her skin, soaking the front of her gown, clinging silk to skin. She did it again—each drop calming the heat inside her.

For a moment, she felt as if the night itself had paused to watch her—wind, moon, and memory holding their breath.

Jonathan hadn't slept. He lay in the dark long after his candle had burned out, the flickering shadows now gone, replaced by silence and the restless thoughts that kept circling back to her.

He rose quietly and wandered to the window, looking out over the pastures where moonlight stretched like silver mist over the grass. Then, movement caught his eye—off to the side, near the garden fountain. He leaned closer and stilled. Elly.

She was sitting on the edge of the fountain, her nightgown glowing pale beneath the moonlight. His heart thudded hard in his chest. He knew he shouldn't go to her. He knew it too well—but knowing wasn't the same as doing.

Drawn by something he couldn't name, Jonathan stepped out into the corridor, moving barefoot and shirtless through the sleeping house.

The night air kissed his skin with every step. The door she had come through still hung open, and he slipped outside without a sound.

Elly hadn't noticed him yet. The wind played gently through the garden, stirring leaves and whispering through the branches. From his place at the threshold, Jonathan saw her clearly. She had splashed herself with water, and now the silk of her nightgown clung to her form. He could see the line of her back, the elegant curve of her shoulders, the silhouette of her body softened by the moonlight.

He paused, torn between desire and decency.

Not wanting to startle her, he cleared his throat softly, just enough to make his presence known.

Elly turned swiftly, startled at first. For a moment, she thought it was Stephen. But as he stepped into the light, she saw the outline of Jonathan—bare-chested, barefoot, his hair tousled, eyes fixed on her with a mixture of apology and something deeper.

She stood quickly, instinctively crossing her arms over her chest. "Jonathan—what are you doing here?"

"Grant offered me a room for the night," Jonathan said gently. "It was late, and I appreciated the kindness."

"Oh."

Elly shifted slightly. The wind continued to dance around her, lifting her nightgown just enough to keep her on edge—aware of every sensation against her skin. The air between them thickened.

"I should go back in," she said, her voice more breath than words.

"No—please," Jonathan replied, taking a step closer but still leaving space between them. "If I've overstepped, say so and I'll leave. I just... saw you here, and you looked so peaceful. I didn't want to disturb that. This is your place, not mine."

You haven't offended me," Elly said, her voice quiet. "You're welcome here. It's just…" She trailed off.

Jonathan waited, watching her. The way she avoided his gaze, the way her arms crossed, how she turned her back to him—all of it suggested more than words ever could.

"It's just what?" he asked, softly.

She didn't turn to face him. "It's nothing," she whispered, but her tone betrayed her.

Jonathan felt something stir—not just desire, but a deeper curiosity. Hope. Was she struggling with the same feelings he had tried to keep at bay? Or was he imagining it?

He moved toward her slowly, as though closing the distance might shatter the moment. He stood just behind her, close enough for her to feel the warmth of his bare chest against her back. When his hand lightly touched her arm and his lips brushed the curve of her neck, she didn't pull away. Instead, she leaned into him, her head tilting back in surrender.

Her breath quickened, the beat of her heart loud in her ears. His hands circled her waist gently—firm, steady, but not forceful. Her whole body trembled under his touch, lost in the moment.

Then, like a snap of waking from a dream, Elly pulled away.

She turned to face him, holding her hands up between them, her eyes wide, unsure. Her breath caught in her throat. "We shouldn't," she said, her voice shaking slightly.

Jonathan stopped, his hands falling to his sides. He didn't move forward again. Instead, he searched her face, waiting—not with pressure, but with quiet understanding.

"My lord… oh, my lord, what am I doing?" Elly whispered, her hand trembling as she pressed it to the side of her head. She looked around frantically, avoiding his gaze, as if trying to anchor herself to the moment and pull away from what was happening between them.

This is wrong. I am married—this is very wrong," she said, voice cracking under the weight of her own denial. She began pacing nervously, fingers clutching at her temples, hiding her eyes behind trembling palms.

Jonathan opened his mouth to speak, but she cut him off sharply. No, please—I beg you—just leave me alone. Now. Go." Her voice shook, thick with suppressed tears.

I love you," Jonathan said softly, barely above a whisper.

Please... go. Now. Hurry." She buried her face in her hands, the tears finally spilling free.

Jonathan hesitated only a moment before turning away. He retraced his steps back into the mansion, his heart heavy as he climbed the stairs to the guest room Grant had prepared for him. Quietly, he dressed—boots first, then shirt—and made his way to the stables. Mounting his horse, he slipped away from the estate, obeying her desperate plea.

Elly waited inside until she was sure he had returned to his room, then retreated to her own chamber. Closing the door behind her, she lit a candle and stood before the mirror. The flickering light cast soft shadows on her face and body, her wet nightgown clinging to her curves, the delicate silk revealing the outline of her breasts.

She wiped away the last traces of tears, took a shaky breath, and reached up to touch the place on her neck where Jonathan s lips had brushed her skin. She could still feel the warmth of his breath, the closeness of his body—the memory, a spark that ignited a confusing ache inside her.

She tried to banish the thoughts of him, but the tingling in her skin persisted, relentless and alive.

Finally, she lay down, curling into a tight ball on her side, knees drawn to her chest as if to protect herself from the storm within. She closed her eyes and surrendered to exhaustion, drifting slowly into a troubled sleep.

CHAPTER TWENTY

A knock at the bedroom door stirred Elly from sleep. She stretched and yawned, blinking against the daylight now spilling into the room. Dora, the servant, entered quietly.

Good morning, my lady," Dora said, walking to the window and pulling open the curtains.

What time is it?" Elly asked, still lying in bed.

It s eight o clock. The painter will arrive shortly. He left explicit instructions to have you ready by the time he returned."

Elly sighed. Yes." Her tone was flat, lacking any enthusiasm. She was not at all thrilled about sitting for her portrait today—or any day.

Grant s companion, Jonathan—did he leave yet?" she asked after a pause.

Yes, my lady. He must have left early. His room was empty this morning, and he didn t stay for breakfast."

And Stephen?"

He left early as well," Dora replied as she pulled back the blankets, urging Elly to rise.

Elly got out of bed and walked to the mirror. She stood silently, studying her reflection. Her nightgown had dried overnight and no longer clung to her skin the way it had last night. For a fleeting moment, she wondered if everything that had happened had been a dream. She tried to convince herself it was, but deep down she knew the truth. It had been real. The memory still lingered, as did the sensations that had coursed through her body.

Staring into her own eyes, she made a silent vow: it would not happen again. She would not allow herself to be placed in such a situation with Jonathan.

Elly finished dressing, slipping into the red satin gown she had worn yesterday for the portrait. She brushed her hair back neatly in the same style as before and made her way downstairs. As she descended the staircase, Pedro and his two apprentices arrived.

Ah, good morning. Just as beautiful today as you were yesterday," Pedro said with a warm smile.

Thank you, Mr. Santiago. Shall we begin?" Elly replied politely.

Yes, we have lots of work to do." Pedro moved into the room where his supplies were laid out.

Elly took her seat on the stool by the window, positioning herself exactly as she had the day before. In her hand, she held a white rose. The two young assistants worked around her—adjusting her hair and pulling the curtains to let in more light.

Pedro painted steadily throughout the day, allowing only short breaks and a two-hour lunch so Elly could eat and rest. His goal was to complete the outline of the portrait, which he could then take back to his shop for finishing. He mentioned he would only need one more session with her, scheduled for the following week, to finalize the details.

By the time the day ended, Elly was thoroughly exhausted. She hadn't slept well the night before, and the long hours of sitting had worn her down.

Later, as the afternoon faded, Stephen returned home early from town. He found Elly in the library, seated comfortably with a cup of tea in her hands.

My dear, how is your painting coming along?" he asked, leaning down to kiss her cheek.

"Very well. I believe Pedro will be completing the portrait in his shop. I dread the thought of having to sit on that stool again," Elly said, rolling her eyes.

"I'm sorry for the discomfort," Stephen replied sympathetically. "But he does excellent work. You know, he studied the techniques of Francisco Goya while living in Spain."

As he poured himself a cup of tea, he continued, "Elly, I was wondering if you might have some free time tomorrow."

"Of course. What do you need?"

"I was hoping you could take a trip into town—to Pedro's shop. He recently received a shipment of his work from Spain, and I'd like to purchase several pieces for the ballroom. Very large, framed paintings—the bigger, the better. Do you think you can choose at least seven?"

"Yes, but wouldn't you prefer to pick out the ones you'd like?" Elly asked.

"No, I have far too much work to do. I'm sure whatever you choose will suit me just fine. Have fun with it—you're the more cultivated one, after all. Just select the paintings and have them delivered. I'll settle the price and payment with Pedro," Stephen replied.

"Alright. I'll take Dora with me and have her stop by the market on Decatur Street while I visit Mr. Santiago. I'm very tired, Stephen. I think I'll turn in for the night."

"Are you feeling ill? Should I have your dinner brought up?" Stephen asked, his voice full of concern.

"No, I just need some rest. Good night," Elly said, rising from her seat and leaving the room.

Stephen remained, finishing his tea in quiet thought.

The next morning, Jacob drove Dora and Elly into town by horse-drawn carriage. He dropped Elly off at the far end of Decatur Street, in front of a small, two-story building.

The building had a charming French-inspired exterior—trimmed in yellow-painted wood, with black wrought iron railings along the upper balcony. A hand-painted sign nailed to the door read: *Artist Pedro Santiago.*

Elly waved to Jacob. "I'll walk down Decatur Street toward the market when I'm done. Take Dora ahead of me," she instructed.

The carriage rolled away, and Elly stepped inside the small gallery.

The room was packed with crates, some stacked so high they created a maze-like path through the space. She made her way carefully around them until Pedro greeted her.

"Mrs. Bentley, your portrait is coming along well. You are here to look at some of my work, yes?"

"Yes. My husband would like several large, framed paintings—the larger, the better."

Pedro put a thoughtful finger to his chin as he scanned the crates, deciding which pieces to show her first. He called out to the same two young assistants who had helped at her home, pointing to several wooden boxes on the floor.

He switched between Spanish and English as he gave instructions. The men opened one crate, revealing two paintings wrapped carefully for protection. They gently uncovered the first and held it upright, each supporting one side.

It was enormous.

The painting depicted an outdoor scene—rolling hills scattered with wildflowers and trees. In the distance sat a small stone villa, nestled peacefully at the foot of the hills. The colors were vivid, and the composition so realistic it felt as though Elly were gazing out of a real window into the countryside.

"Stunning. Absolutely stunning!" Elly exclaimed as she admired the large painting.

"You like?" Pedro asked with a smile.

Yes, I do. We'll take this one. Please, show me more."

Pedro's assistants moved quickly but carefully, unpacking several more paintings of similar size. Each depicted vibrant outdoor scenes—lush forests, tranquil oceans—rendered in brilliant, captivating colors.

My husband will settle the bill with you later. When do you think you can have them delivered?" Elly asked.

I'll have them packed and delivered at once," Pedro replied with a respectful nod.

Alright then. Good day, Mr. Santiago." Elly stepped out through the front door.

The afternoon was still young. Sunlight poured down over the narrow walkways of Decatur Street, warming the cobbled paths and bustling storefronts. People moved along both sides of the street, weaving through the steady foot traffic.

Elly wore a pale yellow dress, casual yet elegant, with delicate ruffles at the neckline and cuffs. A matching hat sat jauntily atop her head, angled slightly to the side. Her long black hair was neatly pinned up off her neck. She carried a matching parasol, using it to shield herself from the sun's heat.

As she made her way down the narrow street toward the market, she spotted a man walking toward her from the opposite side. It was Jonathan. Their eyes met—he had seen her too. He stopped, clearly intending to cross.

Caught off guard, Elly watched as he waited for a break in the flow of horses and carriages passing down the center of the street. Before he could reach her, she turned quickly and slipped into a crowd of passersby, blending in with their movement.

Jonathan lost sight of her.

But Elly could still see him as she moved farther away. He had crossed the street and now stood near the shop she'd been in, scratching his head and peering into the window, scanning for her.

Satisfied that she had evaded him, Elly turned and continued toward the market. A small smile crept across her face. She felt clever—pleased with how smoothly she had maneuvered away, leaving Jonathan searching for her with such persistent confusion.

Elly caught up to Jacob, who was waiting by the carriage. At the same time, Dora arrived, her arms full of parcels from the market. Jacob quickly jumped down to help her with the items she had purchased, then they all began the journey back to the Bentley mansion.

When they arrived, Jacob pulled the carriage up to the front door, allowing Elly and Dora to disembark. Stephen was standing on the front porch, his expression grim and distraught. The sight of him sent a jolt of fear through Elly.

"Stephen, what's wrong?" she asked, her voice trembling. As she stepped closer, her arms began to shake. A terrible thought pierced her—something had happened to her father.

"I'm sorry, my dear. Antonio..." Stephen's voice faltered as he stepped forward, catching her as her knees buckled.

"No, tell me he's alright," she pleaded, desperation rising in her voice.

"Elly... it was his heart..." Stephen struggled to find the right words.

Elly collapsed into Stephen's arms and began to weep.

CHAPTER TWENTY ONE

Antonio's final resting place was a quiet plot in the Bentley cemetery. Theresa insisted on a traditional burial, wanting him laid to rest underground in a casket. She believed the crypts and above-ground vaults common in town cemeteries were like ovens in the heat, and she had heard unsettling stories of tombs being broken into—bodies disturbed by thieves or twisted rituals. She found greater comfort knowing he would rest in peace beneath the earth.

The thought of returning his body to Spain had crossed her mind, but she ultimately chose to keep him close—to her and to Elly.

After the funeral, Elly withdrew into herself. She avoided everyone, refusing to speak or engage, hiding away in her room until well into the afternoon. The household staff grew increasingly concerned. She was barely eating, and whenever anyone entered her room, she would pull the sheets over her head and scream for them to leave her alone.

Meanwhile, Stephen was busy handling Antonio's affairs. Amid the paperwork and estate responsibilities, he spoke with Theresa and asked her to move into the Bentley mansion to be closer to him and Elly. Theresa agreed—but first, she wanted to return to Spain for a short time, to visit family and grieve in her homeland. The loss had pierced her deeply, and she couldn't imagine making the journey alone. She wanted Elly to come with her.

Stephen, however, was deeply concerned about Elly's condition. He called for the family doctor, who examined her and strongly advised against any overseas travel. In her fragile state—physically and emotionally—she was vulnerable, especially with her poor appetite and emotional detachment. A long voyage could put her health at serious risk.

A THREAD BETWEEN LIVES

Still, Theresa was determined. She insisted on going back to Madrid, if only for two or three weeks. She and Antonio still had family there, and she longed for the familiar embrace of her homeland.

After several tense discussions, Stephen agreed to accompany her. It would give him a chance to settle Antonio's international business matters and perhaps find one of Antonio's brothers—someone capable and willing to take over the business Antonio had worked so hard to build.

Stephen himself was beginning to feel the wear of constant travel between the plantation and town. He was tired. With Antonio gone and no longer issuing demands or pulling him away, Stephen yearned to slow his pace, to work from home on the land he loved—and to spend more time with his wife.

Stephen arranged their Atlantic passage, securing two places aboard one of the larger, more reputable ships. He and Theresa would depart in a week. Before leaving, he made sure every detail was handled. He promised Elly he would return as soon as he could, though he wasn't sure she heard him. Grant was assigned to oversee the shops in town, while Chestin would manage the affairs of the plantation.

Still, Stephen hesitated. Leaving Elly behind in her fragile state worried him deeply. But Veronica assured him she would stay close, keep an eye on her, and try to lift her spirits when she could. Grant, too, promised to look in on her regularly. With these assurances, Stephen found some peace of mind—enough to hope that this trip, though long and tiring, might soon grant him the time he'd longed to spend with Elly and Theresa once it was over.

By the time the week passed, Stephen and Theresa had boarded the ship. The vessel was sturdy and commanded by a seasoned captain Stephen knew well. He trusted the man and believed the voyage, while long, would be as safe and smooth as the sea allowed. Still, he worried for Theresa. The Atlantic could turn wild and unforgiving, and the sheer distance was

169

daunting. At her age, such a journey was not without risks. He watched her closely, careful to ensure she ate, rested, and was kept warm.

Back at home, the world continued to turn—but not for Elly.

She barely noticed her mother, and Stephen had gone. Time blurred. The days passed in silence. She remained tucked in her room, buried beneath the covers, often sleeping for long stretches or lying still for hours at a time. When she did emerge, it was only for a few moments, her eyes swollen, her voice hollow.

She was angry—angry at her father for dying without giving her a chance to say goodbye. Angry at him for never letting her live her own life. He had dictated everything: who she married, where she lived, what she was allowed to dream. Now, he was gone. And he had left her with no final words, no apologies, no peace.

Her grief came in waves, following no pattern at first. She denied the truth, unable to fully accept his absence. Then, the anger consumed her, burning through her memories with bitterness. She was numb for a time, lost in a fog of sleeplessness and sorrow.

But eventually, slowly, the numbness gave way to quiet acceptance. Antonio was gone. And though it broke her heart to think of him leaving this world before she had found her own voice, she knew that her healing—her becoming—had to begin somewhere.

After weeks of hiding in her room, Elly finally stepped outside.

She wandered into the garden and settled at the small iron table near the rose bushes, their soft blooms gently swaying in the morning breeze. Dora appeared shortly after, setting down a delicate china cup of tea and a warm, sugar-dusted beignet.

Elly's eyes were rimmed with dark circles, her face still puffy from days—weeks—of crying. She looked weary, fragile, but for the first time in a long while, she was no longer buried under covers and silence. As she cradled the teacup in her hands, she let the breeze soothe her like a balm. She closed her eyes.

Then came the memories.

She thought of Jonathan—his striking features, his intense eyes that seemed to read her soul. For weeks, she had pushed away those thoughts, terrified by how deeply he had unsettled her heart. His arrival, so sudden and magnetic, had stirred something inside her she hadn't been ready to feel.

And then—her father's death.

The grief had come so fast, so raw, she had locked herself away. It had been easier to hide than to feel. Easier to pretend the world outside her bedroom no longer existed. Including Jonathan. Especially Jonathan.

Why had he affected her so strongly? What power had he held, what secrets lay behind those eyes that had slipped past her guard?

She exhaled slowly, sipping her tea.

Just then, a pair of hands gently covered her eyes from behind. She flinched, startled, but the touch was familiar.

"Guess who?" a warm voice said behind her.

She smiled faintly. "Hmm... Could it be my bright young brother-in-law?"

Grant laughed and removed his hands, stepping around the table to face her. "How did you know? And more importantly, does this mean you're feeling better?"

"I don't know," she said truthfully, her voice soft. "Maybe. I hope that was the worst of it. I wasn't prepared... for any of it."

171

I know what you mean," Grant said, his expression turning somber. "When Samuel died, it hit me like a wall. I tried to drink the pain away."

"I know," Elly replied. "You two were very close."

Grant nodded, taking a deep breath before shifting the mood. "Well," he said, brightening slightly, "since I finally have you out of that house, why don't you go get dressed and let me surprise you?"

Elly gave a tired half-smile, shaking her head. "I don't think I'm up for doing anything, Grant."

"No, no, no—you are *not* getting out of it that easily," Grant insisted, shaking his head. "I've spent *hours* planning this, and the carriage is already waiting for us. Please don't disappoint me. I *promise* you'll enjoy yourself."

He looked at her with wide, pleading eyes, so earnest that Elly couldn't help but roll her own.

She sighed. "Alright. But I'm warning you—I don't want to be out late."

"Perfect!" Grant clapped his hands, delighted. "Now go get dressed. And make me happy—wear something formal."

"Do I *have* to?" she asked, raising an eyebrow. "What exactly do you have planned?"

"Hurry! Just do as I say—and trust me." Grant grinned and practically shooed her off to her room.

While Elly changed, he slipped into his formal black tuxedo, then waited in the carriage, nervously adjusting his cufflinks. When Elly finally emerged—dressed in a long deep green gown with a delicate lace overlay—she froze when she saw him.

"You're in a tuxedo?" she asked, eyeing him suspiciously as he stepped out to help her into the carriage. "You'd better tell me what this is all about."

"All right," he said, offering her his gloved hand. "But get in first, and I'll explain on the way."

Elly folded her arms and gave him a skeptical glance but stepped up into the carriage. Once she was seated, still eyeing him expectantly, he smiled and said, "I have tickets to the opera at *Le Petit Théâtre du Vieux Carré*."

Elly blinked. "The opera?"

"Yes. I know how much you love the opera when it's in town. And this is a one-night-only performance. It won't be back once it leaves for New York."

The small theater was one of the first opera houses in the South—modest compared to New York's grand stages, but beautifully adorned with elegant French décor. A local treasure.

"Grant... I'm not sure I feel up to this." She turned her face toward the window, the flicker of doubt returning. "What will people think? I'm still in mourning for my father."

Grant reached out and gently placed his hand over hers.

"Please, Elly. Just give it a chance. I'm worried about you. I *miss* the Elly I used to know. You have to keep living. You can't stop your whole life." He gave her a cheeky smile. "Besides, who cares what those old stuffed shirts think, anyway?"

Elly let out a quiet laugh, touched by his sincerity. "Alright. You win again. Thank you, Grant."

"No need to thank me just yet," he said with a grin. "Just to sweeten the deal—it's *Mozart's Don Giovanni* tonight."

Her eyes widened, and her posture lifted. "Don Giovanni? *Really?*"

"Yes. And this will be the only showing in town before they leave for New York."

A smile bloomed on Elly's face for the first time in weeks. "Now *that* is a surprise. I *do* love Mozart."

As the carriage pulled up in front of the theater, Elly leaned forward, peering through the window. The glow of dusk painted the sky in streaks of orange and soft blue, casting a warm light over the bustling crowd. Women in fashionable gowns sparkled beneath the streetlamps, their jewels catching the last of the sun, while men in tuxedos and polished top hats greeted one another with formal bows and low laughter.

Elly smoothed the folds of her black satin gown. The high collar fit snugly at her neck, and the lace sleeves added an air of grace and solemn elegance. Thin black gloves clung delicately to her fingers—she was dressed perfectly for the occasion, yet she could not shake the nervous flutter in her stomach.

She closed her eyes and drew a deep breath of evening air, holding it in for a moment before releasing it slowly. *Everything will be all right,* she told herself. *I will survive this. I will move on.*

Grant stepped down from the carriage first and turned to offer his hand. "Here we are," he said brightly, glancing over the crowd.

Elly accepted his hand and descended gracefully.

"Shall we go in?" she asked, glancing toward the theater doors.

"Just a moment... Ah—here he is!" Grant waved enthusiastically toward someone approaching.

Elly followed his gaze—and froze.

What?" she said in a hushed, alarmed voice. Her eyes widened. Grant... I don t think this is a good idea."

But Grant was too focused on the approaching figure to hear her.

Isn t this great? Jonathan was the one who managed to get our tickets on such short notice!" he beamed as he greeted him.

Good evening, Elly," Jonathan said as he came to stand beside them. I m very sorry about your father. Please accept my condolences—to you and your mother."

Elly hesitated. She wanted to step back, to keep her distance. But under Grant s watchful eye, she extended her gloved hand.

Thank you," she replied softly, keeping her eyes downcast. Then, turning quickly toward the doors, she added, Shall we go in?"

Of course. What seats did we manage to secure?" Grant asked.

Jonathan smiled. We have the conductor s private box. I ve known him for years."

Wonderful! Isn t that terrific, Elly?" Grant said, nudging her gently.

Elly offered a small, polite nod but said nothing. A quiet tension had settled over her since they arrived. Grant noticed but said nothing, trying instead to keep the mood light.

Inside, an usher in a crisp red uniform guided them through the marble-floored lobby and up the narrow staircase toward the private box. The air was rich with perfume and velvet, the low hum of conversation blending with the distant sound of the orchestra tuning their instruments.

As they walked, Elly felt the eyes of patrons upon her. Some turned discreetly, others less so. She could almost hear their thoughts: *What is she doing here? So soon after her father's death? And with not one, but two gentlemen?*

She kept her chin high, but inside, her pulse quickened.

The box was elegant, with gold-trimmed velvet chairs and a perfect view of the stage. As the usher pulled out her seat, Elly realized she would be sitting between the two men. The space was narrow, and the closeness made her uneasy.

She settled in, her gloved hands folded tightly in her lap. Grant on one side, Jonathan on the other—both looking toward the stage, but she could feel their attention flicker toward her. The lights dimmed, the murmuring crowd hushed, and the first notes of *Don Giovanni* rose into the gilded ceiling.

Elly tried to lose herself in the music, but her thoughts remained knotted—between mourning, memory, and the quiet storm brewing in her heart.

Throughout the performance, Elly struggled to keep her thoughts from drifting toward Jonathan. He sat so close—too close—and his presence unsettled her. A part of her resented the boldness of his plan, arranging to accompany her to the opera under the guise of a surprise. Yet, another part of her—the part buried beneath grief and silence—felt warmed by it. She had been so lonely. So hollow.

As the haunting melodies of *Don Giovanni* unfolded across the stage, tears welled in her eyes. They slipped silently down her cheeks—not tears of sorrow or pain, but of love, beauty, and longing. The music stirred something deep in her soul. In that moment, surrounded by elegance and art, Elly remembered what it meant to feel alive.

When the final notes rang out and the curtain fell, the audience rose in thunderous applause. It was a stunning performance. Elly felt grateful she hadn t missed it.

She remembered coming to the opera with Carolyn in years past—two wide-eyed girls wrapped in silks and pearls, dreaming of love, passion, and possibility. New Orleans rarely saw such performances, with most great productions reserved for New York, but the city was growing fast. And tonight, it had brought something magical.

"Excellent performance, wouldn't you say?" Jonathan asked, glancing at both Grant and Elly.

"Yes, it was smashing," Grant replied with enthusiasm.

"It was... very moving," Elly added softly, turning her gaze to Jonathan. Their eyes met.

Jonathan tilted his head slightly, raising one eyebrow, studying her as though waiting—for her to speak more, or perhaps to reach for something unspoken between them.

A tremor fluttered through Elly's chest. Her breath caught. Her knees gave way beneath her and she stumbled, falling gently into Grant's side.

"Elly!" Grant caught her quickly, his arm steadying her. "Are you all right?"

She nodded, trying to steady her breath. "Yes... I'm sorry. I haven't been eating much. I just feel a little weak. I need to lie down."

"We'll take you home," Grant said, concern knitting his brow. "You should eat something before bed. I'll have the servants bring up some soup."

The theater was emptying now, voices echoing in the high ceilings. The night air had grown cooler as they stepped outside. The carriage waited at the curb, lamps glowing softly in the dusk.

Jonathan stepped forward and opened the door. He helped Elly inside with gentle hands, then paused, holding her gloved hand lightly in his.

"Thank you for your company," he said, his voice low and sincere. "Please—try to rest."

Elly gave a faint nod. Her limbs ached and her head was light. She let herself sink into the velvet-lined seat, the leather warm against her back. She closed her eyes, letting the lingering notes of the opera swirl in her mind like a fading dream.

By the time they reached the house, she was barely awake. Grant lifted her gently and guided her inside. The servants moved quickly—preparing warm broth, bringing a damp cloth for her forehead. She lay in her bed, too tired to speak, sipping the soup spoon by spoon.

Grant remained by her side until her eyes closed and her breathing slowed.

Only then did he rise quietly, leaving her room with a final glance before retreating to his own chamber.

CHAPTER TWENTY TWO

Elly awoke feeling refreshed and strong. Sunlight streamed into her room through the open curtains—Dora must have drawn them back early. She soon appeared with a tray of breakfast: freshly squeezed orange juice and pancakes drizzled with maple syrup. Elly, famished, ate every bite, then rose from bed to get dressed.

It was a lovely day, far too nice to be spent indoors.

Though still in mourning, Elly continued to wear black. Today, she chose a more casual dress than the formal evening gown from the night before. It was simple and understated, with a modestly lowered neckline.

She stepped into the garden and took a seat beside the fountain. A short while later, her sister-in-law Veronica arrived.

Veronica was a small woman with brown hair and equally brown eyes. Her hair, as always, was pulled back into a neat bun. She, too, wore a black dress in mourning. Though Antonio was not a blood relative, she deeply felt the weight of his absence within the family.

Veronica was a plain woman—nothing about her appearance or manner was extravagant—but she possessed a quiet strength that Elly had always admired. She had borne and raised five children, something Elly could not help but envy. There was an ache inside her, a lingering emptiness, and a longing she rarely spoke of.

Veronica approached, leaning in to kiss Elly on the cheek.

You look lovely, my dear," she said with a warm smile, settling across from her.

Thank you. I'm starting to feel much better. Grant insisted I go out last night—exactly what I needed."

Oh, wonderful. Where did you go?"

One of his companions had tickets to the opera—*Mozart s Don Giovanni*. It was superb."

Oh, I envy you! That sounds splendid. We ve just received word that your mother and Stephen arrived safely in Spain. It seems they ve already been there a couple of weeks, though overseas news travels so slowly. I expect we ll have a letter from them soon."

I should have gone with them," Elly said with a sigh.

I don t think you were quite ready, dear. The doctor was concerned, and we all were too. I m simply glad to see you returning to your old self."

Veronica, I m planning to take my horse out for a run. Would you like to join me?"

I m afraid I can t. I ve such a list of things to do today."

As the two women sat in the garden, sipping their tea and chatting quietly, they noticed two men rounding the side of the house. Jonathan and Grant emerged into the garden, walking side by side.

I thought I might find you out here," Grant said, approaching with a warm smile. He leaned down to kiss both women on the cheek.

Veronica, I d like you to meet Jonathan Tate," Grant said, gesturing toward his companion.

Jonathan took Veronica s hand and kissed it gently, his eyes fixed downward, not meeting hers. Elly observed the formality of the gesture—

the difference in how he greeted Veronica compared to the way he had looked into her own eyes when he kissed her hand. His polite detachment was unmistakable.

"My pleasure," Jonathan said, a smile curling on his lips, dimples appearing on either side.

"Mine as well. Thank you," Veronica replied softly, a touch of shyness in her voice.

Veronica, married young to Chestin, had never been courted by a man so outwardly charming. Jonathan was gracious and courteous as he spoke with her, but his glances repeatedly strayed toward Elly—often enough that even Veronica noticed and followed his gaze.

"How are you feeling today?" Grant asked, giving Elly's leg a gentle pat.

"I'm feeling much better. Thank you for watching over me last night. I saw you there as I fell asleep," she said with quiet gratitude.

"It was nothing. I like looking out for you," he replied with a half-smile. "Besides, Stephen would kill me if I let anything happen to you."

"Pardon me, I really must be going," Veronica said, rising to her feet. "Grant, do you have time to go riding with Elly? She asked me, but I've too much to do today."

"Actually, I need to go into town to take care of some matters," Grant said after a pause. "Jonathan, what about you? Do you have some free time to accompany Elly?"

Before Jonathan could respond, Elly spoke up.

"No, that's all right. I don't need a sitter. I'll be fine," she said firmly.

I would love to go for a ride with you—if you're comfortable with that," Jonathan offered gently.

Elly didn t want to make a scene or seem reluctant. She hesitated only a moment.

Of course I m comfortable. I just don t want to take up your time. I imagine you ve got much to do, especially with the new play coming up," she replied, glancing everywhere except into his eyes.

Actually, I m ahead of schedule and have no pressing plans this afternoon. I d be honored if you d allow me to escort you," Jonathan replied.

Great, then it s settled," Grant said with a nod. I ll walk you out, Veronica. Is Chestin in the fields right now?"

Yes, Grant, he is," she answered. Good day to you, Jonathan." She inclined her head politely. Elly, I ll call on you tomorrow. Be safe." She leaned in to kiss Elly s cheek.

Jonathan stood as Veronica rose to leave. Grant kissed Elly on the cheek as well, then walked with Veronica toward the front of the house.

Now alone in the garden, Jonathan and Elly sat in the same spot where, just a few months ago, they had shared one reckless, unforgettable night. The memory lingered between them, unspoken.

Jonathan noticed Elly seemed a little uneasy. The conversation, which had flowed easily just moments before, had now faded into silence.

It s a lovely day," Jonathan said, grasping for something to say.

Yes," Elly replied softly, still looking away. Her hands rested in her lap, fingers nervously twisting—an old habit she d had since childhood.

Shall I have your horse saddled?" Jonathan offered.

Yes, that would be nice. I ll go get ready and meet you out front." Elly rose gracefully and walked back into the house.

Jonathan made his way to the stables and asked Jacob to prepare Elly s horse. His own brown mare still stood tied near the front, where he had left her upon his arrival.

He waited patiently until Elly returned. Jacob soon brought out her gray dappled thoroughbred and helped her into the saddle.

Thank you, Jacob," Elly said, taking the reins from his hand.

Jacob nodded silently and returned to the stables.

Elly and Jonathan rode out into the open pastures, their horses galloping side by side. The wind swept through Elly s hair as they picked up speed. She loved the sensation of riding—the raw power of the horse beneath her, the freedom of the wind rushing past, the feeling that, just for a moment, she was flying.

Jonathan watched Elly as she rode ahead, the wind tugging gently at her hair. Her expression was one of comfort and pleasure, but he could still sense the barrier between them. She was holding something back—keeping him at a distance. Yet he knew there was passion beneath the surface. He just needed to help her feel safe enough to release it.

All right," he teased, breaking the moment with a grin, let s see if you really know how to ride that horse."

With that, he kicked his mare into a steady run. Elly's eyes narrowed as she saw him pull ahead.

Oh no you don t!" she shouted, kicking her own horse into motion.

Her thoroughbred surged forward, closing the gap and then overtaking his mare. Younger and lighter, her horse had the advantage. They raced across the open field, laughter trailing behind them like ribbons in the wind, until they reached the edge of a shimmering lake. There, they pulled gently on the reins, bringing their horses down to a walk.

That felt amazing," Elly said between breaths, her face glowing with exhilaration.

You definitely know how to ride," Jonathan chuckled. My mistake."

We should let them rest and drink," she suggested, glancing at the water.

Jonathan dismounted first, then stepped over to Elly s side. He reached for her, steadying her horse before placing his hands on her waist to help her down. He eased her to the ground, but lingered for a heartbeat too long—his hands still around her, his body close.

Elly looked up into his eyes, her breath catching, her body trembling ever so slightly.

Thank you," she whispered, breaking the moment by turning toward the water.

She loosened her grip on the reins, allowing her gray dappled stallion to lower his head and drink. She walked slowly along the water s edge, letting the breeze calm her nerves. Then, sensing his gaze still upon her, she turned.

Jonathan s eyes were fixed on her, unreadable but intense.

We shouldn t play these games with each other," she said softly. What do you want from me?"

Games?" he repeated. By no means am I playing a game with you."

Come now, be honest." Her voice trembled. You re toying with my emotions."

Jonathan stepped forward, slowly, as if not to startle her. His voice dropped, almost pleading.

"When I first saw you—at the masked ball—I haven't been able to think of anything else since. You move through my mind even when I try to resist. You control me without even knowing. I think... I *hope*... that you feel the same way."

Elly's expression faltered. Her gaze drifted downward as she answered, barely above a whisper.

"I'm married."

"I know you're married. I know you don't love Stephen—at least, not the way your eyes suggest," Jonathan said as he stepped closer.

Elly had stopped walking. She turned toward him, only to feel the rough bark of a tree pressing into her back.

"You don't know that..." she began, her voice faltering.

Before she could finish, Jonathan reached for her. He placed both hands on her cheeks, holding her face gently but with conviction. Then, without hesitation, he kissed her—desperately, as if time were slipping through his fingers. His lips, smooth and urgent, pressed firmly against hers, moving with wild passion.

Instead of pulling away, Elly melted into him. She wrapped her arms around his shoulders, her fingers digging into the fabric of his coat. His body leaned into hers, muscles taut as he pinned her softly against the tree. Her breath caught, her chest rising as his mouth moved from her lips to her neck, each kiss awakening something deep and long-suppressed.

Elly tilted her head, her breathing growing quicker, heavier. His kisses traced along her throat, sending shivers across her skin. Reaching behind her, she braced against the tree, then slowly slid down to the grass, her dress flowing around her.

Jonathan followed, lowering himself on top of her, never breaking contact. His hands traveled from her face to her waist, pulling her closer. One arm wrapped securely around her while the other gently touched her lips. She kissed his fingers, her lips trembling against them.

He moved lower, kissing the exposed skin above her neckline—slow, reverent touches that made her shudder. His fingers traced her mouth, and she opened to them, kissing them with the same heat she had felt since their lips first met.

Their mouths found each other again—this time with an unrestrained hunger. His tongue met hers, dancing, tasting, pulling her deeper into the moment. The weight of him on top of her was grounding, real. She felt the warmth of his body, the rhythm of his breath, and the urgency of his desire pressing into her.

One of his hands slid downward, caressing the shape of her thigh through the fabric of her dress. He tugged the hem gently, lifting it inch by inch until he found bare skin. His large hand splayed out, palm flat, sliding slowly against her leg, sending a surge of heat through her body.

Elly s mind raced, her heart pounding like thunder in her chest. She didn t want to stop. She didn t want to think. She only wanted him—this man, in this moment.

She reached up, wrapping her arms around the back of his neck, pulling him closer.

I want you so much," Jonathan whispered into her ear.

Elly continued to take deep breaths, her body melting beneath Jonathan s touch.

I want you too," she whispered.

But as the words left her lips, something in her shifted. She broke the kiss, placed her hands on his shoulders, and gently pushed him away.

Stop. Please," she said, her eyes locking with his.

Jonathan obeyed without hesitation. He lifted himself slightly, leaving space between their upper bodies, though the weight of his lower half still pressed softly against her. His breath, like hers, was deep and ragged, a mixture of desire and restraint. A tension wrestled inside him, aching.

Elly... don t stop," he pleaded softly.

We can t, Jonathan. I can t," she said, voice trembling. I m married. What are we doing? Why do I long for you like this? Your touch—it melts something in me. But... please, stop."

Jonathan rolled off her, lying flat on the grass beside her. One knee bent, the other leg extended, he placed an arm across his forehead, shielding his eyes from the sky. The other hand reached out, fingers brushing Elly s.

She sat up slowly, resting her back against the tree. Her chest still rose and fell with every breath. The silence hung between them, filled only by the sound of the breeze and the soft rustle of leaves.

What do we do now?" Elly asked, her voice barely more than a whisper.

Jonathan sat up, turning toward her. He shifted until he was sitting cross-legged on the grass, then gently took one of her hands into his.

Elly, leave Stephen. Come with me. We could go to New York, start over. I can work at the playhouse. We ll find a way," he said, eyes bright with urgency. We don t have to live like this—not in silence."

I can t leave him," Elly said, shaking her head. My mother is here, my life is here... I don t know. I just don t know."

Her eyes searched his face as if it held answers her heart couldn t yet find. Her mind was clouded with doubt, but her heart still reached for him.

She leaned forward and wrapped her arms around his neck. Jonathan responded instantly, encircling her waist and pulling her close. They sat in the quiet field, clinging to one another, suspended between reality and longing.

Tell me what to do," he whispered. Anything. I would do anything if it meant you d come with me."

Elly pressed her face into his shoulder, her voice choked by emotion. I want to... I do. But not here. Not now. Please, just hold me."

A single tear slipped down her cheek as he held her tighter, anchoring her in the storm of her own heart.

Jonathan and Elly remained under the tree by the water for hours, speaking softly, comforting one another as the afternoon slowly slipped away. When the sun began its descent, they knew it was time to return to the mansion—Elly didn t want to alarm anyone with their extended absence.

Before parting, they made a plan. Jonathan would return. He would find a reason to come to the estate again, to see her.

When they arrived at the mansion, a message was waiting from Chestin and Veronica. They had invited Elly to dinner. No one suspected what had happened between her and Jonathan, but Elly felt as if the truth were written all over her face. She didn t want to draw attention to herself, so she sent a messenger back with a note accepting the invitation.

She and Jonathan said their goodbyes quietly. As he took her hand and kissed it, he raised his eyes to meet hers, and with a small, knowing smile, winked.

Elly smiled back, watching him as he rode away through the front gates of the estate.

Later that evening, she arrived at Chestin and Veronica's home for dinner. Their family welcomed her warmly, but she could barely concentrate. She stayed only a short while, offering a polite excuse to end the night early. Her thoughts were elsewhere—waiting to return to the quiet of her own room, where she could be alone with her memories of the afternoon.

Once home, she hurried to her bedroom and closed the door behind her. She lay on her bed, fully dressed, letting the memories flood back. She replayed every moment with Jonathan: his hands on her body, his breath on her neck, the way he looked at her like she was the only thing in the world.

A fluttering sensation stirred in her stomach as she recalled each detail. The memory thrilled her. She relived it over and over again, savoring the feeling to keep it alive.

But despite her efforts, she couldn't block out the image of Stephen. At the thought of him, the warmth in her belly turned into a tight, fearful knot. She didn't know what to do.

She had married Stephen because it was what her father had wanted. And now that her father was gone, she tried to convince herself that she had chosen this life, that this was what *she* wanted. But deep down, she knew the truth.

This—*this*—was what it should have felt like. To fall in love with someone she had chosen. Not someone chosen for her.

Her mind spun with emotion. Grief. Guilt. Excitement. Confusion. She was still mourning, still vulnerable, and the weight of everything pressed down on her.

Eventually, exhaustion overtook her. Elly drifted off to sleep, her dress still on, a soft smile on her lips, and a thrill humming through her soul.

CHAPTER TWENTY THREE

Elly had awakened and dressed for the day. She had chosen her red satin evening gown, the same one she had worn when her portrait was painted.

She needed to go into town to see Pedro Santiago for the final touch-up. He had notified her that the portrait was nearly complete, but he needed to see her one last time. He had sent instructions for her to bring a white rose from her garden so he could seat her in the same position, with everything identical to how it had been while he painted her.

This excited Elly. Now she had a reason to go into town and an opportunity to stop by the playhouse and see Jonathan.

As Elly was leaving the mansion, Veronica stopped by with a letter. It was from Stephen. The letter informed her of his travel plans and assured her that he and her mother were safe and well. Their business had concluded, and they were returning by boat. By the time the letter reached New Orleans, they should already be sailing for the United States. He hoped they would arrive back in New Orleans by the end of the week.

Elly's expression as she read the letter puzzled Veronica. It was as if she wasn't hearing a word Veronica was saying; her thoughts clearly elsewhere.

"Are you all right, my dear?" Veronica asked.

"Oh... yes. I was lost in thought. Thank you for delivering the letter," Elly said, reaching over to kiss Veronica's cheek.

She then turned toward the carriage. Before stepping in, she glanced back and gave Veronica a wave goodbye.

During the ride into town, Elly's mind rushed with contemplation. Thoughts spun through her head, wild and unrestrained.

What if she packed her things and left for New York with Jonathan? What would happen then? Would Stephen try to find her? Would she ever truly be free from her life here on the plantation?

Her thoughts turned next to Stephen himself. Life with him hadn t been bad, not at all. He had given her everything she desired. He was kind to her, a good and honest man. He had taken care of her father, and now had crossed the ocean with her mother so she wouldn t be alone.

Elly s excitement about going into town slowly began to shift into a heavy sadness. Her emotions swung wildly, like a carriage on a crooked path, and she could hardly control them.

The horse-drawn carriage came to a stop in front of Pedro Santiago s studio. Elly stepped down and entered the small shop, where Pedro greeted her warmly. It didn t take him long to finish the final touches on her portrait.

When he was done, he turned the easel around so Elly could view it while still seated on the stool.

It was beautiful, so lifelike, it felt as though she were staring into a mirror. Pedro s talent was unmistakable; his use of color, the elegance of his brushstrokes brought the painting vividly to life.

Elly praised him for his work, but she was in a hurry to leave. Her thoughts of seeing Jonathan consumed her with every passing second.

She arranged for her portrait to be shipped to the house. The other paintings had already been delivered, and the servants were currently placing them in the ballroom. One space on the wall remained empty; that spot was reserved for her portrait.

Elly left Pedro s studio and made her way down Decatur Street. The playhouse stood on Toulouse Street, next to a brothel where Grant was known to spend many hours of the day.

She had visited the playhouse before, but only as a patron, attending plays or operas during the evening hours. This would be her first time entering during the day, and not as a guest.

Elly stepped through the front door and into the large entryway, where a young boy was mopping the floors. He looked no older than ten or eleven, with dried dirt on his face and dressed in worn-out knickers and an oversized shirt.

"Excuse me, please," Elly said, looking down at him. "I'm looking for Mr. Tate, the director. Do you know where I might find him?"

"Yes, ma'am," the boy replied, stopping his mopping. He wiped his nose on his shirt sleeve, then pointed toward a set of doors with the same arm. "You can find Mr. Tate through those doors. He's in rehearsal."

"Thank you," Elly said softly as she walked toward the doors.

The boy watched her for a moment, then turned back and resumed mopping.

Elly pushed through the double-door entryway, which led to the back of the theater. She had never entered through these doors before. Her usual entrance was upstairs; she had permanent box seats on the second level. The lower level was open to the general public, while the upper tier was reserved for the wealthy and elite.

She held the door, letting it close gently behind her so as not to disturb the activity inside. The room was dimly lit in the back, the stage illuminated in warm light. Elly stood still for a moment, her eyes adjusting. She watched as the stage crew moved props and the actors rehearsed their lines. Her gaze scanned the space, searching for Jonathan among the crowd.

Elly scanned the stage carefully until she finally spotted Jonathan near the far end. He was standing with his back to her, leaning casually against some crates while speaking with a young woman. The woman looked to be in her early twenties, with short blonde hair and a slender frame. She laughed as they talked, twirling a strand of her hair around one finger.

They stood close. Too close.

Before Elly could react, one of the actors on stage noticed her standing in the back and called out.

"Yes, ma'am, can we help you?" a voice projected from the stage.

"Yes, I'm looking for Mr. Tate," Elly replied, beginning to descend the narrow steps toward the stage.

Jonathan turned his head sharply at the sound of her voice.

"Come on down, don't be shy," the man called, gesturing toward the crates. "He's right over there."

Jonathan immediately stepped away from the young woman and began walking toward Elly. He jumped down from the stage, then climbed the stairs to meet her halfway in the seating area.

Elly gave a polite smile to the man who had spoken to her, then glanced back toward the stage where the blonde woman still stood. Her expression was unreadable, but her eyes lingered a moment longer than necessary before she turned back to Jonathan.

Their eyes met as he approached.

"What a nice surprise," Jonathan said, smiling. "What brings you here?"

"I wanted to see you," Elly replied, looking up at him. "Can we go somewhere to talk privately?"

Jonathan looked around, then glanced back toward the stage, as if considering something.

"If this is a bad time..." Elly began, her voice tentative.

No, no, this is great. Just a moment." He turned and called toward the stage, "Take a lunch break; be back in one hour!"

He turned back to her. "Are you sure this isn't an inconvenience?" Elly asked.

"No, this is wonderful. You look stunning. I'm so happy to see you. Come, this way."

Jonathan gestured and led her out through the same doors she had entered, down a short hall, and into a room with his name printed on the door.

As soon as they stepped inside, Jonathan closed the door and turned toward her. Without a word, he wrapped his arms around her waist, pulling her close. He kissed her deeply, pressing his body into hers.

The force of his passion caught Elly off guard, and she lost her balance, falling back against the door. Jonathan held her firmly, keeping her from falling hard. She wrapped her arms around his neck, their lips meeting with fierce intensity.

Elly tilted her head back, allowing his lips to travel across her cheek and down her neck. His kisses were urgent, hungry. She struggled to catch her breath, which had escaped her the moment he touched her.

She whispered his name softly into his ear, which only deepened Jonathan's desire. He responded with even greater intensity.

Elly kissed him back, then slowly placed her hands on either side of his face, gently pulling him back to look at her.

"We need to talk," she said, her voice steady despite the fire in her chest.

"Yes, yes, whatever you want, the answer is yes," Jonathan said playfully, resuming his kisses.

I m serious," Elly laughed softly, trying to speak between his kisses. Stephen is on his way home from Spain. What am I to do?"

Let us run away and leave all this behind," Jonathan said, only half-joking. My desire for you is hard to resist. You burn my soul, my mind, I can think of no one but you, my dear sweet love. Take me away from my agony," he pleaded, as if reciting from a script.

Hmmm, dear sir... you are a good actor," Elly teased, smiling at him.

Jonathan pulled her closer in his arms.

I m not acting. There are some scenes a heart cannot reproduce. This is love; pure and sweet. And you, my dear, are the cause of it," he said, continuing the playful tone.

No, my kind sir, you must be mistaken. Your love is only a whim, a small fascination of some sort that will end without a thought, I am sure," Elly replied, her voice light with mockery.

Not at all," Jonathan said. Must I show you my love? Taste the sweetness of my soul and feel my lips upon your luscious body. Truly, I hold you most dear to my heart, and never shall anyone take that place."

He kissed her hand and looked deep into her eyes.

Oh, you are truly a good actor," she whispered, smiling. You make me feel as if I am barely breathing. If it were not for my heart rushing a thousand beats per minute, I would surely think I had died and you were an angel, my angel, coming for me."

Come with me, then. Let us leave and never look back," Jonathan said, his eyes eager and fixed on hers.

We can t do that," Elly said, her voice softening into seriousness. We must not let anyone see how we feel... not yet. Until I can sort this out, I m so confused. I don t know what to do."

She paused, looking into his eyes.

"Jonathan, please... tell me. You're not playing with my heart? I have to know for sure."

"Don't be confused, just follow your heart," Jonathan said, reaching out to hold her.

A knock at the door startled them both. They quickly stepped away from each other just as the door opened.

The young woman Jonathan had been speaking with earlier onstage entered the room.

"Oh, excuse me. I thought you were alone," she said, her eyes shifting from Jonathan to Elly with mild surprise and something sharper just beneath the surface.

"No, I'll be with you shortly, Betsy. I have a matter to tend to," Jonathan replied, his tone suddenly professional.

Elly turned away from them both, facing his desk with her back rigid, her body still.

"Okay, just remember my appointment too," the young woman added as she popped her gum, shooting a sour glance at Elly before walking out and closing the door behind her.

"She's a student actress," Jonathan said quickly, smiling awkwardly. "I'm helping her with her lines."

He stepped back toward Elly, wrapping his arms around her again.

"Now, where were we?" he murmured, nibbling at her ear, making her laugh despite herself.

"You need to get back to work," Elly said, gently pulling away. "And I need to go home. I'm sorry for keeping you from your play."

"Nonsense. You're far more desirable than any play," Jonathan said. "When can I see you again?"

"I'm not sure. I'll get word to you," she replied.

"I don't know if I can wait that long."

"You'll survive. You have plenty of attractive women to keep you company," she teased, tapping him on the shoulder with her gloves in a playful gesture.

"None as stunning as you," Jonathan said, catching her hand. "Alright, go if you must. But know that when you walk out that door, my heart will be broken until you mend it again with your presence."

"I will see you soon," Elly said softly, kissing him one last time before walking to the door.

She left, while Jonathan remained inside, giving her time to walk out of the playhouse unseen. Elly made her way back down Toulouse Street toward Pedro Santiago's shop, where Jacob would be waiting with the carriage.

As she exited the playhouse, Grant had just come out of the brothel next door. He thought he saw someone who looked like Elly, but quickly dismissed the thought. She wouldn't have any business in this part of town, he reasoned.

During the carriage ride home, Elly gazed out the window, her mind spinning with thoughts of Jonathan and the proposal he had made, to leave everything and start a new life with him.

She thought of the way his hands felt around her waist, the tingling sensations his touch stirred in her. He made her feel powerless, as though he could do anything to her and she wouldn't resist. A part of her wanted that, craved that freedom and abandon. But what would life with him really be like? And what would her mother think?

She tried to convince herself she wasn't doing anything wrong, but those thoughts dissolved the moment Stephen entered her mind.

Stephen was a good-hearted man. Intelligent. Reasonable. Maybe she could talk to him, explain her feelings for Jonathan?

That fantasy, too, evaporated. Deep down, she knew Stephen wouldn't understand. He wouldn't let her go. And it would devastate him.

Her thoughts grew heavy, too tangled to unravel, so she let them go. Instead, she turned her mind to something less complicated.

She began to daydream about Jonathan again. His arms around her. The warmth of his embrace. The way he looked into her eyes, those deep, dark brown eyes that seemed to see right through her.

Those thoughts comforted her, lifted her spirit, and brought a sense of peace, at least for the moment, as the carriage carried her home.

CHAPTER TWENTY FOUR

The end of the week arrived, and so did the boat that brought Stephen and Theresa back from Spain.

It had been a wonderful trip for Theresa. She had visited relatives and taken time to grieve with Antonio's family. She returned with stories and gifts she was eager to share with her daughter.

Elly, however, found it hard to sit and listen. As her mother and Stephen spoke, her mind drifted, again and again, back to Jonathan.

Theresa noticed something had changed in Elly. She was no longer sad and distraught, as she had been when they left. Theresa assumed that time alone had done her good, that the solitude and mourning had helped her regain strength.

Stephen, too, observed the difference. Elly seemed more alive. Her spirits were lifted. She smiled more often and carried herself with a lightness he hadn't seen in years.

His time away from her had left him feeling empty, both in soul and body. He longed for the night, when he could finally return to her chambers and be alone with his wife again.

Stephen was happy to see her like this; relieved even. She didn't appear burdened with depression anymore, as she had when he departed for Spain.

Perhaps, he thought, she had missed him as deeply as he had missed her.

He admired the glow in her expression, a glow he hadn't seen in such a long time.

And he wanted to share some good news with her: he would now be spending more time with her at home, on the plantation. One of her cousins, Francisco, was due to arrive soon to take over the business in town; her father's legacy.

They had finalized the arrangements, allowing Theresa to collect royalties and commissions from the shop's transactions. The business would remain within Antonio's bloodline. He had worked tirelessly over the years to build something that brought him great fortune, and it was only right that his legacy continued through his family.

Francisco, young and eager, was excited to make his way to the Americas. The trip to Spain had proven productive for Stephen, both personally and professionally.

That evening, Stephen watched Elly closely, anticipation growing with the thought of finally spending quiet time alone with her.

Elly, however, retired to her chambers early, just as she had done on many other nights.

After a brief conversation with Chestin, Stephen excused himself as well, using the fatigue from his journey as an explanation. He cleaned up and changed into his nightwear, then walked down the hall to Elly's room.

He knocked lightly, but there was no response. He noticed there was no light beneath the door. Perhaps she's already asleep, he thought.

Stephen hesitated at the door, just for a moment. The ache of loneliness and his longing for her outweighed his uncertainty.

Inside, Elly lay in bed, wide awake and silent. She had expected Stephen to come to her tonight and hoped he would think she was asleep and leave.

She heard the doorknob turn, then sensed him entering the room, each step bringing him closer to her bedside.

Elly? Are you awake?" Stephen's voice was quiet, tentative.

Elly remained still, her eyes closed, holding her breath.

Stephen sat down gently on the bed and placed his hand on her forehead, brushing her hair back. He could barely make out her face; only the soft contour of her features in the dim light. The moon was hidden behind thick clouds, offering no help.

He bent down and kissed her cheek, then softly pressed his lips to hers.

Elly, can you hear me?" he whispered.

Elly turned her head away from him and rolled over, feigning restless sleep. She muttered a few indistinct words that Stephen couldn't understand.

He sat there a few more moments in the darkness, wrestling with the desire to reach for her. But he didn't. Instead, he took a deep breath, sighed, and stood.

I love you, Elly," Stephen whispered as he quietly closed the door behind him.

Elly turned back to look at the door, just to be certain he had gone.

A wave of guilt washed over her. She had never denied him before; not like this. She had always obliged him, always allowed him to share her bed when he needed comfort or closeness.

Now she lay alone in the dark, her heart pounding, her thoughts racing. What was she doing?

A THREAD BETWEEN LIVES

The next morning, Stephen sat quietly at the breakfast table, unusually silent. He didn't behave like his usual self. He seemed agitated, his temper short, especially toward the servants.

Elly kept her distance. She felt exposed, like he could somehow see her guilt, the longing she carried for another man.

Stephen noticed her subtle detachment but couldn't understand the reason. Still, he chose not to press. He would give her space. Perhaps some time apart would help.

So, he decided to head into town to take care of some business.

As Stephen was preparing to leave, two horses pulling a wagon came through the front gates.

It was Pedro Santiago and his two apprentices, delivering the portrait he had painted of Elly.

Stephen stopped to greet them, offering clear instructions: "Please take it to the ballroom. The servants will hang the portrait where it belongs."

"Good afternoon, my friend. Do you like the selection of paintings your beautiful wife has chosen?" Pedro waved his hand cheerfully at Stephen.

"Yes, fine work. I can hardly wait to see this one," Stephen replied, mounting his horse.

"Where are you going? You should be resting from your long journey and spending time with your wife," Pedro said with a smile, lifting his eyebrows suggestively.

"Thank you for your concern. Did you receive the payment we agreed upon?" Stephen asked, returning the smile but ignoring the implication.

Yes, yes, my good friend. Come to my shop anytime, see more of my work," Pedro nodded.

All right. Thank you and good day." Stephen tipped his hat and rode out through the front gates.

Pedro finished his business by delivering the painting to the servants, reminding them to take special care with his work. Then he too began his journey back into town.

Stephen spent the afternoon in town tending to business at the shops, preparing the financial books for the upcoming transfer to Francisco. He worked quickly with his mind elsewhere; wanting to return home in time to sit with Elly and try again to reach her.

When he arrived, dinner was just being served. He joined Elly and Theresa at the table.

Did you take care of your business in town today, Stephen?" Theresa asked.

Yes. I believe everything will be ready by the time Francisco arrives," Stephen replied. I ll just need to get him familiar with the area and the shops, and then I intend to sign the books over to him."

Very good. Francisco is a good man. Antonio would be pleased." Theresa made the sign of the cross, then looked upward. God rest his soul."

Elly remained quiet, eating her dinner as Stephen and her mother engaged in conversation. They had spent the last few months in each other s company and had grown accustomed to sharing conversations over meals.

Thank you for allowing me to have Carolyn s room. It s lovely. I ll enjoy living here with you; it would have been far too lonely living alone in that big house," Theresa said warmly.

"You're welcome. We're glad to have you here," Stephen replied. "Are the servants managing the packing of your belongings all right?"

"Yes, I believe so. I'll need to go over and look through the house once they've finished, but everything seems to be moving along smoothly."

"I can ride over tomorrow and check on things for you," Elly interjected. She jumped into the conversation quickly, hoping this might be a way to see Jonathan without raising suspicion.

"Yes, what a lovely idea. We could go over together," Theresa offered.

"No, I can go alone. There's no need for you to ride that distance. Meanwhile, you can stay here and oversee the placement of your personal belongings," Elly insisted quickly.

"Oh," Theresa hesitated, surprised. "Well, I suppose you're right," she agreed.

"Would you like me to escort you, my dear?" Stephen asked Elly, his tone gentle.

"No, I would like to ride my horse. You have other matters to attend to. There's no need to burden yourself with this. I can handle it," Elly said firmly.

"Very well. If you change your mind..." Stephen began.

"Thank you, I'll let you know," Elly interrupted, cutting him off gently but decisively.

After dinner, Elly once again retired to her room early. She hurried to change into her nightgown, blew out the candle, and lay still under the covers in the dark. She knew Stephen would likely visit her again that night, and this time, she wasn't sure how she would refuse him.

Shortly after she had settled into bed, Stephen followed his usual routine: cleaning up, then heading quietly to her room. The door was shut, and there was no answer to his soft knock. He opened it anyway, stepping inside and finding her lying motionless in the darkness.

Stephen entered and sat down beside her on the bed. By now, he was certain Elly was avoiding him. She had never acted like this before. She used to stir when he entered, acknowledge him, and willingly submit to his desires. But now, she remained silent and still. He wondered what had changed while he had been away. Was she upset with him for leaving during her time of grief? Had she believed he didn't care?

A dozen thoughts ran through Stephen's mind, each more troubling than the last. He felt the weight of guilt settle on him.

Still, he didn't try to wake her. Instead, he lay down beside her, wrapping his arms gently around her. Eventually, he drifted off to sleep, holding her in silence.

Elly remained very still in the darkness, offering no sign that she was awake. After a while, with her body locked in tension and her mind spinning, she too finally fell asleep, still lying in Stephen's arms.

CHAPTER TWENTY FIVE

Elly awakened in her room to find that Stephen had left as quietly as he had entered. On the pillow beside her, where he had slept holding her through the night, he had left a single rose.

She sat on the corner of her bed, staring at it, contemplating everything she was doing. Right or wrong no longer seemed to matter, she simply couldn t control her feelings for Jonathan. Thoughts of him intruded constantly into her daily life, no matter how hard she tried to suppress them.

Quickly, she got dressed, not wanting to waste a moment. She crossed the room to the small writing desk in the corner, pulled out a sheet of paper, and scribbled a short note:

Jonathan,
I will be at my mother s house this afternoon. If you are able, please meet me there.

—Elly

She folded the paper, sealed it, and addressed it: Jonathan Tate.

Hurrying down to the stables, she found Jacob filling water buckets behind one of the stalls.

 Jacob, I need you to deliver this letter for me, immediately. No delays. And please, keep this between us. Not even Mr. Bentley is to know. Mr. Tate has offered to assist me with planning an upcoming event," Elly added, offering him a plausible reason for the secrecy.

She felt confident entrusting this task to Jacob. He was loyal and, being illiterate, would not read the contents of the note.

Yes, ma am. I ll leave right away," Jacob assured her, taking the letter carefully.

Also, will you have one of the other stable hands saddle my horse? I ll be leaving shortly," Elly said, turning back toward the house.

Inside, Theresa was in the foyer, sorting through some trunks the servants had delivered earlier that morning.

Is everything coming along without trouble, Mother?" Elly asked.

Yes, there s just so much. I don t know which items I want to keep out and which to have stored away," Theresa said as she opened another trunk.

Where is Stephen this morning?" Elly asked.

Oh, he and Grant went back into town to the bank. They had a meeting scheduled today. He said he d be home before dark—he doesn't want to stay in town tonight."

I m going to leave now and ride over to the house to make sure the servants haven t forgotten anything. Will you be all right?" Elly asked.

Yes, oh yes. I have plenty to keep me busy. Be careful. Are you taking Jacob with you?" Theresa asked.

No, I ll ride myself. It ll be much quicker, and I really wanted to ride today, the weather is so lovely." Elly walked over to her mother and kissed her cheek before heading for the door.

One of the other servants had already brought Elly s horse out front and was waiting with it when she stepped outside. She mounted quickly and took off down the road.

It didn t take long to reach her family s house. Two hours had passed since Elly entrusted Jacob with the letter for Jonathan, plenty of time for him to receive it and arrive.

As she rode through the front gates, she saw another horse tied out front and a man standing on the porch. As she approached, she recognized him immediately, it was Jonathan.

He stepped down from the porch and walked toward her. Before she could even bring the horse to a full stop, he reached up, took her by the waist, and helped her down into his arms. He kissed her strongly, urgently, pulling her tightly against his body.

I missed you so much," Jonathan breathed heavily.

Is anyone here?" Elly asked, holding herself back slightly from Jonathan.

No, the servants left a short while ago," he replied, moving closer to her and kissing her again.

Let s go inside. I don t want anyone to see us out here," Elly said, beginning to walk to the door.

Jonathan tied her horse next to his at the water trough, then hurried to the front door where Elly waited. They both walked inside; the house was almost bare. White sheets covered some of the furniture that would remain in the house. The room was dim, with a sliver of sunshine peeking through the drawn curtains.

We need to talk, Jonathan. I don t know what to do. Stephen is starting to notice that I m not behaving the same," Elly said.

Jonathan wrapped his arms around Elly s waist, pulling her to him and continually kissing her neck as he spoke.

Elly, I need you. Let s not talk of Stephen or anyone else," he whispered.

Elly felt his tongue caress her skin and his powerful lips sucking at her neck. He took her breath away. Her knees weakened, her stomach fluttered, and her heart seemed to drop to the floor as she pushed her body toward him. She wanted him to touch her more, her mind forgetting everything else. Once again, she found herself helpless to his touch.

Jonathan was more eager and aggressive than the other day at the lake. He picked Elly up in his arms and kissed her as he carried her. As he walked with her upstairs to one of the bedrooms, he kicked open the door and laid her gently on the bed.

She lay back and watched as he undressed, first removing his shirt, revealing his bare skin and the hair across his chest. Then he slowly unbuttoned and removed his trousers. The sight stirred a rush of desire in Elly. She reached out her arms to him, summoning him to her.

He climbed onto the bed and began untying the silk ribbons that held her dress together. Elly could barely control herself as he slowly loosened each one, further stirring her passion. She wanted him to touch her, to see her, to taste her skin.

They became entangled, rolling over one another, kissing and exploring each other's bodies. Elly felt alive and burning. After they had exhausted themselves, they lay together, naked, Elly's head resting on his chest.

"You send chills right through me, Elly," Jonathan said as he looked up at the ceiling while they lay there.

"What are we to do? Do you think we could really go to New York? Just leave right now?" Elly asked as she lifted her head and looked into Jonathan's eyes.

"Yes, we could go to New York. Although now wouldn't be the right time. I have the new play that's about to open. What would the poor actors do, and how would they feed their families? We need to hold off just until after we open. Then I can leave," Jonathan said as he looked at her.

He moved his hand behind her head, pulling her down onto him to kiss her.

You know we need to wait, don't you?" Jonathan asked.

Yes, you're right. I don't want to cause those families any pain," Elly said, looking into Jonathan's eyes.

I would love to spend the whole day with you, but we need to go. Can we meet here again?" Jonathan asked as he got up and started to get dressed. He reached back down to kiss her, lifting her up off the bed by her arms. Elly began getting dressed as well.

I'll have to send word again with Jacob. I have to see you, I would melt away without your touch," Elly said, pausing her dressing and walking back to Jonathan to kiss him again.

They both finished dressing and started to walk out the front door. They were talking and laughing as they stepped onto the front porch.

Just then, Stephen rode up on his horse. Elly turned, looking up at him, slightly startled.

Hello. I was in town and thought I'd come by to see if you needed a hand. Jonathan, how are you?" Stephen asked, looking down at them as he sat atop his horse.

I..." Elly began, but Jonathan cut her off.

I ran into your servants. They said Elly would be out here alone. I thought it only polite to offer my assistance. I'm glad to see that you returned safely from Spain," Jonathan replied, his tone courteous, his expression unreadable.

Yes, thank you. I appreciate your efforts," Stephen said, watching him closely.

Elly stood between the two men, her face flushed and her composure visibly shaken. She avoided Stephen's eyes, and he noticed immediately, her hair wasn't neatly combed, strands clung loosely around her face. He assumed the disarray was from the ride over, but her discomfort did not go unnoticed. Her nervous glances and fidgeting stirred something uneasy within him.

He looked back at Jonathan, searching his face, but found no sign of impropriety, no smirk, no arrogance, no guilt. Nothing to give him pause, but still, the feeling lingered.

"Shall I ride back with you, Elly?" Stephen asked, his voice gentler now, as if trying to understand something unspoken.

"Yes," Elly replied quickly. "I was just leaving."

She turned to Jonathan. "Thank you for your company. It was very kind of you. Good day."

Jonathan nodded, stepping forward to help her mount her horse. As he handed her the reins, his fingers brushed hers. Elly looked away quickly. Stephen mounted his horse beside her, and they rode off together while Jonathan stood back, watching them go. After a moment, he turned and made his way back to town.

During the ride home, Stephen couldn't shake the tension in his chest. He glanced sideways at Elly, who kept her gaze ahead, silent.

"My dear," he finally said, "that man, he didn't offend you in any way, did he?"

Elly laughed, too quickly, too lightly. "No," she said, still avoiding his eyes. "Don't be silly. I was delighted to have his help."

Her words sounded casual, but Stephen noticed the strain in her voice. He didn't press further. Still, the way she spoke, the way she looked; something was different. Off. But without evidence or reason, he let the moment pass.

When they arrived home, Elly dismounted and hurried inside, claiming fatigue. Stephen stayed behind, handing off his horse to the stable hand and giving quiet instructions on grooming.

212

Upstairs, Elly entered her room and immediately collapsed onto her bed. She wrapped her arms around herself, a smile slowly spreading across her lips. Her heart was still racing, not from fear, but from memory. The images of Jonathan, his hands, his breath, the way he had looked at her, played over and over in her mind like a treasured scene from a play. She could still feel his touch, as if it lingered on her skin.

A sudden knock at the door yanked her back into reality.

Her smile vanished.

It was Stephen. She had known he would come, but she hadn't expected him this soon. She sat up quickly, pulling the blanket around her as the door opened. Stephen stepped inside without hesitation, his gaze drifting toward the window as he spoke.

Elly, is there something wrong? Something that I have done to make you upset with me?" Stephen asked.

No, not at all," Elly replied.

Then why have you been avoiding me? I did not mean to leave you when you were so depressed and needing me. It's just that I did not want your mother to travel alone." Stephen now stood at the window, keeping his distance but watching Elly as he spoke.

Elly looked at Stephen and could see the hurt in his eyes, the caring and longing expression that had once drawn her to him.

No, believe me, I am not upset with you. You did a wonderful duty escorting my mother on such a long journey. I wish I had been well enough to go with her. I'm still having a difficult time, and I need to think matters over. I don't mean to push you away, but I'm afraid I can't be close to anyone right now," Elly said, looking up at him.

Let me help you through this; whatever it is that's pressing on you," Stephen pleaded.

I have to work through my feelings and thoughts myself. Trust me, I'm all right. I don't want you to worry or fuss over me. I just need time. Can you give me that?" Elly asked gently.

Yes, my love. I will do whatever you need to help you. You do know I love you?" Stephen smiled as he walked over, picking up her hand and gently kissing it.

Yes, I do know," Elly said, then looked away. She could barely stand to meet his eyes, knowing that she was the cause of his sorrow.

I'll leave you alone to rest. If you need me, don't hesitate to let me know," Stephen said quietly as he turned and shut the door behind him.

Elly sat on her bed as a tear welled in her eyes. She felt torn, caught between the comfort of Stephen's love and the passionate fascination that Jonathan stirred within her. She tried to convince herself that Stephen didn't deserve her, that he was too good a man and should have a woman who could truly love him in return.

Elly got up from her bed and washed her face in the porcelain basin filled with water that sat at the end of her dresser. Then she returned to her bed, lay down, and fell fast asleep.

Stephen had left her room and walked downstairs into the study. This room had hundreds of books placed upon shelves that covered the walls from the ceiling to the floor. Stephen had read many of the books on these shelves in his younger days, but now he hardly found the time to read anymore.

He poured himself a large glass of brandy and sat down in the chair in front of the fireplace. No logs were burning tonight; it was a warm night. He sat drinking from his glass, staring into the empty hearth, his mind replaying his visit to Theresa's house that afternoon. The way Elly had been smiling and laughing with that man as they walked out the front door. Her hair slightly tousled, her manner toward Jonathan shifting the moment she realized Stephen had ridden up.

Jonathan's keen ability to remain calm and natural struck him. Stephen recalled the night Grant had invited Jonathan to stay for dinner. He remembered catching Jonathan gazing at his wife, not once, but several times during the evening.

Stephen continued to replay these thoughts in his mind, his grip on the brandy glass tightening. The strain showed in his hands, his fingers and knuckles turned white from the pressure. He kept drinking heavily throughout the night until he eventually passed out in the chair where he had been sitting.

CHAPTER TWENTY SIX

Theresa finished her move into the Bentley mansion. She adored Carolyn's room, it had a large terrace balcony that overlooked the gardens and the water fountain. She had moved all of her bedroom furniture from her old house into her new room and decorated it with bright colors, replacing the curtains with new ones. She enjoyed living at the Bentley mansion; it allowed her to be close to Elly. They would sit together in the garden and have tea, just as they had done when Carolyn was alive and would join them.

Stephen continued to work, allowing Elly to have her time and space without feeling pressured by him. He watched her closely but from a distance while staying at home on the plantation. Grant would stop by and visit, but Jonathan did not accompany him. Stephen noticed how Elly would continue to glance at the door after Grant arrived, as if she were expecting someone else to enter. She would engage in conversation with Grant, asking him how Jonathan's play was coming along. Grant would answer politely but would quickly shift the subject away from Jonathan.

Stephen tried not to let her see that he noticed her interest in the other man. He would hide his anger, clenching his teeth and forcing a smile. He harbored no ill feelings toward Elly, his anger was directed entirely at Jonathan. Sometimes, he couldn't help himself and would make a snide remark about actors: how they lived in a fantasy world, leeching off others for charity.

Elly would defend the actors and remind Stephen how much she herself loved the theater. This only worsened the burning sensation that crept into his soul.

Stephen had thought about riding into town and confronting Jonathan with his suspicions, but he could not find the courage to do so.

He was afraid that his worst fears might be confirmed and he wasn't sure he was ready to face that possibility.

Finally, word arrived from town that Jonathan's play was finished, and a private gathering was to take place after the performance on opening night. A special invitation arrived by carrier, inviting Elly, Stephen, and Theresa to both the play and the post-performance party. Opening night was scheduled for this evening, and formal attire was required.

Theresa was thrilled to receive the invitation. She and Elly went through boxes of dresses, trying to find something just right for the occasion. Elly had mentioned the play to Stephen but assumed he wouldn't attend, as he had little interest in plays or the theater. To her surprise, Stephen agreed to go, he did not want to miss any opportunity to observe Elly and Jonathan together. He wanted to see them interact, to confirm whether his suspicions were true.

They all dressed in elegant formal wear. The women wore gowns that draped gracefully off their shoulders, while Stephen wore his black long-tail tuxedo and top hat. He had recently started carrying a cane as a walking stick, though he didn't actually need it for support.

They arrived at the theater a little earlier than Elly usually did for a performance. She walked beside Stephen, her hand resting lightly on his arm. As they entered the grand entryway, a young boy stood at the door handing out playbills for the evening's performance. The boy looked up and smiled at Elly.

"Hello again, ma'am," he said brightly.

Looking down, Elly recognized him as the same boy she had seen mopping the floors during her visit to the playhouse to meet Jonathan that afternoon.

"Oh, hello, young man," she replied, smiling as she continued walking past him.

As she moved forward, a burning sensation rose in her cheeks, they had flushed from being recognized.

That young boy seemed to know you," Stephen noted to Elly. Oh no, I think he must have mistaken me for someone else," Elly replied quickly, then tried to change the subject.

Are you having a pleasant evening?" she asked.

Yes, it is nice to be here with you," Stephen said, tightening his hold on her hand.

Elly noticed that his grip was slightly firmer than usual but assumed it was because they had walked into a crowd, and he didn t want to lose hold of her. As they were being escorted to their seating area, Grant arrived and caught up to them.

The play turned out to be a wonderful performance, even Stephen seemed to enjoy it. After the final curtain fell, the actors and director came back on stage to thank the audience and remind them that a small gathering would follow for opening night, with entry strictly by invitation only. The audience continued to clap, offering their recognition for a job well done.

Jonathan made a small bow before the curtain fell, gesturing as he blew a kiss into the audience. Elly smiled, a warm feeling rushing through her, she knew the kiss had been meant for her. Stephen noticed it, too, and tried to mask his jealousy.

The four of them remained in their box seating while the lower-level audience exited the building. An usher then escorted them to the room set up for the opening night party.

The gathering was not quite the elite crowd Stephen was used to mingling with. The room was filled with business owners and shop managers, respectable people, but not of the same social standing or wealth

A THREAD BETWEEN LIVES

as Stephen. Grant, however, seemed to know nearly everyone by name and was quite familiar with many of the women as well.

Several of the female guests were clearly present to entertain the gentlemen and fulfill their desires. The room was smoky with the scent of cigars and cigarettes, and loud piano music played from the back. It was a small space, with a bar and a table offering pastries. Most people stood in small groups, chatting and mingling freely.

Stephen was unimpressed. He turned to Theresa and Elly and asked if they were comfortable, clearly eager to leave.

This is not at all suitable for you ladies. Shall I call for the carriage?" Stephen offered.

I am fine," Elly said as she moved closer to her mother and pointed discreetly across the room.

Mother, look—there s the actor who played the lead," Elly added with excitement.

Stephen looked disappointed and quietly walked over to the bar to get a glass of whiskey.

I ll be right back. I see someone I need to speak with," Grant said to Elly and Theresa as he stepped away.

Jonathan, standing across the room, noticed that Elly was now alone with her mother. He leaned toward one of the actors he had been speaking with and whispered something. The man nodded, and together they walked over to Elly and Theresa. The actor began to engage Theresa in conversation, complimenting her dress and drawing her attention.

Hello, my love," Jonathan said softly, taking Elly s hand and kissing it gently.

Sshhh, someone might hear you," Elly whispered, pulling her hand away with a shy smile.

219

You are very bold this evening," she added.

It s because I ve missed you. How have you been?" Jonathan asked, his tone tender.

Meanwhile, Stephen finished his drink at the bar and ordered another. As he turned to wait for it, he caught sight of Jonathan and Elly talking. He observed them closely, how they smiled and laughed together before taking his drink and walking back toward them, his eyes fixed on both.

Hello, Jonathan," Stephen said as he returned to Elly s side. Good evening, sir. Did you enjoy the play?" Jonathan asked politely. Actually, yes. It was a good performance," Stephen replied.

I ll take that as a compliment, especially knowing that theater isn't your usual interest," Jonathan smiled.

Ah, yes. My wife is the theatrical one in this family," Stephen replied, looking directly into Jonathan s eyes with a measured tone.

Theresa, now done with her chat, turned back toward the group, rejoining the conversation. Stephen also noted that Grant had taken company with one of the female performers and likely wouldn t be returning to join them anytime soon.

Well, I must end this evening early. I have business to tend to in the morning. Thank you for your invitation. We really must go now," Stephen said, reaching out to shake Jonathan s hand.

If you re not ready to leave, Elly, you re welcome to stay. Grant can escort you home later," Jonathan said, looking directly at her.

Elly felt uncomfortable that Jonathan would say such a thing in front of Stephen. She worried he might begin to suspect their secret. Stephen s face began to flush with anger at Jonathan s boldness.

No. My wife will be returning home with me," Stephen said, his voice deeper and more direct now. Realizing his jealousy was starting to show, he quickly softened his tone.

Besides, Grant looks like he's enjoying himself," Stephen added, nodding toward his brother, who was still deep in conversation with a young woman across the room. He chuckled, attempting to brush it off.

Yes, I think it is time we all head home," Theresa agreed, sensing tension between the two men.

Very well. Good night to you," Jonathan said. He reached for Theresa's hand and kissed it. Then, turning to Elly, he took her hand and kissed it as well, giving it a gentle squeeze before letting go.

During the carriage ride home, Stephen remained quiet, staring out the window into the darkness. Elly and her mother discussed the play and the actors. Both women loved the theater and were eager to review the performance. Their lively conversation made the journey feel short, but for Stephen, it seemed painfully long.

His mood darkened with each passing moment. His patience wore thin, and a surge of quiet anger began to build inside him. Every time he looked at Elly, his thoughts turned back to Jonathan, how he had looked at her, and how she had looked back.

Stephen tried to believe it was all Jonathan's fault that Elly was innocent in whatever game Jonathan was playing. But the seed of doubt had been planted, and it twisted deeper with every mile they traveled.

Stephen knew, deep down, that this was simply what he wanted to believe. But in truth, he could see that Elly was responding to this man's attention, willingly, even tenderly. What was he to do? The thought of Elly being with Jonathan was unbearable. Yet, he didn't want to act out of anger or appear controlling. He had spent years building a life with her, crafting a relationship rooted in respect and devotion and now it felt as though it were crumbling before his eyes.

The carriage finally pulled to a stop at the front steps of the Bentley mansion. Stephen helped Theresa and Elly down with his usual courtesy. They exchanged polite goodnights, and each quietly retired to their own chambers, leaving Stephen alone with the weight of his thoughts.

CHAPTER TWENTY SEVEN

The following morning was beautiful. The flowers were in bloom, the sun shone brightly, and the sky was a soft shade of blue, scattered with a few drifting clouds. A gentle breeze moved through the hot summer air, offering relief from the warmth. The pastures rolled with hills of green grass, speckled with patches of yellow dandelions and wildflowers. This time of year, the land was painted with vibrant, tranquil colors that stretched as far as the eye could see.

The stable servants were busy working with a few of the new horses. Stephen had risen early and was sitting on the wooden fence out back, quietly watching the trainers work. He could sit there for hours; he loved horses, and the peaceful routine helped to calm his mind. Still, he was sick with jealousy and anger. He wanted to confront Elly, to demand answers, but he felt foolish. In all their years of marriage, jealousy had never been an issue.

Stephen remained by the stables until late morning, his thoughts drifting through the years they had spent together. He couldn't recall a time when he had ever doubted their relationship. He believed that Elly had grown to love him, and that love had once given him comfort and peace. But now, this man, Jonathan Tate, an actor, seemed to have entered their lives and unraveled everything Stephen had worked so hard to build.

Desperation had begun to settle in. He felt as though he was losing Elly, piece by piece, with every passing day. Stephen knew he needed to channel his anger into action before it consumed him entirely. He resolved to learn everything he could about Mr. Jonathan Tate. And the most logical place to start was with Grant. After all, Grant was the one who had introduced Jonathan to Elly at the gala.

With that decision made, Stephen waved to the horse trainers and headed back to the house to change his clothes and prepare for his trip into town. As he stepped inside, he saw Theresa coming down the stairs toward him.

Stephen, my dear, Elly and I are putting together a ball. We want to display the fine artwork you purchased from that talented young artist. You know, the portrait he painted of Elly is simply wonderful," Theresa said.

Splendid idea," Stephen replied as he continued walking upstairs, passing Theresa as she came down. He seemed slightly distracted, which did not go unnoticed.

Are you all right?" Theresa asked.

Hmmm? Oh yes, I just have some business to tend to. The party is a wonderful idea. When will it be?" Stephen paused and turned around briefly to speak with her.

At the end of the week—Friday. Will that be all right?" she asked.

Of course. I ll look forward to a dance with you," Stephen smiled, then turned and continued upstairs.

Theresa, flattered by his words, smiled and laughed quietly to herself before continuing down the staircase.

Later, Stephen arrived in town and made his way to the pub where Grant was known to spend many of his afternoons. When he pushed through the wooden doors, he saw Grant sitting at a table with five other men. The room was thick with smoke from cigars and cigarettes, and the men sat around a table cluttered with whiskey glasses, playing cards in their hands, and a pile of silver coins and paper money in the center.

Stephen approached the bar, deciding not to interrupt the game until the hand was over. Grant looked up, spotted him, and gave a wave to let Stephen know he had seen him. Stephen nodded and ordered a drink. He had two glasses of whiskey while he waited.

Finally, Grant finished the hand and walked over to join him.

"Hello, my good brother! What brings you out this afternoon? Are you going to retire and start playing poker with me and the boys?" Grant grinned as he reached out to shake Stephen's hand.

"No, I just had something to take care of in town and thought I'd stop by to see how you're doing," Stephen replied.

Grant looked at Stephen long and hard, though he kept a smile on his face. Stephen avoided meeting his eyes.

"Sure... now tell me the real reason you're here. Have I done something wrong?" Grant asked, still smiling.

"No, no, nothing like that. I just wanted to ask you about your friend Jonathan Tate. What do you know of him, and who exactly is this character?" Stephen asked, motioning for another whiskey. Grant could see that Stephen was serious, though he was trying to sound casual.

"Jonathan? Why do you ask?" Grant said.

"I don't want to get into it. Just tell me what you know."

"Well, let's see. I know he came over about a year ago from Europe. He traveled around a bit and then started directing theatrical performances. From the stories he tells, he's done quite well for himself. He's made a lot of friends since he's been here. I don't know, is that the kind of information you're looking for?" Grant asked.

"Is he seeing any particular lady friends?" Stephen asked.

Grant laughed at the question.

"He's seeing a lot of lady friends. He's got a long list of hearts waiting for him to call on them. Though, of course, his list isn't as long as mine." Grant grinned. "I don't know which one he's serious about right now—he hasn't mentioned it lately. We usually share our tales."

Stephen continued drinking his whiskey, falling quiet as he mulled over what Grant had said.

Why do you ask? Jonathan s a pretty good fellow," Grant said.

I m not sure... I just get a strange feeling when he s around Elly," Stephen replied.

I already warned him that she was taken. I could tell he was interested in her the first night they met. I made it clear Elly is a married woman and that he should look elsewhere. I surely wouldn t think he d try to pursue her," Grant said, placing a hand on Stephen s shoulder.

Please don t mention my thoughts to anyone especially Jonathan. I could be mistaken. I just wanted to find out about his past," Stephen said.

No, I won t say anything to him. But I ll keep a watchful eye," Grant replied. He paused for a moment, as if recalling something. You know... I do believe he once told me that he is or was married. Said his wife is from a wealthy family in London, something like that. I m not sure, but I can find out."

Stephen s heart started to race; this new piece of information sparked his full attention.

Yes, do that. When can you confirm it?" Stephen asked.

I have a ship captain due back from Europe, an old friend of Jonathan s who knows him better than I do. He d know whether or not Jonathan has a wife abroad. I ll let you know what I find out. Don t let it trouble you, Stephen. Elly adores you," Grant said, trying to offer reassurance.

Yes, you re right. I ll try to put this out of my mind. Still, do look into it and let me know as soon as you confirm anything, either way." Stephen downed the rest of his whiskey.

I need to get back home. I ll see you later. Oh, by the way, Friday evening Theresa and Elly are hosting a ball. Dress for the occasion and bring a lady friend, if you like."

Stephen turned to leave.

Alright, I ll see you then," Grant said as he finished his drink and returned to the card table.

During the ride home, Stephen s mind replayed the news Grant had shared. Could it be true? Did Jonathan have a wife and possibly even a family in Europe? His thoughts raced as fast as the hooves of his horse. Rage surged through his body at the idea of Jonathan deceiving them and possibly pursuing Elly while already committed elsewhere. Still, Stephen resolved to say nothing to Elly until he could verify the truth. Until then, he would wait and watch.

When Stephen arrived home, it was already getting dark outside. Dinner had ended, and the women had retired to their chambers for the evening. Tired from his journey, Stephen sat down in the library and soon fell asleep while reading a book.

CHAPTER TWENTY EIGHT

The week had filtered to an end, the final preparations were completed, and the party was to take place this evening. Theresa had awakened early. She was busy rushing around the house, making sure the servants were polishing the marble floors in the ballroom. All of the chandeliers were polished, and the silver shone, cleaned to perfection. The field workers would not be picking cotton or tobacco today; instead, they would change into their uniforms designated for these special occasions and help with the party. Each person was assigned a specific duty, and it was considered a holiday for the field workers to be allowed to work close to the mansion. On these special days, the workers were given better food, and the labor was much lighter.

Elly had made it a point to stay close to the kitchen today, ensuring that everything was done correctly for tonight's serving. She tried to stay busy, hoping it would help ease her thoughts of Jonathan. It had been over a week since she had seen him; since she had spent those tender moments in his arms. The thought of seeing him tonight gave her the extra energy to get through the day.

Grant arrived early that afternoon. He came into the house carrying his tuxedo and handed it to one of the servants to lay out in his room for the evening. Stephen had seen Grant ride up on his horse and followed him inside. This was the first time he had seen Grant since their conversation at the pub earlier in the week.

"Grant, I'm glad you made it back early today. You've been spending your days and nights in town quite a bit," Stephen said as he walked over and shook Grant's hand.

Theresa walked into the room just as the two men greeted each other.

A THREAD BETWEEN LIVES

My, you look lovely this evening, Theresa," Grant said as he bent down to kiss her on the cheek. She was already dressed for the evening s affair. She wore a purple satin and lace dress, the front adorned with sheer mesh lace that covered her neckline, with ruffles curling around the sleeve cuffs and collar.

Thank you, Grant. I m glad you could make it. I m excited about the ball this evening. The ballroom looks grand with the new portraits hanging on the wall; it gives a special touch to the room," Theresa said.

Yes, Pedro did a wonderful job. Please excuse me. I need to get dressed for tonight. Elly will shoot me if I m not standing at the door when our guests arrive," Stephen smiled at both of them.

I have things to tend to. I ll see you later," Theresa said as she walked out of the room and toward the ballroom.

Stephen," Grant said, his voice low, I found the information you asked for. I was right, he does have a wife. I ll talk with you more about it this evening. Go get ready."

Alright, tonight," Stephen replied, then turned and started up the staircase. His heart began to beat faster, jealousy tightening its grip on his chest with every step. The thought of Jonathan still overwhelmed him with anger.

On the way to his chambers, Stephen stopped by Elly s room. He gently knocked on the door and pushed it open slightly, peering inside. Elly was sitting at her vanity, looking into the mirror as she arranged her hair. She didn t turn to look at the door, instead, she kept her eyes on the mirror, where she could see Stephen s reflection standing in the doorway.

Hello, Stephen. Is something wrong?" Elly asked, still focused on her hair.

Stephen hesitated for a moment. Part of him wanted to tell her right then what he had learned about Jonathan, but the words wouldn't come. He couldn't bring himself to say it.

"No, I just wanted to see how you were doing this evening. Everything looks wonderful. You've done such a good job taking care of things," he said from the doorway.

"Thank you, it's kind of you to say. Are you going to get dressed soon, or do you have other matters to tend to?" Elly asked, her tone neutral but pleasant.

"No, I'm going to get dressed now. I'll see you downstairs, my dear," Stephen said as he started to turn away. Then he paused and looked back at Elly.

"Elly..." he said, then stopped.

"Yes? What is it, Stephen?"

Stephen hesitated for a moment.

"Nothing. It's just that... you look beautiful tonight. I love you," he said, then closed the door without waiting to hear her response.

Elly sat and stared at herself in the mirror, a tear welling in her eye.

Stephen finished getting dressed for the evening's event and went to the library to sit and have a drink while waiting for the guests to arrive. When he walked into the room, he saw that Grant was already there, dressed and seated with a glass in hand.

"Grant, looks like we both had the same idea, to have a drink and bide our time in here where it's quiet," Stephen said, walking over to pour himself a glass of whiskey. He held the bottle up toward Grant, gesturing to offer a refill.

Grant nodded. "Yes, I'll have another one."

Stephen poured him a drink and handed it over.

"What I found out," Grant said, lowering his voice slightly, "is that Jonathan does indeed have a wife back in London. A very wealthy wife, in fact. She appears to be supporting his lifestyle, his fun and leisure. She's an older woman and apparently knows about Jonathan's... extracurriculars. She tolerates it, as long as he finds his way back home now and then."

Stephen clenched his jaw.

"Then the question is, what does he want with my wife? Is she just another game to him?" he said, his voice tight. His face turned red with anger, and he could feel his body trembling as he tried to control the flood of emotions rising inside him.

"Stephen, you don't know anything for certain," Grant said calmly. "Whether or not Jonathan has broken trust, he's always been kind and generous to me. I find it hard to believe he'd do something like this to a friend. Let's not jump to conclusions. You need to talk with Elly, let her know what you're thinking. She might not even be aware of any of this."

"I will talk to her tonight, after the party has ended. Do me a favor and keep an eye on Jonathan tonight. I really don't want him spending any time alone with Elly," Stephen said.

Just then, Elly walked into the room as Stephen finished mentioning her name.

"I heard my name. What would you two gentlemen be saying about me?" she smiled, walking over to Grant and offering her hand for him to kiss.

"Stephen was just saying what a wonderful job you did planning this evening's ball and how stunning the portrait of you looks in the ballroom," Grant said smoothly.

"Have you seen it?" Elly asked.

No, as a matter of fact, I ll go take a look right now. And maybe snatch a few fresh pastries while I m at it. I m famished," Grant replied, standing and placing his glass down before leaving the room.

Shall we go wait for the guests to arrive? They should be here any minute," Elly said.

Of course," Stephen replied, following her toward the large foyer.

Guests soon began to arrive, filling the Bentley mansion with voices and laughter. Many on the guest list were longtime family friends, some through business, others through wealth and public standing. The men wore formal tuxedos, and the women donned elegant gowns. Nothing was spared in making the event lavish, a clear display of the Bentley family s prestige in the town s growing society.

An orchestra was set up on one side of the ballroom and had already begun playing. People danced gracefully across the polished marble floor. Large chandeliers overhead sparkled with dozens of candles, bathing the room in a warm, golden glow as guests mingled, laughing and talking in lively groups.

Typically, the large windows in the ballroom would be open to allow for ventilation, but tonight they remained closed. A storm was setting in—the wind had picked up, and a light drizzle began to fall. The once clear sky had turned to deep shades of blue and black. Lightning slashed across the heavens, sending jagged flashes through the turbulent night. Yet inside, the joyful music of the orchestra drowned out all signs of the reckless weather beyond the walls of the Bentley estate.

About an hour after many of the guests had arrived, Jonathan entered the foyer. He was damp from his ride in from town and handed his coat to one of the servants to be dried. The servant also polished his shoes before Jonathan made his way into the ballroom with the other guests.

Elly had been patiently watching and waiting. When she noticed his arrival, her heart began to race, and she could hardly resist the urge to rush out to meet him. Stephen also noted Jonathan's entrance. Though he remained engaged in conversation with guests, laughing and appearing relaxed, his eyes and thoughts remained fixed on Jonathan.

Elly had scribbled a note on a small piece of paper, folded it tightly, and printed Jonathan's name on the front. The letter asked him to meet her in her room at exactly nine o'clock. She felt confident that she could slip away unnoticed. Stephen would likely assume she had gone to the kitchen to check on things, just as Carolyn used to do.

Elly found Jacob, who was dressed in a white waistcoat with black pants and gloves, serving pastries to the guests. She walked over to him discreetly, handed him the folded note, whispered something, and pointed toward the foyer where Jonathan was still waiting for his jacket. Before glancing around the room, she quickly checked to see if Stephen had noticed. He turned his head away just in time, so Elly assumed he hadn't seen the exchange.

It was now eight-thirty, and the party was alive and vibrant. Guests danced and laughed, smoke drifted lazily through the air, and the sweet aroma of pastries and fresh fruit mingled with the scent of polished wood and candle wax. Outside, the storm raged on, thunder roaring across the hills and flashes of lightning streaking down across the open countryside.

Jacob stepped away from his serving station and started toward the foyer, scanning the area for Mr. Tate so he could deliver the note. Just before Jacob reached Jonathan, however, Stephen intercepted him in the hallway outside the ballroom.

"Jacob, give me the note that Mrs. Bentley passed on to you," Stephen said in a stern voice.

Sir?" Jacob replied, his voice shaken. Mrs. Bentley said no one was to see this except Mr. Tate." He looked down at the ground, uneasy about the position he had been put in.

Jacob, give me the letter—now. Then you may leave and go back to your cabin. I am not asking again." Stephen could hardly control his anger as he stared directly into Jacob s eyes.

Yes, sir. I was only doing what Mrs. Bentley asked of me." Jacob handed the note to Stephen.

Jacob, it s all right. I am not angry with you. Please go to the kitchen and take some food home for your family. Do not go back to Mrs. Bentley tonight," Stephen said, his tone now softened as he took the letter from Jacob s hand.

Jacob turned and walked away, doing exactly as Stephen asked. He knew Stephen was the master and his owner and he would never cross his wishes.

Stephen unfolded the note and read it silently. The words tore through his body like a sword slicing his skin. His heart felt as though it had dropped into his chest, and he found it suddenly difficult to breathe. He leaned back against the wall for support. A lump grew in the back of his throat, making it hard to swallow. Stephen felt his entire world crumbling down around him. The room seemed to spin, and the voices of the guests faded into a distant hum. All he could hear was the pounding of his own heart, louder with each beat, harder and faster.

A business associate walked up to him and touched his arm.

Mr. Bentley, sir... are you all right?" the man asked.

Yes, yes, I am all right," Stephen snapped back into reality and walked away from the man. He left the foyer and entered the library, needing to be alone to sort out his thoughts. Walking over to the side table, he poured himself a large glass of whiskey from the flask and drank it down in one long swallow. The burn in his throat helped relieve the tight knot that had formed there.

Stephen pulled out the pocket watch attached to his vest by a gold chain and flipped it open. On the inside lid, the engraving read: To Stephen, with all my love — Elly. It was now five minutes until nine o clock. He knew Elly would be waiting in her chambers for Jonathan.

He poured and drank a second glass of whiskey before making his way up the stairs, each step heavier than the last.

Upstairs, Elly had asked the servants to light a fire in her fireplace. The storm had cooled the evening air, and though she had opened the doors to her balcony, the room still felt brisk. She stood outside, letting the cool breeze wash over her skin as she gazed into the moonlit night. The wind played gently with the loose strands of her hair, and she closed her eyes, taking in a deep breath of fresh air, exhaling slowly. Her thoughts wandered back to the night Jonathan had found her in the garden, how he had looked at her, how her heart had raced. A smile curved on her lips.

Inside the room, the door opened and closed quietly. Elly, certain it was Jonathan, didn t turn around. She heard the soft thud of footsteps on the rug and the faint crackling of the fire as a log shifted.

Stephen had entered the room. He walked to the fireplace and stood silently, staring into the flames. He reached into his pocket and pulled out the letter, her letter to him, and dropped it into the fire. The paper curled and blackened quickly, the words disappearing into ash.

Stephen braced himself against the mantel, leaning in as the firelight reflected in his eyes. They had gone dark and cold. His face was pale, expressionless, carved into stone.

From the balcony, Elly called out gently, Jonathan?"

She turned from the balcony and walked back into her room. But as her eyes adjusted to the firelight, she froze. The man standing by the fireplace was not Jonathan.

It was Stephen.

Her breath caught in her throat. She lifted the back of her hand to her lips and whispered, "Stephen..." Her voice was low, trembling.

A wave of fear swept over her. She could feel it in her chest, cold and heavy. He knew. She was certain of it now. Her mind raced, thoughts colliding. What had he read? How much did he know?

She dared not meet his eyes.

Stephen turned from the fire and looked directly at her. Her face, once flushed with anticipation, was now pale and drawn. He saw the fear in her expression. He saw the tears beginning to well in her eyes.

Elly began to turn away, but Stephen strode toward her and grabbed her by the arms, his hands firm and trembling with rage.

"Look at me," he demanded, his voice low but rough as he gave her a hard shake.

Elly gasped. Her body felt weak, trembling beneath his grip. Tears streamed down her cheeks as she stared at the floor, unable to meet his gaze.

"Why?" he shouted. "Why, Elly? I don't understand! I will not let this happen."

She collapsed, crumpling to the floor at his feet, sobbing uncontrollably. Her hands covered her face as if to hide from the truth now crashing down around them both.

Stephen stood above her, breathing hard. Slowly, his fingers uncurled, and he released her. He stepped back, shaken by the intensity of his own fury.

Realizing what he had done, he turned and walked out of the room. The door closed behind him with a heavy thud.

Outside, he staggered down the hall a few steps and slammed his palm against his own forehead once, then again, harder, punishing himself. He paced the corridor, back and forth, fists clenched, his mind a storm.

Breathe. Breathe. Calm yourself, he told himself silently. She is your wife. Jonathan can't take what you've built with her. He's the one to blame. It's him.

But even as he tried to believe those words, they rang hollow. The betrayal cut too deep.

He remained outside her door for a while longer, fighting to steady his breath, wrestling with the fire raging in his chest.

Stephen returned to Elly's room. She was no longer on the floor, she had composed herself and was now standing outside on the balcony. Her hands rested on the railing, her gaze lost in the darkness as lightning flashed across the stormy sky.

Quietly, Stephen walked up behind her. Without a word, he slipped his arms around her waist and leaned close, whispering into her ear.

"I am very sorry, my dear Elly. I just love you with all my heart. Jonathan can't touch what we have. You are mine. I can give you everything," he said, his voice trembling. "You do love me, Elly... don't you?"

Elly nodded slowly, unable to speak. Her face was still turned away, and her eyes welled with tears she struggled to keep from falling.

"We need to get back to the guests," Stephen said after a moment, more composed now.

"Yes," Elly replied softly. "Let me freshen up, and I'll meet you downstairs."

Of course," Stephen said gently. He let go of her, turned, and left the room.

As he stepped into the hallway, Stephen began to shove everything back down inside. He wanted this night to return to how it was supposed to be, a celebration, a display of wealth, beauty, and pride. Denial crept over him like a blanket, suffocating the rage and betrayal simmering beneath. He didn t want to think. He didn t want to feel. He just needed to pretend.

Stephen reached the staircase and stopped at the top, resting his hands on the carved wooden railing. He looked down at the ballroom floor below, guests twirled in elegant dance, laughter echoed off the marble walls, and the chandeliers glimmered like constellations overhead.

Then, his eyes locked onto one man standing alone.

Jonathan Tate.

He was standing directly in front of the large portrait of Elly, staring up at it in contemplation. Stephen narrowed his eyes and descended the stairs, weaving through the crowd until he reached the spot beside him. The two men stood shoulder to shoulder, both silently gazing at the painting.

Stephen clasped his hands behind his back and said evenly, A lovely portrait of my wife, wouldn t you say? Beautiful, is she not?"

Jonathan didn t look away. His voice was low, his tone sharp with implication. Yes... it s a fine piece of work, sir. I m sure you re very proud to own her."

The word own pierced through Stephen s restraint like a knife.

He turned slowly toward Jonathan, his jaw clenched tight, his breath deliberate. The flicker of rage in his eyes betrayed the calm in his posture. He could barely contain the storm within him.

Hear this, Jonathan," Stephen said, his voice low and cutting. I love my wife, and she returns my affection. Leave her alone... or there will be consequences." Without waiting for a reply, Stephen turned sharply and disappeared into the crowd.

He moved quickly through the ballroom, the pressure in his chest growing heavier with each step. His hands were clenched at his sides, his teeth grinding in frustration. The orchestra played on, the sound of laughter and clinking glasses surrounding him like an unwanted fog.

Grant spotted him and stepped into his path, grabbing him lightly by the arm.

What s wrong?" Grant asked, catching the look in Stephen s eyes.

I was right," Stephen said, barely able to control the trembling in his voice. Jonathan is making advances on Elly. I can t discuss it now. Just, find him and make him leave."

Before Grant could respond, Stephen broke away and continued walking. A guest stopped him mid-stride, eager to speak. Stephen forced himself to smile and nodded along, pretending to engage in polite conversation, though his mind was burning with tension.

Upstairs, Elly had finished freshening up and stepped out of her chambers. Her heart was heavy, her thoughts scattered. As she reached the top of the staircase, she paused, just as Stephen had done, looking down at the sea of dancing guests, glittering lights, and carefully arranged perfection. Her eyes scanned the room, searching.

Then she saw him.

Jonathan stood in front of her portrait, just as Stephen had left him. His posture was still, his eyes fixed on the painting. Elly s breath caught. She needed to warn him, Stephen knew everything. He had read her note. She had to find a way to end this... or at least protect Jonathan from Stephen s rage.

She began descending the staircase when a voice called out to her from the crowd.

Elly, my dear, come visit us!" It was an older woman, smiling and waving enthusiastically.

Elly smiled faintly and raised her hand, gesturing for the woman to wait. Her path was already chosen. She continued down the stairs, her eyes never leaving Jonathan's figure.

Stephen, now free from the guest's conversation, heard the woman call Elly's name. He turned and followed her movement with narrowed eyes. When he saw the direction she was heading, his stomach dropped. It was toward him.

Jonathan had turned now, catching sight of Elly descending the stairs. Their eyes locked. He started moving toward her, unaware of the storm building around them.

They walked toward each other, drawn together in the center of a grand ballroom full of people, yet oblivious to them all.

Stephen broke into a stride.

Just before Elly and Jonathan could reach each other, Stephen appeared. He stepped between them and seized Elly's arm firmly, pulling her toward him. Her eyes widened in shock.

My dear, I have been looking for you. May I have this dance with my lovely wife?" Stephen asked.

Of course," Elly replied.

As Stephen began to escort her to the dance floor, she glanced back at Jonathan, who stood watching her as she walked away from him.

Grant, having observed what had just happened and seeing Stephen take Elly to dance, moved across the room. He approached

Jonathan, placed a firm arm around his shoulder, and began guiding him toward the foyer.

Jonathan, walk with me this way, my friend," Grant said casually.

Grant, how are you doing? Have you any special company this evening?" Jonathan asked with a smile.

Grant didn t respond to the question. Instead, he led Jonathan to the foyer and signaled for a servant.

Fetch Mr. Tate s coat and hat," he instructed.

Jonathan looked puzzled. What is this all about, Grant?" he asked.

You are not welcome here anymore," Grant said bluntly. I trusted you, only to find that you abused that trust. Elly is a married woman, and if you ve forgotten, she happens to be married to my brother. So leave, please."

As he spoke, Grant adjusted his collar slightly, a subtle warning in his posture that he was ready for confrontation if it came to that.

I don t know what this is all about—" Jonathan began, but Grant cut him off.

You re a married man. Are you planning on leaving your wife in London? Does Elly even know about her? Just go, before my patience runs out."

The servant handed Jonathan his coat and hat and opened the door.

Without another word, Jonathan stepped outside.

Grant remained in the foyer for a moment, then turned and made his way back into the ballroom. He scanned the room until he spotted

Stephen and Elly on the dance floor. He paused, watching them move together to the music.

Grant exhaled deeply. A weight pressed on him, the guilt of having brought Jonathan into their lives. He felt responsible for allowing the man to get so close to his family.

Stephen and Elly continued to dance. Elly felt weak from emotion, her mind clouded and uncertain about everything that was happening. It all felt unreal, like a dream and she was sure she would wake up to find that everything was fine.

You look lovely tonight, Elly," Stephen said softly.

Thank you," Elly replied, keeping her answer brief.

These people are here for you, my darling. They are our friends and guests. They adore you, just as I do," Stephen said, gazing into her eyes with a pleading expression.

I know, Stephen. You re a wonderful man... you do so much for me. Things I do not deserve," Elly said, looking away as a tear welled in her eye.

My darling, you deserve even more," Stephen responded.

I m tired. Will you excuse me for the evening? I d like to go to my chambers and sleep. Please send my servant Dora to prepare my bath," Elly said, gently pulling away and ending their dance.

Of course... but what about the guests?" Stephen asked.

They re here for you. Please offer my apologies as you bid them good night," she said quietly.

Stephen leaned in to kiss her lips, but Elly turned her head. His kiss landed on her cheek instead.

Good night, Stephen."

Elly left the ballroom and ascended the grand staircase to the second floor. She walked down the hallway and entered her chambers. A young servant woman followed shortly behind, dressed in a black-and-white maid's uniform.

"Please run me a hot bath and turn down my bed," Elly said without looking up.

"Yes, my lady. As you please," Dora replied softly.

Tears swelled in Elly's eyes. She sat down at her vanity and stared at herself in the mirror. She picked up her brush and gently stroked her hair. She continued to look at her reflection until she finally lowered her head onto the table, covering her face with her hands, and wept.

"My lady, what is wrong? What can I do for you?" Dora asked with concern.

"Nothing. I'm just tired. Please go. I need to be alone," Elly replied, trying to hold back her tears.

"Shall I get Master Bentley?" Dora asked hesitantly.

"No. Leave him with the guests. I just need to be alone," Elly said firmly.

"Yes, my lady. Good night." Dora quietly left the room after preparing the bath.

After the servant left the bedroom, Elly's tears began to fall once more down her cheeks.

As she sat crying at her nightstand, she heard a gentle knock at the door. Grant opened it slowly and saw Elly with tears rolling down her face. He stepped inside, shutting the door behind him. Walking over to her, he gently pulled her into his arms, comforting her.

Hey, none of this now. No more crying," Grant said softly, holding her close.

Grant, what am I doing? What have I done?" Elly sobbed, trying to find the words to explain her turmoil.

Listen... it s over. I told Jonathan to leave. He won t bother you again," Grant said as he moved his hands to her face, gently holding it so she would look at him.

Elly continued to cry. You don t understand... I—" she began.

No, it s alright. I know," Grant interrupted. Jonathan didn t tell you about his wife. I understand. I just feel horrible for trusting him around you. And then I think about all the times I pushed him to go riding with you..."

He paused and shook his head. But it s over now."

Elly was stunned by the news of Jonathan s wife. Her tears slowed as she struggled to process what Grant had just said. She tried to hold herself together, her body stiff with shock, her eyes searching Grant s face for answers.

Stephen didn t tell you? That Jonathan has a wife in London?" Grant asked.

Elly slowly shook her head. Her entire body felt numb. Her mind raced to deny it, this couldn t be true. Someone must be mistaken. Someone had misinformed them.

No... I didn t know," she managed to say.

It s alright now. He won t pursue you anymore. Try to get some rest. We ll talk more in the morning," Grant said gently.

He kissed her softly on the cheek and gave her a reassuring smile as he turned to leave the room.

Grant had no idea that Elly had returned Jonathan's affections. From what Stephen had told him, he assumed it was only Jonathan who had been pursuing Elly.

Elly sat for a long time in front of her mirror at her nightstand. Her mind raced with the possibilities of what she had just discovered, what if it was really true? Elly tried to recall every second she had spent with Jonathan. How could I have been so wrong? she thought.

She could no longer bear another moment of her mind spinning back and forth with thought after thought. In a sudden impulse, she changed into her riding clothes, stepped onto the balcony, and quietly climbed down the side of the house into the garden. Moving swiftly through the shadows, she made her way to the stables, where she found one of the servants sweeping.

Upon her request, he saddled her horse without question.

Elly had decided: she was going into town to find Jonathan. He had to answer her face-to-face and tell her the truth.

As she rode into town, her thoughts swirled with emotion. She thought of all the pain she had caused Stephen these last few months. She remembered the only time she had seen him truly angry, the day he cried in her room after cutting his hands on the flowers from the garden.

She thought about what Grant had said, how Stephen had known about Jonathan but chose not to tell her, not wanting to cause her pain or distress. He had sacrificed his pride to protect her. That was the kind of man Stephen was, always putting her first.

Tears welled in Elly's eyes as she splashed through puddles along the misty road. She searched her heart with each beat of the horse's stride and realized that, no matter what Jonathan's answer was, she would end the relationship. She would return to Stephen and beg for his forgiveness.

She loved him, more than she had ever known. She relied on his strength, his patience, and his unwavering support. He had given her everything, without hesitation, without limit. Jonathan had entered her life during a time of grief and emotional turmoil, when she was angry and lost after her father's death. She now understood that what she had mistaken for love was merely the rush of infatuation, a reckless escape.

Her clothes were soaked from the fine rain, and her hair clung to her back in damp strands. The ribbons that once held it neatly had long blown away in the wind.

Elly arrived at the playhouse and entered through the front doors, which were unlocked. It was dark inside the large foyer; she could see a light glowing down the hallway toward Jonathan's office. Elly walked slowly in that direction, her nerves tightening with each step. The darkness of the empty building at night made her uneasy.

As she approached Jonathan's office, she heard laughter, light, flirtatious laughter that grew louder and clearer with every step. It was unmistakably a woman's voice, and then she heard Jonathan's voice as well. Elly's heart began to race. She stopped in front of his door and stood silently in the shadows, listening.

Then, unable to stop herself, she opened the door and stood in the doorway, staring in disbelief.

Jonathan looked up at her. The young blonde actress whom Elly had seen speaking with Jonathan during her last visit to the playhouse was lying naked on his desk. Jonathan was on top of her, kissing her neck, when the door opened.

Their eyes met.

Elly turned and ran back down the hallway. Jonathan bolted after her, catching up just as she reached the front doors. Elly had struggled to find her footing in the darkened corridors, unfamiliar with the layout of the building. Her breath was shallow, her chest tight, her mind reeling with what she had just witnessed.

Elly! It's not what you think!" Jonathan pleaded, grabbing her arm.

Yes, Jonathan, it is," Elly said, her voice shaking with fury. I was so blind... What was I thinking?"

She wasn't crying, her grief was buried beneath a wave of anger.

Jonathan reached for her again, but she yanked her arm away, stepping back.

Do not touch me. I do want you to know, I came here tonight to say goodbye. We were a mistake, and I've realized that. I am going to beg Stephen for forgiveness. I do love him. You took advantage of me when I was weak. But it was my fault, and I'll have to live with that. But never again."

Elly turned to walk away from him.

Elly?" Jonathan said.

Do not ever try to contact me again." She hesitated, then turned back to him.

Answer me this, when were you planning on telling me about your wife?"

Elly waited, but Jonathan didn't respond. He just stood there, silent, his expression heavy with regret.

I thought so," Elly said flatly, then turned and walked out, closing the door behind her and stepping into the cold, rainy night.

She mounted her horse and rode quickly toward home. The rain had started falling harder, and the thunder was deafening. Wind whipped through the trees, tossing their branches violently. Dark clouds moved swiftly across the sky, masking the moonlight.

As soon as she was far enough from the playhouse, Elly began to cry again, tears of anger, shame, and heartbreak. She cursed herself for allowing this to happen, for letting her emotions cloud her judgment. She urged her horse forward, pushing it to go faster; faster than the storm, faster than her thoughts.

The rain became a steady downpour. Visibility was poor, and Elly struggled to see the path home.

Just as she approached the gates of the Bentley estate, a roar of thunder cracked through the sky. A bolt of lightning struck the ground directly in front of her horse.

Startled, the horse reared up on its hind legs. Elly lost her balance and was thrown backward off the saddle. Her head slammed against a tree stump with a sickening thud. Her neck snapped forward before her body collapsed lifelessly onto the muddy ground.

The horse bolted toward the stables, galloping in panic.

Elly lay motionless, rain pooling in the red-tinged water beneath her head. Her eyes were closed. Her chest did not rise. The storm raged on, but Elly was still.

The stable servant who had saddled Elly s horse saw it galloping back alone. Alarmed, he ran out and grabbed the reins to calm the panicked animal. He led it into the barn, glancing anxiously out into the dark night. But there was no sign of Elly.

Worried, he hurried up to the main house and asked to speak with Mr. Bentley.

Stephen was still dressed from the party, though the guests had left hours ago. He and Grant were sharing a quiet drink when a servant came in to summon them both to the front door.

There stood the young stable hand, soaked from the rain, visibly shaken.

Sir," he said to Stephen, Mrs. Bentley came down to the stables and asked me to saddle her horse. She rode off into the night. A little while later, the horse came back alone, still saddled. I looked for her, but couldn t find her anywhere."

A wave of panic surged through Stephen. Without a word, he rushed up the stairs, calling out Elly s name. He burst into her room and found it empty. He turned and flew back down the stairs, running outside to join Grant, who was already heading toward the barn.

They shouted her name as they searched.

Grant, take a horse and cover the other side of the stables," Stephen ordered. I ll go this way."

Stephen, we ll find her," Grant reassured him as he mounted up.

Stephen didn t wait for his own horse, he mounted Elly s and took off at full gallop. Several of the other stablemen had already begun searching. Suddenly, a voice called out near the front gates.

She s here!" someone yelled.

Stephen s heart nearly stopped. He dug his heels into the horse, pushing it harder. As he approached the gate, he saw a group of men with lanterns gathered around something, or someone, on the ground.

When he saw her still form lying in the wet, muddy earth, his heart broke.

He jumped off the horse, stumbling in his haste, and ran to her. Dropping to his knees, he gathered her limp body into his arms.

No... No, no, no!" Stephen cried out, his voice raw and broken. He looked up at the stormy sky, rain streaming down his face with his tears, and yelled, Why?!"

He rocked her gently, pressing her to his chest, kissing her cheek, her forehead, her lips, begging for a breath, a sign of life that never came.

Grant arrived and watched silently, his own heart aching as he saw his brother clinging to Elly's lifeless body. He stepped forward, but Stephen shouted through his sobs, Leave us! All of you, just go!"

No one dared disobey. One by one, the men stepped back and turned away, leaving Stephen alone in the rain with his wife.

Eventually, Stephen lifted her gently in his arms and carried her back into the house. Up the grand staircase. Into her room.

He laid her on the bed and sat beside her, soaked and trembling. He held her hand, brushed the wet hair from her face, and wept silently beside her; his world, now shattered.

CHAPTER TWENTY NINE

Nothing had ever been the same for Stephen after Elly died. He became a broken, bitter man. Most of his days were spent locked away in his room, drinking heavily. He stopped listening to anyone, refused help, and seemed to have no will left to live.

His body weakened from the neglect. Days would pass where he wouldn't eat—just whiskey, glass after glass. Eventually, Stephen signed over ownership of the estate and named his two brothers, Chestin and Grant, as the sole beneficiaries. They mourned not only the loss of their beloved sister-in-law, Elly, but also the slow, hollow death of their brother Stephen. In many ways, it felt as if he had died that cold, rainy night as well.

Jonathan had heard of the accident that claimed Elly's life. Upon learning of it, he quietly left New Orleans and returned to London. He knew Stephen and Grant would surely blame him for her death. Within a day of her passing, he had booked a transatlantic passage and vanished.

What Stephen never knew was that Elly had gone to see Jonathan to say goodbye. She had told him it was over—that she loved Stephen and intended to return to beg for his forgiveness. And Stephen, had he known, would have given it to her gladly.

But the truth died with Elly.

Instead, Stephen lived on, tormented by the belief that Elly had given her heart to another man—that she had chosen Jonathan, and was riding away from him, not back to him, when the accident occurred. He had no idea that she was on her way home, her heart full of regret and love for him.

The thought of Elly in Jonathan's arms haunted him relentlessly. It gnawed at his soul. He drank until unconsciousness overtook him, praying that sleep would spare him the visions of Elly and Jonathan together.

At one point, Stephen tried to find Jonathan—to exact revenge, to bring pain to the man he believed had destroyed his life. But he failed. His attempts to locate him were erratic and uncoordinated, and in his near-constant drunken state, he couldn t organize any real pursuit. Rumors varied: some claimed Jonathan had returned to Europe; others said he had gone north, to New York. No one knew for sure, and Stephen, too broken to persist, let the trail grow cold.

The years passed by, and life at the Bentley estate continued—except for Stephen. He remained trapped in his sorrow, drinking heavily and staying bitter and angry at the world and everyone in it. Eventually, he moved out of the Bentley mansion and into a flat in the city. He wanted to be closer to the pubs and brothels where he now spent most of his days and nights—often in the same drinking establishments Grant had once frequented for hours on end.

Stephen aged poorly over the years. His body grew frail and weak from malnutrition. His once-vibrant hair had turned gray, long, and greasy. He often went unshaven and unbathed for weeks. The men who had once known and respected Stephen now passed him by without a glance. To them, he was just another broken drunk.

Despite appearances, Stephen still had plenty of money to live on. But you wouldn t have known it by the way he chose to live.

One cold November night, Stephen sat slumped at the bar in a small local pub. A half-empty bottle of whiskey sat in front of him as he leaned forward, eyes closed, looking as though he might be asleep sitting up. He was in one of his usual drunken stupors.

A man entered the pub and took the stool next to Stephen. He set down a black top hat and a cane on the bar, then removed his gloves and laid them neatly on top of his hat. The bartender walked over.

What ll it be?" the bartender asked.

Double whiskey, straight up," the man replied.

The bartender paused, eyeing the man closely, as though trying to remember him.

The man extended a hand.

It s been a long time. Remember me? Jonathan Tate—I used to be the director at the playhouse," he said.

Stephen had heard Jonathan s name. He looked over at him and stared as the man sat talking to the bartender. Stephen s heart began to beat faster, and his mind was racing—faster than his body could respond. He lost his balance and stumbled toward Jonathan. Jonathan caught him and helped steady him.

Easy, good man. You ve had a little too much to drink," Jonathan said.

Don t mind him. He s just an old drunk," the bartender muttered to Jonathan. Then he turned to Stephen. Stephen, I m warning you—keep to yourself, or I ll have you thrown out of here," he snapped, before walking down the bar to tend to other customers.

Jonathan turned to look again at the drunken man who had now slumped over the bar, mumbling incoherently. But then, beneath the layers of filth and years of wear, Jonathan recognized the face. It was Stephen Bentley—the man he once knew. He stared in disbelief, wondering how someone so full of life and strength could have ended up in such a pitiful state.

A few minutes later, the door opened, and Grant entered the pub. He walked straight toward the bar where Stephen was leaning heavily against the counter. At first, Grant didn t recognize Jonathan.

Grant, how are you?" Jonathan asked with a smile.

Grant looked at him for a few moments, squinting, until recognition dawned.

Jonathan," he said flatly.

Yes, you remember me?" Jonathan replied.

How could I forget? Stephen is a constant reminder of you—every single day," Grant answered, his voice cold and stern.

He slid Stephen s arm over his own shoulders and lifted him to his feet.

Come on, big brother. Time for bed," Grant said gently, guiding Stephen toward the door.

What happened to him?" Jonathan asked quietly.

Let me put him to bed—and I ll be back," Grant replied.

I ll be here," Jonathan said as Grant carried Stephen out of the pub.

Grant returned a short while later to find Jonathan still at the bar, now sipping his second glass of whiskey. He sat down beside him on the stool Stephen had occupied earlier.

What brings you back here?" Grant asked.

I m just passing through. I don t plan to stay more than a day or two," Jonathan replied.   How long has Stephen been sick?"

He s been like this ever since the night Elly died—when she was supposedly on her way to be with you," Grant said, signaling to the bartender for a drink.

Be with me? You must be mistaken," Jonathan said, turning to face him.

She had left that night in the rain to go to you, or so we thought. Her horse threw her, and she hit her head. She died shortly after. Stephen was overcome with grief and despair," Grant said, his tone quiet.

"No... she wasn't coming to be with me," Jonathan said softly. "She had already come to see me. She told me she never wanted to see me again. She said she loved Stephen and was going back to him—to beg for his forgiveness. She told me she was wrong about a lot of things... it's hard to remember everything she said, but she was resolute."

Grant looked at Jonathan, stunned. He sat in silence for a moment before speaking again.

"Stephen has believed all these years that Elly was leaving him to be with you. That she died running away," Grant said, shaking his head, sorrow clouding his eyes. "That belief destroyed him."

"I'm sorry," Jonathan said. "I never meant to hurt anyone."

"It's been a long time... and the damage is done," Grant replied, his voice low and firm. "I can't offer you forgiveness, if that's what you're after by talking to me. I appreciate the truth you've shared, but I must go now. Don't try to contact Stephen. He doesn't need any more pain—especially not from you."

Grant stood, tossed a coin on the bar to cover his drink, and turned to leave.

"I understand. Good night, Grant," Jonathan said quietly.

The next morning, Grant returned to Stephen's flat. He had waited, thinking it best to speak to his brother after some rest. He wanted to tell him what he had learned about Elly.

But when he arrived, a doctor was already by Stephen's bedside, examining him. A blood-stained bandage was wrapped around Stephen's head, another around his chest.

Grant's heart sank.

A young servant girl approached him quietly.

"Your brother... he fell down the steps," the young servant girl cried, trembling as she spoke. "He was trying to leave—he stumbled into the street. A horse was coming... it couldn't stop. It ran over him." She broke down in sobs, collapsing into Grant's arms.

"It will be alright. Pull yourself together, girl," Grant said gently but firmly, lifting her off him and handing her over to another servant for comfort.

He turned to the doctor, trying to steady his own nerves. "Doctor... will he be alright?"

The doctor removed the stethoscope from his ears, looked at Grant, and slowly shook his head.

"I'm sorry," he said solemnly. "Your brother is very weak. He's lost a great deal of blood, and the fever has set in. Given his condition... there's not much I can do."

Grant stood still, stunned, staring at Stephen—unconscious, pale, and broken. After a moment, he turned to one of the servants nearby.

"Send word to Chestin. Have him come at once," Grant instructed.

Then he pulled a chair to the bedside and sat down quietly beside his brother.

"What do I need to do to keep him comfortable?" Grant asked the doctor.

"My nurse will remain here and tend to him," the doctor replied. "But... you should say your prayers for him now." With that, he closed his black satchel, gave a respectful nod, and left the room.

Grant stayed there with Stephen, refusing to sleep. He watched over him through the night, looking for any signs of consciousness. The nurse worked gently, dabbing Stephen's forehead with a cool cloth in an attempt to lower his fever.

The room reeked of alcohol—the smell rising from Stephen's sweat was nearly unbearable, as if every ounce of whiskey he'd consumed was now seeping from his pores.

Then, Stephen began to mumble.

His eyes fluttered open slightly, unfocused. He was struggling to see. Grant immediately leaned forward, sitting on the edge of the bed, and took his brother's hand in his own.

"It's me, Grant. You gave us quite a scare," Grant said softly as he leaned closer to Stephen.

Stephen's grip tightened slightly around Grant's hand.

"Squeeze my hand if you can understand me," Grant said.

Stephen squeezed his hand again.

"Good," Grant continued gently. "I need to tell you something important, and I want to make sure you understand."

He paused for a moment, then spoke carefully.

"I saw Jonathan this evening. He told me some things you need to know. Elly wasn't leaving to be with him. She had already gone into town to see him—and she was returning. She was coming back to you, Stephen. She told Jonathan goodbye and told him never to try to see her again. She told him it was you she loved—it had always been you. She realized she made a mistake, and she was returning to beg for your forgiveness. She loved you, Stephen. She always loved you."

A single tear slipped from the corner of Stephen's eye. He closed his eyes tightly, gripped Grant's hand firmly—and smiled faintly before taking his final breath.

His body became still.

Grant remained at his side, leaning in close. He whispered through the heavy silence.

Rest now, in peace, my brother. You'll find her on the other side."

These were Grant's final words to Stephen.

Part III
Jake, Claire, Stephen and Elly
Past and Present day

CHAPTER THIRTY

The morning was peaceful and quiet. The sky, painted in vibrant shades of blue, appeared to be streaked with splashes of orange and yellow as the sun began to rise over the streets of Birmingham. The cool air blew leaves across the front lawns, while tree branches danced wildly to the rhythm of the wind. On this beautiful Sunday morning, nothing had yet begun to stir in the neighborhood nestled just outside the city of Detroit. Most people were still asleep in their beds, except for the early risers: the paperboy, who had already made his rounds delivering the Sunday news, and the local baker, who had opened his shop and finished baking three batches of donuts.

Jake lay awake in bed, staring up at the ceiling fan spinning slowly above him. He pulled the pillow out from beneath his head, placed it over his face, and pressed it down tightly. He felt his own warm breath against the fabric as he exhaled into it. In the silence, his thoughts spoke louder than words.

Why am I having these dreams? he asked himself. Why can t I sleep through the night without being haunted by these memories—these people from another time?

Jake s thoughts drifted back to a conversation he once had with Royce about a dream study clinic. As he lay there, still and tired, he decided he should visit Royce, maybe even ask about a medication that could help him sleep, something non-addictive. He didn t want to go to any of his colleagues at the hospital for a prescription. That would mean explaining why he wasn t sleeping and Jake knew how quickly innocent conversations could spiral into hospital gossip.

He had been the subject of rumors before, many times, thanks to the "eligible bachelor" label that clung to him. Any time he showed interest in a nurse or fellow doctor, whispers would begin, often ruining any chance of a genuine relationship before it had a chance to begin.

As Jake lay in bed, uneager to get up, he heard Maria moving about in the living room, busy with her cleaning. The soft hum of the carpet sweeper clicked on and off, and he knew she was making her way back toward his room. With a sigh, Jake decided to get out of bed and start his day, despite having nothing planned.

He walked into the bathroom and stared into the mirror. His eyes locked with his reflection, as if searching for answers buried deep behind them. He had always felt that something more was calling to him, pulling him toward an unknown purpose. But he had never been able to figure out what he was searching for, or what that "something" truly was.

After finishing in the bathroom, Jake walked into the living room. As he entered, Maria spotted him and quickly shut off the sweeper.

Did I wake you, Doctor Jake?" Maria asked.

No, I was just tossing and turning," Jake replied with a smile.

I left some fresh pastries on the counter for you, in case you get hungry," she said.

Thank you, I ll grab some in a little while." His eyes drifted to the boxes near the couch. What are these?" he asked, pointing to the three boxes stacked on the table and floor nearby.

Oh, those are just some things I brought down from the attic," Maria said as she continued cleaning. I was tidying up and putting things away when I came across them. I thought maybe you'd want to look through them. One of the boxes has your father s personal things; books, pictures, and other little items. The other belonged to your mother. The one on the floor holds your baby things. You were such a handsome boy," she added with a smile, reminiscing as she worked.

Jake sat down on the couch and opened the box that belonged to his father. He began rummaging through it. Even though he had looked through these things before, it always felt as if it were the first time. He pulled out a notebook containing some of his father's early short stories and flipped through the pages. Jake wasn't interested in the content of the writing; instead, he focused on his father's handwriting. He missed both his mother and father deeply.

Next, he opened his mother's box and carefully lifted out a silk scarf. Holding it up to his nose, he closed his eyes and inhaled. He remembered how the scent of his mother had lingered on the scarf for a long time after her passing. Now, only the strong scent of cedar remained.

As Jake explored the items, Maria looked over and commented on what he pulled out. "Oh, I remember that," she would say, or offer a fond remark. Maria had been very close to his family, and she was Jake's only real connection to the past and the parents he no longer had with him.

He then opened the last box, the one with his baby clothes and photos from the hospital where he was born. Maria paused her cleaning, sat down beside him on the couch, and picked up a few items from the box.

"Oh, now I remember this!" she exclaimed, holding up a small blue and white baby outfit with matching booties. "You wore this home from the hospital. You were so cute."

"Imagine that," Jake replied playfully, his cheeks reddening. He embarrassed easily.

He reached into the box again and pulled out a small wooden jewelry box. He opened it, and music began to play for a few seconds before stopping. Jake closed the lid, turned the box over, cranked the handle, then flipped it back upright and opened it again. The music played once more.

Whose stuff is this? I know I didn't wear jewelry as a child," Jake joked, glancing at Maria with a smirk. You guys didn't make me wear this stuff, did you?"

Let's see," Maria said, reaching over and pulling a rosary with a cross from the jewelry box. This was from when you were baptized. Your grandmother gave it to you," she recalled warmly.

Jake then pulled out another necklace, a delicate chain of pearls with a small gold heart pendant hanging from it. He studied it closely, his brow furrowing. There was something familiar about it, he felt as if he had seen the necklace before, and not too long ago.

Was this my mother's?" Jake asked.

No, let me see," Maria said, taking a closer look. Oh, I remember, such a strange story. When you were just a newborn, a tiny little fellow at the hospital, your mother went to the nursery where all the babies were lined up in their cribs, sleeping by the window so people could see them. She came across a woman in a hospital gown standing there, looking at you. Your mother said she was lovely. But she was also very ill, cancer, I believe."

Maria paused, remembering.

The woman died at the hospital the next day. Afterward, a nurse brought this necklace to your mother and said it was meant for the baby boy. The woman's dying wish was to give it to you, a gift that would bring you happiness someday. Your mother didn't want to accept it at first, but when she heard the woman had passed, she took it out of courtesy. I didn't know she kept it all these years. It really is lovely, the pearls still shine."

You can have it," Jake said, offering the necklace to her.

Oh no, Doctor Jake," Maria said, gently nudging his arm with a smile. You should keep it for yourself or for your wife someday."

Jake continued sorting through the items in the box, though his attention kept drifting back to the necklace. He picked it up again and stared at it, turning it slowly in his hand. Closing his eyes, he saw a vivid image: a young, beautiful woman wearing a red dress, holding a white rose, the same necklace draped around her neck. The vision flickered for just a moment, then vanished.

He opened his eyes and looked down at the necklace again, letting it dangle from his fingers. Then, with a quiet sense of reverence, he closed his fist around the heart pendant and the pearls, gripping them tightly. Slowly, he stood up.

Thank you for the walk down memory lane. I think I ll go for a ride or something," Jake said as he walked toward the kitchen.

Yes, have a nice day," Maria replied, resuming her cleaning.

Jake finished getting ready by taking a shower, then dressed in a pair of faded blue jeans and a plain white T-shirt. He left the necklace on top of his dresser, he wanted to keep it in sight, hoping it might trigger more memories of the woman in the red dress. After grabbing a pastry and a cup of coffee for the road, he got into his car and started to drive. He had no destination in mind, but he figured he d end up somewhere in the city.

While driving, Jake picked up his cell phone, hit the number two on his speed dial, and pressed redial. The line began to ring.

Hello?" Marcia s voice came through the receiver.

Hello. I heard you needed a doctor to make a house call?" Jake teased.

Oh yeah? Well, I think you need to go back to the psych ward, because you are one very disturbed, crazy man," Marcia laughed.

Jake smiled. What are you doing today? I m bored."

Oh, thank you. So nice to know you only call me when you're bored," she quipped, seizing the opportunity to tease him.

Stop. You know what I mean. Do you have any plans today?" he asked.

No, not really. What do you have in mind?" Marcia replied.

Well, I was thinking I could meet you downtown at the art museum. They usually have some kind of display on the weekends."

Alright. I'll meet you out front in about an hour. Will that work?" she asked.

Perfect. I'll grab the tickets and meet you by the fountain. Goodbye," Jake said, ending the call.

Jake smiled as he drove toward downtown and the art museum. He thought to himself what a kind and thoughtful person Marcia had turned out to be. She'd become a good friend, one he genuinely enjoyed spending time with. It wasn't typical for them to hang out on weekends. They had gone to a few art shows in the past, but only once or twice, and usually with other people tagging along.

As he drove, Jake recalled what Mike Wilson had asked him during their racquetball game the other day. Mike wanted Jake to find out about Marcia's personal life, specifically, whether she was seeing anyone. He also asked Jake to casually hint around to see if she might be interested in going out with him. Jake found himself thinking how mismatched Mike and Marcia would be as a couple. Still, he figured it was only fair to let Marcia know about Mike's intentions and let her decide for herself.

About an hour later, Marcia arrived. Jake was already seated on the fountain ledge out front, waiting for her. She wore light tan khaki pants and a short-sleeve white cotton button-up blouse. Her soft, silky hair was pulled back in a ponytail, tied with a scarf, and she wore brown leather sandals. She looked effortlessly pretty, so different from how Jake was used to seeing her at the hospital, usually dressed in baggy scrubs and a white lab coat.

"Have you been waiting long?" Marcia asked as she approached.

"Only a few hours," Jake replied with a playful grin.

Marcia laughed. "I'm really glad you called today. I didn't have anything planned, just housework. You know, some of us *don't* have the luxury of a maid to tend to our every need."

"Yeah, yeah, whatever. You poor helpless, struggling doctor," Jake teased.

"Are you ready to go inside? By the way, do you know what exhibits are on display this weekend?" she asked.

"Marc Chagall," Jake answered. "They've got some of his work from private collectors and other museums. Have you heard of him?"

"Yes, I love his work!" Marcia's face lit up. "Now I'm really glad you called," she said, smiling warmly at him.

The two headed inside, strolling through the museum while chatting about hospital matters and upcoming educational projects they were working on together. It felt good to walk in a casual setting and simply enjoy each other's company. Marcia listened to Jake intently as he spoke, her eyes never straying. She laughed at his jokes and responded with genuine warmth. Jake felt completely at ease around her, and he began to wonder: did she feel the same comfort with him? Did she sense the easy rhythm of their friendship as much as he did?

"Oh, by the way, someone was asking about you the other day. He wanted to know whether or not you were seeing someone special," Jake said, pausing to look at Marcia.

"Really? And who would this 'someone' be that's so curious about my love life?" Marcia asked, tilting her head and eyeing Jake with interest.

266

Well... I m not sure if I should tell you, unless you share your part of the story first," Jake replied with a teasing smile.

Oh, is that how this is going to go?" Marcia raised an eyebrow, playing along. Well, let s see. Yes, I am interested in someone. But it s complicated. I can t afford complications in my life right now. Maybe someday... I don t know," she added, her eyes meeting Jake s with a quiet intensity.

Let s sit here for a minute," Jake said, pointing to a bench welded to the floor in front of a large painting. The portrait showed an 18th-century mansion with water fountains in front and a green pasture that rolled into distant hills, vanishing into the clouds. It gave the illusion of endless land, stretching beyond the horizon.

A small gold plate affixed to the frame read: Pedro Santiago, 1845.

Jake sat down, staring at the painting as his mind began to drift. A strange, overwhelming sensation came over him, his breath caught, his chest tightened, and his face flushed. He stared at the portrait, transfixed.

Well? Aren t you going to tell me who was asking about me?" Marcia asked, noticing the sudden change in his demeanor. Are you okay?"

Jake snapped out of his trance and returned to the conversation.

Yes—um... well, let s see. Complications, huh? I don t buy that. You re going to have to be a little more specific," Jake said, trying to keep his tone light, though his gaze continued to flicker back to the painting.

You don t want me to be more specific, trust me," Marcia said quietly, turning her eyes away from him.

He senses that he s touching a tender spot and decides not to toy with her emotions.

Mike Wilson! He was the one asking about you. I know you must love his shy, quiet, and subdued personality," Jake says with a smirk, fully aware that Mike is anything but shy, quiet, or subdued.

Mike Wilson? I m afraid not, even if his life depended on it. Oh my gosh, he s so... so..." Marcia pauses, clearly struggling for the right words. I can t even describe him without sounding horribly mean. What did you say to him?"

Nothing really," Jake replies casually. I just told him I d check it out for him."

Marcia looks at Jake with a flicker of hesitation, and he can tell she wants to say something more.

What? What is it?" he asks.

Nothing," she says, shaking her head. Just do me a favor and tell Mike I m seeing someone else. Make it interesting, really sell it, so he leaves it alone."

She stands and pulls Jake s arm. Come on, let s walk some more."

Jake rises and glances once more at the portrait of the mansion hanging on the wall, then turns and walks with Marcia.

Did you like that house or something?" she asks, noticing his lingering look.

I don t know... it just seemed familiar somehow. Never mind. It s probably just my strange mind playing tricks on me again," Jake replies.

You are strange," she jokes, nudging him lightly.

The afternoon passed quickly as they continued walking through the museum for nearly four more hours, admiring the many works of Marc Chagall and other artists whose pieces had been collected over the centuries. As the sun dipped lower, Marcia realized it was getting late and that she needed to end the day.

They said their goodbyes and drove off in separate directions, each heading home, each carrying their own unspoken thoughts.

During the drive home, Jake thought about Marcia's words. He knew, or at least believed, that she had been talking about him. That he was the special someone she was interested in but hesitant to name. He had been tempted to press her further, to gently coax it out of her, but the truth was, he was just as afraid to hear those words as she was to say them.

If she admitted her feelings, he would be forced to make a decision about their relationship and he wasn't sure he was ready for that. Marcia was right: it would be complicated. They worked closely together, and Jake held a supervisory role over her, which could raise concerns if anyone were to find out. For now, it seemed safer to keep their feelings unspoken.

By the time Jake finally arrived home, the sun had disappeared below the horizon, and the sky had deepened into darker shades of blue, edging toward black. He was tired from all the walking and decided to skip dinner and go straight to bed.

He had to work early at the hospital the next morning and wanted to leave in time to stop by Royce Webster's office afterward. It had been a good day overall, and Jake hoped for a long, peaceful night of sleep, without the dreams that so often haunted him.

CHAPTER THIRTY-ONE

Claire awakened earlier today, much earlier than the day before. She felt agitated and irritable from not sleeping comfortably, as she would have in her own bed. Living out of a suitcase was difficult, and it was unsettling knowing that people had been watching her as she slept.

Still, Claire reminded herself that the sleep study program would only last a little while longer, and it had already helped her recall specific details from her dreams, things she might never have remembered on her own without Dr. Webster's help. She had begun to recall names like Bentley, and she was almost certain that the setting of her dreams was New Orleans or some other southern town. Though she couldn't be sure of the exact time period, it appeared to be the early to mid-1800s.

Claire remained confused about the man she saw in her dreams, the one who made her heart flutter. She believed that Elly, the woman she somehow was or saw through, was married to Stephen but loved someone else. The thought troubled her deeply. Personally, Claire did not accept infidelity or betrayal in relationships, and the emotional conflict left her frightened and unsettled.

As she was leaving the clinic that morning, the nurse at the front desk handed her a slip of paper. It had tomorrow's date on it, along with a time: four o'clock past midnight.

"Dr. Webster would like to meet with you and go over his notes. Will this be an acceptable time?" the nurse asked.

"Yes, I'll meet him then. Thank you," Claire replied, then stepped outside and hailed a taxi.

Back at home, Claire fed her companion, Lucy, and then changed into a pair of jogging pants and a sweatshirt. She tied her hair back into a ponytail and began stretching in the living room. After her warm-up, she turned on the television, popped an aerobics videotape into the VCR, and worked out for the next forty-five minutes.

By the end, Claire had worked up a good sweat. The collar of her shirt was darkened with moisture, and tiny beads of sweat dotted her brow. She licked her lips—her mouth was dry, and she could taste the bitter salt from her perspiration. It had been a solid workout, exactly what she needed. Claire always felt better after exercising, and with the tension she'd been carrying lately, this was her personal remedy to restore a sense of calm.

After Claire showered and finished getting dressed for the day, she started to head out the front door to meet her brother at the music shop and check if she had any scheduled classes to teach. Just as she was closing the door, the telephone rang. She ran back into the apartment and picked up the receiver.

"Hello?" Claire said.

"Bonjour, Claire—is that you?" a voice crackled through the line.

"Yes... Pierre?" Claire asked.

"My sweet friend, hello! I think I have a bad connection—these damned lines. It's taken me nearly an hour to get through. Can you hear me alright?" Pierre asked.

"Yes, I can hear you fine. It's good to hear your voice. I received your letter the other day—it sounds exciting, the opening of your new shop."

"My good friend, the reason I'm calling is because I need to ask you a very big favor. I wouldn't ask unless it were extremely important," Pierre began.

"I'm sorry, I can't come to Paris right now. Something's going on in my life, and I can't get away," Claire said.

No, it's not Paris—although I wish I could get you to come. I was hoping you could fly to New Orleans for a day. Just overnight, then straight back home to Detroit the following day," Pierre asked.

Why New Orleans?" Claire replied.

Donnell was supposed to make the trip, but he got delayed and won't be able to go tomorrow when the shipment is scheduled to be packed and sent out. I've purchased a collection of very old paintings and other antiques, many of these items were imported to the States from Europe in the early 1800s. They're worth a great deal of money and are extremely precious. I'd feel much better knowing someone with my best interests at heart is there to oversee the packing and inspect the items," Pierre explained.

Gosh, I'm not sure I can. I really want to help, but I just have so much going on right now..." Claire hesitated.

Claire, my good friend, this is very important, please? I'll arrange your airline tickets and hotel accommodations. All I need is twenty-four hours of your time. I'll even throw in one of the items you'll be inspecting. I might pick something out from the shipment and consider it yours for helping me. I know how much you love antiques and trinkets. What do you say? Appealing enough yet?"

Claire let out a long sigh before answering.

All right, you know I couldn't say no to you. You are a devilish man. New Orleans, eh?" Claire said.

Yes, wonderful! I owe you big for this one. I'll fax you the details and the address of the building you'll need to be at tomorrow at ten o'clock in the morning. I'll have your airline ticket waiting for you at the front desk. I need to go now and take care of everything. Look for the fax this afternoon. Goodbye, my friend, and thank you," Pierre said.

Goodbye," Claire replied, hanging up the telephone.

She paused for a moment, then picked up the phone again to call the sleep clinic. Claire informed the nurse that some unexpected business had come up and that she'd be leaving town for a few days. The nurse agreed to pass the message along to Dr. Webster and assured Claire that it would be fine.

Claire was somewhat thankful that she would be able to sleep in her own bed tonight instead of at the clinic. She figured her flight would be early in the morning and didn't want to stay overnight at the facility—especially since the technicians had been waking her during the previous nights.

She poured herself another cup of coffee and headed downstairs to tell her brother about her change in plans. As she walked, her thoughts returned to her dreams. She wondered again if the characters she had been seeing were, in fact, from New Orleans.

Claire spent the rest of her afternoon working with her brother in the music shop. Later, she finally received the fax from Pierre, informing her that her flight from Detroit to New Orleans would depart at six o'clock in the morning, and her return flight would leave the following day at eleven o'clock. He had arranged for her to stay in the French Quarter at the Sheraton Hotel. He included a map and detailed instructions about whom she would be meeting and what she would be inspecting.

Pierre simply wanted to ensure that the merchandise he was purchasing was in good condition and of high quality before it was packaged and shipped to him in Paris. Some of the antiques were estate items from large plantations around New Orleans, and most of them had been appraised as being over 150 years old.

Claire finished up early at the music shop and returned to her apartment to wash some clothes before packing for the overnight trip. She was beginning to feel excited—she had never been to New Orleans before and hoped to squeeze in some shopping after the business meeting was done. She sent an email back to Pierre, letting him know she had received the fax and thanking him for persuading her to go. She felt the short trip would be a welcome break, something she truly needed.

After packing, Claire snuggled into bed, hoping to fall asleep quickly and get plenty of rest before morning. She had a full day ahead and wanted to feel refreshed for her travels.

The night was cold and dark. Tree limbs danced fiercely, waving in the wind. Rain steadily fell from the sky, forming puddles across the land. A woman rode through the night on horseback, galloping across fields into the shadows. Her clothes were soaked from the rain, clinging to her skin. The ribbons that once held her long black hair back had slipped loose, her wet hair now draping into her eyes. She was crying as she rode her horse across the rain-soaked green pastures.

Claire woke in the middle of the night, her face damp with sweat and her heart pounding as tears fell from her eyes. She sat up in bed and turned on the nightlight on the table beside her. Brushing her hair back from her face, she could feel the wetness of both sweat and tears. Claire sat there, crying, overcome with sadness she couldn't explain.

She got out of bed and walked to the bathroom, turned on the faucet, and splashed cold water on her face. Then she stood staring at herself in the mirror, closed her eyes, and silently wished that these feelings would go away.

This dream had been different from the others. In the past, her dreams had always taken place inside the mansion, in a ballroom filled with people and celebration. But this time, she had been alone, riding a horse through the night in the pouring rain.

Claire could feel she was getting closer to something she couldn't quite explain. Her emotions were overwhelming, and she felt a longing that she couldn't control or understand.

She took a sip of water and returned to bed. Glancing at the alarm clock, she saw it was only two-thirty in the morning. She turned off the light and lay there in the darkness, eventually drifting back to sleep.

CHAPTER THIRTY-TWO

Jake arrived early at the hospital today, feeling refreshed after a weekend off without any complications. He hadn't really accomplished anything during his time off except relaxing, sleeping in, and wandering through the art museum. Today, however, was already proving to be busy—he figured it was the universe's way of balancing out his uneventful weekend.

Shortly after arriving, Jake was called to the emergency room to assist his intern in placing a catheter in the pulmonary artery of a fifty-year-old man who had arrived in full cardiac arrest. After twenty minutes of chest compressions and ventilating with an artificial airway, the trauma team finally managed to get a pulse back. The man's cardiac rhythm remained unstable, and he would require close monitoring.

Jake allowed his interns to lead the code and make decisions regarding the patient's care. He stepped in only when his expertise was needed or if their actions risked harming the patient. He was a skilled teacher, known for his patience in guiding new interns through high-pressure situations, always mindful to teach the art of practicing medicine. Jake remembered his own internship all too well; the grueling hours on call, working the units while residents rested in their call rooms.

Mike Wilson, the intern handling this morning's case, was confident in his skills but preferred having a second set of hands nearby. He knew delicate procedures like catheter placement could become complicated, and having a backup was a precaution he didn't take lightly.

Once Jake finished assisting Mike, he returned to his office to tackle the stack of charts that had accumulated over the weekend. Paperwork consumed most of Jake's days and nights. Often, he found himself wishing he weren't in a supervisor's role, longing instead to be one of the emergency room residents, putting in his hours and going home.

Jake finished reviewing some of his charts and stopped by the secretary's desk as he was leaving for lunch.

"Betty, I'm going to be out late for lunch today. Page me if you need me," Jake said as he walked past the desk where the older woman sat typing a paper.

"Yes, Doctor Miller. Have a nice lunch," Betty replied.

"Thank you," Jake said, continuing past her on his way out.

He drove to the address printed on Royce's business card. The building and office décor of the sleep clinic impressed him. The facility was modern and tastefully designed, giving off a professional yet welcoming atmosphere.

Jake entered the office with Royce Webster's name displayed on the door.

"Hello, I'm Dr. Miller. Is Dr. Webster available?" he asked the receptionist sitting behind a half-open glass window.

"One moment, please. I'll check for you," the young woman said with a polite smile.

A moment later, she looked up from the telephone. "Dr. Miller, he'll be right with you. Please take a seat."

"Sure, thank you." Jake walked over and sat in the waiting area.

The room featured a large 36-inch color television on one wall, tuned to a game show. Oak-framed chairs upholstered in paisley fabric lined the room, with matching curtains and a couch that added an elegant touch. Jake noticed a photograph hanging in a gold frame, a picture of himself, Royce, and several other college friends on graduation day. He and Royce stood side by side, looking quite different from their college days.

Jake waited only a short while before Royce appeared through a door marked "No Entrance." Royce walked up to him and extended his hand for a handshake.

"Jake, good to see you," Royce said, shaking his hand.

"Same here. I hope I didn't catch you at a bad time. I just thought I'd stop by and see what kind of operation you've got going here."

"No, this is actually a slow day. I'm not seeing any patients, just reviewing some tapes and going over notes. Come on, I'll show you around," Royce said as he led Jake through the door he had come from.

Royce and Jake toured the building. Royce showed him the sleep rooms and various labs set up to monitor patients. After the walkthrough, they returned to Royce's office. A row of five television monitors was built into the wall, with recording equipment and VCRs installed beneath them. Royce picked up a remote control and pressed a button, starting one of the recordings.

Jake watched the screen as images of sleeping patients appeared. A cardiac rhythm strip and other digital readouts were displayed at the bottom of the screen.

"These are the patients in my current study," Royce explained. "I monitor their brainwave activity and review notes. There are a few interesting cases."

"You've got a really impressive setup here. I can see why you went into private practice," Jake said. "Have you been able to figure out what's causing these sleep disorders or the strange dreams?"

"Some cases are straightforward, others not so much. It depends," Royce replied. He pointed to one of the monitors. "Take monitor number three, for instance."

He pressed a button to zoom in on the person sleeping in the bed.

"This woman has an intriguing case. She's been having the same recurring dream since childhood. Usually, she wakes up without remembering much detail, but she's emotionally drained. We've only been working with her for a short time, but she's made progress. She's now able to see faces and recall names from her dreams. I'm considering hypnotism to see if we can go even further."

Royce's gaze stayed on the screen. Jake looked as well, watching the image of the young woman sleeping as the camera zoomed in closer.

"Can you zoom in more on her?" Jake asked.

"Sure. Do you know her?" Royce replied, adjusting the controls.

"Yes... well, no, I'm not sure," Jake said, leaning closer to the screen. His heart fluttered with a jolt of recognition. The woman on the monitor was the same young woman he had seen playing the violin at the coffee shop. "Yes, that's her. I saw her playing the violin at a coffee shop not too long ago."

Royce nodded. "Yes, she teaches violin."

"Have you figured out what's causing her dreams? Is she dreaming about her past?" Jake asked.

"That's where it gets complicated," Royce said. "It goes beyond her past. Some people struggle with the idea of past lives, but we try not to dismiss any possibility. It's not a straightforward medical issue. It's a radical theory, but we gather the data and treat with medication and therapy where possible."

Jake was thoughtful. "What do you think? Do we live past lives, moving from one body to another?"

Royce smiled and let out a soft chuckle. "I try to keep my personal opinions neutral. I think there are things we can't explain and things we can. You seem pretty interested in this sort of topic; maybe you chose the wrong field of practice."

Jake smiled back. "No, I m still a firm believer in the medical side of things. Scientific proof is the answer."

Royce grinned. "So, are you going to tell me about your dreams, or do I have to guess?"

"Honestly, I think all I need is something to help me sleep. My dreams aren t that bad. I don t think that s the real problem," Jake said.

"Alright," Royce said, nodding. "Let me ask you a few questions, and then I ll prescribe a mild sedative to help you sleep better. We ll take it from there."

Jake glanced back at the screen showing Claire sleeping. His eyes lingered on her image as Royce rummaged through his desk, searching for a notebook. Without looking up, Royce continued his interview, starting with routine questions before moving into those about Jake s dreams.

"Tell me, in your own words, what you re dreaming about," Royce asked.

"Well, let s see. Most of the time, I m dreaming as if I m someone else. Sounds strange, but I actually feel the emotions this other person feels. It s like I m seeing through his eyes. When he gets angry or sad, I wake up feeling the same way. But I don t recognize anyone in these dreams. They re all just faces in a crowd, no one familiar. It s sort of silly," Jake said, trailing off.

"You re doing well. Keep going," Royce encouraged. "Do you recognize the surroundings? Do you hear names of the people in your dreams?" he asked as he reached over to switch on a tape recorder. "Sorry, I like to record these sessions so I can take notes later. Go on."

Alright," Jake continued. "It's usually the same theme. It's like a masquerade ball, where people are dressed in 18th-century clothing. There's a man—he seems to be married to a beautiful woman—and he's jealous of her, or maybe angry. He goes to her room; she's standing on a balcony. They argue, or something like it, and he grabs her, shakes her until she collapses on the floor crying. That's when I usually wake up."

Royce leaned forward, his attention sharpened. "Do you recall anything specific about the room? The clothing? Jewelry? Do you hear any voices when you dream?"

"I don't know. I have a hard time remembering," Jake admitted. "I try not to think about it too much when I wake up. I did hear the name Jonathan... or Stephen. One of those, maybe both. I'm really not sure. Honestly, I feel a little silly talking about it. I'm sure it's nothing important, probably just nonsense."

"Hey, listen," Royce said, leaning forward. "There's nothing wrong with you coming here and talking to me. This is what I do. Even if you think it's nothing, the fact is, it's keeping you up at night. It doesn't hurt to explore the reasons. Don't start getting all stubborn on me now."

"Alright, alright," Jake said, relenting. "So what do you think?"

"It'd be nice if I could give you all the answers just from hearing about your dreams," Royce said with a wry smile. "But it's not that simple. I need your help. I'd like to get you into my study. Can you come in so we can monitor you overnight?"

Jake hesitated. "I don't know if I can find the time."

Royce nodded, as if he expected that answer. "Alright then, let's move to hypnosis. It could help you remember more details from your dreams. Can we at least try that? I'll start you on something mild to help you relax at night, but I want you to write down anything you can remember when you wake up."

Jake sighed, considering. "Okay. I can go along with the hypnosis, and I'll try writing things down, though it usually isn't much. I'll give you a call next week."

"How about you give me a call in a couple of days?" Royce said with a grin.

"Persistent. Some things haven't changed since our younger days," Jake said, reaching out to shake Royce's hand.

As they shook hands, Royce added, "Jake, one last question. Do the names Claire Strauss or Elly Bentley mean anything to you?"

Jake paused, hesitating for a moment as if searching his memory.

"I don't think so. Maybe Elly sounds familiar, but I don't know anyone by that name. Why do you ask?" Jake said, curious.

"Nothing important, just wanted to ask," Royce replied casually. "Oh, one more thing. If you happen to see the violinist playing somewhere, remember to respect her privacy. Don't mention you saw her on a tape in my office, alright?"

"Sure thing, doc. Bye," Jake said as he walked out of Royce's office.

He stopped in the hallway, the names Royce had mentioned still lingering in his mind. Elly. The name tugged at something in his memory, but he couldn't place where he had heard it before or why it seemed familiar. Shaking off the thought, Jake continued on and left the building.

He drove back to work to finish out the rest of his day, feeling better about his visit with Royce. There was a sense of relief in knowing he had someone to talk to about his dreams, someone who wouldn't judge him as incompetent or crazy for experiencing them.

CHAPTER THIRTY-THREE

Claire's flight from Detroit to New Orleans was smooth and without delays. It was a nonstop trip, and she was glad there were no other connections. Flying itself never bothered her, but takeoffs and landings always unsettled her. Multiple connections often meant more motion sickness, something she tried to avoid.

She arrived in New Orleans at eight o'clock in the morning, took a cab to the Sheraton in the French Quarter, and checked in. Pierre had made all the arrangements in advance, including prepaying for her accommodations. Waiting in her room was a fruit basket with a note from him, thanking her for doing this favor.

Claire had packed lightly, bringing only an overnight bag that she carried on the plane. After quickly freshening up from the flight, she left the hotel, hoping to explore the shops for a short while before meeting the men with the shipment at ten o'clock.

At the concierge desk, she asked for a map of the city. A young man with a thick Creole accent handed her a tourist map, then used a black marker to draw a line from the hotel to her meeting place that afternoon. He suggested a route, pointing out interesting shops along the way. He also recommended that she visit one of the many restored plantations surrounding the city, many of which offered tours and even lunch or dinner packages. Claire thanked him but decided not to commit to any set plans, unsure how long her meeting might take.

She began her walk down Canal Street, eventually making her way along the water's edge near Riverfront Park. Large steamboats were docked nearby, and casinos lined parts of the shore. She browsed a few local shops, content with just window shopping. At a small café, she ordered an espresso and a beignet, a deep-fried local pastry dusted generously with powdered sugar, before continuing on her way.

It felt nice to be outside, walking through the lively streets. Claire didn't mind being alone in a new city; in fact, she felt comfortable sitting at a table by herself, watching the steady stream of people pass by. Tourists filled the narrow streets of New Orleans, their voices mixing with the distant sound of street musicians.

After finishing her coffee and beignet, Claire continued her walk across the French Quarter until she reached the building where she was to meet the seller of the antiques Pierre had arranged to buy. She arrived a little early and paused to look through the window. Inside, a young man in a suit and tie moved between rows of antiques and paintings, jotting numbers into a notebook.

Claire tapped lightly on the window to catch his attention. He glanced up, then walked to the door and opened it, greeting her as if he had been expecting her.

"You must be Claire," he said. He had black hair, a thick beard, and a faint Middle Eastern accent. His English, however, was fluent and precise.

"Yes. I'm a little early, I hope you don't mind," Claire said, extending her hand. As he shook it, she caught the strong scent of his cologne. She couldn't place the brand, but it smelled refined and expensive, nothing like the cheap, overpowering scents she disliked.

"No, not a problem. This works out well. We can go through the inventory together before the shippers box it up. By the way, my name is Armad Bekar." He handed her a business card.

"Pierre and I have done business before. He's a good man," Armad added, guiding her toward a desk where his briefcase rested.

"Yes, he is. He sent me a list of items he was concerned about. Should we start with those first?" Claire asked, passing him the paper.

Yes, that would be fine. Let's get started. Would you like a cup of coffee?"

No, thank you. I stopped at a coffee shop on the way," she replied.

Claire and Armad spent the next two hours examining the items that would be packaged and shipped. When the men arrived to begin packing, they spared no expense on foam and padding, securing each piece so it would remain snug and protected during transport. Claire was impressed by the level of care and attention Armad showed, ensuring that everything was handled with delicacy.

The last pieces to be prepared were small trinkets laid out on a table covered in soft velvet.

These are small items picked up at estate auctions. Some of them are over a hundred years old," Armad explained. They'll be tagged and wrapped separately."

Claire picked up a few of the objects, glancing at each before setting them back down. She was about to step away when a glint of silver caught her eye. Moving a hairbrush that partially covered it, she lifted the object — a silver pocket watch on a chain.

She turned it over in her hand, studying it closely, a faint feeling of recognition stirring. Flipping open the lid, she read the engraved inscription:

To my darling husband, Stephen, from his loving wife, Elly.

For a moment, she stood frozen, staring at the delicate script. Armad noticed her interest and looked over to see what had caught her attention.

Do you collect pocket watches?" he asked.

Claire didn't respond. Her eyes remained fixed on the watch.

Claire," he said again.

She blinked and looked up, startled. "Oh... yes. I m sorry, what did you say?"

"I asked if you collect pocket watches. You seem to like that one."

"No, not really. I just... like this one, though I don t know why. Do you know where it came from?"

Armad flipped through several pages in his notebook, then looked up. "No. Some of the smaller items were bought at estates or donated as tax write-offs. I can have one of my buyers check if he remembers its origin. What I do know is that it dates back to around the 1840s and was made by a local watchmaker of that time. So it s definitely from here."

"No, that s alright. It s not important to check on, I was just curious. I do want to keep this, though. Pierre said I could choose one of the items, and this will suit me fine," Claire said.

"Are you sure? There are so many other pieces to choose from. Pierre left a message with me to make sure you pick something nice," Armad replied.

"This will be fine. I think everything looks in order. You ve taken very good care to make sure everything is complete." Claire glanced around the room before meeting his eyes again.

"Thank you. I take this business very seriously," Armad said. "I just need you to sign a few documents, and then we re finished. Would you like me to package the watch for you?"

"No, I ll just carry it, but thank you for offering," Claire replied.

"What are your dinner plans this evening? Could I take you out for some local cuisine?" Armad asked with a smile.

"Thank you, but I think I'll have dinner at the hotel and call it an early night. I'm still tired from the flight. I appreciate your offer," Claire said, returning his smile as she handed back his pen.

"It doesn't hurt to try. If you change your mind, my number's on the business card. It was nice to meet you, Claire. Have a nice afternoon," Armad said, shaking her hand and walking her to the door.

Claire stepped outside and headed back the way she had come. When she reached the street corner, she paused, pulling the silver watch from her pocket. She opened the lid and read the inscription again, her mind drifting back to her dreams.

The woman in her dream was named Elly, and her husband's name was Stephen. Could this really be connected? She wasn't even sure if the people in her dreams were real or only figments of her imagination. Yet here was a watch, engraved with those very names.

It was strange — too strange — to dismiss.

Claire slipped the watch back into her pocket and began walking toward the center of town.

She stopped in a few more shops, browsing without finding anything that caught her interest.

As Claire walked past Market Square, she noticed rows of vendor booths set along the edge of the grass, each selling handmade goods. A young girl sat on the cement playing with a small kitten, while beside her an older woman with long gray hair and deeply tanned skin sat in a chair. The woman's clothing was a mismatched collection of layered fabrics, and her eyes were a cloudy blue-white, the corneas pale and opaque. She swayed slightly in her seat, hands resting on the table before her, staring straight ahead at nothing.

The young girl looked up as Claire passed.

Lady, come sit with my grandmother. She is the wisest around, she can answer all your questions. Come sit," the girl said.

Claire smiled politely, slowing her pace, and shook her head. No, thank you," she replied.

Lady, come. She is the best. Only pay if she helps you. Come sit with her," the girl s small voice called after her.

Claire glanced at the older woman again. The clouded eyes confirmed her suspicion that the woman was blind. An empty chair sat on the other side of the table. Claire had never had her palm read or her fortune told. She had always believed it was a hoax — vague words that could be twisted to fit anyone s life.

She was about to decline again, but something made her hesitate. On impulse, she turned back and approached the table.

All right. But you said I only pay if the information is good," Claire said, reinforcing the girl s earlier promise.

Yes, yes, lady. You pay what you wish. My grandmother is the oldest and wisest. She can see the future and the past. Place your hands on the table," the girl urged.

Claire set her hands down, and the old woman reached forward, taking them gently. Her skin was soft but lined with wrinkles, and Claire felt an unexpected sense of comfort in her touch. The woman turned Claire s palms upward and began to sway, her head and body moving side to side as she murmured words Claire could not understand.

Ask me your question," the woman mumbled.

Claire hesitated. A creeping doubt settled in, this could all be a setup. She didn t believe in this sort of thing and began to pull her hands away. But the older woman s grip tightened.

Claire, your violin sounds so lovely," the woman muttered.

Claire froze. How did you know that?" she asked, staring at her in disbelief.

You are almost there. Keep searching, and you will find him," the old woman murmured before resuming her low chant.

Find who? Who am I looking for?" Claire pressed.

I can see you, Elly. Go to this address. You will see."

The woman, still gazing straight ahead, reached for a scrap of paper and scrawled an address across it.

Why did you call me Elly? How did you know?" Claire began, but the woman offered no further reply.

Claire picked up the paper, the handwriting uneven but legible. The young girl placed a tin can on the table for payment. Claire slipped a twenty-dollar bill inside, feeling both unsettled and strangely curious.

As she walked away, she studied the address. Her thoughts swirled with the woman s words.

A taxi was idling at the corner. Claire approached the driver and held out the paper. Excuse me, sir. Do you know where this place is?"

The man studied it. Yes. That s the old plantation on the north side of town."

Is it very far?"

No, only about twenty minutes."

Can you take me out there, then back to the Sheraton?"

Sure, but if you plan on going inside, I ll have to charge an extra fee if you want me to wait," the driver said.

That s fine, as long as it s not unreasonable," Claire replied, opening the back passenger door and sliding into the seat.

The drive to the north side of town was quiet and peaceful. The plantation lay far enough outside the city that it felt like the countryside. The road followed the edge of a lake, and Claire gazed out the window at the empty, rolling pastures, admiring the scenery. She tried to summon any memories the fortune teller's words might have stirred, but nothing came.

After a short ride, the taxi turned into a driveway off the main road. Massive oak trees lined both sides, their branches arching overhead like a natural tunnel. The cement drive curved ahead, leading to the front of a grand white mansion. At its center stood an elegant fountain, the driveway circling around it. Neatly sculpted bushes framed the outer edge of the circular drive.

The house itself was large, built in a stately colonial style with white brick and stone. Four towering pillars rose from the porch floor to the roof, and the wraparound porch was furnished with wicker chairs and tables along one side.

The cab pulled to a stop at the front steps.

"Thank you, I'll only be a short while," Claire told the driver.

"I'll be over there under those trees," he said, pointing to a small parking area.

Claire climbed the steps to the wide porch, taking a moment to look around. A small group of visitors emerged from the front door, chatting as they made their way past her. She stepped aside, then entered through the same doorway.

Just inside, a small table with a cash register had been set up. Behind it sat a young woman dressed in a blue jacket over a white blouse and skirt.

"How many tickets?" the woman asked.

"One, please," Claire replied.

Would you like a guided tour, or do you prefer to walk through on your own?"

I'm not sure. How long does the guided tour last?" Claire asked.

The woman glanced at her watch. Actually, it's too late for a guided tour. We'll be closing in about twenty minutes. I can give you a brochure."

All right." Claire handed the woman three dollars, accepted the brochure, and stepped into the foyer.

Twin grand staircases swept upward from the lower level to the second floor, framing the space in symmetry. Claire paused in the open foyer, gazing up at the chandeliers glittering high above. The entryway was vast, filled with light and air.

She tilted her head back too long, and a wave of dizziness washed over her. Closing her eyes, she stood still, trying to steady herself. Footsteps passed nearby, the murmur of voices drifting toward the door, growing fainter as the other visitors left. Her heartbeat quickened, heat flushed her face, and her breath came shallow until she instinctively held it, which only deepened the lightheadedness.

The sensation lasted only seconds, yet it felt like hours. Then she heard it — faint music coming from her left. An orchestra was playing the same haunting melody she had heard countless times in her dreams.

Claire opened her eyes. For a moment, the mansion around her was gone, replaced by the place from her dreams. People in fine clothing moved past her, speaking to her, laughing, twirling on the polished floor.

Drawn to the sound, she walked toward the ballroom just off the foyer. The tall double doors stood open, offering a full view from the entry and the staircases. Inside, couples danced in elegant gowns and black tuxedos beneath the glow of crystal chandeliers.

She crossed the dance floor, her gaze drawn to a portrait hanging on the far wall. It depicted Elly, the beautiful woman from her dreams, wearing a deep red gown and holding a white rose.

From her post at the cash register, the young woman in the blue jacket watched Claire enter the empty ballroom. The day's last customer seemed to move in a strange, dazed manner.

Claire stopped directly in front of the portrait, staring up at the delicate brushwork. Then the room began to spin — slowly at first, then faster and faster. Her legs weakened, her body went limp, and with her eyes closing, she collapsed to the floor, unconscious.

The woman at the desk in the foyer, who had been keeping a close eye on Claire, saw her collapse. She immediately picked up the telephone and called the manager for help. Moments later, a young man in his thirties entered the ballroom through the garden doors. Without hesitation, he rushed to Claire, lifted her into his arms, and carried her to a couch in the foyer.

Another staff member hurried over with a cold, damp cloth and a glass of water. She pressed the cloth gently to Claire's forehead and patted her hand.

"Dear, can you hear me?" she asked softly.

"Do you want me to call an ambulance?" another woman inquired.

"Not yet," the first replied. "She's breathing, and her pulse is strong. She probably just fainted. Look—she's coming around."

Claire mumbled something before slowly opening her eyes. The faces of strangers hovered above her. Feeling the cool cloth against her forehead, she reached for it and tried to sit up.

"What happened?" she asked weakly.

"You fainted in the ballroom, my dear," the woman replied. "Have you eaten today? Do you take any medications?"

"Yes, I've eaten. No, I'm not on any medications," Claire said. "I... I don't remember going into the ballroom. Wait, yes, I do. I was looking at the portrait of Elly."

"Elly?" The man who had carried her spoke up for the first time. "How did you know that was her name?"

Claire turned her gaze toward him.

"My name is Charles Bentley," he said. "I own this estate and the plantation. There's no nameplate on that painting. How did you know the woman's name?"

Claire hesitated, then asked quietly, "I'm feeling better. Could we speak in private?"

Charles looked unsure, but after a moment, he nodded. "Yes, that would be alright."

The two women who had been tending to Claire exchanged glances as they left, moving toward the front to finish closing for the evening.

Claire waited until they were gone before speaking again. "This may sound strange, and I don't know if you'll believe me, but I've been having dreams—dreams that led me here. I know it sounds crazy, but I promise I'm not. I just need to know about Elly and Stephen. Who were they?"

Charles studied her, suspicion and curiosity mingling in his expression.

"I can tell you what I know," Charles said after a pause. "It does sound strange, you dreaming of this place. I'm not one to put much stock in that sort of thing."

I understand. Honestly, I don t either," Claire replied. It s just… odd. Please, just a few moments of your time. A little information, and I promise I won t trouble you again."

Charles nodded slowly. Stephen Bentley was my great-uncle, my grandfather s older brother. There were three boys: Stephen, the eldest; Chestin, my grandfather; and Grant, the youngest. Stephen married a woman named Elly, and they lived here in this mansion from the time Stephen was a boy until after Elly s death in the 1840s or 50s. Stephen died shortly after her. From there, my grandfather took over the estate, and it has been passed down through the family ever since — to my father, and then to my wife and me."

Do you know how Elly died?" Claire asked.

As the story goes," Charles began, she had an accident while horseback riding. There s another part to it, family whispers, really. Elly had been involved with another man. She ended that relationship, but tragedy followed. She was on her way home, intending to beg Stephen s forgiveness. It was a stormy night, and she never made it back. Stephen never knew the truth — that she was returning to him, ready to vow her love. Not until he was on his deathbed did he learn the truth. By then, it was far too late. He died a broken man, consumed by grief. My grandfather spoke of it sometimes to his brother Grant. I was just a boy then, and the details are hazy, but it s always been one of those sad family stories passed down through the generations."

Claire s eyes drifted around the foyer as Charles spoke, her mind turning over every word.

This is the place I ve seen in my dreams," Claire said softly. I ve never been here before, but I could describe the inside in perfect detail. The ballroom looks exactly the same as in my dreams. Upstairs, on the second floor, Elly s room was at the end of the hallway on the right. It had a fireplace and a balcony overlooking the gardens. Stephen s room was smaller, two doors up on the left, with a view of the stables. Being here feels so strange."

Charles stared at her for a moment. What you say is correct... but I don t understand how you know this. Forgive me, but I ve never been one to believe in supernatural things or ghost stories."

I understand. I know how it must sound," Claire said, rising from her seat. I should be going. Thank you for your time and for sharing your family history."

You re welcome. I hope I ve been of some help," Charles replied, extending his hand.

Claire shook it, then began to walk toward the door. Halfway there, she turned back.

Charles, if you don t mind my asking... do you know what kind of horseback riding accident Elly had?"

It was lightning," Charles said. They believe it startled her horse. She fell and struck her head on a rock near the front gates of the estate."

Thank you."

Claire stepped through the tall entry doors into the warm air outside. She crossed the drive to the taxi and tapped on the window, waking the driver who had been dozing in the front seat. The man straightened, rubbing his eyes, as she opened the back door and slid inside.

Sheraton Hotel in the French Quarter, please," she said.

Claire sat in silence on the ride back, gazing out the taxi window as her thoughts circled around the story Charles had told her. The revelation still felt unreal; the people she had been dreaming about for years were not figments of imagination or fairy tale characters, but real individuals who had lived, loved, and died long ago. The realization left her shaken. Why had she been dreaming of them? They were of no relation to her. How could she possibly know events that had taken place more than a hundred years ago?

Perhaps Dr. Webster could help her find the answers. Now that she knew her dreams mirrored real history, she hoped he could explain why.

By the time she reached her hotel, exhaustion weighed on her. The long day, the unexpected truths, and the strange emotions left her drained. In her room, she ran a hot bath, then ordered a sandwich and a cup of tea from room service. An unfamiliar emptiness pressed against her chest, and a lump rose in her throat. She felt on the verge of tears without knowing exactly why.

After her bath and dinner, she curled into bed. That night, no dreams came to her — only deep, undisturbed sleep. Moonlight spilled through the window, painting soft shadows across the room, while the wind whispered a gentle tune against the glass. Wrapped in warmth, Claire felt safe, as if she were back in her own bed at home, and drifted peacefully into the night.

CHAPTER THIRTY-FOUR

Claire returned to Detroit the following morning, her mind scattered and racing as she tried to piece together the facts she had uncovered in New Orleans. She did not understand why this was happening to her or how it was possible that she could dream about people from another time. Her memories of these dreams stretched back to early childhood. Because she was an intelligent, well-adjusted child, the doctors had always told her parents that she would eventually grow out of it, or that she simply had an overactive imagination.

Throughout most of her teenage years, Claire denied having the dreams, not wanting her parents to think she was abnormal or different. But as she grew older, instead of fading, the dreams only became more frequent and more disturbing. Now, this was her final hope of finding answers and putting an end to them. Claire placed great hope in Dr. Webster to provide those answers when she returned home.

As soon as Claire's plane landed in Detroit, she called the sleep clinic and asked the receptionist for the next available appointment with Dr. Webster. The receptionist checked the schedule and booked Claire for that afternoon. A note attached to her chart from Royce stated that he needed to see her as soon as possible, and the staff had been instructed to keep trying to reach her until they did. What the receptionist did not mention was that Dr. Webster was just as eager to meet with Claire as she was to speak with him.

After hanging up the phone, Claire caught a taxicab back to her apartment. She fed her furry companion, Lucy, then settled onto the couch with a hot cup of tea. Pulling her long hair back from her face, she ran her fingers through the silky strands and let her thoughts drift. She remembered standing inside the mansion's ballroom, the same place she had dreamt about for years. She thought, too, of the blind fortuneteller who had given her the mansion's address in New Orleans. The old woman had told her to keep searching for "him" and had said something about being close. But who was she talking about?

All the men who appeared in Claire's dreams would be long gone by now, dead from old age. They would have been gone for many years.

Claire glanced at the clock. She still had a few hours before she was supposed to meet Dr. Webster. For a moment, she considered going downstairs to the music shop, but she knew Bobby would ask too many questions, and she did not feel like talking about it until she knew more. She feared he would think she was imagining things, and wanted answers for herself before telling him anything.

She picked up the stack of mail from the coffee table and began sorting through what was important versus the endless pile of junk that filled her box each day. A bright red envelope caught her eye. The address read: Miss Claire Strauss, Sleep Clinic. Inside was an invitation to spend a weekend up north at the Rothschild Resort in Houghton Lake, compliments of Dr. Webster, for her participation in the clinic.

The invitation mentioned two workshops and strongly recommended attending. It also said she could bring a guest to enjoy the weekend of relaxation, bike riding, fishing, golfing, or horseback riding. Claire checked the date and realized it was for this weekend. She set the envelope down, wishing she had been given a little more notice. So much had happened in the past twenty-four hours that all she really wanted now were answers—answers she hoped Dr. Webster could provide.

Claire arrived at the sleep clinic early and sat in the waiting area with two other people who were there to see Dr. Webster's colleagues. Three psychologists were listed as practicing at the clinic. Claire was relieved to know she would be the next one in to see Dr. Webster. She hated doctor's offices and the long waits that often stretched to an hour.

Feeling a bit impatient today, she stood and began walking around the room. As she moved through the nicely decorated space, she noticed several framed photographs of the doctors and staff on the walls. One photo, in a gold frame, caught her eye—a graduation picture of Dr. Webster with five of his colleagues. A gold engraved plate beneath it read "University of Texas Health Science Center" along with the year of graduation.

Claire studied the row of men until she spotted Dr. Webster. He looked quite different back then, with long hair, a beard, and a mustache. Her eyes lingered on the young man standing beside him. There was something familiar about him, though she could not place where she had seen him before. He was handsome, with a warm smile, and she tried to think harder about the memory tugging at her.

Just then, the office door opened and a nurse appeared, calling her name. Claire followed the nurse into Dr. Webster's office, where he stood up from behind his desk as she walked in.

"Claire, it is nice to see you," Royce said.

"Yes, I am glad you were able to see me today. So much has happened over the last twenty-four hours," Claire replied, speaking without taking a breath.

"Slow down, please sit. What do you mean over the last twenty-four hours? I had a message that you went out of town on business," Royce asked.

Claire spent the next few minutes recapping everything, starting from her arrival in New Orleans all the way up to the present. Royce turned on a tape recorder and was taking notes as she spoke.

"So what do you think this all means? And what can I do to make these dreams stop?" Claire asked.

Claire, what you have just told me is outstanding. It is hard to believe." He looked at her and saw the disappointment in her expression.

But I do believe you, and I think something is guiding you. I have some thoughts that I cannot yet discuss with you, thoughts that may pertain to your case. You are going to have to trust me and give me time to put the pieces together. I feel we are getting close—very close." Royce reached across his desk and touched her hand to reassure her.

I am just tired and need to find the answers," Claire said, her voice shaky as if she were about to cry.

I know. I believe we will find the answers," Royce said gently.

Do you think I am crazy? Does all of this sound strange to you?" Claire asked.

No, you are not crazy. I cannot disclose much, but I have another client who is experiencing the same things you are, so you are not alone," Royce told her.

Claire looked up at Dr. Webster. She held a tissue in her hand and wiped away a tear that had started to fall.

What do you mean, someone experiencing the same thing? You mean the same dreams?" Claire asked eagerly.

I cannot go into details, but I do believe they are related. We need to take this slowly. I was hoping we could continue your sessions under hypnosis. You will not need to stay at the clinic overnight—we can schedule sessions here to help you remember more of your dreams," Royce said.

Hypnosis? Is that dangerous or anything?" Claire asked.

No, not at all. By the way, did you get the invitation to the resort for this weekend? I was really hoping you would go. In fact, I think it is very important for you to be there," Royce said.

I was not planning on it. I only found out about it this morning. But if you think I should, I suppose I could arrange to go. Will the lady who is having the same dreams be there too?" Claire asked.

Yes, my other client will be there, but you must not question anyone about it or try to seek this person out. That is very important," Royce replied firmly.

Alright, I am trusting you to find the answers and get me through this ordeal. I just want the dreams to stop and for my life to be normal again. I guess I will go home and pack. It feels like I have not slept in my own bed for a very long time," Claire said.

I think you will find the resort a very good experience. Use the time to relax and enjoy yourself. I will introduce you to some other people there. My fiancée, Elizabeth, will be joining me, and we can all have dinner together," Royce said.

Claire stood up and shook Dr. Webster's hand. I will see you at the resort," she said.

Be careful driving up. Stop by the secretary's desk and she will give you a map. Goodbye," Royce said.

As soon as Claire left his office, Royce pressed the intercom button and called for Sharon Richardson, his assistant. A tall, slim young woman with blonde hair and contemporary-framed glasses entered.

Royce, what can I do for you?" Sharon asked.

I need your help this weekend. Sit down and I will fill you in on the details," Royce said.

Royce spent the next hour going over both cases with Sharon, showing her the tapes and playing the recorded conversations. Sharon's interest was piqued when she realized that both individuals were experiencing the same dreams, and that the subjects in those dreams seemed to have lived real lives in the past. At first, Sharon wondered if Jake and Claire might have known each other as children, but Royce assured her that was impossible.

He explained that he wanted to observe Jake and Claire together in an open environment to see what might happen. He and Sharon worked out a schedule to help monitor them both over the weekend. Royce planned to call Jake and insist that he attend, not allowing him to decline the offer. He was not sure what he would discover or where this would lead, but the case was unusual and fascinating to say the least.

Afterward, Sharon left to make her final arrangements. One of her tasks was to research the Bentley family, which Claire had mentioned earlier. She needed to gather as much as she could from articles, newspaper clippings, and any other sources she could find. Royce then picked up the telephone and dialed Jake s office.

CHAPTER THIRTY-FIVE

The week passed quickly, and Friday arrived before Jake knew it. Meetings and paperwork had consumed most of his time and energy. During the week, he had filled the prescription Royce had given him. The medication was the newest sleep aid on the market. It was becoming popular for its short onset time and because it lasted only a few hours, allowing patients to wake without the groggy, drugged feeling caused by many other insomnia medications. Jake now had no trouble falling asleep, but the same dreams still woke him in the middle of the night, leaving him just as exhausted as before.

That Friday afternoon, Jake sat with his feet on his desk tossing a baseball into the air and catching it with a glove on his left hand. It was something he often did to calm himself, clear his mind, and think. He was also simply bored, tired of paperwork, and longing for play. Jake was still adventurous and always looked forward to some weekends when he didn't have to deal with hospital responsibilities.

The telephone rang. Jake set the ball and glove aside and picked up the receiver.

Hello, this is Dr. Miller," Jake said.

Jake, how are you doing?" Royce's voice came across the line.

Royce, hey, I was just thinking about you," Jake chuckled.

Yeah, sure you were. Listen, I was wondering what your plans are this weekend. I've booked a resort about four hours north at Houghton Lake, and I want you to come," Royce said.

Resort? What are you having, a family picnic?" Jake asked.

No, I do this every year for the staff and the clients. It's actually a write-off because we have therapy sessions scheduled. The rest of the time is for fun. I have one more room left and thought you'd be the perfect guest. Come on, you'll have a good time," Royce said.

"Write-off, eh? I swear I must be in the wrong practice. I don't know..." Jake hesitated.

"Listen, you can bring a friend, you do have some, don't you?" Royce teased.

"Yes, I have one or two. You said it was for your clients. Will the violinist be going?" Jake asked.

"I think so. But if she does, remember not to mention anything about what we discussed. I still have patient confidentiality to keep in mind, even with you being a doctor," Royce said.

"My lips are sealed. I guess I can make it. I'm not on call this weekend. Should I go up tonight or in the morning?" Jake asked.

"Whichever you prefer. I'll fax you the directions and see you there. Oh, by the way, I'll have a hypnotist there performing sessions, so think about that, alright?" Royce said.

"Alright, I'll see you there. Goodbye." Jake hung up the phone, picked up his ball and glove again, and continued tossing the ball into the air. He smiled to himself, thinking about the girl he had seen in the coffee shop playing the violin.

Shortly after his call with Royce ended, Jake heard a light tap on his office door.

"Yes, it's open. Come in," Jake called out. But no one entered. A few seconds later, he heard the tapping again.

"Come in!" Jake yelled. Again, there was no reply, and no one entered. A few more seconds passed, followed by another tap at the door. This time, Jake stood, walked over, and opened it. Marcia was leaning against the wall outside.

About time you got your lazy butt up," she said with a smile.

How did you know I wasn t on the phone?" he asked.

Who would be talking to you on a Friday afternoon? You know we re the most boring people who work in this hospital," she joked.

Well, that may be your story. I, on the other hand, have an exciting life and really fun plans for my weekend," Jake replied, squinting his eyes with a devious grin.

Really? You re not just pulling my leg?" Marcia asked.

Actually, I m not. I talked to Royce Webster a little while ago. He asked if I wanted to join his staff and clients at a resort he rented out for the weekend," Jake said.

Sounds nice. He must be doing well if he can afford that," Marcia replied.

It s a write-off. He says he does it every year. He had an extra room and asked if I wanted to come along. I guess there ll be a couple of therapy sessions and even some hypnosis," Jake said.

Gosh, sounds like fun. I guess I just don t know the right people," Marcia teased.

You can come if you want. I don t know how much fun it ll really be," Jake said, glancing at her and then back down at his desk.

Really?" Marcia asked, surprised.

Sure. He said I could bring a friend, that is, if I could find one," Jake said with a smile.

I m not on call this weekend. That sounds like fun. No work, just relaxing," Marcia replied.

Now, he did say there was only one room left, so we'd have to share it, if that wouldn't be too uncomfortable for you?" Jake said.

Get out of here, you're so strange. Why would it be uncomfortable for me? Are you going to be all right with that? I don't want to make you feel uncomfortable," Marcia teased, smacking Jake lightly on the arm.

You must think I'm so amoral and delicate. Gosh, I do have male friends, you know?" Marcia added, giving him a look.

No, really? I thought I was the only one. Oh, and by the way, since you're not delicate, you can sleep on the floor," Jake said with a grin.

We'll see about that. What time are we going?" Marcia asked.

Well, we can skip lunch, call it an early day, and go home to pack. It's two o'clock now, I can probably pick you up around six or seven tonight," Jake replied.

How about I just drive to your place and leave my car there? That way, you don't have to come back into the city. Your place is on the way up north, and we can get an earlier start. I can be at your house by five," Marcia suggested.

Alright, that works for me. Royce is supposed to fax me the directions. As soon as I get them, I'm heading out of here. And hey, let's not tell anyone about our weekend plans, you know how rumors can start," Jake said, giving her a look as she started toward the door.

Yeah, and I wouldn't want my pure, delicate reputation ruined by hanging out with you. Just kidding, I know what you mean. I'll see you tonight," Marcia replied, leaving and closing the door behind her.

Jake sat back down in his chair, picked up his glove, and began tossing the ball into the air again.

He finished his work at the hospital and drove home to Birmingham to pack for the weekend. He packed two small pieces of luggage and carried his blue suit coat on a hanger. On his dresser, he noticed the pearl necklace from his childhood memory box and decided to take it with him, slipping it into the pocket of his suit jacket.

As he packed his overnight bags, the thought of Marcia spending the weekend with him stirred an uncomfortable feeling. He wondered if it was a mistake, especially since they would be sharing a room at the resort. The possibility of his colleagues finding out made him uneasy as well—he knew how quickly rumors spread and how hard they were to explain away.

At the same time, he couldn't ignore his excitement. A weekend away with Marcia promised fun and relaxation. They shared so much in common, and this would be a completely different setting for them both. Finally, Jake concluded he was spending far too much time worrying. He decided to let go of what others might think and simply enjoy himself.

Shortly after five o'clock, Marcia pulled into the driveway in her black Mustang convertible. Jake heard the engine and met her at the door.

"Do you want me to drive, can we take my car and you drive?" she asked.

"No, that's alright. Let's take my vehicle. I've got four-wheel drive, and I'm not sure what the roads will be like up there," Jake replied.

"Alright, let me grab my suitcase. Are you ready to go?" she asked.

"Yes, my bags are in the car. Maria packed a dinner basket for the road, and I already gassed up on the way home from work," Jake said as he picked up the cooler. He walked to his Lincoln Navigator, opened the back hatch, and tossed in some extra blankets and a flashlight before closing it again.

"I think we're ready." Jake smiled at Marcia, then walked around to open her door.

Thank you. This is going to be a great weekend. It worked out well that we're both off and not on call at the same time, that doesn't happen very often," Marcia said.

"You're right," Jake replied.

Their four-hour drive north brought them to the resort just as the sun was beginning to set. The lodge stood at the north end of the lake, tucked deep into the woods with its edge right against the water. Jake pulled the Navigator up to the front entrance beneath the covered driveway, where a bellhop in a red velvet jacket stepped forward to greet them.

"Do you have a reservation with us this evening, sir?" the bellhop asked.

"Yes, Jake Miller. We're here with the sleep clinic's group for the weekend," Jake replied.

The young man glanced down at the clipboard in his hands. "Ah, yes, here you are. Room 220, Dr. Miller. I'll have your baggage delivered to your room. We also provide valet parking, if you need your vehicle, just call down to the front desk and we'll bring it around. If you'd like to check in at the desk now, your luggage will be delivered shortly."

"Do you know if Dr. Webster has arrived yet?" Jake asked.

"I believe so. He and his guest arrived a few hours ago. You might check by the bar inside to see if they're there," the bellhop replied.

"Alright, thank you," Jake said as he stepped out of his vehicle, allowing the bellhop to take it.

Marcia and Jake went to the front desk to check into their room. They asked the clerk if the room assigned to them had two double beds, which it did. Afterward, they made their way to the bar to see if Royce was there.

You re lucky our room has two beds. That floor would have been hard on your back," Marcia teased.

Yeah, we would ve been arm wrestling for the bed. But you did say you re not a delicate girl. See, I remember those things," Jake replied as they stepped inside the bar.

Jake scanned the room until he spotted Royce seated at a table with a woman. He pointed them out to Marcia and guided her in their direction. As they drew closer, Jake recognized the woman with Royce, Elizabeth Rohn, the young woman who had come into his emergency room and lost her mother the night he was on duty.

Hello," Jake said to Royce and Elizabeth as they reached the table.

Hey, glad you were able to make it. Did you already check in?" Royce stood and reached for Jake s hand.

Yes, we re in room 220. This is Marcia, she s a resident at Mercy General. And this is Royce... and Elizabeth?" Jake glanced at Elizabeth as he introduced them.

Nice to meet you," Marcia said with a smile.

Sit down, have a drink. I m waiting for Sharon, my assistant, to bring me a copy of tomorrow s agenda," Royce said.

Jake and Marcia accepted the offer, sat down, and ordered a drink. Marcia and Elizabeth began a conversation about the resort. Since Elizabeth had stayed there before, she shared details about special activities, points of interest, and the spa hours. Meanwhile, Jake and Royce discussed the practice at the sleep clinic, including the different grants allocated for the study program. Their talk eventually drifted to fishing. Houghton Lake was known for some of the best fishing spots, and they hoped to carve out time early one morning to go.

Shortly after their drinks arrived, a tall, slender blonde woman walked over to the table and handed a schedule to Royce.

Sharon, this is Jake Miller and his guest, Marcia. They'll be sitting in on some of the sessions tomorrow," Royce said, introducing her.

Sharon reached out to shake Jake's hand, then Marcia's. Nice to meet you. If I can be of any assistance, please don't hesitate to ask. I believe Royce mentioned you'd be participating in the hypnosis session. I'll let you know when your scheduled time will be tomorrow."

Alright. If you run out of time and don't have any sessions available, that's fine, just let me know," Jake replied with a smile.

Don't worry, I think we'll have you covered. Again, it was nice meeting you both. Enjoy your stay. I'm calling it a night—the fresh air here makes me sleepy. I'll see you in the morning. Good night." Sharon left the bar.

I think she has the right idea. We'll call it a night, too. We'll see you down here for breakfast or coffee," Royce said as he and Elizabeth stood to leave.

Alright, sleep well," Jake said.

Good night, and thank you for inviting us," Marcia added as Royce and Elizabeth headed off to their room.

They finished their drinks, then decided to walk around the grounds for a short while before heading up to their room. A full moon shone beautifully across the water, casting light over the still surface of the lake. The silhouettes of trees stood in the darkness, and the cool night air was refreshing. Crickets filled the silence with their steady rhythm, and the scent of pine lingered in the air.

There was something clean and invigorating about being outside at night, the glow of the moonlight pressing softly against the skin as the cool air wrapped around them. Each breath numbed the chest as it sank deep into the lungs, and as they exhaled, a white cloud drifted up into the sky.

They walked along the water's edge near the boat dock. No one else seemed to be around, just Jake and Marcia alone in the darkness. Jake stopped and looked up at the sky, his hands tucked into his pockets as he bounced slightly, giving the impression that he was chilled.

Marcia glanced at him as he stood in the moonlight. The alcohol had just touched her senses, and as she watched Jake's figure and his face turned upward to the sky, her body began to shiver. If it wasn't from the night air, it was from the feelings swelling inside her as she stood watching him.

Jake turned toward her and caught her staring. "Are you alright? You're not about to fall into the water and make me rescue you, are you?" he asked with a smile.

"I'm alright. Just getting a little tired. It's colder up here than in the city," she said.

Jake noticed Marcia shivering. He slipped off the denim shirt he wore over his T-shirt and draped it around her shoulders. "I'm sorry, here, take this," Jake said.

"I'm all right, you don't have to give me your shirt," Marcia replied, though he wrapped it around her anyway.

"Thank you. Shall we go and see if our luggage made it to our room?" she asked.

Jake glanced at his watch, trying to catch the time in the moonlight. "Yes, I think we'd better call it a night. I'm pretty sure Royce wants to use me as a guinea pig tomorrow," he said.

I ve always wanted to see if I can be hypnotized. I just don t know if I can," Marcia admitted.

Good, then you can take my session time, and I ll go fishing," he said with a smile.

They walked back into the resort, found the elevators, and rode up to the second floor. Their room was numbered 220.

Don t expect me to carry you in or anything," Jake teased.

Yeah, yeah, you re just the comedian tonight, aren t you," Marcia said as she opened the door.

Their luggage sat neatly in the center of the room. Two double beds waited, linens folded back with chocolates placed on the pillows. The room was moderately large and tastefully decorated, with a sliding glass door leading to a balcony that overlooked the lake. Gold, black and woodstone tones filled the space, with matching curtains and bedspreads. It was clear the resort had been remodeled with a modern, elegant style. This was no budget inn; the place radiated class, and Royce s choice reflected his refined taste.

Marcia quickly claimed the bathroom, showered, and changed into her pajamas. When she returned, her hair was damp, and she brushed it out before climbing into her bed, pulling the covers around her as she sat up.

I hope you don t sleep in the nude or anything," Marcia teased.

Oh, I forgot to tell you—I also snore and have a tendency to sleepwalk," Jake replied, tossing his pillow across the room at her.

Laughing, he headed into the bathroom to get ready for bed. When he returned, he climbed under the covers and reached for the light switch.

Are you going to sleep, or do you want to watch television or read?" Jake asked.

No, I m tired. I think I can fall asleep. Goodnight."

Goodnight."

Jake turned off the light. For a few moments, he lay in the darkness, listening to the stillness of the room. His eyes grew heavy, and soon he drifted into sleep.

The sky in his dream was pitch black, with no stars to be found. Heavy clouds smothered the moonlight as they dragged across the heavens. Cold rain stung the face of a man riding hard through the night on a gray-dappled stallion. His expression was pale and hollow, his dark eyes blurred by the downpour. His soaked clothes clung to him as he urged the horse forward like a madman toward the flickering lanterns at the gates.

He hardly waited for the horse to stop. Swinging down, he ran to the still figure of a woman lying on the cold, wet ground. Dropping to his knees, he gathered her in his arms, rocking her against his chest as despair ripped through him. Blood darkened the puddles beneath her head. Her eyes were closed, her sweet face locked in a lifeless calm as raindrops traced her cheeks.

The man s cry tore through the night. Those who had gathered looked on only briefly before retreating toward the distant house and stables.

In the resort room, Jake tossed in his sleep. Sweat ran down his temples, his chest heaving as he muttered and clenched the sheets. His lips struggled to form a single name, crying it into the darkness.

Elly!"

Marcia was jolted awake by Jake s cries. She sat up quickly, her eyes darting to his bed where he thrashed and muttered. Flicking on the light, she rushed over, calling his name. Fear gripped her as she saw his pillow drenched in sweat, his face twisted in agony, his eyes clenched shut.

Jake! Jake!" she cried, her voice rising as panic set in. She reached for him, shaking his shoulders, then pulled him against her, wrapping her arms around him.

At her touch, Jake stilled. He clung to her tightly, whispering in a broken voice, Don t leave me, Elly. Please don t go." His body finally relaxed, the tension melting away as his cries faded.

Marcia held him close, tears slipping down her own cheeks. Wake up, Jake," she whispered desperately.

His eyes fluttered open. Blinking in confusion, Jake pulled back, startled by her tear-streaked face.

What happened?" He touched his forehead, wiping away the sweat dripping down his temples.

I don t know. You must have been having a terrible dream. You were calling out names, I couldn t wake you." Marcia steadied her breathing and brushed at her eyes.

Oh my gosh, I m so sorry. I didn t mean to scare you. These dreams... they don t stop. I wake up like this—sweating, exhausted. I m so sorry. Are you alright, Marcia?" Jake reached out and touched her arm gently.

Yes. You just frightened me. You looked like you were in so much pain," she said softly.

That s why Royce wanted me to try hypnosis, to see what I can remember. I shouldn t have dragged you into this when I m in this kind of state. I feel terrible."

Don t," Marcia said quickly. It was just a dream. Everything s fine now." She tried to smile through the heaviness in the room. Though you weren't kidding about snoring. Only it wasn't snoring—it was yelling."

Jake managed a faint laugh, but his eyes searched hers. "Are you alright? Will you be able to sleep?"

"Only if you can," she replied gently. "Do you think you'll dream again?"

"Usually, it happens just once. Then I can settle back down." He leaned against the headboard, still catching his breath. "Will you be okay?"

"Yes, I usually don't have any problems sleeping," Marcia said.

She moved back to her bed and slipped under the covers. Jake reached for the light, switched it off, and lay back down. In the darkness, he glanced over at her.

"Thank you. I'm sorry I scared you," he whispered.

"Everything is alright. Goodnight," Marcia replied.

CHAPTER THIRTY-SIX

Claire arrived at the Rothschild Resort early Saturday morning. She had decided not to drive up Friday night in the dark, wanting instead to enjoy one more night in her own bed. Leaving Detroit around five o'clock in the morning, she reached Houghton Lake at about nine-thirty.

Pulling up beneath the covered entryway of the hotel, Claire rolled down her window as a young bellhop hurried to her driver's side.

"Good morning, ma'am. Do you have a reservation with us?" he asked.

"Yes, my name is Claire Strauss," she replied.

The young man checked his clipboard, then looked back up at her.

"Ah, yes. Here we go. You're with Dr. Webster's group," he said.

"Yes," Claire confirmed.

"You're in room 218. You may leave your vehicle with me and go inside to the desk to pick up your key. We'll deliver your luggage to your room and park your car. If you need your vehicle during your stay, just call the front desk and we'll have it ready for you. I believe the breakfast buffet is still being served in the main dining room if you'd like to stop by there."

"Thank you." Claire stepped out of her vehicle, leaving the engine running. She watched as the young bellhop slid behind the wheel of her Honda Accord and drove it away. Claire rarely used her car in Detroit, since the city's people movers and taxi services were so convenient. She usually kept it in storage, bringing it out only for road trips.

Once the bellhop pulled away, Claire made her way to the front desk to check in. An envelope was waiting for her with the daily schedule of sessions. Inside, she found a note about a brief introduction meeting arranged for all attendees. It was scheduled for eleven o clock in Conference Room One. Checking her watch, she saw it was still before ten. Deciding she had time, she headed to the dining room for a light breakfast before freshening up for the meeting.

At the reception desk, she asked for directions to the conference rooms, then carried a stack of hotel brochures with her to the dining room. Sitting down, she looked through the amenities the resort offered. Everything was included in the package except spa treatments, which were charged separately. Meals and recreational activities, however, were part of the stay. Claire noted with interest that the resort offered horseback riding and thought it might be fun to try.

After finishing her breakfast, she took the elevator up to the second floor and found room 218. The décor was done in mauve and tan, warm and inviting. A king-size bed dominated the center of the room, looking almost oversized against the wall. The bathroom featured grey and white marble tiles with gold-plated faucets and fixtures, giving it an elegant finish.

A small area between the bedroom and bathroom held an extra sink and countertop space. On the counter sat a coffee machine with an assortment of gourmet coffees and teas, and beneath it was a fully stocked refrigerator. The carpet was brown and plush, soft enough that Claire felt her feet sink slightly as she walked across the room. She slipped off her shoes and enjoyed the comfort against her tired feet. The room had a clean, elegant atmosphere, and Claire thought to herself that Dr. Webster must be spending quite a bit of money for accommodations like this.

After brushing her teeth and combing her silky blonde hair, Claire left her room and headed toward the conference area. As she walked down the hall, she opened her purse, digging through it for the schedule she had tucked inside at check-in. Focused on the contents of her bag, she didn t notice Jake coming around the corner at the same time. He was carrying a small ice bucket and also looking down. They collided, bumping shoulders just as the ice bucket tilted, spilling a few cubes onto the carpet. Claire dropped her purse, and as they both bent to retrieve their things, their heads bumped together.

"Oh, I'm sorry," Claire said with a small laugh.

"No, no, it was my fault. I should have been watching where I was going." Jake rubbed the spot on his head where they had collided.

"I wasn't looking either. I'm sorry I made you drop your ice." Claire smiled at him.

"Not a problem. Are you alright? I didn't give you a concussion, did I?" Jake grinned back.

"No, I'm fine. Again, I'm sorry," Claire said as she started to step around him.

Jake looked back at Claire, his gaze lingering for a moment. "Do I know you? You look very familiar," he said. He didn't realize she was the woman he had once seen playing the violin at the coffee shop.

"I don't think so," Claire replied with a smile.

"My name is Jake Miller. Nice to meet you," Jake said, extending his hand.

"Claire Strauss," she answered, shaking it.

"Claire Strauss... that sounds familiar too. Are you from around here?"

"No, I live in the city, Detroit. I'm sorry, but I need to go or I'll be late for a meeting. It was nice to meet you, Jake. I hope you enjoy your stay." With that, Claire turned and walked away.

Jake headed toward his room, but before opening his door, he glanced back, hoping to see her again. She was already gone. He swiped his key card and stepped inside.

Meanwhile, Claire turned the corner toward the elevator, but her thoughts lingered on Jake and his smile. A warm feeling stirred in her chest, and on impulse she turned back, hoping to catch one last glimpse of him. But when she peeked around the corner, he had already disappeared. She stood there for a moment, smiling softly to herself, before making her way to the elevator.

Claire arrived at Conference Room One, which had been arranged with a podium at the front and six neat rows of chairs facing it. About a dozen people had already gathered. Off to the side of the podium, Dr. Webster stood reviewing paperwork. Claire lingered near the back, alone, taking in the scene as she waited for the meeting to begin. Royce soon noticed her standing by herself and walked over.

"Claire, I'm so glad you came," Royce said, reaching for her hand.

"This is a really nice resort. Thank you for inviting me," she replied.

"Did you bring a guest?" Royce asked.

"No, it was kind of a last-minute plan for myself. That's alright, I'll enjoy the time relaxing," Claire said.

"I'd like you to join my table for dinner tonight, if that's alright. There are a few people I'd like to introduce you to," Royce offered.

"That would be fine. What time?" Claire asked.

"We have reservations at seven o'clock," Royce answered, then waved for Elizabeth to join them.

"Claire, I'd like you to meet Elizabeth Rohn, my fiancée. Elizabeth, this is Claire Strauss," he introduced.

"Nice to meet you," Elizabeth said, reaching to touch Claire's hand.

I think we can get started now," Royce said as he excused himself and walked to the front of the room. Taking his place at the podium, he leaned into the microphone.

Welcome. If you'd like to take a seat, we can begin the introductions."

Claire walked to a row of chairs near the back and sat down.

I'm glad you were all able to make it," Royce began.

As he continued his opening remarks, Jake and Marcia entered the room and took seats in the front row. Claire's eyes lifted and found Jake as he sat down. She kept watching him until he glanced back, scanning the room. When his eyes met hers, she quickly looked away. Jake studied her for a few seconds, hoping she'd look back so he could wave, but she kept her gaze fixed on Royce. With a small sigh, Jake turned back to the podium. A moment later, Claire's eyes drifted back to him.

Royce spoke about the therapy sessions planned for the weekend and the scheduled times available. He emphasized that the goal was for everyone to relax and enjoy themselves. After a while, he announced a short break so the group could grab refreshments or use the restrooms before the first session, which would be led by his assistant, Sharon Richardson.

As the room stirred with movement, Royce made his way over to Jake, shook his hand, and then called Claire over.

Claire, I would like you to meet a good friend of mine, Dr. Miller, and this is his friend Marcia. They both work at Mercy Hospital," Royce introduced.

Yes, I already met Jake." Claire reached out to shake Marcia's hand.

Royce looked puzzled. You already met?"

Yes, we sort of bumped into each other in the hallway. I wasn't looking where I was going," Jake laughed.

No, it was me. I wasn't paying attention. I think I gave him a concussion," Claire teased with a smile.

I'm glad you've already met. Jake and Marcia will be joining us for dinner tonight as well," Royce said. "Claire came up for the weekend alone, so don't let her feel like a stranger."

Well, I feel relieved knowing that if I need medical attention, there are so many doctors here," Claire joked.

You're right about that," Elizabeth chimed in as she walked up and slipped her hand through Royce's arm.

What are your plans this afternoon, Claire?" Marcia asked.

I'm not sure. I thought about going horseback riding, I saw it listed in the brochure," Claire replied.

That sounds like fun. I haven't been riding in such a long time," Marcia said warmly.

Why don't you come along?" Claire offered.

Alright, I'll look for you after the session." Marcia turned to Jake. "Sounds like fun. Will you come with us?"

Sure, why not? You might fall and need a doctor," Jake joked, smiling at Marcia before glancing at Claire.

She quickly looked away, though she could still feel his eyes on her.

I'd better go see about making reservations for this afternoon," Claire excused herself. "I'll be right back."

Claire left, and a few moments later Marcia and Elizabeth excused themselves to check on spa appointments for later in their stay, leaving Jake and Royce alone.

Is Claire the woman in the tapes, the violinist?" Jake asked quietly.

Yes. You caught me off guard, already meeting her," Royce replied.

I didn t recognize her at first. There s something about her... I just don t know." Jake paused, searching for words. I feel out of place here with Marcia. We re only friends, but somehow it makes it harder to meet anyone else."

You two are just friends. No harm in looking elsewhere." Royce gave him a playful slap on the arm.

Yes, I suppose you re right. Well, let s get started," Jake said with a sigh.

The rest of the morning was filled with a lecture from Dr. Roberts, a professor at the University of Michigan. He spoke on the latest breakthroughs in sleep disorders and the medications now available to treat patients. He also touched on non-conventional therapies, presenting different approaches to understanding and managing sleep-related issues.

Before the group broke for lunch, Sharon approached Jake and Claire. She asked if she could schedule both of them for a hypnosis session the next morning at nine o clock, since some participants needed to leave early and the afternoon slots were already booked.

Neither Jake nor Claire looked thrilled at the idea, but they both agreed. Royce had suggested it, and each felt it might be worthwhile.

After Sharon left, Claire turned to Jake. I didn t know you were a patient of Dr. Webster s."

Actually, I m not. I m not really being treated by him," Jake explained. He just wants me to do this hypnosis thing, to help me figure something out."

Then it sounds like you re being treated," Claire said with a small smile.

Jake rolled his eyes and smiled back at Claire. Well, I suppose you re right, even though I don t like the thought of being treated by him."

All you doctors are just alike, aren t you?" Claire teased.

Hmmm... and what exactly does all just alike mean?" Jake asked, giving her a playful, lingering look. Then he added with a grin, Now be nice. Remember, you could be a patient of mine someday."

You don t mind treating others, but you can t accept help when you need it yourself." Claire looked away as she spoke. The weight of his eyes on her stirred something deep inside, an unfamiliar feeling she hadn t known in years, except in her dreams. Jake intrigued her far more than she wanted to admit, but she fought to steady her thoughts, reminding herself that he was here with someone else.

Alright, I guess I can buy that," Jake said lightly.

Just then, Marcia walked up and slipped into the conversation. I think we re done here for the day. Now we can just have fun. You both have your sessions scheduled for tomorrow, right? Good, that means I can sleep in."

I m going to go change into some blue jeans. We ve got horses reserved at one o clock. Do you want to meet at the stables?" Claire asked.

Sounds like a plan. We ll see you there," Jake replied, giving her a small wave as she walked off.

Marcia noticed how his eyes followed Claire until she disappeared around the corner. She gave him a playful smack on the arm.

What?" Jake asked, smiling.

Put your tongue back in your mouth," she teased, waiting for his reaction.

I m sorry, I was just being nice. Does it bother you if I hang out with her?" Jake asked.

Gosh, no. I was joking. She seems like a very nice girl," Marcia said.

I get these strange feelings around her, like I know her from somewhere," Jake admitted.

You re strange. What you re feeling is the male hormonal thing," Marcia shot back with a smirk.

No, it s something different. I don t know." Jake shook his head, then glanced at her. Anyway, what do you want to do until one?"

I need to go change, too, if we re riding horses. Let s head back to the room," Marcia said, leading the way out of the conference area.

Both Sharon and Royce had been quietly keeping an eye on Jake and Claire. They had already noticed the spark of attraction between them, and Sharon had purposely scheduled their sessions for the following morning, giving them the afternoon free to spend together.

By one o clock, Jake and Marcia met Claire at the stables for their hour-and-a-half trail ride. The afternoon group was small, just three other riders besides them and their guide, a man named Buddy. He looked every bit the cowboy with spurs on his boots, a weathered hat pulled low, and a wad of tobacco tucked in his cheek. Every so often, he d spit to the side, always with a quick apology.

Claire was matched with a sleek gray stallion named Silver, Marcia with a brown-and-white spotted horse called Spot, and Jake with a towering black stallion named Trigger. Once everyone was mounted, Buddy gave a short briefing before setting out.

The line of horses fell into order behind Buddy's mount, with Marcia taking the lead among the riders and Jake and Claire riding near the rear. Conversation was sparse, the single-file line making it difficult to talk, so they rode mostly in silence, listening to the steady rhythm of hooves.

The trail wound deep into the woods and then opened along the edge of a shimmering lake. Afterward, Buddy guided them off the main path, up a hillside, and into a wide pasture. Tall grasses in shades of green and yellow rippled in the breeze, stretching toward the horizon.

Buddy turned in the saddle and called back, giving them a grin. He suggested they let the horses run for a bit, but only two at a time, riding to the end of the field and back to stretch the animals' legs.

Since there were six riders altogether, not including Buddy, he paired them off and sent them in turns. Marcia went first with the woman riding ahead of her. She urged her horse forward, racing across the field with a burst of laughter, the power and speed of the animal giving her an exhilarating rush.

Next, it was Claire and Jake's turn. Claire nudged Silver into a run, taking off ahead of Jake. She glanced back over her shoulder and laughed as she kept in front of him. Jake spurred Trigger forward, quickly closing the gap. Near the end of the stretch, he urged his horse around hers and cut into the lead.

Cheater!" Claire called after him, laughing as she tried to catch up.

Jake grinned back at her, his horse holding just enough of an edge to keep him in front. He looked over his shoulder again, laughing, but when his eyes met hers, Claire's smile faltered. Her expression went blank. She eased her horse's pace and let the race go.

In that moment, an image flashed in her mind—Stephen, the man from her dreams. It wasn't Jake's face she saw but his, smiling at her with the same wind-swept hair and glowing expression. The memory was so vivid it startled her.

Jake reached the group a few seconds before Claire did. When she caught up, she managed a smile, but it lacked the carefree warmth of before. Jake immediately noticed the change.

"Are you alright?" he asked.

"Yes, I just got a little winded. I'm fine," she replied, forcing another smile.

The horses fell back into their places on the trail, with Claire riding behind Jake. Every so often, he glanced over his shoulder to check on her, though she pretended not to notice.

The guided tour was nearing its end as the group followed the path back behind the stables. Just as they emerged from the woods, a bee landed on the back of Claire's horse and stung him. Silver jolted forward, colliding into the rear of Trigger, who was blocked by the horse in front of him. Feeling crowded, Trigger lashed out with his hind legs, kicking at Silver.

Jake grabbed his reins, trying to steady Trigger, while Silver reared up on his hind legs and stumbled backward. Everything happened so quickly that before Buddy, the guide, could even react, Silver bucked and threw Claire from his back. She tumbled to the side, rolling instinctively to keep clear of the horse's hooves.

Jake finally brought Trigger under control. He leapt from the saddle and ran to Claire, dropping to his knees beside her. She had landed face down, her hands pressed beneath her as if bracing herself. Jake's heart pounded, fear surging through him, his hands trembling as he touched her arm.

"Claire, are you alright? Don't move, you need to stay still," he urged, reaching to check her pulse at her neck.

Claire felt his trembling fingers against her skin and slowly rolled onto her back to look up at him.

"Yes, I'm alright," she said.

But as Jake gazed down at her, a chill ran through him. The scene mirrored the dream he'd had the night before: a woman lying on the ground, and a man at her side, overcome with anguish. The same fear and despair welled up inside him now, tightening his chest and shaking his voice as he tried to speak.

"You need to stay still, you might have broken something in the fall," Jake said, carefully checking her for any sign of bleeding or injury.

Marcia had jumped down from her horse and now knelt beside him. "Are you alright?" she asked.

"Yes, I'm fine," Claire replied, starting to get up. Jake and Marcia helped her to her feet, but she lost her balance and stumbled into Jake's arms.

"See, you need to sit back down and let us check you over," Jake said, steadying her.

"I'm just a little shaky still, but believe me, I'm alright," Claire insisted.

Buddy returned to check on her, then rode off to catch Silver, who had bolted ahead toward the stables. Jake and Marcia walked Claire back the short distance, then called the resort for a golf cart to take her to the main building. Jake kept his arm around her as they walked, giving her support. His steadiness had returned, no longer shaken the way he had been when he first touched her on the ground.

"Did I scare you, Doctor?" Claire asked with a faint smile.

Yes, you did. You re only allowed to do that once per trip, though," Jake replied with a smile of his own. Still, the memory of seeing her on the ground lingered. He thought about the enormous wave of fear that had poured over him. He had faced countless emergencies, seen all kinds of trauma, yet this moment had rattled him more than anything he could remember. For a few seconds, he had felt like he was losing control, his heart hollow, his mind gone blank.

I think you should lie down and rest. I d like to stay with you and make sure you re alright," Jake said.

Nothing personal, but I think I d prefer a woman doctor if you insist I need to be checked out," Claire replied, meeting his eyes. She, too, was unsettled, frightened not just by the fall, but by the unexpected feelings stirring inside her for a man she hardly knew.

Oh yes, of course. I am sorry, I did not think of that," Jake says.

I will examine you, and I won t even bill you for it," Marcia says with a smile toward Claire.

Thank you," Claire replies.

The golf cart arrived and brought them back to the resort. Royce was waiting out front, having been notified by the manager of the accident.

Is everything alright?" Royce asked.

Yes, everything is fine. Claire is going to lie down, and Marcia will make sure everything checks out," Jake says.

They helped Claire up to her room, then left Marcia alone with her.

Claire lay down on the bed as Marcia began a quick exam. She looked into Claire s eyes, checked her pupils, then felt for pulses in her arms and legs. Marcia pressed gently around Claire s abdomen and hips to make sure there were no tender spots.

"Everything appears fine," Marcia said, still sitting on the edge of the bed. "I think you're going to live. Nothing broken or damaged."

"Great, thanks a lot. I really appreciate your and Jake's concern. You have a nice companion," Claire says. She wanted to ask more about Marcia and Jake's relationship, but didn't quite know how.

"Yes, Jake is a good man," Marcia answers.

"How long have you both been dating?" Claire asks, gathering her courage.

"We're just good friends. We're not together," Marcia says, looking away as she spoke.

"Oh, I'm sorry. I thought since you were in the same room, you must be a couple," Claire says.

"No, just friends. What about you? Are you with anyone?" Marcia asks.

"Oh no, that's a complicated one. I usually meet the kind with lots of baggage or the over-controlling type," Claire says with a roll of her eyes and a laugh.

"Believe me, I know the type," Marcia says. "Well, I'll leave you to rest and come back to check on you shortly. Are you still coming down for dinner with us?"

"Yes, I think I'll rest for a while. Thank you very much, Marcia," Claire says.

"No problem, get some rest," Marcia says, giving Claire's leg a light tap before leaving the room.

Jake and Royce were waiting in the hallway. Marcia told them that everything was fine, and that Claire was going to rest and still meet them for dinner that evening.

329

I think I ll go freshen up and relax before dinner as well," Jake says.

Marcia and Jake returned to their room, assuring Royce they would keep an eye on Claire. Royce then went back to the session still taking place in conference room one.

About thirty minutes before dinner, Marcia called Claire s room to check on her. Claire sounded refreshed, assured her that everything was fine, and agreed to meet them in the dining room.

Jake and Marcia arrived at the table where Royce and Elizabeth were already seated. Jake had changed into more casual dinner wear: khaki pants, a white shirt, and a blue suit coat. Marcia wore a brown silk dress that fell just below her knees, the neckline cut low enough to offer a flattering view of her cleavage.

Claire arrived shortly after, wearing a red dress that fit snugly against her slender, firm figure. She took a seat across from Jake, trying not to look at him too much during dinner, though she felt the weight of his gaze on her. A tingling sensation stirred in her stomach, her nerves heightened by his nearness. Her chest felt as though it might burst as her heart pounded heavily. It was hard to catch her breath, as if the air had been stolen from her lungs.

Claire focused on eating her meal, joining in little of the conversation at the table. Jake spoke with Royce but continued to glance at Claire, offering her small smiles. Marcia sensed Jake s interest but chose not to comment on it.

She valued his friendship, and although she too had strong feelings for Jake, she did not want to interfere if he was interested in someone else. After dinner, while the rest of the table ordered coffee, Claire excused herself. She said she was going to take a walk and then turn in early. She assured Dr. Webster that she would be at the session the next morning, ready to go. Claire stood up and left the table.

Jake said nothing, only watching as she walked away. Silence settled over the group for a few minutes. Everyone knew what the others were thinking, but no one wanted to say it. Finally, Marcia broke the silence.

You should go after her and walk with her to make sure she's alright," Marcia said to Jake.

Good idea," Royce added.

You think so? Would you be alright if I left?" Jake asked Marcia.

Of course. Get out of here. I'll see you back at the room." Marcia waved him off. As Jake left the table, Marcia watched him go. A lump formed in her throat, but she forced a smile at Royce and Elizabeth, doing her best to hide the ache inside.

Jake caught up to Claire as she walked along the dockside by the lake.

Hello, would you mind if I joined you?" Jake called out.

Claire stopped and turned around when she heard his voice.

You didn't have to come. I don't want to pull you away from your friends," she said.

I see them all the time, don't worry about that. Are you feeling alright?" Jake asked.

Yes, I just have some things on my mind," Claire replied.

Anything you'd like to talk to a doctor about?" he teased with a smile.

You're a nice man. I appreciate yours and Marcia's kindness," she said.

Jake looked out over the water. They had stopped walking, and Claire was leaning against a pole. He bent down, picked up a rock, and skipped it across the surface, the stone bouncing three times before sinking. Claire watched his movements, and once again she felt her body tremble.

Jake turned and looked at her, the moonlight shining down on her. She looked so beautiful standing there against the pole. He stood quietly for a moment, just gazing at her. When she finally looked back at him, he slipped off his suit coat and draped it over her shoulders. Claire held the jacket close, trembling not entirely from the cold.

I don t know why I have these feelings when I m around you. It s making me embarrassed because it feels like it s written all over my face. Every time you look at me, it s like you can see right through me. Can you?" Claire asked.

I feel the same way. Why is that? I don t want to be away from you. It s so strange. I don t want you to think I m just trying to pick you up or something, but when I look at you, I can t stop my heart from racing," Jake said.

He walked over to her, standing just inches away. Claire looked up into his eyes, her knees suddenly weak. Jake leaned closer, his lips nearing hers—then footsteps broke the moment. Royce and Elizabeth were walking up from the side.

Jake backed away quickly, his expression lost and pleading. Claire looked away as Royce approached.

Hey, I found you two. Is everything alright?" Royce asked.

Yes, I was just going back to my room. I ll see you in the morning. Goodnight." Claire used the interruption as her chance to leave. She waved, glanced at Jake once more, then walked away, still draped in his suit coat.

When she reached her room, she slipped the coat from her shoulders. As it fell to the side, something dropped from the pocket. Claire looked down and saw a pearl necklace with a gold pendant lying on the ground. She bent to pick it up, and her body trembled as she recognized it—the same necklace Elly had worn in the portrait at the Bentley mansion.

Her mind went blank. How could Jake have this necklace in his pocket? Where could he have gotten it? Unsure, she decided to wait by the elevators on the second floor, planning to return his coat and ask him about the necklace.

Meanwhile, Jake was still outside with Royce and Elizabeth.

Did I come at a bad time? What were you two discussing?" Royce asked.

I don t know, Royce. It s strange. We both feel something for each other, but we don t even know why. It s a different kind of attraction, and I can t explain it," Jake said.

Listen, get some sleep. I ll see you in the morning. I have news for both of you, and I think it will help. Trust me, just go rest, and I ll talk to you then," Royce said.

Jake agreed, said goodnight, and headed back. When he stepped off the elevator on the second floor, he saw Claire sitting in a chair.

Sleeping in the hallway tonight?" Jake teased with a smile.

No, I just wanted to return your coat," Claire said as she handed it to Jake.

You didn t have to wait for me. I could have picked it up in the morning," Jake replied.

Claire s mind raced. She wanted to ask about the necklace but felt hesitant.

333

Jake, can I ask you something?" Claire struggled for the words.

Sure." Jake turned toward her, his eyes intent on hers.

The necklace in your pocket dropped onto the floor. I picked it up and couldn t help noticing how beautiful it is. Can I ask where you got it?" Claire held the necklace out to him.

A woman gave it to my mother a long time ago, around the time I was born," Jake said, avoiding the full story about the woman in the hospital.

Did your mother know her well?" Claire asked.

No, I don t think so. It s supposed to bring me happiness," Jake said with a small roll of his eyes.

Really? I could use some of that sometimes," Claire said softly.

Here, you take it. Maybe it ll work for you. It s worth a try." Jake placed the necklace back in her hand.

Oh, I can t accept this. It s far too expensive to give away," Claire protested.

I didn t pay for it. I really want you to have it. If you can t accept it as a gift, then think of it as being loaned, and to be returned one day. You can return it if it doesn t bring you happiness." Jake smiled as he gently closed her hand around the necklace.

Thank you. Goodnight, I ll see you in the morning," Claire said, then walked to her room.

Jake went to his own, pausing outside the door with a smile. His thoughts lingered on what he had told Claire about the necklace bringing happiness, and how he realized it did.

Inside, the lights were already out. Marcia lay in bed pretending to sleep, not wanting to talk about Claire. Tears welled in her eyes, though she kept them hidden. She and Jake had always been good friends, never more, yet tonight she felt the sting of something deeper.

Jake closed his eyes and drifted off, his last thoughts filled with Claire standing in the moonlight—her soft hair waving in the cool breeze, her blue eyes gazing deep into his soul. Unconsciously, he whispered to himself, Goodnight, Elly."

CHAPTER THIRTY-SEVEN

Jake slept through the night without waking. He had a peaceful night's rest, without the taunting feelings and exhausting emotions that usually filled his nights. He felt refreshed and in good spirits. Marcia was still lying in bed when Jake awoke. He jumped in the shower and dressed. He did not want to be late for the therapy session he had scheduled that morning.

Before Jake left the room, he went over to Marcia's bed and sat on the corner of it. She felt the depression in the mattress from his weight, then rolled over to look at him. He looked so awake and refreshed. She pulled the pillow over her head.

"Don't look at me. I feel like a zombie today," she said.

"You look like one, too," Jake laughed.

Marcia took the pillow off her face and hit Jake with it.

"Have a nice session. I hope you find some answers," Marcia said.

"Me too. I'll see you in a little while," Jake replied. He stood to leave, but Marcia grabbed his hand and pulled him back.

"Wait a minute," Marcia said, still holding Jake's hand. He sat back down and looked at her hand. He reached and held it in his.

"Marcia," he began.

"Listen, Jake, I like you as a friend. You are a wonderful, terrific friend to me. If you like Claire, that is all right with me. I will still be your friend. It would be complicated for us anyway. I just wanted to let you know where I stand," Marcia said.

Jake lifted Marcia's hand to his lips and gently kissed it.

"Thank you. You mean a lot to me. I don't want to do anything to jeopardize that," Jake said.

Marcia felt the knot swell in her throat again and thought she had better make him leave, or she might start to cry.

"Alright, get out of here then," she teased in an authoritative voice. Jake smiled as he got up and walked out of the room, leaving Marcia in bed. She kept her eyes on the door for a few moments, hoping he would return, though she knew he would not.

Jake arrived in the conference room and grabbed a cup of coffee from the back table, which was set with pastries and coffee pots. He ate a donut and waited for Claire. A thought crossed his mind, maybe she had left the resort. He wondered if he had scared her off, that she might have slipped away in the middle of the night just to avoid seeing him again.

While these doubts filled Jake's mind, Claire walked in through the same doors he had entered only ten minutes earlier. She walked up to him and smiled.

"You look wide awake today," she said.

"I feel pretty good this morning. What about you?" he replied.

Claire glanced around the room as if searching for someone, barely paying attention to Jake.

"Is there someone you're looking for?" he asked.

Claire's eyes shifted back to him after scanning the gathering crowd.

"Actually, yes. I'm looking for another patient of Dr. Webster's. She's supposed to be here," Claire said.

"What's her name? I can go ask Royce," Jake offered.

"No, that's not necessary. He didn't want me to talk to her. I guess we're having the same dreams, and I just wanted to see if I could pick her out of the crowd," Claire explained.

"So you're having bad dreams? What are you dreaming about, if you don't mind me asking?" Jake said.

Claire looked at him and was just about to answer when Royce walked up.

"Good morning. Are you two ready to get started?" Royce asked.

"I suppose I'm as ready as I'll ever be," Jake said.

"Good. Both of you can come with me." Royce gestured toward the door and led the way.

They entered a smaller room next to conference room one. The curtains were drawn shut and the lights dimmed low. Two couches sat side by side, both facing the same direction. At the end of one side, a single chair was positioned between them. Off to the side was a table with two chairs and a tape recorder set up on it. An older man with thick gray hair stood at the table, adjusting the recorder.

"This is Dr. Richardson. He will be hypnotizing you today," Royce said, introducing him.

"Hello," Dr. Richardson greeted, reaching out to shake Claire's hand, then Jake's.

"Dr. Richardson, what if I can't be hypnotized?" Jake asked.

"I don't think we'll have that problem," Dr. Richardson replied. "But I do have some medications that can make it easier if you're unable to relax. Why don't you both take a seat on the couches and lie down."

Claire looked at Jake, then back at Dr. Richardson.

"We're going to do this at the same time? I don't understand why," she said.

"It's alright. We're trying something a little different. Please, try to relax," Royce reassured her.

Both Claire and Jake walked over to the couches and lay down. They were about two feet apart, their heads aligned in the same direction. Dr. Richardson sat in the chair positioned at the end of the couches near their feet.

He spoke in a low, soothing voice, guiding Claire and Jake through deep breathing exercises until he felt they were both at ease. Then he began to lead them into the hypnotic state.

Jake slipped into hypnosis more quickly than Claire, so Dr. Richardson continued working with her until she finally relaxed enough to enter the same tranquil phase. To confirm, he asked them both a few simple questions, making sure they were under his influence.

Satisfied, Dr. Richardson began guiding them back, starting from the present day, then moving farther and farther into the past. He brought them to the moment of their births, and then beyond, into a previous life they had both lived.

"What is your name and where do you live?" Dr. Richardson asked Claire.

"Elly Bentley. I live in New Orleans," Claire said, her voice soft and low.

Dr. Richardson asked Jake the same question.

"Stephen Bentley. I live in New Orleans," Jake answered. He turned his head as if growing restless.

Dr. Richardson told both Jake and Claire that they could hear each other's voices and reminded them they were together in the same room. He glanced at the tape recorder to make sure it was running.

"Stephen, I cannot see you. I am trying to find you. Where are you?" Claire cried, moving her head from side to side restlessly.

"Elly, my love, I am here. Don't go. Please don't leave me again," Jake said, his voice shaking. Tears slipped down his face while his eyes remained closed.

"I am sorry, Stephen. I made a mistake. I love you. I have always loved you. I have to tell you this tonight and beg you to forgive me. It is so cold and the storm is so bad. I have to get to you. Please don't leave me," Claire cried as she shifted and writhed.

"I forgive you, my darling Elly. I never stopped loving you. I thought you did not love me. My life was nothing without you. I love you so much," Jake said, crying harder.

"Stephen, don't leave me. Where are you? Where did you go, Stephen? Please come back." Claire collapsed to the floor. Dr. Richardson rose to help and tried to bring her out of the hypnotic state, but she continued calling for Stephen. Jake, still lying nearby and crying, pushed Dr. Richardson away and fell to the floor beside her. He reached for Claire and held her tight as he sobbed.

"I am here and I will never let you go," Jake said, holding Claire in his arms.

"It is cold, Stephen. I am frightened. I love you so much, my husband," Claire whispered as she clung to him, their bodies molding together.

Dr. Richardson regained his balance and continued speaking softly to bring both of them out of hypnosis. When Jake and Claire opened their eyes, they were still holding each other. Both faces were flushed and wet with tears. They would not let go.

"It's you," Claire said.

"You are what I was looking for. I spent my whole life moving toward you, searching for you," Jake said.

"I still love you, Stephen," Claire replied.

"I have always loved you, Elly," Jake said. He gently kissed her on the lips, then pulled back and looked deep into her eyes. Claire kissed him back, this time a longer, more passionate kiss. She rested her head on Jake's shoulder and held him tight.

Royce opened the curtains, letting sunlight pour into the room.

"Are you both all right?" Royce asked.

Jake and Claire nodded. Jake rose from the floor and helped Claire up. They sat together on one of the couches, Jake's arm wrapped around her shoulders as she leaned close.

"This was very unusual. I want to make sure you are both all right. You experienced a lot of emotion," Royce said.

"Yes. I think we are. I feel really drained," Jake replied.

"Me too," Claire added.

"You found each other. I believe your dreams will stop now. You told each other what you needed to say a hundred years ago. I believe Stephen and Elly's souls will rest. We will have to see if this theory is correct, but I do believe so," Royce said.

"Jake was the other person having the same dreams?" Claire asked Royce.

"Yes. I could not tell you before," Royce replied.

"I thought it was another woman having the same dreams," Claire said, then looked at Jake. "I felt an attraction to you and I did not know why. I felt like I knew you, and you brought out emotions I had not felt in so long."

"I felt the same way. I saw you once before, though," Jake said.

Claire looked at him. "Where?" she asked.

"In the coffee shop, you were playing the violin with two other girls," Jake said.

Claire hesitated, as if searching her memory, and then she remembered. She recalled looking at him while he sat at a table with Marcia.

"I remember now," Claire said.

"What happens now?" Jake asked Royce.

"I don't know. That is up to you, both of you," Royce replied.

Jake turned back to Claire, staring into her eyes.

"Where do we go from here? I don't want to lose you again," he said.

"You won't," Claire answered with a smile. She leaned in and kissed his tender lips.

As they sat together, their lips melting into each other, nothing else in the world seemed to matter. All the noise faded away. The room seemed to spin gently around them, music filled their ears, and happiness filled their hearts.

Some people believe that life always has a plan, that everything falls into place for a reason. That fate is predestined, and true love never dies. That love will find a way to survive, no matter the odds. Jake and Claire believed that now. They had lived separate lives, yet every path led them toward each other. Hidden forces pulled them together until they reclaimed the love that had slipped away many years ago.

Two souls searching for each other. Two voices longing to say the words they never had the chance to speak on that cold, rainy night.

Always remember: never let go. Do not allow the chance to slip away to say the words that mean the most today. And believe in "the thread between lives."

Made in the USA
Monee, IL
18 October 2025